FIELDS OF ASPHODEL

FIELDS OF ASPHODEL

CALLIE ROWLAND

47NORTH

Published by 47North, Seattle

www.apub.com

EU product safety contact:
Amazon Media EU S. à r.l.
38, avenue John F. Kennedy, L-1855 Luxembourg
amazonpublishing-gpsr@amazon.com

ISBN-13: 9781662539794 (paperback)
ISBN-13: 9781662539800 (digital)

Cover design and illustration by Edward Bettison

Printed in the United States of America

For Nana and Weeza, who heard this story (and many others) long before I was ready to share it with the world

Chapter One

A garden is a deceptive landscape. At first glance, it appears docile enough. Flowers bob and sway in a breeze scented by their blooms. Butterflies alight on tender petals, tongues unfurling to suckle sweet nectar from their depths. Sunlight filters through a canopy of leaves, dappling the flowers like so many gold coins. All is light. All is life.

Perhaps that was why no one would expect the goddess of flowers to try to destroy the king of the underworld. Yet here Del stood in her kitchen, intertwining the roots of a narcissus, poppy, and aconite plant for that exact purpose.

Grafting different flowers required immaculate control of her magic, and she grimaced as she wove her fingers through the air. The roots followed her movements. With each stab of her finger, she imagined another strike at her father. *That* was for kidnapping her mother. *That* was for tricking her mother into a marriage vow.

Hades had controlled Persephone since before Del was born, but that would end tonight, when she would feed him this flower at the Farewell Festival.

The three strands of roots braided together, and she whooped before wiping sweat from her brow. She buried the plants in one of her windowsill flower boxes and settled her hand atop the soil. The force of her will sent the stem shooting upward in search of the sun, revealing a bloom that combined all three flowers. It had the hooded shape of aconite, but it was as red as a poppy, and beneath its hoods grew a yellow fan just like a narcissus.

She smiled. Perfectly innocuous.

With a slice of her finger, she snipped the bloom from the flower box. She carried it to the domed oven that climbed one of the walls, plucking the purple hoods. Imagining she was tossing her father into the pit of Tartarus, she dropped them into a pot of boiling water. While she stirred, she hummed a funeral dirge and looked out at her cottage.

The one-room space was small, but the windows were open, filling it with a floral-scented breeze from her garden. Blue butterflies flitted over the flowers, and the waves of the Aegean Sea crashed in the distance. Vines of bindweed crept across the pale limestone walls, and in the washbasin splashed a red-throated swallow. Del smiled. On her Isle of Flowers, she lived alone, but she always felt connected to the world.

The pot began to waft a thick floral aroma, and she peered down to find the water had turned the red of fresh blood. Her lips curled into a smile.

Then there came a knock at the door.

"Zeus's name." Del startled. She looked out the window to find a black structure standing on the beach of the Isle, evening sunlight streaming past its ebony walls. She cursed under her breath, then her grandmother threw open the door.

"Seedling!" Yaya swept toward Del, who pressed herself as close to the oven as possible, trying to hide the steaming pot. Yaya wore the same deep-red color as Del, which everyone would wear tonight at the Farewell Festival. She wrapped her granddaughter in a hug, enveloping Del in her scent of mint and sun. Del stiffened, and the wicker Cornucopia of Life pressed against her stomach.

"Relax." Her grandmother pulled away with a laugh. She looked Del up and down, squeezing her upper arms. "You look beautiful."

Del had the same hair as Yaya. It was long and curly, so dark brown it was almost black, and she had arranged it in a braided updo with a few strands hanging down. A crown of bindweed snaked through the top. The tiny white flowers contrasted well, and she liked to remind Hades that while he might be her father, she did not belong to him.

She would wear a living thing even in the realm of the dead.

"Thank you, Yaya." She managed a tense smile. "You look lovely yourself."

"Oh, you know I hate this festival," Yaya said, but she gave a twirl. The Cornucopia of Life swung out from her body on a thick leather cord.

Behind her, Hecate smiled. "I think Demeter had a little too much wine before we left the farm." The goddess of witches was tall and slender, with pale skin and eyes. She placed her hands on Yaya's shoulders, bringing her to a stop.

"Now, Cate." Yaya's lips curved upward. "We both know I didn't indulge by myself."

"A little too much wine can be excused tonight," said Del.

"Indeed." Yaya glared at the Cornucopia of Life with an intensity she often reserved for Del's father. "Would that this Cornucopia could free your mother from Hades forever, rather than just half the year." She sniffed and looked up at the steam curling through the air behind Del. "What is that, a new concoction for the Spring Equinox Festival?"

"It's—it's tea," Del said. Yaya had long given up on saving Persephone from the underworld. If Del said she could dissolve her mother's marriage vow and failed, she would never forgive herself. No, she would wait until she could give Yaya the greatest surprise of bringing Persephone home. She would be the opposite of her mother in every way possible.

She would make Yaya proud.

"It smells delightful—like poppy and narcissus." Yaya reached for the wooden spoon Del had been using to stir the flower essence. "Can I try it?"

"No!" Del grabbed the spoon and tossed it out the window. When it vanished into a bush of pink roses, a swallow flapped into the air. A rabbit dashed down the path.

Cate and Yaya stared.

"I mean, it will spoil your appetite for the Farewell Festival," Del said.

Yaya furrowed her eyebrows. "It's tea, seedling. Nothing more."

"I'll bring it with us." Panic twined through Del's limbs, but she tried to act calm. She needed an excuse to bring the flower essence to the Farewell Festival. "We can have it with the banquet." Her fingers shook while she searched the counter for a small enough jar.

"Here." Cate handed her one. It was black with an orange cork. "Are you sure you're all right? You seem distressed."

"Just tired, that's all. You know I hate going to the underworld."

"What about one of your dates? That should help." Yaya searched the counter, which was cluttered with all the goods Del would sell at the Spring Equinox Festival on Mount Olympus tomorrow. White lily poultice for healing wounds. Fresh lotus flowers for inducing relaxation. "Ah, here we are." Yaya uncorked an orange clay jar and shook a dried date into her palm. "There. Here you go."

Del took the brown, shriveled fruit and stuffed it into her mouth. Energy surged through her, and she gave Yaya a smile. "Better."

Yaya patted her arm. "You need to be more careful about overextending yourself."

"I know." Del poured the flower essence into the black clay jar. She stuffed it into the pocket of her robe, then she swept into the garden with Cate and Yaya. White lilies swayed over the pebbled pathway, surrounded by bushes of pink roses. Most of the blooms were shut tight inside green buds, but the garden would be a riot of color before long.

When they passed through the pair of chaste trees at the edge of the garden, the Isle of Flowers opened up around them. An orchard of almond, pear, lotus, and fig trees stretched to the woodland, where deer and rabbits frolicked. As they strode through the crocus lawn, purple blooms brushed their ankles. Del had grown every plant on the Isle herself. All of them were enhanced with her magic, and some could be found nowhere else.

"How was your time at the temples?" she asked Yaya when they reached the beach of the Isle. On the morning of the Farewell Festival, Yaya always communed with the mortals.

Yaya scoffed. "Terrible. All the mortals can talk about this time of year is your mother—how she will finally return to the living world for the spring and summer." They waded into the Aegean, warm water lapping at their ankles. "All it does is remind me what I have lost. Be grateful I have kept you a secret on this Isle since you grew old enough to leave the farm."

"I am grateful," Del said while Cate pulled an intricate key from beneath her robe. She slid it into the spell-room door, which was carved with a rabbit trying to outrun a dog.

The spell room traveled through the space before, after, and between realms. Inside, the walls were filled with spell scrolls and hydromancy bowls. Bundles of dried herbs dangled from the ceiling, giving the air a thick, cloying smell. A fire burned in the hearth, and three cups of tea steamed on the worktable. Cate handed one of them to Yaya, then she raised her eyebrows at Del. "Do you want me to manifest your curse before we go?"

Del nodded, and Cate lifted both arms. A hum filled the air like the plucked string of a harp, and glowing red threads materialized atop Del's skin. They covered her from head to foot, but they were thickest around her heart.

"Still nice and strong," said Yaya, and Cate lowered her arms. The red threads sank into Del's skin, and she hugged herself. She knew her curse was unbreakable, but she liked to see her protection before venturing into the underworld.

She would never be like her mother, and this curse proved it was so.

Cate handed Del her cup, and the three women gave a toast before swallowing the tea in one gulp. Del wrinkled her lips. "Gods, it tastes like pure sugar. Do you have to put so much yewberry paste in this?"

"Yewberry is a necessary evil," Cate said.

While she stacked the cups on the worktable, Yaya took out a mint leaf for herself and Del. "Maybe your new tea will not be so awful," she said, and Del forced out a laugh. She placed the mint leaf on her tongue, clutching the jar in her pocket while the sweet, clean taste flooded her mouth. It was difficult to act normal when she knew this might be the last time any of them entered the underworld. If her flower essence worked, tonight their lives would change forever. And Hades would finally receive the punishment he deserved.

"Ready?" Cate walked to the door.

Del and Yaya nodded, and Cate turned her key in the lock.

Chapter Two

Del sat at the banquet table in the grand ballroom of her father's palace.

The space was cavernous, but her family filled it with talk and laughter that mingled with lyre music drifting from shrouded corners. Yaya smiled at the center of the table, where a roasted pig held a pomegranate in its mouth. She gave Cate a kiss on the cheek while Persephone chastised the triplets a few seats down. They were yanking at the Furies, but the three old women lost patience and flared their batlike wings.

The triplets went flying. Persephone covered her mouth, but instead of falling to the black marble floor and cracking their skulls open like geodes, Mel, Mak, and Zag gripped the glowing tree roots that dangled from the ceiling. Swinging wildly, Mel called out to Cerberus, and with shrieks of laughter, the triplets let go of the roots. He caught each of them on his three necks, then he trotted them safely away from the fury of their aunts.

Del could not help but smile at that. At a mere eighty years old, the triplets were inexhaustible bundles of deviousness. They could be curbed by no one other than—

"Cerberus!" Her father's voice shook the tree roots. "Heel!"

With a low whine, Cerberus hung his head, and the triplets slid off his necks. They returned to the banquet table, but Del glared at the arch of pomegranate trees at the far end of the ballroom, where her father stood with Thanatos.

She gritted her teeth, turning over the jar of flower essence in her palm. Of course he was talking to Thanatos. The god of death was his right hand, and although the Farewell Festivals were supposed to be family-only affairs, Thanatos had always been central to the ceremony that happened here. His back was to her, his wings of glistening black feathers twitching in a way that reminded her of Yaya's drakones. The wings rose above his head and brushed the floor, so she could see no more of him save his unkempt black hair.

"Del!" Mak tugged at Del's robe. Del momentarily lost her balance, almost dropping the jar of flower essence to the floor. "Come watch what we can do with the roasted pig. We have been practicing our magic, and we're much stronger now."

Letting out a deep breath to calm her racing heart, Del followed her little sister to the head of the table, where Hades always sat. A cup of red wine stood beside his obsidian Cornucopia of Death. The cup was nearly filled to the brim, and thanks to the wine's red coloring, the flower essence would blend right into it. Del glanced up at her father, who still stood beneath the arch of pomegranates. Zag yelled, "Del, watch this!"

The young god of rebirth slapped the roasted pig with both hands. The air around it rippled, and it shrank into a live, squealing piglet that raced down the table, hooves clattering against platters and wine casks. The triplets and Cerberus scrambled after it. Everywhere Cerberus ran, purple blooms of aconite grew behind him. The Furies screeched with laughter, and Persephone clapped. Yaya and Cate cheered for the triplets.

Del started working the cork off the jar of flower essence. She almost had it when a scream ripped through the ballroom, and the jar fell from her hands. Still uncorked, it splashed into the cup. Wine speckled her robe. With a muffled curse, she lifted her hand. She intended to fish out the jar, but Mak yelled across the ballroom, "Del, did you see that?"

"I sure did!" Del looked up to find Mel had snatched the piglet from atop Cerberus's central neck. As the goddess of nightmares, her magic was much less showy than that of the other triplets, but she made up for it in sheer audaciousness. The piglet screamed and wriggled, but Mak laid her hands on it. Eyes closed, the goddess of blessed death murmured a prayer, and the piglet morphed back into a roasted pig. None of the triplets were old enough to reveal themselves to the mortals yet, but a few decades from now, Mak would reap souls alongside Thanatos. She always gushed about their lessons when she visited the farm.

"You were right," Del said when Mel dropped the pig with a thud. "All three of you are much stronger than you were last year."

"Than helped us." Mak pointed at Thanatos, but when Del turned to the arch of pomegranates, she saw her father striding toward her. Dread pooled in her stomach.

He must have seen her drop the flower essence.

Her mind struggled to come up with a lie while he drew closer. He had a hooked nose. Square jaw. Short-cropped black curls. He was perfect, as a corpse done up for burial is perfect. He unsettled Del. Made her throat close up. Made her want to turn and run, as her mother had been too stupid to do all those years ago.

But she did not run. She met his death-dark eyes, awaiting the accusation, but all he did was gesture at the arch of pomegranates. "I want to introduce you to Than."

Del blinked. It was so far from what she had expected him to say that it took her a moment to process. She peered at the arch of pomegranates, where Thanatos stood with his arms crossed, looking up at the tree-root chandelier.

"In all these years," Hades said, "I don't believe the two of you have properly met."

"We haven't." Del narrowed her eyes. This made no sense. Her father scarcely spoke to her at the Farewell Festivals. He knew she hated him. She did not trust this show of kindness, but she also didn't want to make him suspicious. So, while the rest of her family plucked aconite from where Cerberus had run, she followed him to the arch.

"Del!" Thanatos said when they reached him. His blue eyes darted from her to Hades, and a flush bloomed across his high cheekbones. "We were just talking about you. I mean, about the—" Hades lowered his eyebrows, and Thanatos cleared his throat. "Anyway. I have something for you." He reached into the pocket of his red tunic and pulled out a necklace. A small coin was knotted in a nest of silver. "Oh, it's all tangled." He grimaced and unwound the chain with careful fingers. Del shifted on her feet, feeling distinctly uncomfortable. "There." He smiled. "I know it might be a bit soon to give you an obol, but . . ."

Del took the necklace, trying to remember what an obol was. Noticing that the coin was carved with a pink rose bloom, she frowned. Her mother wore a similar necklace, though it was carved with a pomegranate instead of a rose. Hades had given it to her when he stole her away to the underworld, and she never took it off. Perhaps this necklace was some sick homage, but if so, Del did not want to confront her father about it right now. She needed to play nice if she wanted to save her mother from the underworld.

When she slipped the obol around her neck, Hades scowled. "I think this conversation will go more smoothly if the two of you talk alone." Without giving either of them time to respond, he lifted his ruby cloak and swept toward the banquet table.

"Well," Thanatos said after a moment. He was so tall that he had to tip down his chin to look at Del. "I have to admit, I am a bit surprised by all this. But I'm glad to see you wearing the obol. It goes well with . . ." He gestured to her and swallowed. "Anyway. I'm pleased to see you. I always looked forward to seeing you at these festivals."

"Thank you . . ." Del examined his flushed face and tight smile. She could practically see his heart pound. Which was odd. Up until now, he had always avoided her at the Farewell Festivals. He had never tried to visit her in the living world. If he found her attractive, surely he would have made some sort of effort before now.

"Why did you give me this?" She gestured at the necklace.

"Oh." His smile dimmed to a frown. "Well, I suppose it makes sense that you would not be familiar with the customs of the underworld. But

I thought you might know, being the goddess of flowers and all. You see, it's a rose. It's a symbol of—"

"It's a symbol of love. Yes, I know. So why would you give it to me? We barely know each other. We see each other one night a year."

Thanatos nodded. "It is presumptuous. I'm sorry. I know. I would never expect you to feel the same way right now." When Del raised an eyebrow, his eyes bulged. "Not that *I* feel the same way right now. Not that I feel that way at all." He covered his face with both palms and groaned. "I am just saying, even though I know the circumstances are not ideal, I hope someday we find it possible to be as in love as your parents are."

"It's not possible," Del said, and his face fell. She resisted the urge to roll her eyes at him. He had lived with her parents since he was a child. Over the years, they must have told him why a relationship with her was doomed to fail. "Look, this is a lovely necklace. It truly is. But my parents must have told you I can't—"

She broke off when the funeral dirge began to play, signaling the start of the ceremony. Thanatos cinched his eyebrows as though he wanted to say more, but Hades strode up and clasped his shoulder, turning him away from Del. The rest of the family joined them in a flurry of activity, and Mak handed the bouquet of aconite to Del. Thanatos caught her eye, but he remained beneath the pomegranate arch with Hades and Persephone.

Del would have to talk to him after the ceremony. In the meantime, she needed to figure out how to retrieve the jar of flower essence without her father noticing.

She barely listened to his speech about how he would miss Persephone. While the lyres strummed their haunting melody, she glanced at the banquet table surreptitiously. She could knock over his wine, grab the flower essence, and pour it into the cup when she refilled it. Once that was done, she could finish turning down Thanatos.

Simple enough.

She returned her attention to Thanatos when the ballroom fell silent. His face was no longer flushed, and his wings were fanned out behind him, cheekbones sharp beneath the light of the tree-root chandelier. He looked calm. Undeniable. As mortals must see him when he reaped their souls. "We are gathered here," he said, "for the yearly vow renewal of Hades and Persephone's marriage. Long ago, when Persephone first came to the underworld, Hades fed her half a pomegranate from his Cornucopia of Death."

With this, Hades lifted his obsidian Cornucopia. He reached inside it and pulled out a pomegranate half, and Thanatos took two seeds from it. Then he took a small jar from the pocket of his tunic. He uncorked it, and black water dripped onto the pomegranate seeds before trailing down his hand. Now that the seeds had been doused in water from the river Styx, he handed one to each of Del's parents.

"Eating from this pomegranate granted Persephone safe passage to the underworld, but she needed to eat from the Cornucopia of Life to return to her mother's farm."

Yaya lifted her Cornucopia of Life and pulled out another pomegranate half. Thanatos plucked two seeds from it and doused them in water from the Styx. Hades and Persephone took them, and together they ate the seeds from both pomegranates.

"Hades ate from the pomegranates alongside her," Thanatos said, "vowing on the river Styx to live with her forever." He raised both hands, placing one of them in front of Persephone and the other in front of Hades. As he lifted them, their chests began to glow with white light through their robes. The air around them grew dark, and the lights rose up their throats before reaching their mouths. Wind whipped their hair and clothes. Thanatos's blue eyes glowed. When he spoke again, his voice reverberated through Del's bones.

"With this binding of their immortal souls, Hades and Persephone became one. Should anything threaten Hades, it will threaten Persephone as well. Therefore, they shall always protect each other as fiercely as they would protect themselves."

The white lights threatened to spill from Hades's and Persephone's lips. This was the power Thanatos held. He did not only reap mortal souls. With his control of the river Styx, he could call forth the souls of gods. Only he could officiate vows.

Yes, Del's father was the one in control. He had bewitched Persephone into thinking she loved him all on his own. But without Thanatos to bind their souls, Persephone could never have been locked in the underworld.

Before Hades's and Persephone's souls could escape from their mouths, their kiss sealed the vow renewal. The light of their souls flowed back into their chests, and they embraced while the triplets cheered and Cerberus howled. Del clapped politely, though she and Yaya exchanged a disgusted look. The shadows receded, but Hades did not announce that it was time for the meal. Instead, Thanatos turned to Del.

"Just as Hades gave his pomegranate to Persephone, today I have given you my obol." He smiled. "When a mortal perishes, their loved ones place a single coin beneath their tongue. This coin is called an obol, and it pays for their safe passage to the underworld."

He gestured at the necklace Del wore. "I am honored that you have accepted my offer of safe passage. While a betrothal is perhaps not the best way to enter our marriage, from the moment our vow is completed, I will care for you as I would myself. You will want for nothing so long as you live in the underworld."

Silence. A rush of blood in Del's ears. She must have misheard him. Surely there was no way he had just said what she thought he had. But her whole family was staring at her, and Yaya's face had drained of color, her eyes lit with an infuriated glint.

Del glared at the god of death. She meant to verbally eviscerate him, but all she managed was a stuttered, *"What?"*

Yaya clasped her shoulder. "Persephone, what is the meaning of this?"

Persephone opened her mouth, but it was Hades who said, "I believe the meaning is clear." He turned to Thanatos, who looked like he wanted to melt into the floor. "Did you not discuss the betrothal with Del after I left?"

Del stabbed the aconite bouquet at the god of death. "You *betrothed* me to him?"

Hades lifted his eyebrows. "I did."

Del stood, the bouquet limp in her hands. She was still trying to wrap her mind around what was happening here. She felt like she was watching the scene play out from far above while hanging from the tree-root chandelier. All her plans to free her mother from the underworld, and she should have been saving herself.

Thanatos gestured to where they had spoken before the ceremony began. "I—you—we just talked . . ."

The reality of the situation crashed down on her, and she threw the bouquet at him. The flowers merely drifted to the floor, but when she spiraled her wrist, a vine covered his lips.

She whirled on her father. "You betrothed me to a man *I cannot fall in love with*," she snarled, her body flourishing with hatred. "Did you forget about that? About the curse I have had since I was born? Oh, no, of course you did not forget. You simply do not care. Just like when you kidnapped my mother. Because you are a sick, twisted monster who only cares that he gets what he wants, regardless of how it hurts anyone else."

Thanatos looked from her to her father, wings thrashing while he tried to speak through the vine that covered his mouth. "Hades," said Yaya, "stop this nonsense at once."

"It is not nonsense." Hades spoke with infuriating calm. His gaze settled on Del. "We need your marriage to officiate an alliance with—"

"Of course!" Del barked a laugh. "Of course an alliance is the reason I am to be traded for the best offer. Traded like one of Yaya's drakones." She faced her mother, who had just disintegrated the vine around Thanatos's mouth. "Are you hearing this? Do you see how he ignores the curse you gave me when I was born? You cannot believe this is love."

Persephone hesitated, placing her hand on Hades's arm. "Asphodel," she said, but Del shook her head when understanding dawned. She stared at her mother, hearing her own voice as though it came from someone else.

"You knew about it. You knew about the betrothal."

Persephone's face crumpled. "Please listen, Asphodel—"

But Del was already backing away from them. As her footsteps echoed through the ballroom, Yaya slapped her father across the face. Her mother called her name. Thanatos took a step forward, looking her way. Then the ballroom doors slammed closed, and she was running through the black marble halls.

Chapter Three

The halls flickered with sconces of blue fire and shadow. Del stumbled through them, the forest of white poplars a silvery blur through the windows.

This was the sight she would wake up to each morning when she was locked in the underworld. Rather than the sun, she would open her windows to snowflakes that hung in the air, glistening like stars. Her slow mornings spent wandering through the dewy grass of her Isle would be gone. She would no longer pluck sun-warmed figs from her orchard or arrange bouquets of freshly picked flowers on her windowsills. The life she had made for herself would be stolen. She would be taken from her home. She knew this was so, because Thanatos was crucial to the functionality of the underworld. Without him to reap mortal souls, mortals would stop dying as they should. Chaos would erupt in her father's realm.

Slowly, Del came to a stop.

When Hades had abducted Persephone, Yaya had halted the seasons in the living world. She had become a problem the other gods could not ignore, and Hades had been forced to let Persephone return to the living world. As the goddess of flowers, Del was not nearly as powerful as Yaya. She could not stop the seasons, but maybe her solution was much more simple. Maybe she needed to stop only one god.

While her tears dried and her breathing evened out, she saw the field of asphodel that filled the hall. Woody stems bloomed with star-shaped white flowers, surrounding her as they always did when she felt lost. Slicing her finger through the air, she disintegrated them. Then she took a deep breath and walked over to the nearest window, hoping the view would orient her to where she was in the palace halls.

From here, she could see where the white poplar forest split around the Fields of Punishment. The charred landscape was threaded through with the Phlegethon, the fiery river snaking toward the pit of Tartarus, where it rained down on the vile entities incarcerated there. Del had never seen it up close, but Yaya had told enough stories for her to know that the pitch-black sweltering conditions would soon have her begging for death.

But that did not mean she would quietly become Death's wife.

Now knowing where she was in the palace, she rolled her shoulders and wove through the halls. She did not let herself consider how out of her depth she was. As a flower thinks only of turning its face toward the sun, ever intent on survival, she kept her mind trained on her goal. When she at last reached the looming, curved black doors of the throne room, she closed her eyes, loosed a breath, and pushed on the talonlike handle.

The well-oiled doors swung open silently, the lack of sound more frightening than the expected groan. Her footfalls echoed through the domed chamber, which was encircled with black marble pillars. All of them were carved with her father's most famous forms of torture, and the frieze of Tantalus gave her pause. Here was a man condemned to forever reach for fruit from within water he could never drink. He was doomed to spend eternity within a handbreadth of his goal, the nearness of his triumph making his loss all the more painful.

With a swallow, Del climbed the steps to her own goal: the throne.

Though the walls around it burgeoned with a conflagration of gemstone flowers, such as roses hewn of ruby and irises of amethyst, the throne itself was an austere structure of bleached bone. Femurs for the legs. Humeri and ulnas for the arms, which ended in delicate finger bones. One set of finger bones clutched her father's scepter, which was shining black and ringed with gold. It was tipped with an obsidian raven named Coronis, whose wings outstretched before the fused rib cages that composed the back of the throne. They formed a cruel imitation of an embrace when her father sat on the seat of pelvic bones.

Her father had used the scepter to steal her mother all those years ago.

Staring at its black-and-gold length, she felt her fingers grow cold. Squeezing her eyes shut, she pressed her lips into a firm line, reminding herself it was just an object. It could not hurt her. On its own, it was just a tool. A tool she could use to save herself from her mother's fate, should she be brave enough to do so. She could take the scepter, find where Thanatos slept in the palace, and wait until he retired from the festival. Yes, everyone would wonder where she was, but no one would dream she had stolen from her father's throne. Not even Mel, Mak, and Zag would dare attempt such a stunt, and they were the heirs of the underworld.

No, when she failed to return to the festival, Hades would send the Furies to search for her in the palace gardens, or somewhere similarly innocuous. Meanwhile, Del would hide in Thanatos's rooms. When he opened the door, she would lift her father's scepter and—

"Del?" Thanatos's voice echoed off the walls.

Heart racing, Del spun around. He stood in the center of the throne room, wings flared, carved pillars rising around him as he fisted, then flexed, his long-fingered hands. "I am so sorry about what just happened. I should have guessed based on our conversation. Your curse—I had no idea. I swear, I thought that . . ." He trailed off when she took the scepter from the throne, his eyes darting from her face to her outstretched arm. "What are you doing?"

Del took in his tall, slim stature. His high cheekbones and full parted lips. He lifted his leg to walk toward her, and in that moment, she imagined what would happen if she acquiesced. She saw herself descend the steps and walk, stiff and silent, back to the ballroom with him. She would sit beside Yaya, who would promise to help her find a way out of this. She would try to fish the jar of flower essence out of her father's wine cup, but everyone would be watching her. She would be trapped. The reality was, it was now or never.

The Fates would not grant her another chance.

Before Thanatos could finish taking a step, she locked her eyes on his. "I'm kidnapping you," she said.

His mouth dropped open. He beat his wings, but before he could take flight, Del raised her arm toward the ceiling, her fingers splayed upward in a clawlike shape. With a room-shaking rumble, the marble floor beneath Thanatos gave way, and with a yelp, he fell into the trunk of a gnarled laurel tree. While the branches curled around his flared wings, holding them in place, Del lifted the scepter and called Coronis's name.

With a caw, the raven sprang from the scepter. Del gave him instructions, and his obsidian wings clacked against each other as he flapped to the ceiling. There, while the god of death was encased in the laurel, no longer able to scream, the raven pecked at the marble until it cracked loudly enough to make Del's ears ring. Rock and dirt cascaded into the throne room, through which Del wove the laurel's vast network of roots. Hands shaking, she placed the scepter back in the grip of the throne just as Coronis returned to dead stone. Fear stabbed through her when she heard leathery wings flapping beyond the doors of the throne room, but she did not stop. It was too late for that now.

Burying her fear as she might bury a flower bulb, she wrapped her arms around one of the laurel branches and swung herself up with a grunt. Her robe pooled around her waist. She clung, knowing each plant yearned for only one thing.

The laurel was no exception. Its bark covered Thanatos's wide blue eyes, at last cocooning him entirely, and its roots yanked it upward in search of the sun. Through its rustling leaves, Del glimpsed the Furies burst through the doors in a whirlwind of leather and talons. They screeched when they saw her, but then the throne room was gone, and her hair was flying around her face while the laurel soared through the gloomy sky of the underworld. Breathing in the heady scent of balsam from the poplar forest far below, Del caught a glimpse of her father's palace. Then she squeezed her eyes shut and pressed her face to the branch she held.

In a rush of air and leaves, Del stole the god of death from the underworld.

Chapter Four

"It's not like I make a habit of kidnapping people," Del said. "I've never done this before."

Thanatos gave her a withering frown. "I feel so special."

Around them, sunlight streamed through the cottage windows. Roses spilled over the sills, and a swallow swooped low over the garden, twittering its song.

"Locked in a cage of vines," said Thanatos, "listening to darling birds lament the dawn. Perhaps I should join them. I have a nice singing voice, and we caged birds must find some way to spend the time."

"Do *not* victimize yourself." Del stabbed her finger at the flowers that bloomed across the cage vines. Their white petals were half translucent in the golden light. "I did not want to trap you on my Isle, but the situation left me no choice."

"No *choice*? I was right there in the throne room, ready to talk. I had no idea you didn't know about the betrothal. I mean, for Zeus's sake, you accepted the obol!"

"You said yourself that I do not understand the customs of the underworld. Why not explain those customs to me, then, instead of stuttering like some lovesick fool? You would not be trapped here if you had managed to form a coherent thought."

"I would not be trapped here if you had stopped to think about your actions before you chose how to act. Do you think Hades will not demand my return? Of course he will. It's only a matter of time before he tells Zeus what you have done." Thanatos stepped forward, gripping the cage vines. His voice was soft. "I know you love your Isle. Persephone says you cultivate it with immaculate control. But we gods are not merciful. If you do not let me go, Zeus will destroy your home with storms."

Del swallowed. She did not regret stealing Thanatos, but she knew it had made her an enemy of the underworld. It had taken all night to bring him to her home. For the first time in her life, she had wished she could open a path straight from the underworld to her Isle. Instead, she had directed Coronis to peck a tunnel to Yaya's farm, where she harnessed a pair of drakones to the chariot she had learned to drive as a child. The horse-size serpents had wings like white doves, and they flew across the Aegean Sea surrounded by twinkling stars. She had sagged in relief when they reached the Isle just before dawn.

Leaving the drakones on the winding path through the garden, she had wriggled her fingers, causing the laurel to scuttle on its roots into the cottage. When she lowered her opposite hand in a spiral, the branches receded, granting the trunk enough space to scutter past the living space into the kitchen. She spiraled her other hand upward, and the laurel sank into the floor, giving way to vines of bindweed that braided together until the god of death was caged like a bird, trying to manipulate her into letting him go. The idea of her Isle's destruction sent panic twining around her heart, but she could not let it show.

If she wanted her way, she had to maintain control.

"You cannot convince me, Thanatos." She stepped into his shadow, chin upturned to meet his eyes. All that separated them were the cage vines. "My father may want you returned to the underworld, but without my permission, no one can set foot on my Isle. It has no connection to the earth, so pathways cannot be opened to the underworld. No one is coming to save you, which means the only way out is with my help."

Thanatos dug his fingernails into his biceps, and Del noticed that his arms were all muscle. He swallowed, and Del watched his throat bob. "And what must I do to earn your help?"

"Easy." She stepped back into the sunlight, spreading her hands wide. "All you have to do is vow on the river Styx that you will not marry me, and you are free to go."

Thanatos blanched. "But—"

"But what? You told me in the throne room that you thought I had agreed to the betrothal. I thought that meant you wanted our marriage to be consensual. But I suppose that would not matter to you. I doubt any of the souls you reap want to go to the underworld."

"The deaths I give are *peaceful*—" Thanatos squeezed his eyes shut, his mouth forming a thin line. She watched him take a deep breath and saw there was a slight crook in his nose. Strands of black hair fell across his cheekbones.

"Look," he said, and she ripped her gaze away when he opened his eyes. "I understand why you're upset. Hades never should have approached me about the marriage without first asking for your consent. Until I made my announcement, I thought you had given it."

Del raised an eyebrow. "You thought I had agreed to a loveless marriage."

"I didn't know about that."

Del barked a laugh, but when Thanatos only stood there with his jaw locked, she frowned. "My curse. The one that prevents me from falling in love with gods of the underworld. My father must have told you about it before you agreed to the betrothal."

Thanatos shook his head. "No."

Del sucked in a breath, then blew it out. "All right. Well. My mother cursed me when I was born. To protect me from being taken to the underworld."

"But why would she do that? Persephone and Hades are in love."

"They are not."

"Yes, they—" When Del glared at him, Thanatos closed his mouth. An absurd laugh bubbled from his lips. "Okay. Fine. They aren't. But if Persephone gave you that curse when you were born, why would she agree to our betrothal?"

"I don't know." Del reached up and yanked the obol from around her throat. When the silver chain snapped, she tossed it to the floor. It skidded behind the washbasin built into the wall. Thanatos watched it go. "What I know is that I do not agree to it, and you will vow never to marry me if you want to go home."

Thanatos looked up at the ceiling. He blinked at Del. Then he scrubbed his eyes with both hands and let out a sound caught between a growl and moan. "I can't, Del."

"Oh, so binding my parents in marriage is not enough. You just *have* to tie our souls together as well."

"No. I mean, I already gave your father my marriage vow."

Del stared at him. Everything inside her went still.

"He wanted an alliance with my mother." Thanatos dropped his hands to his sides. "That was the alliance he mentioned at the festival. She is the goddess of night, he is the king of the underworld . . . He said the alliance would strike fear in mortals. Mortal fear leads to more sacrifices, more prayers, more temples." His wings flared, then drooped to the floor. "He thought I would want my mother to return to the underworld. Now, maybe if he had been talking to my sister Keres, that would have worked. But my mother abandoned me as a child. Why would I want her to come barging into my home?"

"So you made this vow for no reason." Del felt numb. "You did so out of pure, unquestioning loyalty to my father. You really are his hellhound."

"What? No! That is not why I made the marriage vow."

"Then why? Why else?"

"Oh. Um." Thanatos looked her up and down, clearing his throat. "It was . . . Well, it was . . . um." He glanced up at her, his face red as a rose. "Gods. I'm sorry, Del."

"Just to be clear—you vowed you would marry me on the river Styx."

"Yes, I did."

Del turned to the window, taking a deep breath. Watching her garden always helped her calm down. She loved looking long enough to admire the details. She appreciated each hum from a bee. Each sway of a tight green bud. She saw the marching ants, crawling ladybugs, zipping lizards, and hopping birds. Every flower bed was its own unique world, all of which she had set in motion with the flowers she had grown. It was beautiful and controlled.

Looking at her garden now, she tried to breathe through the thicket of panic in her throat. Maybe if she completed her half of the marriage vow, she would eventually be able to grow a flower that could dissolve it—like she had planned to do for her mother's marriage vow at the Farewell Festival. But she had not been able to test the flower. It might fail. She couldn't trap herself in the underworld when she had no idea whether her escape plan would work.

Which meant that if Thanatos did not marry her, he would break his half of the vow, forever banishing him from the company of other gods. He would no longer be able to reap mortal souls, and slowly but surely, the mortals would forget who he was. He would be forced to spend eternity alone and forgotten. For a broken vow was the closest thing to death for a god.

Thanatos had put himself on the line, which meant Del had no leverage. No one would side with her if it meant Thanatos would be banished from doing his work forever. But because vows on the river Styx were so dangerous, their wording had to be careful. If Thanatos had given her father a poorly worded vow, there was still hope.

All she had to do was find the loophole.

She turned back to him. "What were the exact words of your vow?"

"Listen," he said as her eyes adjusted to the cottage shadows, "I know I should remember the words. I know. But I . . . Look, Del. I was in shock. Hades already knew what he wanted me to say. He gave me this paper. He had it written down. It all happened very quickly, but here, let me see. Let me help. I'll try to remember now." He squeezed his eyes shut, tapping his fingers against his thigh. "It was something along the lines of . . ."

Del made a frustrated sound. "I don't need *along the lines of.* I need exact words. Get your story straight. Don't lie."

"I am not lying!" He yelped when she lifted both hands, thickening the cage vines. "You can trust me. I swear it. I would never want to hurt you, ever. But I was nervous. I was trying to wrap my head around the fact you had said yes—"

"Well, you had better start praying to Mnemosyne, because until your memory starts working properly, you will remain trapped."

"But you *must* free me." He leaned forward, eyes pleading.

"I must do nothing. That is the whole point of this kidnapping."

"Del. Listen to me." He crushed a pair of white flowers when he gripped the cage. "I know you love the living world. I know you want to keep it beautiful. But without me, horrible things will start happening."

Del clucked her tongue. "No. The underworld will suffer without you, but the living world will not. Mortals will go on living because you are not there to reap their souls. I am sure that without you, they will see a much more beautiful world."

"What . . . ?" Thanatos shook his head. "No. Do you forget? I am not the only god of death. I am the god of *peaceful* death. Without me, mortals will be at the mercy of my sister Keres. She will kill them violently—"

"If your sister cares so much about her work, then where is she? My mother says she has not been to the underworld since she slapped you across the face at that Farewell Festival. Which happened when you were, what, a hundred and twenty years old?"

"That doesn't mean she has stopped working. She works every day—"

"So let her come find you! Let her come fight to set you free. But maybe she would like to see you stowed away. Maybe she sees this as her chance to become my father's preferred plaything." Del flicked her gaze over his tunic, which was plain red linen save for gold trim. "Not that he dresses his toys very well, I must say."

"I am not a plaything. I am a force of nature. And I don't like ostentation. I find it looks redundant on me."

"Redundant," Del sneered. "What does that even mean?"

A cloud passed over the sun, swathing the cottage in shadow, and he locked his eyes on hers. "Death need not prove it should be taken seriously."

His voice was soft, but it rushed through the cottage like wind over a wheat field. And just as wheat bows, shivering, to the wind, Del felt cowed.

This was the danger of him. No violence. No shouts or shrieks. The danger was that he could simply wait. Quiet against the wall, until Del dared to grow lazy. Then he would exploit that laziness for his own gain. She might have locked him in a cage, but he would be freed. It was an inevitability. Somewhere, deep in the thicket of panic, she knew that. So did he. That was why he concealed the words of his vow. Because he knew soon enough, Hades would return him to the underworld.

Despair seeped through Del like rain. The packed-earth floor fissured around her feet, making way for woody stems that crept up to her knees. Thanatos parted his lips, but before he could speak, Del swept her finger in a slicing motion, causing the budding asphodel to disintegrate. No. She must not douse her rage. Not while a way out still remained.

Her feet smothered the cracks in the floor when she stepped toward the cage.

"You claim to be sorry," she said. "You claim I can trust you, but when I look at you, do you know what I see? I see someone who obeys my father unquestioningly. Who always believes he is doing the right thing. You want to maintain your loyalty, so you do not want to tell me the words of the vow you made. I understand this loyalty, but it does not make you trustworthy. In fact, it makes you the opposite of trustworthy in my case."

While she spoke, Thanatos pressed himself against the limestone wall that formed the opposite side of the cage. He watched her run a finger over one of the vines, her voice carrying on the sweet spring breeze. "My father controls you with this loyalty, you see. I hate him, but I understand his ways. Until you tell me the words of your vow, I will do much worse things to you than simply locking you in a cage."

Without warning, she spun both hands in blurring spirals, sending a cascade of vines roping around his ankles, wrists, and wings. She glared at him, his eyes wide as a final vine covered his lips. "I may look delicate, darling Thanatos, but I will bring you to your knees. A few days with me, and you will be begging for release."

Chapter Five

Del opened her mouth to say such a position would encourage Thanatos to think. Then her eyes caught on movement through the window at the edge of his cage. One of the only people who could visit the Isle without permission was striding up the pathway.

Her mother. Persephone.

"For Zeus's sake." Del marched to the doorway. She already had to deal with one god who had arranged her marriage today. She did not need another. Especially not the one who was the hardest to hate, because in many ways they were the same.

Like Persephone, Del had been born in Yaya's farmhouse on the day summer vanquishes spring. Asphodel had bloomed across the bedsheets, just as narcissus had grown around Yaya when she gave birth to Persephone. While Persephone grew up, the yellow horn-shaped flowers had bloomed around her whenever she felt pleased. When she flew a chariot for the first time. When she learned to dive to the bottom of the lake. When she flounced through her favorite meadow on hot summer days.

Yaya did not tell these stories with the fond, airy tone mothers reserve for the triumphs of their children. Rather, over bedtime cups of kykeon, with the windows latched against the winter chill, she told Del these stories as though her daughter had died long ago. And in a way she had, for Persephone became a different person when Hades stole her from the meadow. She no longer flew chariots or dove into the lake. She rarely smiled, and she walked with a stiff, cutting stride, as though the very air needed to be repelled.

This was how she met Del on the pathway beside the chariot and drakones. But Del spoke before she could open her mouth. "Yes, I stole Thanatos. No, I won't be giving him back. If my father misses him so much, he must figure out how to wed him to someone else. Someone who is willing. Someone who knows about the proposal before their fate has already been decided by everyone else."

Persephone's pink robe billowed around her ankles. Beside her, the winged serpents flicked their tongues through the air. "You have every right to be angry," she said. "This is not how you were meant to find out about the betrothal."

"And the obol? What was that for, to make me look like a fool?"

Persephone shook her head. "Than did that on his own. Hades and I didn't know about it until the Farewell Festival. When Than gave it to you, Hades was shocked."

"He didn't seem shocked. He seemed like himself."

"Not to mention"—Persephone held up a tiny clay jar—"I found this in his wine cup. I recognized it as part of the set your grandmother gave you when you moved to the Isle. When I showed it to Cate this morning, she said its contents looked like poison."

"It's not really *poison*."

"Asphodel, what were you trying to do to your father?"

"What was *I* trying to do? He betrothed me without my knowledge."

"I was the one who wanted to wait to tell you about the betrothal."

Del took a step back. "What?"

Persephone squeezed her eyes shut. "I felt it would be best if I could explain it to you while living at the farm during the spring and summer. I wanted to tell you about the alliance, and I wanted you to get to know

Than." Her eyes opened, though they were narrowed to slits. "Perhaps I was wrong about that, but I did not expect you to steal him."

"What did you expect me to do, just let it happen?"

Persephone shook the jar of flower essence. "I have seen your concoctions at the Olympian festivals. Is this one of them?"

"Give me that." Del grasped at the jar, but Persephone grew a vine of bindweed that slapped back her hand.

"So help me, Asphodel, you will tell me what this is."

Del disintegrated the vine. "Mother, you are bewitched. You think you have power over Hades, but you do whatever he says. My betrothal proves it is worse than Yaya and I thought. This is the essence of a flower I created to dissolve your marriage vow. I wanted to help you return to yourself. And instead, you want me to become as lost as you are."

"Did Yaya know about this?" Persephone went still.

"I wanted to surprise her by bringing you home."

Persephone rubbed her forehead. "The underworld is my home. I agreed to this betrothal because I want you to understand that. I want you to be part of our family, and I think you could be happy with Than."

"I cannot be happy with him." Del waved at the cottage. "Besides my curse, I have a life of my own here. I sell my flowers and fruits and poultices at the Olympian festivals. I *meet* people. I take lovers until I grow bored, then I bid them farewell. I have free will. You think I will allow all that to stop? No. I have already told Thanatos. All he has to do is help me dissolve the marriage vow he gave my father, and I will set him free. Until he does so, he will remain here, with me."

Persephone looked pained. "You are so much like Hades."

"I am *nothing* like him." Del gripped the chariot reins and led the drakones down the pathway. She refused to consider that her decision to break off her engagement made her like her father in any way. It didn't. Hades had stolen her mother without provocation. Del had stolen Thanatos as a means of self-preservation. The two situations were not comparable.

Yet when she led the drakones beneath the three archways of white myrtle, she felt chilled by their shadows. And when Persephone clasped her hand on the other side of them, tears tightened her throat.

"I promise you . . . Look at me." Persephone swallowed, squeezing Del's hand as she spoke. "Than is a kind man. You should see how he is with the triplets. Flying them around the palace grounds, helping them with their magic lessons. Mak thinks he is the best teacher in the world. I know you have your curse, but I never would have agreed to this betrothal if I did not think it would serve you well."

Del watched her mother. In the distance, waves crashed on the beach.

She breathed in sharply and marched to the chaste trees. "If you cared about my well-being, you would have come here to help me. You would not be trying to convince me to set Thanatos free. You would not have betrothed me to a man I am cursed never to love, and you would not have sent the Furies to attack me when I fled the underworld."

"Your aunts were merely doing their job. They are our guards."

"You could have called them off."

"Asphodel! Please. You know it was not personal. When you are one of the gods, family must come second to the balance we uphold."

"Yes, and how well did upholding the balance work out for you, when Zeus gave your hand in marriage to an evil god?"

Persephone sighed. "Hades is not evil."

"No, you wouldn't think so." Del stood in the shadow of the chaste trees, surrounded by their cone-shaped buds. "You ate the seeds of his pomegranate quickly enough."

Lips parted, Persephone blinked. Seeing her mother struck dumb by her insult, Del felt an apology sprout up her throat. She turned to one of the chaste trees and watched a swallow build a nest within its boughs. "At least your mother tried to return you to the living world." She made her voice airy, though tears clogged her throat. "Imagine how it would have felt, if Yaya had given her blessing for you to be stolen out of that meadow."

"Asphodel—"

Del whirled when she felt a palm on her shoulder. *"No."* She raised both hands, causing the nearby rosebushes to rear upward, threatening Persephone with their thorns. "You, of all goddesses, ought to know how this feels. Well do I know how hopeless you are when it comes to defending yourself, but I am your *child.* You might have the triplets now, but I am your first little girl. After everything you did to protect me when I was born . . ." She hugged herself, her voice softening to a broken whisper while the rosebushes shrank back into themselves. "How could you let him do this to me, Maytare?"

Persephone met her daughter's eyes as a cloud covered the sun. For a moment, Del viciously hoped she would reach out and pull her into a hug. With all the hunger of a newly sprouted plant stretching toward the sun, she yearned for her mother to whisper an apology into her hair. She wanted to be a little girl again, who could trust whatever her mother said.

Then Persephone spoke, and the moment passed with the cloud.

"I did not let your father do anything. We made a decision together. If you are determined not to marry Than, you will need to speak with both of us about it." She took the chariot reins and reached toward Del. "Come with me. Hades is with Zag and the girls on the farm." She held up the jar of flower essence. "After *this*, I am not letting you anywhere near him by yourself."

Persephone started to climb into the chariot, but Del spun her wrist in an upward spiral. Vines split the ground and wove around her mother's ankles. "After this betrothal," she said as Persephone looked down, "I have no reason to trust a word out of your mouth."

Persephone sliced her finger through the air, but Del raised her other hand, and new vines grew twice as fast. As the goddess of spring, Persephone's magic was strongest at the height of her season. She was just beginning to regain her strength, but Del retained her magic year-round. After a short struggle, the vines wrapped around her mother's wrists and ankles, and Del climbed into the chariot alone.

"Asphodel." Persephone yanked at her bonds. "Let me go."

Del shook her head. The vines continued to grow, forming a living blanket that wove Persephone into its folds. One of them wrapped around the chariot hook designed to hold a sword. "I will go to the farm, but I will go alone—to see Yaya, the one person who has always had my best interests at heart. Until you prove I can trust you again, you are no longer welcome on my Isle."

Persephone's voice became incomprehensible when the vines covered her mouth. Del made sure they were loose enough for her to breathe easily, then she dragged her mother through the crocus lawn and stopped on the beach.

"I am setting you out to sea," she said while the drakones tugged on the reins. "Do not try to return to this place. You will search for it in vain."

Knowing Persephone would be able to free herself as soon as the Isle was no longer visible, Del snapped the reins. The drakones beat their wings, and she dragged the raft of vines behind her, keeping the chariot just above the waves. She untied the braid of vines from the chariot hook and dropped it into the sea. As it fell, Persephone stared death at her daughter, her hair glittering with salt spray.

Ripping her gaze away, Del gave a double snap of the reins. The drakones shot into the sky, leaving half of her stomach—and a piece of her heart—drifting on the waves.

Chapter Six

Del led the weary drakones into the stables. With soft words of encouragement, she returned them to their stalls, then she opened the cages near the entrance and grabbed a pair of live snakes and clip-winged doves. Grimacing, she tossed one of each animal into both stalls. Then she hurriedly left the winged serpents to devour their meals.

As she exited the stables, she wondered if it was wise to leave Thanatos alone. But she had tied him to his cage good and tight, and no one could visit the Isle while she was gone. Cate and Yaya were the only people who were welcome there at any time, and she was going to see them now. Thanatos would be fine until she returned home.

Meanwhile, she would find out how to end her betrothal.

The farm sprawled at the base of Mount Olympus, the mountain of the gods rising behind it in a haze of blue fog. Because of its height, it blocked many of Zeus's clouds from leaving the farm. This led to more rain, which meant Yaya produced the healthiest crops in the Greek world.

Yes, Yaya's status as the goddess of the harvest had something to do with that as well, but the ensnared clouds helped.

This early in the year, the barley, mint, and wheat fields were still flat green carpets that rolled across the valley from end to end, where the Olympic forest climbed the mountain's lowest hills. They were latticed with aisles of lush grass lined with red poppies, so they formed a pattern of interlocking squares when viewed from above.

As Del walked down one of the aisles now, she inhaled the scent of dew and good soil. The smell sent her back to spring days spent frolicking through the fields while Yaya perused her fledgling crops, pausing every so often to rub a mint leaf between her fingers and remark on the fragrance level.

Del bent down and rubbed her fingers across one of the young mint plants now. Eyes closed, she lifted her fingers to her nose and breathed in the fresh, sweet, and slightly spicy smell. This method of relieving stress had not changed since she was a little girl, and it reminded her that she was still herself, whatever else her actions last night had cost. Muscles that she had not realized were tense calmed, and she stood just as a crane flapped low in front of the house. It bugled its gravelly caw, the sun shining off its red brow.

When the crane vanished into the forest, on its way to the lake that bordered Persephone's favorite meadow, Del remembered how she used to swim there as a little girl. Before the triplets were born, she and her mother would race from one end of the lake to the other. When Del inevitably won, Persephone would hug her beneath the lakeside white willow, the wind spreading gooseflesh across their arms. There had been laughter in those days, and more closeness with her mother than Del could recall anywhere else.

Swallowing the tightness in her throat, Del shook her head and continued toward the house. It rose from the center of the valley, its pale limestone walls partially obscured by the giant yew that shaded the herbs Cate grew for her spells. Del squinted into its shadows, but Cate's spell room was nowhere to be found.

With a sigh, she swept into the courtyard. Clay amphorae lined the walls, filled with stores of grain that Yaya sold to the other gods.

The double-handled jars looked like upside-down lily buds, kept safe from the sun by the walkway that extended from the second floor. Passing beneath that walkway now, Del glanced at the clay oven and found disks of barley bread baking beneath its dome. She opened the kitchen door—

And was assaulted by three young voices and a threefold hug.

"Del!" The triplets squeezed her middle as though she had not seen them only last night at the Farewell Festival.

Zag looked up at her, his gray eyes wide beneath his floppy black curls. "Where's Maytare?"

"She was supposed to bring Than back to us," Mak explained while Del held the three of them close before prying off their arms.

Mel grinned. "He's going to fly us around the farm before we go home."

At Del's raised eyebrows, Zag yelped, "Maytare swore!"

Mel led them back to where the triplets had been eating a late breakfast at the kitchen table. She climbed into her chair and leaned her elbows on the table. Her black eyes glittered with conspiracy when she told Del, "I want him to fly me all the way to Olympus and back."

Del opened her mouth, but before she could explain that Thanatos would not be flying anyone to Olympus or anywhere else, Zag smacked his palm on the table, rattling the cups of honeyed goat milk. "Well, if he's flying you to Olympus, I want him to fly me as well."

"I want to go to Olympus!" Mak's round brown eyes darted from Mel and Zag to Del. "I want to see the festival for the Spring Equinox."

With an eye roll that ended in a long-suffering glance at Del, as though only they understood the world, Mel sighed at her sister across the table. "Mak. You know we can't go to the festival. We aren't allowed." She grabbed a piece of barley bread from the platter in the center of the table, dredging it in a saucer of red wine before popping it into her mouth. "And anyway, Than can't fly all three of us there and back. There won't be time."

Zag and Mak looked at each other, but Del found her voice before they could launch a dual assault. "Thanatos isn't flying anyone to Olympus or around the farm."

The triplets glared at her, and Zag squawked, but she shook her head, keeping her voice calm. "I don't know why Maytare promised he would, but at the moment, he is . . . all tied up." She winced at her choice of words, but the triplets didn't seem to notice, too focused on the loss of their promised flight across the farm.

"But where *is* he?" Zag gripped the edge of the table, leaning toward Del. "When is he coming home? He's supposed to help me practice my magic on the old hellhounds."

"Pretty soon," Del said as she ripped the soft inside of the bread from the crust, "this problem will be solved, and Thanatos will be home to help you with the hellhounds and fly you all around." She smushed the bread into a tight ball, as she had since she was a little girl, then popped it into her mouth. When she spoke, she held the faintly nutty bread against one cheek with her tongue. "Where is Yaya?"

Mak gestured vaguely at the plethora of kitchen utensils that hung along the walls. "She's somewhere," she said, and Del sighed. That was no help. She opened her mouth to ask if Hades was here, but then Cate's black polecat darted across the kitchen tile, chasing a terrified Askalabos.

The yellow, black-spotted gecko frantically scampered behind the clay jars of dried herbs and spices that lined the countertop, trying to outwit Gale. The triplets chanted the polecat's name as she scrambled onto the windowsill. She knocked Yaya's Cornucopia of Life with her tail, and the wicker horn swayed wildly, but the triplets clapped when she shot behind the jars. She shoved them so far outward that one of them crashed to the floor. Dried bay leaves and orange clay skated across the tile.

Del gasped, gaze flying from Gale to the triplets, with no idea how to return the room to its previous calm. The triplets stood in their chairs, whooping while Gale herded Askalabos back to the kitchen washbasin and cornered him on the windowsill. She reared up on her hind legs, her collar of white fur flashing when she opened her pink maw. The triplets' cheering crescendoed—

"What in the name of *Olympus* is going on?" Yaya swept into the room without sparing a glance at the table. A flurry of wheat and barley spun through the air behind her, which was abruptly silent and still. The triplets sat in their chairs, their grins altogether gone.

"Oh, Askalabos," Yaya said while Gale scurried from the kitchen in a rush of clacking claws. She strode to the washbasin, seeds of grain clattering against the broken clay jar. She stilled the Cornucopia and lifted the quivering gecko to her shoulder. "I don't have time to watch you like an eagle. If you do not want Gale to eat you, don't go running off." On the green fabric of her robe, Askalabos curled into a ball.

"Yaya," Del said, amazed at how, even in her harried state, her grandmother had controlled the room without any effort at all.

Yaya startled, another flurry of grain scattering across the floor.

"Seedling!" She stepped over the broken jar to wrap Del in a hug. Del shut her eyes tightly, melting into her grandmother's scent of mint and sun. She had to swallow tears when Yaya pulled away and squeezed her upper arms. "There you are." She glanced behind Del to the window that looked out on the courtyard. "And no greasy raven of a god. Good. Come along." Placing a quick kiss on each of the triplets' heads with a promise to return as soon as she could, she stacked the pieces of the broken jar on the countertop. Then she swept back the way she had come. With a single sip of honeyed goat milk, Del bid the triplets a hasty farewell and hurried after her down the hall.

"Where is your mother?" Yaya asked when Del caught up, the sweet, cold goat milk still coating her mouth. "She went to collect the necrotic scoundrel, I was told."

"She did." Del wiped her mouth, blinking in the alternating strips of light and shadow as they whisked down the many-windowed hall. "She came to the Isle and tried to convince me to let Thanatos go."

"Ah, but you did not." Yaya led Del into the airy sitting room, where the clothes she and Cate had worn to the Farewell Festival were draped over the back of the couch. "Good. I wish I had been able to help you at the festival, but you did exactly what I would have done. Hades needs Thanatos. He will not be able to ignore your wishes now." She set Askalabos on the emerald cushion, and the gecko sped off. With a shake of her head, she gestured with her poppy-printed robe at Del. "Well, what happened when your mother got to the Isle?"

Biting her lower lip, Del watched her grandmother expertly fold the robe and set it in the wicker basket beside the couch. Only when Yaya looked up at her, eyebrows raised, did she reveal, "I . . . might have tied her to a raft of vines and forced her to set sail?"

Yaya pursed her lips, holding Cate's shimmering bloodred cloak to her heart. "Well. That is not ideal. But it is better than you letting Thanatos go and acquiescing to this Gordian knot of a marriage proposal. Hades has corrupted her mind worse than I thought. It is one thing for her to think she loves him, but for her to agree that you should be forced to live in the underworld . . ." She shook her head. "You cannot believe a thing she says anymore."

Del made a dull hum of agreement in the back of her throat. While Yaya folded the clothes, she searched the sitting room, as though the poppy-printed walls and plant-filled windowsills might have an answer to her problems. They did not. Feeling incompetent and small, she shifted her gaze back to the couch. She stared at the dust swirling in a shaft of sunlight that fell across its emerald cushion, tears tightening her throat. "I just don't know . . ."

At the strained wobble of her tone, Yaya ceased folding the clothes. She set Cate's cloak in the basket and wrapped Del in a hug. "Seedling, do not doubt yourself. Know that I am proud." She kissed Del on the nose, as she had every night when Del was a little girl. "You have grown into a strong young goddess who knows how to take care of herself."

Yaya stepped back, eyes turning sharp. "But do not think you will be in this fight alone. As soon as Cate returns to watch the triplets, I will fly to Zeus's palace. All he cares about is upholding balance. When he learns that Thanatos can no longer bring death to mortals, he will put an end to this betrothal. Once I have his support, I will come to the Isle, and all this will be resolved."

She squeezed Del's hands, and Del squeezed back. "Thank you, Yaya." She almost told her grandmother about Thanatos's marriage vow, but it would only make her feel younger and more helpless than she already did. Yaya wouldn't be able to do anything about it. Del's only chance was to convince Hades to tell her the words and then exploit some loophole in them. Hopefully, by the time Yaya returned from her audience with Zeus, the vow would no longer be an issue. Del would have handled at least one thing by herself.

With a nod, Yaya pulled away, returning her attention to the clothes. "No thanks necessary, none at all." She folded Cate's crimson robe with strict, violent movements, as though it had done her wrong. "After this stunt, I hate the man who stole my daughter with all the fire in his pit of Tartarus." She draped the robe into the basket and pressed it down with her palm. "He takes and he takes from this family, but it's never enough, oh no. Even now, you, your mother, and I should be on Olympus for the Spring Equinox, selling your wares and drumming up interest in the yearling drakones. And instead, I am here, trying to keep the triplets happy while Cate entertains your father with her spells. Oh, I know the Fates forbid her from taking sides, but this is her family. Could she not refuse someone just once?"

"So my mother told the truth," said Del. "Hades is here on the farm."

Wheat and barley fell from Yaya's chignon. "He barged in here this morning, no doubt using his path carved under the white willow. When Cate returned from bringing your mother to the Isle, she whisked him off in her spell room. Look, there they are now."

Del turned to the window that looked out at the courtyard, wincing when a grain of barley pinged off her arm. Cate's spell room had appeared on the opposite end of the courtyard, the sun gleaming off its ebony walls.

"I have to go talk to him," she told Yaya.

"What?" Yaya turned Del's face from the window. "No. Seedling, you must not. I know you want him to explain himself. You want a reason for his behavior, but you won't get one. All you need to do is keep Thanatos on your Isle. I can work out everything else."

Del swallowed, lifting her chin to appear braver than she felt. "I know you can. But, Yaya, if I don't stand up to him, he will try to trick me again in a few years, decades, centuries from now. He needs to understand that just because I am the goddess of flowers and he is the king of the underworld, it doesn't mean he can push me around. I am not my mother, and I will not bow to his will."

She stepped up to the sitting-room door, but Yaya took her hand. "Seedling, you misunderstand. I do not mean he *will* not tell you his reasoning, but that he can't. Evil needs no reason to be itself. It simply is."

"I am not trying to change him. I understand who he is. Perhaps I could never convince him to listen to me before, but now I can. I have stolen one of the most important members of his household. I have power now, the only language he understands."

Yaya looked out the window and chewed her lower lip. Finally, she shook her head. "Very well. You can try to make him listen. If need be, Cate will be there to help. Whatever the limitations of her magic, she will not let him do you harm."

Del nodded. "Wish me luck," she said as she gripped the handle.

With a sigh, Yaya kissed her nose. "Tyche be with you, my heart."

Chapter Seven

Releasing a steadying breath, Del strode into the courtyard. The sky was pale blue, and songbirds flew overhead. When she reached the spell room, the door creaked open of its own accord. Breathing in the scent of herbal smoke, she stepped into the shadowed room and found the goddess of witches sitting on the hearth, ladling yewberry tea into two cups.

"Selene came and talked to me this morning," Cate said without looking up. "Last night, she saw something very unusual. There were heavy clouds, but she swears she saw a pair of drakones pulling a chariot that carried a laurel through the stars." She set one cup on the worktable. "She said even for the goddess of the moon, it was a shock."

"Indeed, it was." Hades sat at the end of the worktable, gaze boring through Del while Cate handed him the second cup. He was swathed in a black diamond-encrusted cloak. Looking at him made Del tremble, but she forced herself to keep her chin up. She could not show weakness. If she did, he would cultivate it into a thriving field of doubt.

"Do you realize," he said, "that by keeping Than on your Isle, you doom our realm?"

Del swallowed. "I realize that he will not return to the underworld until he has dissolved his marriage vow. Until then, he will remain on my Isle, where you cannot reach him. If you want the underworld to function, you will tell me the words of his vow. Now."

Hades took a sip from his cup. "And what of the little jar Persephone found in my wine cup? Was that your attempt to poison me at my own table?"

Her body flooded with embarrassment and doubt, but Del kept her voice level. "Perhaps it was. There are plenty of poisonous plants on my Isle, and I am not opposed to using them on Thanatos. It might be fun to see how long it takes to bring Death to the brink of himself. Poetic enough torture for Homer's little storybook. Don't you think so?"

Hades tightened his mouth and furrowed his eyebrows, as though she were a young hellhound trying to threaten one of the adults. He glanced at Cate, who merely sipped from her cup, before he drawled, "Very well. The words of the vow are: 'I, Thanatos, vow to wed Asphodel, the eldest daughter of Hades and Persephone, after which she will forever reside alongside me in the underworld.'"

A rush of astonishment swept through Del, but it fled when she considered the words of the vow. Her father had not bowed to her will. He had told her the words because, as far as she could tell, there was no way out.

"I suppose," Hades went on, "Than has told you the alliance with Nyx is the reason for your betrothal. I have been asking her for this alliance since before you were born, and she finally agreed to it—so long as you marry her son and live in the underworld. She is the one who decided on the wording of the vow."

"What, and is that supposed to convince me that you care about what I want?"

"No." Hades drained his cup. "I am trying to tell you why this alliance is so important—and why it matters to me and your mother so much."

"Do not bring my mother into this." Del slammed her palm on the worktable. "You have bewitched her. She doesn't know what she's talking about. And Thanatos already told me this alliance is to strike fear in mortals. More temples, more sacrifices, more tales. Are the stories the mortals tell about you and my mother not enough? Do you need more worship than all the prayers you receive for the well-being of deceased loved ones?"

Hades opened his mouth, but then the spell-room door swung open, banging the wall, and he leaped away from the worktable with an undignified yelp. Gale scrambled out of his robe and climbed Cate's wine-red gown. She curled her sleek body around the goddess's neck and lifted her head so Cate could scratch the crescent of white fur at her throat.

"Oh, hello, Gale." The goddess smiled. "Did you have a good hunt? I hope you did not terrorize Askalabos *too* much."

Hades folded his arms. "Now, Cate. Do not sabotage—"

"Patience." Cate fixed her pale gaze on the king of the underworld. As she spoke, wind whipped through the spell room and shoved Hades out the door. The door slammed shut behind him, but the rest of the spell room was untouched. Any other day, Del would have laughed at her father pounding on the door, but there was no humor in it now. He had well and truly trapped her in this betrothal, and the only recourse was to lock him outdoors.

"I know you cannot take sides," she said while Cate turned her key in the lock. "But can you not give me any sort of help?"

Cate sighed. "You know I cannot. I can provide time and space for you to make choices, but I cannot make those choices myself."

"Helping others is not the same as making their choices. Everyone helps their loved ones. It is the way of the world."

"It is the way of mortals."

"For Zeus's sake." Del gestured at the bundles of herbs on the ceiling and the stacks of bowls on the shelves. "You could divine my best course of action with a glimpse in a hydromancy bowl or the innards of a flayed dove."

"I cannot interfere with previously cast spells."

"Mel, Mak, Zag!" Hades's voice bellowed. "Come. We're going home."

With a scowl, Del reached out and rubbed a circle on the wall. As though it was composed of soot and not solid wood, a small, round window appeared, just big enough for her to look through to the courtyard. There, a sopping Persephone clutched Hades while they walked to the kitchen door. Del wrinkled her upper lip when the triplets tumbled into the courtyard and crushed them in a hug. "Look how he orders the triplets around like dogs."

Cate hummed as the window returned to ebony wood, leaving Del with the image of her mother hugging herself while Hades carried Mel on his shoulders with Mak and Zag on each arm. "Demeter hates that they stay down there with him during the spring and summer. She wishes they lived with Persephone on the farm."

Del turned from the window. "Don't you wish that as well?"

Cate smoothed one finger up the bridge of Gale's nose. "I think that ever since your mother first went to the underworld, she has lived at a crossroads. And I know she does not want that for her children. She wants each of them to have a home. Which, right now, is where I suggest you go."

Del blinked. "You're kicking me out?"

Cate plucked the empty cups from the worktable. "Your parents are likely not the only people trying to free Thanatos. I may have protected your Isle with my own spells, which I trust more than anything else, but, well . . ." She gave Del a small smile. "When you are flirting with Death, you can never be too careful."

Dread pooled in Del's stomach as Cate placed her key in the door. She opened it to reveal the beach of the Isle of Flowers, and Del took off through the crocus lawn. Heart hammering in her throat, she raced down the pathway through the garden, glancing wildly around to see if there were any signs of trouble. But there were none. The bees buzzed. The birds chirped. The plants smiled at the sun.

She reached the cottage, forcing herself to be logical. Cate liked to stir up trouble, but nothing was wrong. It was impossible. No one could set foot on the Isle without her say-so.

But when she opened the cottage door, Thanatos was not alone.

Chapter Eight

Keres slammed Del against the wall. A flap of white wings, a flash of blond hair, then strong hands flipped her around. Her face crashed against the limestone, and she gasped, pain radiating from her cheekbone. She tried to maneuver her wrists in spirals, but Keres pressed them against her back as the cottage door snapped closed. She hissed in Del's ear, her voice like a sword being whetted on a stone, *"Let my brother go."*

Del struggled to breathe when Keres pressed her full weight against her back. "No."

With a snarl, the goddess of violent death gripped the back of Del's neck, and Del squeaked when she felt the bite of knife-sharp nails. She flipped Del around, and the back of Del's head collided with the wall. Gritting her teeth against a cry, she spoke through the haze of pain and shock. "How did you get onto my shores?"

"I flew." Keres flared her white-feathered wings, and the gust of air sent the blue sofa cushions gliding to the floor. "Then I walked through the door." She yanked one of Del's arms toward Thanatos. "Remove the vines holding him to the wall." She slightly loosened her hold, but when Del twisted her wrist, it still felt like grinding her bone against a manacle.

"Let her go," Thanatos told his sister after the vines disintegrated from around his mouth. "Attacking Del will get you no closer to what Mother wants."

He flapped his wings, moving the sword that lay beside the cage with a gleaming gold hilt. It was obvious Keres had been trying to hack through the vines, but to no avail. The items that Del had planned to sell at the Spring Equinox Festival littered the floor, but the cage was still intact. As the midday sun shone through the vines, their white blooms seemed to glow. The cage was delicate but strong. Dangerous but fine.

Even as fear snarled through her, Del swelled with pride.

"What happened?" she demanded of Thanatos. "How did she get here? How long ago?" If Keres was here, there must be something wrong with Cate's protection spell. Just what Del needed. Another problem. She had a whole garden of them now.

"I think you invited her here by accident," he said, "before you left me here alone."

Del thought back to their argument leading up to when she saw her mother through the window. They had discussed the obol, the vow, the alliance with Nyx. Then Del had challenged Keres to find Thanatos if she cared that he was gone. She had grown so angry that she had mistakenly invited the goddess to her Isle. Stupid. Reckless.

Her father never would have misspoken like that.

"Never mind how I got here," Keres said, tightening her hold on Del's neck. "I have sliced and slashed at this cage for the better part of an hour. Why can I not break his bonds?"

"If you want her to talk," said Thanatos, "loosen your grip on her throat."

Keres narrowed her red-brown eyes, but she did so. Del coughed, sucking down sweet spring air before she was able to rasp out, "The cage is made of bindweed, enhanced by my powers. You will never unravel it by yourself. If you want your brother off my Isle, help me dissolve his marriage vow. And if you want to leave this Isle yourself, let me go."

Keres growled, but Thanatos silenced her with a look. "You said Mother sent you here to talk. Instead of resorting to violence, why don't we try that now?"

"Talk is a waste of time and breath. Words run circles around a problem. Violence cuts straight to the heart."

"I agree with you," said Del. The Twins of Death turned to her with shock, but she could tell that Keres would respond best to straightforward talk. "I stole Thanatos because it was the fastest way to get what I want. What I want is to break off our betrothal. My father told me it was your mother who wanted me to marry Thanatos and live in the underworld, so maybe she can help dissolve his vow."

"That is not why she sent me to your Isle." Keres let go of Del and yanked up her sword. Del feared she would be attacked after all, but the goddess only slipped the blade into the gold sheath at her belt. "In fact, she did not want to send me at all. She said I would be too forceful."

"I can't imagine why," Thanatos drawled.

Keres snarled at Del. "I came here to warn you about the havoc your actions have wreaked on the world."

"Not this again." Del gestured at Thanatos. "I *want* to cause chaos in the underworld. Now that your brother has stopped reaping mortal souls, Zeus will call off our betrothal. My grandmother has already gone to Olympus to explain my terms."

Thanatos cinched his eyebrows, and Keres chuckled. "Oh, little flower girl. Zeus will never agree to your terms. My mother was careful with the wording of the vow. It cannot be dissolved, and if it is broken, Than will be forgotten by mortals. Zeus will not allow the balance to be thrown off. Did you not grow up hearing the story of your mother and father? It illustrates the principle of balance quite well."

"Of course I did, which is why I know—"

"No, you don't." Keres jabbed a finger at Thanatos. "If you refuse to let him go, you do not understand the principle of balance at all. Do you know why it is all Zeus cares about?" She held up her hand. "No, let me talk. It is because we need mortals to care about us. We need them to listen when we argue. We need them to cheer at our triumphs and weep for our losses. We are immortal. We are powerful. Our injuries heal, and we do not grow ill. But these strengths make us vain, and this vanity is our flaw."

"I know that," Del said, then wanted to melt into the floor. She sounded like a reprimanded child whining to an adult.

"When the mortal world is peaceful, the poets have time to write and read their tales. Those who listen may sit around fires and burn offerings as they praise the exploits of us gods. This is how we make sure they worship us." Keres released a clipped sigh, flicking a strand of white-blond hair behind her back. "In times of trouble, though, mortals must focus solely on themselves. Entertainment is a poor substitute for survival."

Thanatos muttered, "Bread and circuses seem to distract them well enough."

Keres bared her teeth at his intrusion, but it reminded Del that she did know what she was talking about. Del's father was the king of the underworld. If she knew about anything, it was death, and pain, and war. She glared at Keres with renewed confidence, bracing herself against a wave of dizziness before she stood from the wall. She mirrored Keres, crossing her arms. "The vast majority of mortal tales take place during wars. That is when heroes can most easily make their marks on the world. Even if Thanatos being trapped here causes more war, the mortals will still worship us. They will pray for victory and a safe return home."

"The concern is not *war*. Somewhere, there is always war. If there weren't, I would not be a god. The concern is that without Than, there will be no peaceful deaths to counteract those wars. Mortals will no longer die of old age. They will no longer find relief from illness. Instead, they will topple down stairs, breaking bones and crying for help that will never come. They will burn with fever from the inside out, sobbing with pain until I reap their souls. How do you think that will make them feel?"

Del swallowed. "They will be angry, of course—"

"And how do you think the gods will respond? Mortal worship is a drug. The more gods have of it, the more we want. As mortals stop worshipping us, the most powerful gods will be the first to go mad from withdrawal. They will lash out at the world you love. They will terrorize the mortals until they give them the worship they want."

"Think about it, Del." Thanatos's voice was soft. "Zeus is the king of the gods. He will go mad first. He will send terrible storms to destroy the world in vast swaths . . ."

Del looked from one twin to the other, feeling hopelessly small. They were right, of course. The first gods to be maddened by lack of worship would be the most powerful. But if the mortal anger went on, the madness would trickle down to lesser gods. It would reach her mother. Cate. Yaya. Only Del would be unaffected, because the mortals had never known she was born. She would be all alone, and the world would be destroyed by crazed gods.

She looked at Keres, tears filling her throat. What had she done? She had doomed everyone she loved. She should beg for forgiveness. She should free Thanatos this instant. She could stomach a loveless marriage. It would be far better than destroying the world. She was not her father. She could not doom the world to please herself.

But when Persephone had been stolen all those years ago, that was exactly how Yaya had returned her to the farm. By demanding her will be done. And when Del thought about spending her days in the underworld, fear snarled through her throat.

"If the gods want mortal worship," she said, her tongue feeling too large in her mouth, "they must find a way to dissolve Thanatos's vow. Because until our betrothal is resolved, he will not leave my shores."

Keres looked her up and down.

Del watched her, feeling numb.

Thanatos warned, "Keres, don't."

Then Keres ran at Del, who experienced savage vertigo. "You will not listen to my words," said the goddess, "so my violence will persuade you now."

The next thing Del knew, Keres had multiplied into three duplicates of herself. The identical goddesses unsheathed their swords, their white-blond manes billowing around their skulls. Their thickets of hair were adorned with pinprick white diamonds, and as the three aspects advanced toward Del, their hair glittered like wet spiderwebs in a storm.

"Having captured my brother," one of them said in her ear, as another tipped up her chin with a pointed nail, "you think yourself ever so smart." The third Keres yanked Del's hands forward and raked her nails up Del's arms. "Your veins flow with power for the first time, and it has electrified you like one of Zeus's lightning bolts."

The first Keres traced her finger around Del's mouth. "You taste the tang of ozone on your tongue as though you are the sky moments before a storm." She dropped her hand and stepped back, making room for the Keres who tipped up Del's chin.

"Now that you feel so large, you want to best Hades and his underworld." She dragged her nail down the center of Del's throat. "But I have watched mortals chew and swallow and choke on power all my life long."

"By now," the three aspects chorused, their words vibrating through Del's skull, "I have a knack for knowing the difference between a predator who can tear into the feast of power and never tire of sucking marrow from bone, and a mouse who will never have the stomach to gorge itself, no matter how dazzled it is by the meal."

The aspects circled Del, so her world became a blur of blond hair and white wings and knifelike nails. "You, little flower girl, are a mouse. Long before you have acquired the taste for electric, bloody power, you will vomit it back up." Their voices were the clash of swords and thunder of feet on battlefields. "I will admit, you wear a nice facade. But I have spent much of my life in the company of mortals who have lost their lives by overestimating themselves, and there is little difference between the hubris of mortals and gods."

The aspects raised their swords, preparing to deal a threefold death blow. Then a voice like a cold wind said, *"Enough."*

The aspects froze. Del managed to spiral her wrists, roping them in bindweed that bloomed with white flowers. When the aspects touched, their skin shimmered, and they melted into each other. By the time the bindweed had constricted Keres from ankle to shoulder, she had returned to one aspect of herself.

"Keres," said Thanatos, his voice sharp and cold, "I know you are angry. I am as well. You think I want to be trapped on this Isle? Of course not. But imagine yourself as Del. Here you are, having lived your whole life hating the underworld, and the one night a year you can stomach being there, you discover your betrothal to one of its gods."

He shifted his gaze to Del, the melody of his voice growing soft. "You panic. Fear chokes you, and the only way to keep breathing is to maintain control. So, you take the god you are supposed to marry to your home. Everyone is telling you to let him go, and in your heart you know you must free him before you destroy the world. But when you think of doing so, fear crushes you in its choke hold."

"So give up." Keres struggled within her bonds. "Face the fear like a hero, knowing your own fate is inevitable, but in accepting it you might save the world."

"Del is no hero." Thanatos looked at Del, and the cool certainty in his voice sent guilt clawing up her throat. This was the tone reserved for children who needed time to admit the adults were right all along. This was how Thanatos viewed her, because he knew—just as she did—that she could not break his vow.

He turned to his sister. "Tell Mother that Del is cursed never to love gods of the underworld. I doubt she knew about that when she asked for my vow."

This finally gave Keres pause. She blinked at Del. "What?"

"It's true." Del swallowed. "My mother cursed me when I was born."

Keres snarled, but it was not directed at either of them. She tilted back her head and blew out a breath. "Fine." She wriggled within the bindweed. "Let me go."

Del raised her eyebrows at Thanatos. "I can trust her?"

Thanatos nodded, and Del was halfway through spiraling her wrists before she realized she had taken him at his word. When the bindweed that encircled Keres fell to the floor, she prepared for the goddess to attack her with her gleaming sword. But Keres merely flared her wings and stalked to the door.

"You should thank every god in the pantheon that you captured him and not me," Keres said when she paused on the threshold. "He gives you grace, though you have declared yourself our enemy. That, little flower girl, is true strength."

She slammed the door and soared from the pathway. But Del felt no relief, because she had not convinced Keres to leave.

No, Thanatos had done that while she was wallowing in self-pity.

"I'm sorry," she said, the apology hanging between them, useless and heavy. She meant to follow it up with some proof of what she was feeling, but freeing him was the only action that would hold any weight.

Her voice cracked when she said, "I'm just not ready."

Before he could say anything, she wheeled around and hurried up the staircase. She batted aside the curtain of ivy and collapsed onto her bed, which was heaped with pillows in all the colors of a springtime flower bed. It took several tries to yank up the ivory linens, and she let out a growl of frustration before tugging them to her chin. Face pressed against the soft, cushioned fabrics, she listened to swallows chirp in the garden. Waves crashed on the shore, and the scent of anise wafted from the giant fennel that bobbed against the windowsill.

It was all so peaceful. That was what Yaya had promised when she gave Del the Isle. Her life would be calm. Her life would be stable. Visitors would come and go, but her life would be her own.

It wasn't anymore.

Shoving her face farther into the pillows, she squeezed her eyes shut and sobbed. She recalled the carving of Tantalus she had seen when she approached her father's throne. Now she felt a kinship with the tortured man after all. She had succeeded in kidnapping Thanatos, but she could think of no way to dissolve his vow. Which meant she was doomed to free him before maddened gods destroyed the world.

With a last racking sob, she wrenched her face up from the pillows. Asphodel swayed over the bed, and her face was wet with tears and snot. Her cheeks were hot, and on the green pillow, she had left twin tear blots. As she rubbed her eyes, she heard Thanatos beat his wings just once, as though testing the sound. She stilled, watching the star-shaped white flowers while she waited for another sound. When he remained quiet, her lips trembled. She curled onto her side, trying to breathe through the body-wide thicket of anxiety and guilt.

The god of peaceful death was down there, knowing she risked destroying the world, and instead of making a nuisance of himself, he was letting her rest up in her loft. Del hated that. She hated it so much. If he had been brutal like his sister, keeping him here would have been easier. Fighting for herself would have felt strong. Instead, it felt like a refusal to accept her inevitable loss. Even worse, Thanatos seemed to know this as well. He had told Keres to leave so Del could process her new reality on her own.

Her breaths buffeted the field of asphodel. She wilted like a flower does when it feels the first chill of frost, weeping until her thoughts dissolved into sleep's peaceful dark.

But, as the world does not remain warm, the dark did not remain peaceful for long.

Chapter Nine

The nightmare began familiarly enough. Del walked up the winding road that led to her father's palace. Cypresses lined either side of it, their pointed tips stabbing the gloomy sky, where snowflakes glistened like stars. When she reached the palace, the doors opened of their own accord, and music spilled from the black marble hall.

Out of no volition of her own, she stepped over the threshold. The doors swung shut behind her without sound, eliciting a gust of air that guttered the sconces of blue fire that hung along the walls. Her hair billowed, and she gripped her red shawl more tightly around herself. As she started down the hall, she was comforted by the soft, warm wool.

The music grew louder while she walked, the sound solemn and low. It was the funeral dirge that always played at the Farewell Festival. But as Del strode toward it, she found herself coming no closer to the grand ballroom, where she knew her family enjoyed their meal. Amid the music, she heard barks of laughter and snippets of their talk.

Her mother asked, "Where is Del?"

Hades snorted. "She probably didn't want to come."

"Good," said Zag.

"It feels weird when she's here," agreed Mak.

Mel giggled. "She isn't like us, Maytare."

A pause, in which the music grew soft. Del tried to call out, but the words snagged in her throat. She tried to run down the hall, but she slipped and fell. Her head hit the marble, and she lay there, pain radiating through her skull.

Her mother sighed. "No, I don't like her much at all."

The words landed on Del like physical stones. They pounded into her back, eliciting disks of pain like ripples on a lake.

And just like that, there she was, in the lake where she used to swim with her mother as a little girl. When she drifted up from its murky depths, she was young again, swimming alongside Persephone to the shore. Her mother was tall and perfectly beautiful, as she had always seemed when Del was small. In the spring breeze, her thicket of brown curls bounced like a cloud. Her almond eyes shone when she lifted Del into her arms. "I was thinking we should braid our hair. To show how alike we are."

"Yes!" Del clapped, and Persephone grinned. Time unfurled while she braided Del's hair. Around them, the narcissus swayed. The lake glittered beneath golden sunrays.

By the time Persephone had finished her own braid, shadows extended from the white willow that shaded the lake. She stood, helping Del to her feet, but then the ground shook, and Del stumbled away. In the dimness, the ground split open beneath the white willow tree. She glimpsed her father's death-dark eyes and Coronis's sharp beak, then with a sweep of his cloak he stole her mother away.

"Maytare!" Del screamed, scrambling away from the hole in the ground, which was extending toward her feet. "Maytare, don't leave me!"

The ground beneath her gave way, and she fell through the dreary sky of the underworld. A glimpse of white poplars, a whiff of balsam, then her head smacked against the marble floor, and she was back in the flickering hall.

All this was familiar. Del had been having this nightmare for weeks. She knew the moment she hit the marble after falling from the lake, she would startle awake.

This time, however, the nightmare changed.

Del remained in the hallway, cold marble pressed against her cheek, surrounded by lapping blue flames. Through the haze of pain, she listened to the funeral dirge as her parents began to speak.

"Than, you understand us," said Persephone.

Hades sighed. "If Del would only let the two of you get married."

"She would see why I left."

"She would see it is better this way."

"She would see," said another voice that Del did not recognize from her nightmares or from reality, "down here, she would not be weak."

The voice was a star shooting down the hallway. Its first words were soft, distant, but it strengthened swiftly, until it was bright and searing in Del's face.

"Down here," the voice said, "she would be queen."

The voice shoved Del over the nearby windowsill. The marble scraped the backs of her knees, and she fell through the snowflakes. All she knew were twinkling stars and cold pinpricks of pain. Darkness spread across her vision like a spilled pot of ink—

Del snapped awake. At first, she thought she was still asleep. It was dark, and pinpricks of cold were falling on her feet.

Then thunder shook the cottage, and she realized the cold pinpricks were rain.

She blinked rapidly, freeing herself from the linen sheets. They were tangled and damp, and at her feet they were sopping wet. Beyond the open window, lightning flashed. The bolt illuminated the downpour of rain. When Del lunged toward the clattering window screens, another thunderclap rattled her teeth. She glimpsed the garden, which was an undulating sea of glistening leaves. Waves pummeled the beach.

Cursing herself for falling asleep, she slammed the window shut and hurried down the staircase. Before she even reached the last step, she spiraled her wrists, and curls of bindweed latched the window screens. The room became instantly quieter, but rain still rattled the wooden slats. White light filled the cottage when another bolt of lightning flashed. She glimpsed Thanatos, who huddled in the back of his cage. He called her name, but she ran past him and threw open the door, determined to keep her Isle safe.

The moment she stepped outside, wind and rain slammed her in the face. Her knees buckled, but she pushed farther into the storm with gritted teeth. Clouds covered the moon. Lightning blazed across the frothing waves. Chunks of dirt slapped her legs. When she tripped over the rosebushes, their thorns sliced her calves. The myrtle archways had blown over, and lily buds smacked her arms. She fought her way to the crocus lawn and dropped to her knees in the slurry of purple muck.

Breathing heavily, she clenched her eyes shut. Her robe clung to her skin, and her hair plastered her neck and arms. She pressed her hands into the mud and imagined the roots of her plants growing stronger. She saw them cling to the ground, refusing to let go. She drained her energy, knees sinking into the sludge, but it was no use. Flowers flew into her face. Rose thorns dug into her legs and arms.

She screamed into the storm and heard an earsplitting crack. The sound reverberated through her bones. There came a great whoosh, and she scrambled out of the way just as an elm collapsed onto the crocus lawn.

She stood, hugging herself, staring at the tree that lay where she had crouched a moment ago. One of its branches had sliced into her forehead on the way down, and a stinging sensation spread toward her temple. Far above, the remaining trees groaned. A bolt of lightning struck her orchard, and the trees fell upon one another, collapsing in a neat row.

This destruction was purposeful. Practiced. Uniform. There was no doubt in her mind—Zeus had sent this storm. Which meant there was nothing she could do.

Her lifetime of work had been destroyed.

Chapter Ten

"Del!" Thanatos leaped to the front of his cage when she stumbled into the cottage. "You're hurt. Why would you go outside? It's the middle of a storm."

"It's my Isle." Del was already crying when she fell back against the door. Black spots danced in front of her vision. She knew what she would find when the storm lifted. Fallen trees like corpses. Jutting bones of splintered limbs. The buds of would-be flowers, shredded like skin. She sank to the floor, arms wrapped around her middle. There was no air. She felt like one of her flowers caught in the storm. Pummeled into the earth by a gale-force wind, deeper, deeper, until she would never see the sun again—

"Breathe," Thanatos said. "Del, look at me. Breathe like this." He crouched on the other side of the cage and breathed in. She imitated him, lungs filling with air. Then she let it out again. "You're panicking," he said. "It happens to me every once in a while. Just focus on being here." He took her hand and rubbed the space between her thumb and forefinger. The rhythmic motion calmed her, and after a few more breaths, she was able to think again.

"Feel better?" Thanatos let go of her hand.

Del shook her head. Without speaking, she went up to her loft to put on some dry clothes. Her body stung from the rose thorns, and her forehead throbbed where the branch had struck. Her wet robe twisted around her hands, and she ripped it while pulling it over her head. When she came back downstairs in a lavender robe, Thanatos was sitting cross-legged in his cage, fingers tapping his knee while he frowned down at his lap. Thunder shook the cottage, and he looked up, eyes catching on hers when she reached the base of the stairs.

"I know you sell poultices at the Olympian festivals." He tapped his forehead. "Do you have anything you could use for that cut on your head?"

"I see what you're doing." Del remained on the stairs.

"I'm trying to help you. You look like you got trapped in the hell-hound puppy pen."

"You're keeping me talking. So I won't go back out there."

"Well, it's working, isn't it?"

Del sighed and walked into the kitchen. "I have white lily poultice." She plucked one of the jars from the floor and struck her twin flint shards. She lit the beeswax candles that lined the countertop, and as they filled the cottage with flickering shadows, she poured water into a clay pot. After placing the pot on the edge of the oven, she held up one of the jars strewn across the countertop. "You crush the bulbs."

She dabbed some of the poultice into her hand. It was a thick pale-yellow paste that smelled of green earth. When she spread it over her arms, it sent a cooling sensation across her skin. Thanatos raised his eyebrows when it sealed the cuts. "That works quite well."

"It is a bestseller at the festivals." Del rubbed some of the poultice on her calves.

"You have cuts all over your face. Come here. Let me help with them."

Del scoffed. "You think I'm going to let you touch my face? Thank you for the offer, darling Thanatos, but I will be keeping you as my captive. Not the other way around."

"If I wanted to hurt you, I could let you run back into the storm."

"Why don't you, then?"

He gestured at the cage. "You told Keres only you can break this cage. To get out of here, I need you in good health." When she glared at him, he sighed. "For Zeus's sake, Del. I hate that this has happened to your Isle. Please let me help."

Del hesitated, but it was true. He needed her on his side if he wanted to leave the Isle. And she had already given him the chance to hurt her when she ran back into the cottage.

Slowly, she walked toward him. "One wrong move and I will tie you to the wall."

"Yes, mistress." He gave her a small smile.

She handed him the jar, and he dabbed some of the poultice into his palm. Del moved her face close to the cage so he could reach her forehead. At first, his fingers were shockingly cold, and she startled. "Sorry," he murmured, and paused. When Del did not move away, he brushed the cut on her forehead again, and now the sensation was pleasantly cool. When he was finished, he handed her the jar. "There you go. Already healed."

She moved back into the kitchen when the water in the pot began to burble. She reached for her jar of mint sprigs and plopped two of them into the boiling water, then she tossed two handfuls of barley in after them. The air filled with the yeasty scent of grain garnished with sweet, clean mint, and she watched the opaque liquid in the pot thicken. The steam cleared her sinuses while she stirred it.

She ladled the liquid into twin cups, and her movements fell into a familiar rhythm. Leaving the cups to cool near the oven, she unfolded the cloth from some day-old bread. She cut two thick slices, then she took a wedge of goat cheese and spread it generously across them. She drizzled honey over the cheese with a practiced hand.

"Have you ever tried kykeon?" she asked.

"Your mother makes it," Thanatos said as she handed him his cup and bread.

"My grandmother used to make it for me every night. We would drink it together in my bedroom. I had this big chair." She lifted her own cup of kykeon, watching shadows dance across the rim. "She would tell me stories while we drank it. She told me about my mother before she was kidnapped."

Thanatos said nothing to that. For a moment, he held her gaze, then his wings twitched, and he lowered his eyes to his bread. Together, they sat in silence and ate, mint and grain and honey filling their mouths while they leaned against opposite sides of the cage. Shadows rippled through the cottage, and the windows clattered with rain. Far off, a tree fell with a deafening crash. Del squeezed her eyes shut. Another death.

"Breathe," Thanatos said. "Tomorrow, you can fix it. When the storm has passed."

She wouldn't be able to fix it, Del almost said. Instead, she lifted her kykeon cup to her lips, speaking into the minty sweetness. "I deserve this."

"Maybe. But that doesn't make it hurt any less."

She sighed and leaned back her head. A short span of time passed. When she heard a rustling sound, she opened her eyes and found Thanatos holding three graphite drawings in his lap. They usually hung on the wall behind him, but she looked up and saw it was now barren. "I apologize if you didn't want me to touch these. I took them down while you were upstairs—so they wouldn't get wet."

"I don't mind," Del said.

A moment of silence, then he tapped the drawing on top of the stack. It was quite messy, with charcoal smudged across the page. Zag had drawn it, and he was not patient by any means. Still, it clearly depicted Cerberus as a puppy, panting with purple blooms of aconite growing around his feet.

Thanatos looked down at it. "I remember that day. It was the Farewell Festival when Hades first gave Cerberus to the triplets. The puppy started to drool, and aconite bloomed everywhere it fell. The shock of it, and all that cracked marble floor . . . I don't think we have ever laughed that hard."

He smiled up at Del, but the reminder of the Farewell Festival sent weeds flourishing through her throat. He was so familiar with her family. With the triplets. It reminded her of the nightmare she had just had. Of her mother saying he understood them. Of her father wishing she would just marry him. If she did, perhaps she, too, would understand. Perhaps she would realize the underworld was not so bad. What was it the other voice had said? Down there, she would not be weak. Down there, she would be—

She would be trapped. And curse her father for telling Mel to send her such nightmares.

"It was a good day." She gestured at the drawing of Cerberus. "But it was a good day because I knew I could go home at the end of it."

"Why is that?" Thanatos set the drawings on the floor beside him. "I mean, I've always wondered. Why do you hate the underworld so much? Your whole family is down there. Why choose to live up here by yourself?"

Del scowled. "My whole family is not in the underworld. Up here I have Cate and Yaya. And I love my Isle. It's peaceful." She looked at the window, throat tightening as she listened to the rain that lacerated her home. "No one can change you while you're alone."

"No one can change you? But that's life, Del."

"Well, look at this." Del turned from the window. "Death teaching me what life is about."

"No, but—" Thanatos looked down, huffing a laugh to himself. "It's just, *death* is peaceful. Life is anything but, on the whole."

Del shook her head. "Death is not peaceful. Not for the scores of tortured souls in my father's realm. And life can be calm, for those of us who do not trouble ourselves with making marks on the world."

"But you are a god. It is in our nature to want to be loved."

Del watched her finger skim the rim of her kykeon cup. "Perhaps it is in the nature of gods who crave mortal worship, but I do not.

Yaya told me when I was young—mortal worship is not worth the cost. Think of my mother. The story of her kidnapping means she will never be forgotten, no, but she will spend half her immortal life in the underworld. She is irrevocably divorced from who she once was and cast out from the world where she used to belong. My mother has no home anymore. And now, thanks to this betrothal, I also won't."

She stared at her cup, throat tight and eyes hard, words hanging in the darkness between her and Thanatos. He stayed quiet, and she tucked her legs toward her chin. Then she wrapped her arms around her calves. She rested her chin on her knees, flicking her eyes up to find him watching her with drooping wings.

"What?" She spoke without lifting her chin.

Lightning flashed, and Thanatos sucked in a breath. The movement made his cheekbones look even sharper than they usually did. He released his words in a rush of air. "Do you really think your mother is bewitched?"

Del stiffened. "Yes. Of course she is. She would never love Hades if she wasn't."

Thanatos shook his head. "But that's just it. That's what I don't understand. The stealing bit. That's just not how Hades and Persephone talk about it."

Del arched her eyebrows and lifted her head. "And how do they talk about it, then?"

Thanatos dipped his eyes to his lap. "Well, Persephone. She says she ran away with him. She loved him, but your grandmother had forbidden their marriage. She asked again and again, but Demeter's answer never changed." He looked up at Del, fingers tapping his knees. "So, when Hades came to visit her in her favorite meadow one day, she just . . . left."

Thunder cracked, and Del stared at him. "People can convince themselves of a lot of things. If you had been there when she was first taken, you would not believe what she says."

"But . . . I was there. I've lived with your parents since I was a kid."

"I don't care what she says!" Her voice was a rose thorn slicing through her lips. "She is bewitched. Hades has convinced her she loves him, and she lets herself go on believing it, because that is easier than facing the full horror of her situation."

Thanatos nodded. "That's what she says, that Demeter refuses to accept how it is—"

"*My mother* is the one who refuses to accept how it is." Del leaned close to the cage. "You may live in my father's palace, you may serve as his right hand, but that does *not* mean you understand what happened."

His blue eyes skated over her face. He ran a hand through his hair and gave a small flap of his wings. The breeze fluttered her hair as he met her gaze. "You're right. I'm sorry. I don't know."

"You *don't* know. Whatever my father has told you, my parents are not in love. They never have been. He only understands possession. That is why he agreed to this betrothal. Because he does not care if we are locked in a loveless marriage."

"Well, I care. Do you honestly think, after all this, I would make you do anything against your will? I *care* about you, Del. And don't say that I do not know you well enough to think so. I have watched you every year at the Farewell Festival."

"Why not speak to me, then? You never talk to me at the Farewell Festivals. You have never tried to visit me on the Isle or on Yaya's farm."

Thanatos clenched his jaw. He shut his eyes and breathed out through his nose. "I could tell you hated the underworld. I figured it was better to keep my distance, rather than get attached to something that I knew was doomed from the start." He closed his eyes and swallowed. "How exactly did it happen, this curse of yours?"

"What does it matter? We can't break it. Curses are unbreakable."

"So are vows, but that hasn't stopped you from keeping me here until you can dissolve my marriage vow."

Del sighed. "Look, I'm sorry, all right? I feel awful. Worse than awful. I don't want to destroy the world. When Keres was here, I should have let you go. But when I opened my mouth, the words just wouldn't come out—"

"I am trying to remind you that wording matters, in curses as well as in vows. Maybe your curse has a loophole, and then our problems will be solved."

"What, because if my curse is broken, we will fall in love, and I will live happily ever after with you in the underworld?" She met his eyes. "I don't care how much I love you, darling Thanatos. I will never willingly live in the underworld."

"I—just—" He scrubbed his face. "For Zeus's sake, Del. Maybe we can work something out. Maybe . . . I don't know. I just want to know what I'm up against, is all."

Del said nothing for a while. She looked out the window while lightning flashed across the Isle. The storm was not slowing down. Her Isle was already gone, and she was doomed to spend eternity in the underworld. If Thanatos thought he had a chance at loving her, she might as well be cordial. Perhaps she could never fall in love, but spending eternity with a good friend might not be the worst thing in the world.

She turned to Thanatos. "It's a long story. Do you still want to know?"

He spread his hands. "You've got yourself a captive audience, Del."

So, with a small smile, Del told him her story while the candles burned low.

Chapter Eleven

Del's story began the day her mother was stolen.

On an early-summer afternoon, Persephone was plucking narcissus in her favorite meadow. Birds chirped overhead. The sun peered through the white willow. Everything was calm. Everything was normal.

Then the ground split open, and in a whirl of twinkling darkness, Hades wrapped her in his arms. Beneath the white willow, he held her close while a stone raven leaped from the black-and-gold scepter he held. With a caw, Coronis pecked at the broken ground, and Persephone vanished with Hades back to his realm.

In the following moments, the ground resealed. The lake glittered. The narcissus swayed. The sun shone through the white willow boughs. Everything looked as normal as it had before.

But now, everything was wrong. Because now, Persephone was gone.

Demeter scoured the farm before she was forced to accept that her daughter was not coming home. She wanted to collapse, to claw at the earth as her tears watered the soil, but grief was a luxury she could not afford.

Not while there was still hope.

In the evening twilight, she swept to the stables. She harnessed a pair of drakones and soared up Mount Olympus, where she found Helios stepping out of his sun chariot. The god of the sun held the fading body of a red-winged little girl.

"Her name is Eos," he said when he saw Demeter. "Please, do whatever you can to save her, and I will tell you anything that has happened under the light of the sun."

Demeter plucked Eos from his arms. She wove her fingers through the air, and soon she held a stalk of heliotrope. It glowed gold, its clusters of purple flowers resembling clouds.

She handed the plant to the sun god and asked him why Persephone had been taken to the underworld.

"She has gone to be with her beloved." Helios cradled the heliotrope in his arms. Sunrays fell from his golden hair as he climbed the front steps of his palace, leaving Demeter alone on the side of the mountain. Darkness descended, and while Selene soared across the world in her moon chariot, Demeter flew to the top of Mount Olympus.

In the audience chamber of Zeus's palace, she found the king of the gods languishing on his throne, which was formed from the trunk of a stately oak. Through the low-hanging boughs, she glared at him as he twirled his beard the color of storms. "Tell me you have not given my daughter to that wicked king of the underworld."

"He loves her," Zeus said. "She loves him. It is easy to understand. She is life, he is death." He gestured to the symmetrical canopy of the oak. "They bring balance to the world."

"Balance," Demeter spat. Zeus only stared at her, his eyes like the sky moments before the first thunderclap, so she left. Feeling numb, she stared out the farmhouse window and waited in vain for Persephone to return home.

Her loss was incredible. Light looked dark. Warmth felt cold. And as the days turned into weeks, her pain changed the world.

Without her magic to cultivate the fields, the summer heat scorched the crops. The mortals burned offerings and begged for her help, but she remained home, buried in her grief as the air turned cold. Snow suffocated the land. Ice paralyzed the seas. Frigid winds brought buildings to their knees.

The other gods begged Demeter to help the mortals, but she would not. Unless Persephone returned, the world would remain cold. She grew poppies to lull her into sleep, and when she was awake, she stared out the farmhouse windows in a daze.

One morning, she awoke to find a gleaming black structure at the edge of the courtyard. The door was carved with a rabbit trying to outrun a dog.

Determined to tell whichever god this was to leave her alone, Demeter wrapped herself in a green shawl and trudged through the snowy courtyard.

"Selene has told me that each night you sit expressionless at your window," a tall, lithe goddess said when Demeter stepped into a dark room filled with herbal smoke. The goddess breezed around a worktable, hips swaying beneath her black cloak. "It is my thought that, when grieving, no one should be alone."

"Hecate," Demeter breathed, realizing who the goddess was. She pressed herself against the door. "You cannot be here. The Fates do not allow it. You must work from afar."

"I may appear to those at a crossroads." Cate poured red tea into twin cups. When Demeter took hers, she smiled. "I came to provide you with tea, and time, and warmth."

"Thank you," Demeter said after she sipped from her cup. "But it will not help. Persephone is gone. I have lost my soul."

Cate clasped her hand. "Souls can be found."

Demeter finished her tea, regretting that the goddess was wrong. She asked, "How did you get to my farm?"

Cate smiled. "My spell room travels where it wills. Anywhere, in any realm."

Demeter took Cate by the shoulders. "Take me to the underworld."

Her grip was tight enough to be painful, but Cate merely lifted a large, intricate key that hung from a cord around her throat. "If it wills."

She slipped the key into the door, but instead of the underworld, it opened to an inn filled with mortals. Torches burned on the walls, but despite the flickering warmth, the mortals huddled on chairs and the floor, mumbling among themselves. A baby cried in its mother's arms against the wall.

These mortals were exhausted. Starving. It was clear they were giving up hope.

"Why did it bring us here?" Demeter pulled her shawl more tightly around herself.

"I suppose we need giant fennel." Cate gestured to the torches that lined the walls. "Thanks to you, this might be the only place with any of it left in the Greek world."

With that, she disappeared down the hall.

Alone in the room of hungry, coughing mortals, Demeter found herself striding to the counter in front of the kitchen, where a boy with drooping eyes lounged. "You want a room?" He waved a hand at where she had been standing moments before. "I saw you and that lady come in together."

Demeter smiled tightly at him. "I would like to purchase your entire stock of kykeon. As a celebration." She gestured to the room behind them. "Everyone may drink of it."

The boy looked her up and down, as though wondering whether she was serious, then he laughed. "Our whole stock? We don't have any stock. After this winter, we scarcely have anything left at all. Even if we did have barley and mint, we would not waste it on kykeon. Demeter has left us for dead. If we manage to survive this, we won't be serving her sacred beverage ever again."

At his words, Demeter stared, feeling something crack in her chest. The winter was not her fault. It was the fault of Hades, who had stolen her daughter, robbing her of any reason to bring life and light to the world.

She did not plan to do it, but in the next moment, the boy had vanished, and she held a spotted gecko in her fist. It screamed, but the mortals did not react to it.

"What have I done?" she breathed when Cate returned with a head of giant fennel.

She showed the goddess the squirming gecko, and Cate frowned. A deep crease formed in the middle of her brow. "Madness," she said, leaning close. She wrapped Demeter in her scent of herbal smoke. "It happened to me once. I turned an ungrateful witch into a polecat. This is how it starts. But if you do nothing, it will get worse."

Demeter stared at the gecko. "How do I stop myself?"

"By finding your daughter." Cate held up the head of giant fennel. "Let us go."

They returned to the spell room, where Cate offered up a glass orb to hold Askalabos, lest he be attacked by her black polecat, Gale. Even still, the beady-eyed creature stared at the gecko, pawing at the orb when Demeter set it on the worktable.

Cate opened the spell-room door, and this time, the cool, clean scent of balsam filled Demeter's nose. When she stepped over the threshold, she found herself in a white poplar forest that twinkled with flakes of snow. The silvery trees extended in all directions, climbing the mountain that composed the underworld. The ground beneath their trunks was brown and cold. The air was thick with smoke, but Cate lit the head of giant fennel and followed Demeter into the silent realm.

"The journey will be dark and long," she said while she closed the spell-room door. "I cannot promise that you will find what you are looking for, but your daughter languishes in the palace on the mountaintop."

Demeter stepped into the silver forest and snow. "She is all that matters anymore."

Yet at the end of it all, after the ashen Fields of Punishment and the pale Fields of Asphodel, the verdant Isle of Elysium glimpsed through the foliage, Demeter did not find the daughter she had been searching for. Instead, she found a woman who greeted her at the palace doors with a flat expression and a voice as hard as the walls of black marble.

"Mother," she said, standing between the cypresses that rose on either side of the doors. Her eyes flicked to Cate. "The goddess of witches cannot help you take me home."

"We have come so far." Demeter lifted the smoldering torch. "Whatever method of entrapment that man has snared you in, I will find a way to break you free of it."

"My husband has not trapped me here." Persephone gestured to the pomegranate trees that lined the hall behind her. "I have willingly eaten the seeds of his pomegranates, and I must remain here. As the queen of the underworld, I will rule beside him." She placed her hand on her stomach. "Until we deem it time to pass the throne to our children."

Demeter stared, gaze flying from Persephone's eyes to the hand on her stomach. Her blood rushed in her ears. "You are with child by that man."

Persephone nodded, wrinkling the pink fabric of her robe as she tightened her grip on her stomach. "I am."

Demeter gripped Cate's shoulder. Her voice broke. "My daughter, I may have lost you to this evil man, but your child must not be born here. Surely you do not want your flesh and blood, a child of the sun, to grow up the heir of your captor's realm."

"He is not my captor," Persephone snarled. "He is my husband. In your refusal to let me grow up, you have made me choose between my home and true love." Her voice and expression softened, her eyes glistening like the snowflakes in the air. "I miss you every single day, Maytare. I miss the flowers and I miss the stars. I love you and the world we have built with all my heart, but I have to live for myself."

With no other farewell, she whirled back into the palace, spiraling her wrist so that vines broke the soil. The vines twined around the doors, slamming them shut. The gust of wind guttered the torch.

"She is bewitched," Demeter said, turning to Cate in the gloomy dark. "Please, you must stay here. Help her, until I find a way to bring her home again."

Cate pursed her lips, flicking her eyes from Demeter to the palace. "Your daughter will remain at a crossroads for many years. I will not be able to stay with her for all of them, but until the baby is ready to be born, I will serve as her companion."

Demeter pulled the goddess into a hug. She allowed herself a few moments to sob. Then she fled down the mountain, torchless, blinded by white trunks and silver leaves until she crossed the river Styx and emerged into the living world.

She flew to Mount Olympus, where she swore to Zeus that she would bring warmth back to the world if he forced Hades to let Persephone return home. Zeus agreed, desperate for mortal love, and that spring, Hades hosted the first Farewell Festival.

The surviving mortals rejoiced at the return of warmth and good soil, but Persephone drifted through the farmhouse like one of the underworld's souls. Demeter fed her poppies to lull her into a peaceful slumber, and as the months passed, her stomach swelled. Until, almost a year after Hades stole her from the meadow, she gave birth to a little girl.

As sunlight poured through the windows, bathing the bedchamber in gold, the bedsheets blossomed with a field of asphodel. Demeter blinked back tears when she looked down at the squirming infant in her daughter's arms. "She is the goddess of flowers, who will bring life to the world. Just as you grew narcissus when you were born."

"The goddess of flowers," Persephone said, breathless as she gazed at her daughter. She looked up at Cate, and her voice and eyes turned hard. "I want you to curse her so she can never fall in love with gods of the underworld."

Cate frowned. "Are you certain? Such spells are irrevocable."

"Of course she is certain." Demeter traced the face of her grandchild, who twitched her nose. "I will raise her here, on the farm, where

I will treasure her with the reverence of my own beating heart." She looked up at Persephone, whose face was stretched with a wan smile. "And you will see her for all the months you are home."

Persephone peered down at the baby in her arms. She pressed a kiss to her forehead, then she looked up at Cate through the asphodel. Under the weight of her words, her voice broke. "Do what you must."

Cate sighed. "Very well."

The goddess of witches raised her hands and blew out a breath that became a cold wind. The room darkened, and when Cate spoke again, her pale eyes rolled into the back of her head. Her black hair billowed, and her posture went rigid. The words spilled from her mouth as glowing red threads.

"Grant this child protection from wild, treacherous, life-changing love," she said, her voice echoing threefold. "Let her never forsake her family for the warmth of another's arms."

The threads wove around the infant, thickening as Cate went on. "Let these threads become a shell, hardening her heart against all creatures of the underworld."

The threads sank into the skin of the swaddled child, and Cate blinked, coming back to herself. With a shudder, Persephone hugged her daughter and named her Asphodel. It was the name of the flowers that swayed over the bed, of the flowers that bloomed through the underworld. It was a name that meant mourning, a flower that symbolized normalcy.

This was fitting, Persephone wept over her child. Because each day she spent in the underworld, separated from her little girl, mourning would become her new normal.

Chapter Twelve

"So you see," Del said in the dark cottage with Thanatos, "no matter how much you love me, or how kind you are, I can never love you in return."

Thanatos took a moment to respond. When he did, all he said was, "That's terrible."

Del folded her hands in her lap, staring at the dying candles. Beyond the windows, the storm howled. "The curse, or the fact that we will be trapped in a marriage devoid of love?"

"Well, both. But I meant the curse."

"Ah. Well. It was supposed to protect me, but here we are."

"I just . . ." He shifted, and Del thought he would take her hand, but instead he ran a finger across one of the white flowers. While he spoke, he watched the movement. "All my life, I have thought you hated the underworld. But really, your heart was hardened against it the moment you were born. You never had a chance to decide for yourself."

Del shook her head. "I did decide for myself. Yaya told me more than enough stories while I was growing up. The Fields of Punishment. Tartarus. The Fields of Asphodel, with its colorless flowers and faceless souls. I hate all of it. I *do* hate the underworld."

She glared at the candles, waiting for a response. When none came, she turned to Thanatos and raised her eyebrows. "What? What are you thinking now?"

He looked up with a mirthless huff, then down at his lap. "I am thinking what a fool I am for believing you would ever want to live in the underworld. I suppose we see what we want to see, and we believe those who promise to give us what we want." His eyes met hers. "I'm sorry, Del. From the depths of my soul, I never wanted to trap you in a marriage you did not want. If you only knew . . ."

"If I only knew what?"

"All I do is trap people. Day in and day out, I trap mortal souls. It is a loving act, and I do not dislike it in itself. When a mortal soul comes to me, they feel relief, and that is all. But I regret how I make the living feel. After I reap the soul of someone they love, they lose vast swaths of what little life they have to grieving the loss." He tapped his fingers on his knees. "But the worst part is that most of the souls I reap are unremarkable. They are neither villains nor heroes. They are normal people. Which means they drink from the river Lethe and lose all their memories before entering the Fields of Asphodel."

In the shadows, Del studied his face. He seemed so pained. "How can you love the underworld, if that is how it makes you feel?"

He sighed. "I admit it is flawed, but are not all worlds? We can love what we have while still daring to dream for more. Perhaps that is why I was so quick to agree to the marriage vow. Your mother suggested that, after you moved to the underworld, you might want to improve the Fields of Asphodel. You are named after them, after all. You must feel connected to them on some level."

Del shook her head. "I do not. The Fields of Asphodel cannot be improved upon. They are a grand nothing. To improve, something must exist at the start."

"Is that how you feel about yourself? Is that the real reason you keep yourself up here alone? We both know the truth. Being alone and forgotten is the closest thing to death for a god. Yet here on this Isle, you are forcing everyone to forget who you are."

"I live alone on this Isle because I cannot *trust* anyone. Did you not hear the story I just told? Yaya warned me when I was little—never let anyone turn you into someone you do not know. The only way to ensure that is to be alone."

"Maybe my mother thought the same thing when she abandoned Keres and me in the underworld." He sighed, watching her with those blue moon eyes while the storm raged outside. "I don't think being alone is good for anyone, but I am sorry I took that choice from you when I made my vow. Perhaps it cannot be dissolved, but . . ." He pulled a clay jar from the pocket of his tunic. It was the same jar he had used during the ceremony at the Farewell Festival. The jar that held water from the river Styx.

"Thanatos," Del said, "what are you doing? Stop." She sent one of the cage vines lashing toward him, but before she could knock the jar from his hand, he tipped a droplet of black water onto his tongue. His eyes began to glow.

Del scrambled back from the cage. Her mind raced, but she had no idea what vow he planned to make. She already had to marry him. She didn't see how things could get worse, but he was a god of the underworld. He spent his days watching the Fields of Punishment torture mortal souls. Whatever vulnerabilities they had just shared, however caged he might be, right now she was in his power. She could do nothing to stop him from making the vow.

"Del," he said, his voice reverberating through her soul, "I, Thanatos, vow on the river Styx to do everything in my power to help you break your curse, and I will not marry you until we have fallen in love."

As he spoke, the storm seemed to seep into the cottage. The wind ripped flowers off the cage and buffeted his hair and clothes. He faded into the shadows, leaching out of existence while his eyes gleamed bright blue. When he spoke the last word, a golden thread wove through the air between them, connecting their hearts.

He snapped back into being, and Del leaped to her feet, glaring at him in shock. "Thanatos! What have you done?"

"Hopefully," he said, "earned a bit of your trust."

"But we cannot fall in love. Breaking my curse will be impossible. I thought you wanted to return to the underworld, but now—" She groaned, waving a hand at the white flowers that drifted to the floor. "When we fail to break my curse, the mortals will forget who you are. Without you to reap souls, the gods will descend into madness." First would be Zeus, then her father, then her mother and Yaya. "How is this supposed to help?"

Thanatos looked up at her, lips quirked. "The way I see it, my situation has not changed much. The only difference is, now there is no risk of entering a loveless marriage. Unless you had changed your mind about keeping me here?" He shook his head. "And all it took was me deciding to stay. If only I had known."

Del growled. "I did want to keep you here. But just until—" She flapped her hands, casting wild shadows on the cottage walls. "I don't want to destroy the world."

"Well, then," Thanatos smiled, "I suppose we better hurry up and fall in love."

Chapter Thirteen

Del gestured at the cottage door. "And how do you suppose we go about doing that? Even if I wanted to break my curse, we can't leave the Isle. I doubt you can fly in such a storm."

"Well." Thanatos leaned back, wings draped across the floor. "I could start by answering your father, who has been hammering on the door of my mind this whole time."

"What?" Del raised both hands, thickening the cage vines. "You have been communicating with my father?" Her stomach dropped as she thought back to everything they had discussed. She could not believe she had told him so much.

"I have not been communicating with him." Thanatos tapped a finger against his temple. "The connection between our minds is useful when I am in the living world reaping souls, but ever since I discovered his dishonesty about our betrothal, I have been blocking him out. I can hear him as though he is knocking on a door, but when he tries to peek through the windows, I snap the screens closed." He gestured at the windows just as another crack of thunder rattled the Isle. "Hades wants you to let him come to the Isle. He says the storm will not stop until you do so, and I assume he wants to force you into letting me go." His voice grew soft. "Instead, you can tell him about my new vow."

Del swallowed. Her Isle was the one place she was safe from her father. It might be destroyed, but if she gave him permission to come here, her final shred of protection would snap. Thanatos would be the only thing between her and a future she hated.

She examined his face, searching for any sign of deception. But he was open to her, his eyes filled with a welcoming innocence. His new vow meant he must disagree with Hades on some level, and not long ago, she had all but resigned herself to a life in the underworld. If letting her father come here meant there was a chance of preserving her freedom, she would take it. It was the best choice she had left.

She breathed out through her nose. "Very well, then."

She sank to her knees on the packed-earth floor. Eyes closed, she imagined roots extending from the Isle. They plummeted into the Aegean, unfurling through the murky depths. When they burrowed into the silt at the bottom, she opened her eyes and stood, feeling light-headed from using so much magic.

"Are you all right?" Thanatos cinched his eyebrows. "You look pale."

Del grabbed the jar of dried dates from the kitchen counter. "Tell my father he has permission to come here for the duration of one hour. After that, his path to the underworld will collapse." When Thanatos kept looking at her, she sighed. "I'm fine, Thanatos."

She stuffed one of the sweet, chewy fruits into her mouth, and it was only after energy flooded through her that Thanatos let his eyes close. A low hum emanated from him, and gooseflesh pebbled Del's skin. She felt a tug of awareness, as though her heart was trying to hear something far in the distance. When he opened his eyes, the hum and tug vanished. Morning light seeped through the window screens, and the Isle fell silent. No rain. No wind. The storm clouds had fled, but the quiet was not comforting.

It was the silence of death.

"I have to go look at it," Del said. She stared at the door, wringing her hands.

"Take me with you," Thanatos said.

"No." She shook her head. "This is my Isle. I need to face it alone."

"That is precisely why you should *not* be alone. This is your home. The thing you love most in the world. And it has been . . . I mean, you know. It's not going to be good out there, Del. I know about loss. I don't want you to face this by yourself."

Del hesitated. After last night, she should have no qualms about him seeing her vulnerable. But this was different. Last night they had spoken of emotions she had felt in the past. This would be showing him her feelings that she had had no time to process.

"And," he said, "we both need to speak with Hades about our marriage. Regardless of what reasons he had for keeping your curse a secret, I am not happy with him. I may not hate him like you do, but I want answers."

"At any moment," Del said, "he could whisk you away with him."

"So make sure he doesn't. You locked me in a laurel tree. I'm sure you can find some way to make sure he doesn't take me away. And, well, you may not like it, but I am close with him. We get along. Having me out there will help."

Del pressed a hand to her forehead. She stood like that for a few moments, letting herself be furious at her situation. Then she looked up at Thanatos. "You asked for this."

She spiraled her wrists, and a net of bindweed folded his wings tightly to his body. He grimaced, and a long vine wrapped around Del's wrist. She thinned the cage vines so he could step through them, then she tilted up her chin to get a good look at him. "Be a good boy while we're out there."

Thanatos shaded her like a tree. "Always, mistress."

Del watched him. His eyes skated over her face, and he parted his lips.

"Right, then." She spun away from him. "Let's . . . let's go face it."

He touched her back with a featherlight hand. "I'm right here."

With a nod and a deep breath, she opened the door—

And that breath felt like her last.

The rows of white lilies on either side of the path were smashed into the mud, spilling pale guts from their green buds. The rosebushes were upturned, roots dangling like disemboweled intestines from the warped white myrtle arches. The ground was so waterlogged that Del's feet squelched when she walked, the hem of her robe quickly turning heavy and brown. The orchard and woodland had become a battlefield of broken limbs, tree trunks jutting from the earth like snapped bones. They reached in vain for the yellow sky, which made the entire Isle look ill.

"It looks like the Fields of Punishment," breathed Del. Feeling as if she was outside herself, she drifted over the trampled crocus lawn. The beach was smeared with purple blooms that had been pounded into the surf. Tree limbs hemmed the shoreline, and seaweed slapped against them with pus-white foam, wafting a warm, rotten smell.

No longer able to hold herself up, Del sank to the ground. She sat on the damp sand, leaning against the elm that had sliced into her forehead when it fell.

Thanatos sat beside her, saying nothing, allowing her to grieve. Unable to look at his face, she lowered her eyes to his hands and saw he was twining crushed crocus stems. She realized that he was making a bracelet. He wore a concentrated frown, shadows dancing across his cheekbones. He really was beautiful. The way his lips swelled from the rest of his profile. The way he sat cross-legged, elbows on his knees, leaning forward so his wings would not brush the tree. Had their situation been different, Del might have considered him for a lover. Just for a season. Then she would have sent him away to be alone again.

But their situation wasn't different. Thanks to their betrothal, he would be a constant, suffocating presence. He would create an idea of her in his head, confining her to his expectations. Over time, she would forget her true self, and she would belong only to him. He was a kind person. She could not deny that. But a silken cage is still a cage, and at the thought of never being her own person again, the bars chafed.

"Here," he said, holding out the bracelet of crocus stems. "Take this."

"What?" Del blinked at him.

He shrugged and lowered his gaze, gently taking the wrist around which Del had wrapped the bindweed leash. He slipped the bracelet over her hand, his fingers cool against her skin. "Sometimes, it helps me when I'm upset. To have something to fiddle with."

He lowered his hands back to his lap, but when Del looked at the thin green bracelet that now adorned her wrist, she still felt the ghosts of his fingertips.

"Growing this Isle took hundreds of years," she said. "I had plants that grew nowhere else in the world. Creations that were entirely my own. They were the first and best versions of themselves, and now they are gone."

"But you are still here," Thanatos said. A breeze ruffled his hair. "You can regrow your Isle after all this. You will keep bringing life to the world even after mastering Death." He gave her a small smile. "The mortals will admire that."

She ran her thumb over the bracelet. "The mortals will never know about this."

"Ah. Yes. You have never experienced mortal worship. I understand shying away from it, but it's not all bad. Calling it a drug . . . I'm not sure Keres was right about that. It is natural to want to be loved, and it is natural to be upset when you aren't."

"We are talking about madness, Thanatos."

"I said it was natural. I didn't say it was good."

"I have no interest in anything that can make young gods lose their souls. Yaya always warned me about what happened to Eos. The goddess of dawn—she went to the mortals when she was only fifty years old, long before she should have revealed herself. She got lost in her magic, and all that remains of her soul is what Yaya could trap in the heliotrope plant she gave Helios. Between that and my mother, by the time

I turned one hundred and twenty years old, I knew I did not want to reveal myself. Instead, Yaya and Cate gave me the Isle."

Thanatos furrowed his eyebrows. "You mean the Isle was not your idea?"

"It was a surprise," Del said. "It was the best gift anyone could have given me."

Thanatos made a noncommittal hum and tapped the sand.

"Whatever you want to say, just say it."

His face scrunched, and he lifted his hands. "I mean, doesn't it seem a bit—forgive me if this sounds terrible—but doesn't it seem a bit wrong? The day you are supposed to make your grand reveal to the mortals, and you were taken to an Isle that keeps you locked away from the rest of the world."

"I did not want to be part of the rest of the world."

"But you deserve praise for what you have done!" He gestured at the Isle. "The mortals should know who controls the sweet-smelling flowers that fill their gardens and meadows. They should know who cultivated the fruits and vegetables on their tables."

Del fiddled with the crocus bracelet. "It's not that I think there is anything wrong with wanting praise for my work. It's just, I grow my flowers because I love doing it. When I'm upset, it helps me calm down. I don't need mortals or anyone else to tell me what I love, and I relish that freedom. I can live for myself." She looked up to find him arching an eyebrow. "What? You asked, and I told you. What now?"

"You have never even wondered how mortal worship might feel."

She looked out at the Aegean. Rage-red flowers climbed up her throat, but even after she swallowed them, her throat still felt clogged. She brought her knees up to her chin, watching the waves pound into the sand in time with her heart. "Fine," she snapped. "Yes, sometimes I wonder how it might feel. But I have never told anyone, and I don't blame Yaya. We all keep secrets tied around our hearts, and I am one of hers. That's all."

"I suppose." Thanatos watched her hands. Or perhaps he was watching the bracelet on her wrist. His eyes caught hers, and he held them as he said, "But can't you breathe easier, having finally let one of yours go?"

Del pulled the bindweed leash taut. "Darling Thanatos, do you expect me to believe you hide nothing in your heart?"

Thanatos cleared his throat. "Well, I might have laughed at you for thinking Hades and Persephone are not in love, but the truth is, I understand it all too well."

"What do you mean?"

"I mean, whether or not Persephone is actually bewitched, maybe it is easier to believe that she is. Because I hate my mother for falling in love, and I understand how it feels to wish your mother would choose you over someone else."

Del waited. She wanted to ask him what he was talking about, but she knew sometimes saying nothing is the best way to convince someone to talk.

When he let out a breath, she tamped down a smile. "Your mother married the king of the underworld." He tilted his head back against the elm, looking at the yellow sky over the Isle. "My mother, Nyx, fell in love with the god of darkness long before I was born."

Chapter Fourteen

Long ago, Nyx called the underworld her home.

Erebos served as the master jailer of Tartarus, where he watched over the cells of fire and brimstone, and as right hand to Hades, Nyx gathered his reports. She had long been enamored with the jailer, but she kept her feelings to herself. Each evening, she had to spread night across the living world, relieving her daughter, Hemera, from bringing day to the world. And while Erebos sent some of his shadows up above, the underworld held his soul.

Such a difference in where their souls were held would only lead to strife between them, so Nyx reasoned it was best to keep what little of Erebos she had than to speak up and lose even that. Each time she met him in his alcove behind the fiery waterfall of the Phlegethon, she reminded herself that these meetings had to keep her content.

And they did. Until at the end of one of them, as the light of the flames coated their skin in gold, Erebos leaned down and kissed her on the mouth.

The kiss was not soft or slow. It was the passionate meeting of two like individuals at last merging into one. And in the wake of it, while her lips tingled and mind buzzed, Nyx listened to Erebos say he had loved her for some time now. Regardless of whether his feelings were reciprocated, he could no longer remain silent. He needed to know how she felt, but as he stood there, black eyes reflecting the flames of the waterfall, Nyx opened and closed her mouth without emitting any sound.

His confession of love was what she had always dreamt of, but now that it was real, she hesitated to begin a relationship she believed was doomed to fail. On her trips through the living world, she had often heard mortals tout that it was better to have loved and lost than to never have loved at all, but that was because everything ended for mortals. It was natural for them to believe love would end as well. The same was not true for gods. To experience bliss for a short time was not worth spending eternity with the loss.

Knowing this, Nyx did not tell Erebos how she felt. At the end of their meetings, he always asked if she loved him back, but she was too cowardly to tell the truth and not brave enough to lie, so she kept her mouth shut. It took years of him never wavering in his love before she nodded when he asked if she loved him as well.

As they kissed, she let herself fall, and she fell with all the light and speed of a shooting star. Each night, while her Cloak of Darkness fanned out around her, painting the sky with twinkling stars, she smiled down at the shadows that rolled across the waves and hills. She took comfort in them until she returned to their maker in the underworld.

In the alcove behind the Phlegethon, Erebos held her all day long. Every morning when she got home, he promised to never let her go, and as the months spun into years, Nyx began to believe she had been wrong. Their differences would not divide them but would make them strong. This realization filled her with life, and she let the death inside her go.

One of her abilities was that she could release parts of herself in the form of a child. She had done this with Hemera long ago, the goddess of day taking on the mantle of bringing light to the world, and now she did the same with Keres and Thanatos. The Twins of Death were hers and hers alone, but Erebos treated them as his own.

While Nyx spread night across the living world, he cuddled them in his Shroud of Shadows. And when Nyx returned home, she practiced flying with them off the alcove. The twins learned how to control their magic, and Thanatos performed his first marriage vow on Nyx and Erebos when he was only sixty years old.

Everything was blissful. Which was perhaps why Nyx failed to notice when Erebos fell out of love. It was not a sudden ending. Not a star plummeting to the ground. Rather, it was the shift from night to dawn. Even if one stands watching the horizon, it is impossible to pinpoint the exact moment the shadows recede. All you know is, at some point, you are standing in the unforgiving light of day.

This was how Nyx felt when, one evening after the twins were in bed, she stood at the edge of the alcove and waited for Erebos. When he arrived home, she stopped him before he could lie down. Arms wrapped around her glittering cloak, she reminded him they had not slept together for some time now. They barely saw each other save for this brief trade-off on the alcove, and he seldom so much as kissed her farewell. The words kept pouring out, and by the time she had finished, tears stung her eyes. She paused, gathering herself.

Then she asked him why.

For a moment, he watched her with his black eyes. His brows were furrowed, and his jaw was locked, forming the same expression he had worn the day he confessed his love. It was the expression he wore when he had a deep, hidden truth to reveal. Though this truth was not really hidden at all, because Nyx had known it from the start. Voice terribly gentle, he told her that he did not blame her for being unable to leave Hemera alone in the living world, but he wanted someone who could remain down below.

Though it shredded her heart, Nyx knew it was best to cut off their relationship now. When she returned from bringing night to the world, she packed up her things and her children and flew off the alcove for the last time. She did not look back. She felt empty and cold. Rather than being reassured that she could at least trust herself, the knowledge that she had always been right only worsened her loss. Because while she hated Erebos for fooling her, more than that, she hated herself for being fooled.

She and the twins took refuge in the palace at the top of the underworld. Hades was often away courting the goddess of spring, so he was happy to let his right hand care for his home while her heart healed. But by the time he married Persephone, Nyx knew her heart would never heal in the underworld. Everything reminded her of Erebos. She had to go. Keres and Thanatos had to remain in the underworld until they were old enough to reveal themselves to the mortals, so Hades agreed to raise them in his home.

Alone, Nyx fled to live with Hemera in the living world.

Chapter Fifteen

"I have not seen her since," said Thanatos. He stared at the Aegean, watching the waves crinkle against the horizon. "I understand why she cannot bear to live in the underworld. You die a little death each day you are parted from the one you love. It must make it easier, maintaining this self-imposed distance from Erebos."

"But she still left you down there." Del searched his stoic expression. "She still went to live with Hemera and left you and Keres alone in the underworld."

His eyes caught on her lips before flicking up to her own. "But I wasn't alone. I resent my mother for leaving, but thanks to your parents, I always had a home."

"And what of Keres? She hasn't lived in the underworld for nearly two centuries now. Did she do something to make them kick her out?"

"Of course not." Thanatos was aghast. He huffed a breath, watching the waves crash against the silty shore. "She lived in the palace with me until we revealed ourselves to the mortals. You remember her from the Farewell Festivals when we were young."

"I remember the last one she attended, when she backed you into a corner and slapped your face hard enough to leave a welt."

Thanatos sighed. "She was trying to convince me to go live with her in Helios and Selene's palace. That is where our mother lives now. Keres left the underworld after that Farewell Festival." His legs were still folded beneath him, and he traced the gold pattern that adorned the hem of his tunic. "She told me she had gone to find out why our mother never came back to visit us after she went to live with Hemera."

"I get it. She wanted answers." Del plucked at the crocus bracelet. "I've always wanted some from my own parents."

"Well." Thanatos cleared his throat. "For a while, she sent lots of letters home. Then out of nowhere, she stopped. Hades sent the Furies to search for her, but they were forbidden to enter Olympus, so they could not reach the palace. For over a century, I never even saw her in the living world. Which was terrifying, because even though there is not much overlap in our reaping of souls, I was used to seeing her every once in a while."

He paused, and Del remained quiet while he gathered himself. She knew how it felt to be held captive by memories you wished would let you go.

"Anyway." He scrubbed his hair. "It went on like that for a while, all of us very hurt and confused by the silence. Honestly, she didn't start speaking to me again until the end of last year. We have lots of shared history, so we are getting back to how we were when we were kids—but it is still rocky, as I am sure you saw. Siblings are your best friends even when you hate them, you know?"

Del thought back to yesterday in the cottage, where Keres and Thanatos had seemed entirely at odds. Yet at the same time, together, they formed a balanced scale. Whether or not they were at each other's throats, they would always be part of one another. The principle of balance made them indivisible.

"What did you say," she asked, "that made her slap you at that Farewell Festival?"

Thanatos flexed his jaw. "I told her I didn't trust a word out of our mother's mouth." He gestured to her with a flippant hand. "What you just said—about wanting answers—Keres always assumed I wanted them as well. And I did, when I was little. Keres and I used to fall asleep in our palace bedroom wondering why our mother left us alone down below."

He brushed sand off his tunic. "But once I grew up, I let all that go. Which is what I told Keres at that Farewell Festival. I told her I have a family. I have a home. I have no interest in forming a relationship with the woman who abandoned me as a child. So I said, why would I want to go live with a person who has always only seen me as a reminder of what she has lost, when I have spent my life feeling loved by these two amazing people?"

His voice faded when he saw the asphodel that poked through the sand around Del. "I'm sorry. Hades and Persephone are not really my parents. They're yours. I know your relationship with them is complicated—"

"No." Del shook her head, making a slicing motion with her finger to disintegrate the asphodel. "*I'm* sorry." She pressed the heels of her hands to her eyes, then she lowered them to her middle, hugging herself. "Zeus's name, I feel terrible."

Thanatos shifted so his body faced hers. "What? Why do you feel terrible? My mother did all this before you were born. None of this is your fault."

His voice was so soft, so gentle. Del wished he would yell. She shut her eyes and leaned the back of her head against the elm. "No, I know. I know it's her fault." She opened her eyes, squinting at the yellow sky over the Isle. "It's just . . . I have always been so jealous."

"Of what?"

"Of you." Del laughed less out of mirth and more to loosen the thicket of guilt in her stomach. She had never even considered that the reason Thanatos was around her family so much was because he had no family of his own.

"I have always been so jealous of you." She swallowed, voice firmer now. "Of the relationship you have with my parents. With the triplets." She plucked at the crocus bracelet. "My whole family loves you so much."

Thanatos was silent, letting her words mingle with the lapping water and rustling leaves from the fallen elm. He placed his hand on her wrist, running his thumb across the bracelet before slipping her fingers through his one by one. "Del," he said when their hands were intertwined on the sand, "I could never replace you. Not in the hearts of your parents or of the triplets. I hope you know that."

"You don't need to comfort me." Del watched their hands. His were so much larger than hers, so pale from the lack of sun in the underworld. "You just told me this awful story. You're the one who needs comforting."

Thanatos shrugged, and their hands shifted on the sand, the grains tickling Del's skin. "I have accepted it. It's the distant past." She lifted her gaze to take in his solemn expression. "Everything your family has done for me and Keres, I appreciate it. I appreciate it so much. I spend every day trying to prove myself worthy of it—"

"You *are* worthy of it." Del squeezed his hand.

Thanatos gave her a small smile. "But you are their child. I know your father does a poor job of showing it, but he cares for you deeply. I'm sure he had a good reason for binding us into this betrothal, and I know he feels horrible about how it has all played out. He told me as much when he said he needed to come to the Isle."

Del sat utterly still while he rubbed the space between her forefinger and thumb.

"And I know your mother loves you more than anything else. She talks about you so much. Always has. It's weird." He laughed, and the sound sent gooseflesh across her skin. "Because even though you and I barely spoke until this betrothal, I feel like I have grown up knowing you so well. You have always been this presence in my life, thanks to the stories your mother tells."

Del looked up, catching his eyes. They were tinged green in the yellow light. "What kind of stories does she tell?"

Thanatos took in a breath, but then the ground beneath them began to rumble. With a yelp, Del scrambled away from the fallen elm. Its leaves shuddered like a child in the cold. "Run!" she said, and dragged Thanatos to the edge of the crocus lawn. Birds shrieked and funneled from the broken woodland in a great black cloud.

In the disorienting blur of shadows, Del stopped, breathing hard. She turned back in time to see the ground crumble from beneath the fallen elm. Still holding his hand, she stumbled into Thanatos. He gripped her shoulders, and Del pressed herself against him while watching the elm. Rock and dirt belched from the hole, obscuring the tattered boughs.

In a whirl of glittering darkness, Hades stepped onto the Isle.

Chapter Sixteen

Del froze. It was just like her nightmare, watching her father emerge from the roots of the white willow. When Hades stepped out from beneath the fallen elm, she lifted her hands to her shoulders and interlocked Thanatos's fingers with her own, gripping them hard. Thanatos squeezed back, and she let out a deep breath while the hole beneath the elm resealed.

The ground settled, and she gently removed Thanatos's hands from her shoulders. She stepped away from him, focusing on her father as he rippled across the shore.

His cloak was mottled with gemstones that swallowed the sunlight and spat it back out, rendering him the colorless center in a cacophony of rainbows. The cloak billowed around his ankles when he flowed to a stop, his death-dark eyes flicking over the bindweed leash that connected Thanatos to Del.

"I regret the destruction of your Isle." He scowled. "But we had to force you to listen before you destroyed the world."

"Rather hypocritical"—Del buried the fear that coiled up her throat—"punishing me for doing the same thing you did three hundred years ago."

At first, Hades did not respond. She met his gaze, and he clenched his jaw. He had never been one to yell. No, his anger was as cold as the jewels that decorated his cloak.

"In the past two days," he said, his cloak billowing like a death shroud, "I have received letters from both gods of war." His voice lowered, and he turned on his heel, spraying sand in the wake of his cloak. "Ares and Athena are demanding I get you in line, threatening me with what will happen if I do not. Your mother has gone to the living world, and rather than enjoy her time with you and Demeter on the farm, she is attempting to pacify rioting cities and battlefields. The triplets are distraught—"

"I know." Del gestured at Thanatos. "I know we have made a mess of the world, which is why I agreed to talk—"

"We?" Hades again turned on his heel, and the spray of sand hissed against Del's robe. "No, Daughter, Than has done nothing wrong. I recognize that your mother and I made a mistake by not telling you about the betrothal before he made his vow, but based on the counsel your mother received, we thought . . ." He shook his head sharply. "It does not matter now. What matters is getting Than back to reaping souls."

Del took a step toward him. "I *know*—"

"Which we could accomplish quite easily, if you would stop being such a selfish, shortsighted child."

"Hades," said Thanatos, startling Del. His voice swept across the beach like a crescendoing note. "*Listen* to your daughter when she talks."

His interruption froze Hades on the shore. Cloak flapping around his still form, he stared at the pale, winged god. In the silence, he dragged his gaze down the bindweed leash to the hand Thanatos rested on the small of Del's back.

"I'm sorry," Thanatos said to the king of the underworld. He brushed his hand lightly against Del's robe before dropping it to his side. "I'm sorry to use such a tone."

"No, I apologize." Hades watched them with a raised eyebrow. "Del invited me here to talk, and I came in on the attack." He turned to Del.

"I know you want to break off your betrothal, but neither Nyx nor I know how. We need Than back in the underworld, so tell me—what else do you want? Merely ask, and it is yours."

"Actually," Thanatos said, "bribing Del won't help."

Hades deepened his scowl. "What is this? Don't you want to go home?"

"Of course I want to go home. But I have no interest in entering a loveless marriage against Del's will. You should have told me about her curse before I made my vow. You did not, so I have decided to remedy the situation in the only way I know how." He took a deep breath and let it out, glancing at Del before he told the king of the underworld about his new vow. "Help us break her curse, and I will return to the underworld."

Hades blanched, but Del spoke up. "Perhaps you could start by telling Mel to stop giving me nightmares about marrying Thanatos. Depriving me of rest will not help."

Thanatos turned to her. "What nightmares?"

"Mel has not been giving you nightmares," Hades said. "I had her promise not to practice on her siblings anymore. She was causing Mak and Zag too much distress. Every night, they were climbing into my and Persephone's bed."

Del arched her eyebrows. "You have two disobedient daughters, then. Because I have been having the same nightmare for weeks, and last night it got worse."

She expected Hades to accuse her of lying, but instead his lips thinned. "What happens in this nightmare?" he asked.

"What does it matter?" The shift in his interest unsettled Del, but it was anger that bloomed from her mouth. "Don't you want to condemn Thanatos for making his new vow? Don't you want to berate me for being a selfish child?"

A muscle ticked in Hades's jaw. "Yes, we must discuss the vow. But first, tell me about this nightmare of yours."

Del opened her mouth to say he had no right to know her fears, but Thanatos placed his hand on her back again. His palm was warm through her robe, and with a glance up at him, she expelled an angry breath. She nodded, half to herself and half to him. Then she turned back to her father and, in as clipped a tone as she could manage, told him. About the endless hallway and overheard conversation. About the lake and smacking her head.

"That is where it used to end." She dropped her wrist when she realized she had been fiddling with the crocus bracelet. "But last night I started hearing a woman claim that in the underworld, I could be queen." She glared at Hades. "What is that, if not Mel enticing me to agree to your marriage plans?"

Hades ignored her jab. "What did this woman sound like?" he asked.

Del ran out of patience. "You already know this!" She zipped her hand through the air with a sharp movement. "The voice looks like a star, shooting toward me. It pushes me out the window, and I wake up while I fall through the snow."

Slowly, Hades shook his head. "This nightmare is not Mel's doing," he said.

"Oh?" Del folded her arms, refusing to acknowledge how a thicket of panic snarled through her chest. "And whose is it, then?"

"My mother's," Thanatos said. "Isn't it?"

Hades sighed. "I believe it is."

"But how?" Del asked. "She is the goddess of night, not nightmares."

"She has powers over dreams. Nightmares and dreams . . ." Hades tilted his hand side to side. "There is not a clean divide between these things."

"But why would she want to frighten me? If she wants to finalize her alliance with the underworld, she should be trying to make Thanatos and me feel comfortable." She gestured at Thanatos. "Maybe, oh, I don't know, she could come discuss things with the child she abandoned until he became useful?"

Thanatos increased the pressure of his palm on her back. "Del—"

"Come to think of it, why does Nyx even want an alliance with the underworld? Thanatos said she left the underworld after Erebos broke her heart. Why would she want to go back? She wanted to get away so badly, she abandoned her children to do so."

"Hades," Thanatos said when Hades opened his mouth, "I apologize. I told her everything just before you arrived." He turned to Del. "I know it is all fresh in your mind, but that stuff happened a long time ago. My mother must have moved on—"

"Than," Hades said. "Than, stop."

Thanatos blinked and dropped his hand from Del's shoulder. "What?" He turned to her father, a breeze ruffling Del's robe where his hand had been.

"I . . ." Hades cleared his throat. "I have not been entirely honest."

Del scoffed. "There's a shock."

Hades closed his eyes for a few moments. "Del," he said when he opened them, "I tried to tell you before."

"Before my betrothal? No, I don't think so."

"In Cate's spell room, when you came to ask me about the marriage vow. This is what I was planning to talk to you about. It is why I wanted to come to your Isle. I thought it might change your mind about the betrothal." He shifted his eyes to Thanatos. "That is, before I learned you had taken matters into your own hands."

"What is this other information?" Thanatos asked. "You didn't tell me about it."

"And I will." Hades held up his hands. "I promise, I will tell you everything, but first I want you to know how sorry I am." He pressed a palm to his chest, rippling the rainbows that sprang from his cloak. "Than, it was selfish of me not to tell you before now. I wanted you to like me for a little longer, and after you hear this story, you won't. I will spend the rest of my immortal life trying to atone, and—though I will never deserve it—I hope someday you will grant me forgiveness for what I have done."

His words settled over them, and Thanatos edged close to Del so that his bound wings could wrap around them both. Del leaned toward him. If Hades was prefacing this revelation with something so dramatic, he was about to tell them something that would likely shift everything about how Thanatos saw the world and his place in it.

Hades lifted his hands, holding them with his palms down, fingers outstretched. Del gasped when the ground between the three of them fissured. Sand and crocus blooms fell into the crevices, and jewels rose up to replace them. Emeralds. Rubies. Diamonds. Lapis. All the earth's riches, subject to her father's command.

"It is true that Nyx and Erebos fell in love and lived together," he said. "But Nyx did not leave the underworld because Erebos broke her heart." The hoard of jewels arrayed themselves across the sand. "She left because I discovered their relationship."

He paused, sweat beading his forehead. Then he strummed his fingers through the air, sending the jewels smoothing into the shapes of two men. One was seated on a glinting throne of opal. The other was shrouded in a white diamond cloud. "Before I met Persephone, I was a bitter, jealous man. Zeus ruled the living world, free to swoop down from Olympus to commune with mortals whenever he wished. Because of this, the mortals built him many temples. They spread his tales like grains of sand."

On the ground, the man surrounded by diamonds swept toward the rolling emerald hills. He alighted on an amber temple, then the temple and all that surrounded it crumbled, raining down on the man seated upon his opal throne.

"Meanwhile, I was trapped in the underworld, tending to dead mortals. Along the slopes of the mountain that composed my realm, I leveled great sections of forest to make flatlands for the Fields of Punishment and the Fields of Asphodel. I dumped the excavated soil into the Lake of Mnemosyne to raise the Isle of Elysium. Before deciding where each mortal soul would go, I granted each of them a fair trial."

The jewels that rained past the throne formed trees of white diamonds interrupted by rivers of amber and sapphire. All of them built atop one another to lift the throne higher and higher, until the man on the throne sat directly below the hem of Hades's cloak. Tiny amethysts darted through the forest, all of them moving away from the throne.

"I earned no appreciation from the souls I ruled. Those who landed in the Fields of Punishment cursed my name." Amethysts burrowed into the barren sand near Del's feet. "Those who wound up in the Fields of Asphodel drank from the river Lethe and forgot everything, drifting aimlessly." Halfway up the diamond slope, amethysts dipped themselves in a sapphire river and roved through a patch of moonstone. "Those who were granted access to Elysium thanked me and ran, fearing I would change my mind about their heroism." Amethysts sailed into a lake near the top of the mountain. They leaped onto the emerald island in the middle of it, and the opal throne became flanked by three winged, topaz women.

"The Furies were my only companions. Rather than their superior, they treated me like a spoiled child. Now I applaud their behavior, but back then I thought no one had it worse off than myself. Fed up, they suggested I visit Tartarus. I had not been there in many years, and they thought Erebos might help me gain some perspective."

The topaz women whispered in the man's ear, and the opal throne dissolved into a long, thin boat. It sailed down the amber river with the women alongside it. When it reached the sand near Del's feet, the women shattered into a topaz waterfall that lifted the boat, disintegrating the diamond forest until the entire mountain became an inferno. Within the flames coalesced a man of onyx. Reaching out an enrobed hand, he pulled the man from the boat onto a patch of sand. Around them, amber jewels glittered and lapped.

"Erebos led me inside his alcove behind the Phlegethon. I am sure he thought I had some issue with how he was guarding the cells, but when he asked me what was wrong, the truth came spilling out. It was as hot and angry as the fire falling around us. He listened well, then he said he understood how I felt. As the god of darkness, he had long been feared by mortals. But he told me this terror inspires respect, which inspires worship."

With a bow to the onyx man, the other man returned to his boat. He rose on a wave of gleaming amber flames, which receded to reveal him seated on his throne. A golden crown appeared atop his head, and the diamond forest lathered the ground.

"Erebos showed me what my true power was. Zeus was a friend to mortals, but I was their common enemy, limitless in the great unknown that follows death. When I returned to the palace, I had gained more confidence. But more than that, I had gained a friend."

Hades paused then. Del glanced up at him, but he was staring at the network of jewels beneath him, face colorless and jaw set. Sweat trickled down Del's neck, the hot, sticky sensation soothed by the spring air. At her side, Thanatos was rigid.

"For years," Hades said, fisting, then flexing his hands, "Erebos and I strengthened our friendship." Del looked back down to see the sand swallow the diamond forest. "Once a week, I gathered his reports as an excuse to pay him a visit." The throne gave way to a sprawling palace of onyx. "But now that I took pride in my work, it demanded more of my time. Before long, I had to ask Nyx to gather his reports in my stead."

In the halls of onyx, the crowned man leaned close to a woman cloaked in obsidian. She bowed and swept her cloak over her shoulder in one fluid motion. It fanned outward, obscuring the palace. Topaz and amber bubbled to the surface, the ground once again devolving into a flaming mass.

"Back then, Nyx was my right hand." Hades's voice flowed in Thanatos's direction. "She had not given birth to you and Keres yet, so she still maintained power over death. She was strict yet gentle, brutal yet merciful. She was the most capable individual I had ever met, and this fueled my obsession. As the goddess of night, she was much older than I was. Really, she and Erebos were a natural fit. But I refused to accept this."

Within the flames, the onyx man held the obsidian woman to his chest. She clung to him, but the flames roared toward them from all directions. Del held her breath.

"When she told me she had fallen in love with Erebos, all my bitterness and jealousy came flooding back in." The amber jewels pummeled the man and woman, shattering them. "The Furies advised me against rash action, but they could do nothing to stop me from locking Erebos in one of the cells of Tartarus. Because of their marriage vow, his imprisonment banished Nyx from the underworld."

The flames near his cloak petered out into a sapphire sky, where the obsidian woman hovered like a single black cloud. The man of onyx curled behind topaz bars.

"To ensure neither of them could escape, I cursed Nyx to chase Hemera across the sky for eternity. Nyx can only return to the underworld after she and Hemera embrace, and until then, Erebos cannot be freed. And with Nyx being the goddess of night and Hemera the goddess of day, their meeting remains an impossibility."

In the sapphire sky, the obsidian woman chased a golden orb that reflected the sunlight. It streaked across the sky far too fast for her to catch, but still she followed it. The beach became a blur of gold and black until Hades snapped his fingers, and the riot of color dissolved into darkness. The crowned man sat at a table in the halls of onyx, flanked by a girl and boy with wings of white and black opal.

Hades directed his voice toward Thanatos. "Because you and Keres could not yet reveal yourselves to the mortals, Nyx was forced to leave you in my care. I wrote to her tirelessly, horrified by my actions, but she never replied to my letters. Finally, I grew desperate enough to travel to Helios and Selene's palace."

The onyx palace sank into the ground, giving way to a blanket of emeralds. Trees rose around citrine-speckled grass, and a patch of diamonds glittered at the clearing edge.

It was a miniature version of the meadow where Del and her mother used to swim.

"I met Persephone while descending Olympus. The sun god and moon goddess had refused my entrance, and feeling defeated, when I arrived in a meadow, I laid down to rest. I awoke to find Persephone picking blooms of narcissus." The crowned man watched a woman of rose quartz gather citrine flowers in the emerald grass. "I was enamored with her instantly, but after everything I had done, I knew I could never deserve her attention. I never would have spoken to her had she not approached me herself."

The rose quartz woman swept toward the man. She took his hand, and they walked to the lake, where at the edge of the glittering diamonds, they kissed. "From that day forward, I was besotted. I told her all my history and was amazed when she said there was still good in me. It made me want to prove she was right to believe in me."

The crowned man leaned down and deepened their kiss, and the darkness that surrounded his body expanded. He and the rose quartz woman stood in the onyx palace, each holding a winged child by the hand.

"When Persephone came to live with me," Hades said, voice wavering when he spoke to Thanatos again, "we decided not to burden you and Keres with the truth of what had happened. We were selfish. But we also wanted you to have a childhood devoid of all that torment. We did not want you to hate the underworld when you had nowhere else to live. I continued writing to Nyx, but she always refused my attempts to make amends. Until this alliance."

The couple embraced the winged children until they all fused together, and Del looked up to see her father slowly clench his outstretched hands. The figures sank into the sand along with the hall of onyx. As the ground became barren save for tattered crocus blooms, Hades dropped his hands. His muscles relaxed, but when he looked up at Del and Thanatos, his expression remained painfully tense.

"I do not know why Nyx wants the two of you to be married," he said, "but it is my hope that with Cate to help break Nyx's banishment, I may finally be able to heal the harm I did." His eyes settled on

Thanatos. "Keres fled the underworld when she learned the truth of this. Though it pained me and Persephone, we could not blame her for hating us." His nose thinned when he sucked in a breath. "Just as I cannot blame you now."

Del glanced up at Thanatos, but he remained silent. He stared at Hades, his mouth quirked upward in strange, serene amusement.

"Than," Hades said while swallows chirped in the broken branches all around them. He took a halting step forward, crushing uprooted crocus blooms. His face crumpled, and he reached out a hand. "Say something," he said, but his hand fell, catching only empty air. "I don't care what it is. Just, not silence."

But silence was all he would get. Because behind him, Del saw Cate's spell room shimmer into existence. It stood on the Aegean Sea, waves splashing against its walls of ebony. The door cracked open slightly.

Thinking only that she needed to give Thanatos a safe space to think, Del tightened her grip on his hand and started running. Her father did not call after them, but nevertheless she pounded across the beach. Thanatos followed her, the bindweed leash swinging wildly as sand flung up in their wake. Plunging through water up to her knees, she tugged the spell-room door open, inhaling the scent of herbs and paper and tea.

Without hesitation, she plunged into the familiar darkness. She tugged Thanatos in behind her, slamming the door just in time to see her father's pathway collapse, the ground beneath him tumbling into the sea.

Chapter Seventeen

Thanatos fell beside her, his wings splayed awkwardly against the door. The impact sent bundles of herbs swinging from the ceiling and jars tumbling from the shelves. When they clattered to the floor, Gale rushed out from beneath the worktable. The polecat squealed and climbed Cate's wine-red robe.

"Seedling!" Yaya rushed toward Del. She tried to pull her away from Thanatos, but the bindweed leash held them close. Yaya frowned and crouched beside Del. "I wish I could have been here sooner. When I went to speak with Zeus, he told me about the storm he sent to your Isle. I was worried you had let Thanatos go back to the underworld."

Thanatos gave a mirthless huff. "I don't think you need to worry about that anymore."

Del turned to him. His forearms rested on his knees, and he was hanging his head. She placed a hand on his arm, swinging the bindweed leash between them. "I am so sorry." She squeezed his arm, feeling the warmth of his skin.

"So." Cate plucked the broken jar of yewberry paste from the floor near her feet, red paste splattering in its wake. "Hades told you the truth about what he did to Nyx."

Del kept her eyes on Thanatos, but he merely stared at the floor. She let go of his arm and let her head fall back against the door. "He is so *awful*."

Thanatos kicked off from the door and strode to the worktable. "Thanatos?" Del said as she followed, but he only leaned against the worktable, hands in his hair. His wings drooped within the bindweed net, and with a slice of her finger, Del disintegrated it. The leash crumbled, and Thanatos rubbed his wrist. He glared at the red paste on the floor, as though it and not Hades had lied to him for all these years.

"I love him," he spat. "That's the worst part. I still love him, despite all of it."

"I know." Del pinched the crocus bracelet between her forefinger and thumb. She had accepted her father's evil long ago, but Thanatos had not. He might be a god of the underworld, but he believed the best in people.

It gave her no pleasure to see him proven wrong.

"Here." She slid the crocus bracelet from her wrist. Then she took his hand and slipped it onto his. His wings twitched, and he watched her movements. Surprise lit his eyes when she laced her fingers through his, smiling tightly at him. He tried to smile back, but it was more of a grimace. He lowered his gaze to the floor and plucked at the bracelet.

"It would be easier if I hated him," he said.

Yaya huffed. "We can agree about that."

"And it would be easiest," Cate said, handing Thanatos a cup of steaming red liquid, "if you could look at him with indifference."

Del looked up at Cate, furrowing her eyebrows. "Wait a moment. You said Hades finally told us the truth about Nyx. You knew about this?"

"Hades has been trying to break Nyx's banishment since before you were born. Of course he has told me about it."

"And you just didn't think to tell anyone else."

"I serve the Fates. I know much that I cannot share."

Del opened her mouth, but Yaya placed a hand on her arm. "Seedling, Cate is telling the truth. If she shares information the Fates don't want her to tell, they might try to trap her soul in the space between realms."

Del whirled. "What is the point of knowing anything if you don't use it to help people?" She glared at Cate. "First you can't help dissolve the marriage vow, and now you can't tell Thanatos the truth about his mother. Can you do anything useful?"

"Seedling." Yaya's tone was firm. "Do not speak to Cate like that. She and I are doing all we can. Now come with me." She gestured to the hearth. "There is something I would like the two of us to discuss alone."

"I don't want to leave Thanatos—"

"It's fine, Del." Thanatos waved her off while Cate sat beside him at the worktable. Del hesitated, but with a sigh, she followed Yaya to the hearth.

While she sat down, Yaya poured each of them a cup of tea from a burbling pot. "Your mother told me about the jar of flower essence she found in Hades's wine at the Farewell Festival." She sat and lifted her eyebrows, taking a sip from her cup.

Del groaned and rubbed her eyes. She leaned back in her chair. "You know how you sealed Eos in the heliotrope plant when you were trying to rescue my mother?" She spoke through her hands, and Yaya acknowledged her with a hum. "Well, ever since I moved to the Isle, I have been trying to grow a flower that can seal the part of my mother's soul that lives in my father. All the plants and flowers I have created were practice. I wanted to surprise you by bringing her home. Otherwise, I would have told you about it a long time ago."

"Oh, seedling." Yaya cinched her eyebrows, lips thinned in concern.

"What?" Del's voice sharpened, and she dropped her hands. "You think I am not strong enough to do it? You think I am not capable?"

"Of course I think you are capable." Yaya took another sip of tea and set down her cup. "Which flowers did you use to create the essence?"

Del took a deep breath. Yaya had not immediately told her the idea was impossible. Good. She had a well-planned answer for this. "I used narcissus."

Yaya nodded. "Because they have always been sacred to her, yes."

"And I used poppies."

"Because that is what I fed her while she was pregnant."

"And I used aconite. Because it brought such joy to all of us at the Farewell Festival where Cerberus first grew it."

Yaya drummed her fingers on the table while Del tentatively lifted her cup to her lips. She was relieved to find the tea flavored with lavender rather than yewberry. No cloying sweetness.

"How exactly did you plan to use it?" Yaya asked.

"I wanted Hades to eat it, and then . . . Well, I hoped it would disagree with his stomach. When he coughed it up, my mother's soul would be sealed inside it. Once their marriage vow was broken, I thought we could throw Hades into Tartarus."

"What is this about throwing Hades into Tartarus?" Thanatos walked up behind her. Del turned and saw Cate standing beside him, Gale perched on her shoulder.

Del met his eyes, but she hesitated. Despite what Hades had done to Nyx, Thanatos had said he still loved him. Their minds were connected. If she told Thanatos her full plan with the flower essence, Hades could know about it in an instant.

"Seedling, don't tell him," Yaya said, and Del was surprised to feel a twinge of offense. All Yaya had done was voice a fear Del shared, but hearing it from someone else made her realize it was ridiculous.

"Thanatos has been loyal to Hades all his life." Yaya took Del's hand. "You cannot speak ill of your father while he is present."

Thanatos raised his eyebrows. "I think we are well past that."

"It's all right, Yaya." Del squeezed her grandmother's hand. "My parents already know about the flower essence, which means they will be too careful for me to ever use it. And . . . I don't think Thanatos will turn against us."

"And why is that?"

"Well." Del glanced at Thanatos and swallowed before she turned back to Yaya. "He has already vowed on the river Styx not to marry me until we fall in love."

Yaya took in a sharp breath and looked up at Thanatos. "You did what?"

His wings twitched. "I have had my doubts about Hades ever since I learned he hid the betrothal from Del. I will not force her into a life she doesn't want, and now that I know what Hades did to my mother and Erebos, I have started to wonder if I want to return to the underworld myself." He looked at Del. "You were right. I always trusted him to tell me the truth, but he lied to me for years. For Persephone to marry him . . ." He shook his head. "She really must be bewitched."

Yaya nodded. "If anyone deserves Tartarus, it is him." She turned to Del. "Go on, seedling. You can tell him."

Burying a sprout of irritation at Yaya's need to give permission, Del told Thanatos her plan with the flower essence. When she admitted how she had dropped the jar into the wine cup, he said, "That's why you kept glancing at the banquet table during the vow renewal. You were trying to figure out how to retrieve it."

"What, do you watch my every movement?"

"I was about to announce our engagement. So, yes."

Del rolled her eyes. She drank some more tea and set down her cup. "Yes, well. I thought I could free all of us. But now my chance is lost."

Thanatos made an uncertain hum. "I'm sorry to say this, but . . . I don't think the flower essence would have worked."

Yaya narrowed her eyes. "Why not?"

"Well." He leaned his hands on the worktable. "A marriage vow on the river Styx does not simply place part of both souls in the other person. It merges their souls into one being." He lifted his hands and nestled them together. "They cease to be what they once were." He dropped his hands back to the table. "What I am saying is, in terms of their souls, Hades and Persephone no longer exist separately from one another. They are one entity, as different to what they were before their marriage as a living mortal is to their soul in the underworld. They gave themselves up for one another."

Del swallowed. Cate wrapped her arms around Yaya's shoulders.

"However," said Thanatos, "I'm not sure we need to split their souls." He looked at Del. "I mean, think about what Hades just told us. According to his story, when Erebos was thrown into Tartarus, my mother was banished from the underworld—all because of their marriage vow. I am not sure we can trust him, but it sounds like if Hades is thrown into Tartarus, Persephone will be forced to live up above."

Yaya raised an eyebrow. "Perhaps so."

"Which means it is my fault," said Thanatos, his wings drooping around him, "that my mother was banished from the underworld."

"What?" Del glared at it him. "No, it isn't. Why would you think that?"

"If I had never given her and Erebos their marriage vow, she never would have been banished. Keres and I could have grown up with her. Instead, I have spent years defending the man who hurt her."

"That is not your fault." Del took his hand in hers. "You were a child, practicing your magic. You could never have known what would happen later."

Thanatos opened his mouth, but Cate spoke before he could. "Del is correct. Nyx's banishment was woven into the great story of the world. The Fates knew it would happen. It could not be avoided. To ensure the future would unfold smoothly, I could not speak about it. But now that you have discovered it," she said, turning her pale eyes on Thanatos, "I wonder if the Fates would allow me to help their little brother."

"Little brother?" Del gaped at Thanatos. "The Fates are your sisters?"

He tilted his hand side to side, face scrunched. "They are, but we have never so much as spoken." He turned to Cate. "Do you really think they would help us?"

"I think you have a better chance than anyone else." Cate removed a sleeping Gale from her shoulders. She set the polecat on the worktable, where the creature curled into a ball. "For me, curses like the one I gave Del—or the one Hades gave Nyx—are unbreakable. But the Fates are much more powerful. If they are willing to rip a few threads in their great story of the world, they may be able to help."

She grabbed the broken jar of yewberry paste from the worktable, but Del placed a hand on her arm. "Cate. I'm sorry I was angry before. Whatever I said, disregard it. I never should have asked for your help. I don't want you to risk your soul."

Cate smiled. "You and this family are my soul." She looked up at Yaya. "For all of you, I will try to bend the rules." She moved to the hearth, but rather than brew a pot of tea and stir some of the paste into it, she took a scoop into her hand. It was as red as an organ.

"Be careful," Yaya said. She hugged the goddess. Then Cate swallowed the paste, and her eyes rolled into the back of her head.

A few moments passed before Cate began to emit a low, continuous hum through her closed lips. She did not so much as pause for breath. Her posture went rigid, and she slipped from where she sat at the edge of the oven.

"Cate?" Yaya grabbed the goddess, slowing her fall. "Cate, can you hear me?" She slapped Cate across the face, but Cate didn't respond. The hum continued, and Yaya looked frantically at Del and Thanatos. "She has never done this during her soul travel before."

"Cate?" Del dropped to her knees while Yaya shook Cate by the shoulders. Gale awoke and ran to the goddess, sniffing her gown before she began to squeal. "Cate, what's the matter?" Her heart thumped wildly, her chest tight with panic.

Suddenly, Thanatos was beside her. "Here, let me," he said, and Del scrambled out of his way. Yaya hesitated, but when Del pulled her away, she let Thanatos lean over Cate. She clutched at Del, both of them watching Cate's eyes move rapidly back and forth while they were still rolled in the back of her head. The floor split to make way for woody stems.

Del disintegrated the asphodel while Thanatos tipped up Cate's chin. He stroked up the column of her throat with one long, slim finger, and the sound faded from Del's ears. Gale still scrambled through the spell room, but Del was enveloped in his voice, which rose and fell in a delicate melody. At first, the notes sailed high, like a bird soaring on an early-morning wind. Then his voice dipped, as though the bird had dived toward its nest.

"Hecate," he sang, drawing out the first half of Cate's name. "Hecate, goddess of witches, lady of crossroads, can you find your way home?" He repeated the lyrics, continuing to stroke Cate's throat. He sang the words three times, lulling Del into a trance while a soft white glow emitted from the base of Cate's throat. At first, the light was so small it was barely there at all, winking in and out like a far-off star. But when he dragged his finger upward, it flowed through Cate's throat until it reached her mouth.

"Hecate," he sang, slowing the deep melody, "goddess of witches, lady of crossroads, you are on your way home." The light threatened to spill from Cate's lips, but Thanatos gently pressed his finger to them. He sang, "Hecate, goddess of witches, lady of crossroads, you have found your way home."

The final note sounded like the sigh of a bird settling down to rest. As it faded from the air, the light receded from Cate's lips. Her eyes flew open, glowing bright white before dulling to their usual milky color. Her posture relaxed, and Yaya buried her face in the crook of her neck. Del threw her arms around both of them while the spell room filled with sound once again. Gale cuddled into them. "Oh, thank Tyche," Del said.

"I assure you, luck had nothing to do with this." Cate gently removed their arms from around her neck.

"What happened?" Del wiped her tears. She raked her gaze over Cate, ascertaining that she looked the same as she always did.

"Was it the madness? Was it my fault? Oh my *gods*. I am so sorry, Cate, Yaya—"

Cate barked a laugh, but there was no mirth in it. "No, that was not madness. You have only held Thanatos hostage for a few days. Zeus may be at risk of madness right now, but at my level of worship . . . No, that happened because the Fates did not want to help their little brother after all. For daring to ask, they tried to trap my soul in the space between realms." She dipped her chin to Thanatos. "Thank you for bringing me back before I was lost."

"Though if you had never vowed to marry Del," said Yaya, her voice cold, "Cate never would have needed to go to the Fates for help."

"I apologize." Thanatos looked from Cate to Yaya.

Del shook her head. "You don't need to apologize. Cate decided to help."

Yaya opened her mouth, but Cate silenced her with a look. "Of my own accord."

"Perhaps my mother would be able to convince them," Thanatos said. "Hades spoke of mortal battlefields. If he was telling the truth, Keres will be there. If we can find her, I can admit how wrong I have been, and maybe she will take us to see my mother."

Cate hummed in thought. "Selene tells me that Nyx has a door that leads directly to the Fates' home. If she were to open it for you, you might be able to earn their help."

"Well, then we should go straight there," said Del. "Forget the battlefield."

Cate sighed. "Visiting the Fates is dangerous—even more so than the soul travel I just attempted. It should only be done when you have exhausted every other option, and I'm afraid your presence on the battlefield is important." She glanced at Yaya, whose jaw was locked. "When we spoke to Zeus, he said the only way to restore balance to the world is through your marriage vow. If you want your freedom, you need to prove him wrong."

Del swallowed. "How?"

"By letting me off the Isle," said Thanatos, "so I can reap souls. You can come with me." He gave Del a small smile. "If it helps, you can regrow that leash to keep me close."

"That's all we have to do?" Del flicked her gaze from Cate to Yaya. "We have to prove that Thanatos can still reap souls, and then it's all over, all of this?"

Cate nodded. "And then it's all over, yes. You can return to the Isle and regrow it. You can stop the gods from descending into madness. You can save the world and go back to living as you did before this betrothal."

Del chewed her lower lip. She finished her tea and looked up at Thanatos, watching him frown at his hands. Feeling the weight of her gaze, his blue eyes met hers. She realized she was waiting for him to say something, but he did not break the silence. He just watched her with his brow furrowed.

Del tried to keep her misgivings from showing on her expression. Finding such a simple solution to her problems was all she should have wanted. But now that she had it, she felt no satisfaction. Instead, she felt like a tree hollowed out by illness. Perhaps because she struggled to believe it. Yes, that must be it. It seemed impossible that all she had to do was let Thanatos reap some souls and she would be free from this betrothal. As soon as tomorrow, she could return, alone, to her Isle.

While she watched Thanatos, she imagined herself walking through the cottage door alone. She saw herself unwind the bindweed cage in her kitchen, her hair fluttering in the spring air. In the quiet, she would begin the arduous process of regrowing her orchard, woodland, and garden. For the rest of the spring, she would make berry wine and dye linens and grind flower petals into perfumes and poultices. Then she would sell her wares on Olympus during the festival for the Summer Solstice. She would find a lover there, whom she would enjoy for the rest of the season. Everything would be normal. Yes, she and Thanatos would still have to dissolve his vow, but this time of closeness would be over.

"I would advise against going to the battlefield." Yaya cut through her thoughts.

"What?" Del blinked as she came back into the present moment. "Don't you want me to be freed from this betrothal?"

"Of course I do. But as I said when you came to the farm, I think you need to keep Thanatos here on your Isle. Let me handle everything else. If you let him go, you have lost your leverage against the underworld."

"But when I stole Thanatos, I thought it would only hurt the underworld. I didn't realize it would cause madness in the other gods." She paused. "Yaya, when you stopped the seasons, how did you reconcile your desire to save my mother with the knowledge that you were risking the destruction of the world you love?"

"I wanted my daughter." Yaya spoke as though this was a ridiculous question. "I wanted her more than anything else. Just as I thought you valued your freedom above all."

"I do, but—"

"Besides, your mother will be at the battle. She has gone to help. Bewitched as she is, if she sees you, she might try to force you into the underworld on her own."

Del shook her head. "She cannot force me into anything. Not this early in the spring. My magic is still stronger than hers." She sighed. "And I should talk to her about my curse. I need all the information I can get, and if nothing else, she can explain exactly why she did it."

"Seedling," Yaya said, "I don't think this is a good idea."

"I am all out of good ideas. I am doing what I have to do to get what I want—just as you did when you were trying to save my mother from the underworld."

"If you stay here on the Isle, I can—"

"The Isle has been destroyed!" Del flung out her hands. "Hades has already been here. The Isle no longer serves as a means of protection, and my curse is clearly no longer working either. It makes no sense to stay here." She took Thanatos by the hand, shocked that she had yelled at Yaya like that. "When we return, we will go to Olympus."

Thanatos nodded, and with some difficulty, Cate strode to the door. Gale dashed across the worktable, but Yaya remained by the hearth. She watched Del as though she no longer knew who she was. Del had never disobeyed her in such a flagrant manner, but regardless of how badly Yaya wanted to protect her, she had meant what she said.

Going to the battlefield was the only way to get what she wanted.

Cate removed the key from her robe. As she slipped it into the keyhole, Yaya strode around the worktable. She reached for Del, but Cate shoved Del and Thanatos out the door.

Chapter Eighteen

The first thing to hit Del was the sound. Clashing blades. Yelling mortals. Feet thundering so nearby, the ground shook beneath her skull. Thanatos had landed on top of her, his wings obscuring her vision while his body pinned her cheek to the ground. But when she shoved him off, too stunned to be embarrassed, she saw it all.

Waves of mortal men pounded into each other on a battlefield. Their once-neat phalanxes were broken, their water-droplet foot soldiers intermingled. Men on horseback yelled a cacophony of orders, the midday sun lancing off their bronze armor and shields. Some of the shields were emblazoned with a pointed arch, while others bore an owl. Everywhere Del looked, men fell. Skewered with spears. Stabbed with swords. Peppered with arrows. Near to where she and Thanatos sat at the edge of the battle, a man fell with his head bashed in with a shield. One of the men on horseback charged over him, leaving him trampled.

Swallowing bile, Del looked up, squinting through the haze of dust. Within the bloody ocean sailed tranquil gods. Unseen by the mortals, Ares strode through the battle twirling his spear, which glowed a subtle gold. Everywhere, men who touched the spear of the god of war descended into the savagery of animals. They attacked their enemies with intent only to kill, with no care for themselves. They took down dozens of men before falling as heroes.

Meanwhile, Athena swooped over the battlefield in the form of a little owl, her spotted brown-and-white plumage catching the sun. The goddess of wisdom landed on the shoulders of soldiers at random, morphing them into momentary strategists. They gathered the men around them and encircled small pockets of enemies, picking them off with lethal precision. They knocked commanding officers from their horses and slung themselves onto the backs of the animals, charging unopposed behind enemy lines. There, they knocked other enemy officers off their horses until they themselves were thrown to the ground.

Among this seething throng, the sight of Keres was the most frightful. She was everywhere at once, having split into countless aspects of herself. Her wild white hair crashed across the ocean of battle like whitecaps, dragging men down to their violent deaths. One aspect dashed out of the miasma and pounced on the trampled man near Del, prying open his eyelids. She kissed both his eyes in quick succession, then sucked in a mighty breath. The man's eyes glowed red before the light poured out of them, curling like smoke into the wings of the aspect. When the last of the light had been sucked in, the aspect's feathers were sheened red. Del gasped, and the aspect whipped up her head. Her expression slackened, then she peeled back her lips. With a hiss, she dove back into the battle and vanished.

Del witnessed all this in the span of a moment. She scrambled to her feet, pulling Thanatos up by the hand. She opened her mouth to lament the sea of violence, but the words died when she saw Thanatos was not looking at the battlefield. Instead, he gazed at the city walls behind it, his expression weighed down by sorrow.

The walls shimmered like a mirage of land beyond the ocean of battle. Their mud bricks were caked with blood and dust, but behind them rose a city on a hill. Limestone structures dotted the hillside, all of them roofed with orange clay tile. Even in the daylight, Del could see firelight flicker in their outdoor braziers. Cypresses grew like needles, pinning down walkways of stone, while olive trees peppered the hill. At the summit of the hill sprawled a white marble temple trimmed in a riot of color, the friezes set against a backdrop of blue and gold.

"The Acropolis of Athens," said Thanatos, squinting at the blinding white temple, and Del cursed herself for not realizing where they were on her own.

Athens. The mortal center of knowledge. The most influential city in all the Greek world. Athena often bragged about it at the Olympian festivals. It was her favorite city, whose patronage she had won by gifting it the first olive tree. The goddess always complained that Ares and his favorite city were trying to invade it due to jealousy.

Thanatos lowered his eyes to the battle. "Sparta is practically at the gates."

Together, he and Del watched all of Keres's aspects slough to the center of the battlefield. On her way there, she sucked down soldiers like a whirlpool. Ares and Athena stood on opposite sides of the battle, both glowing soft gold. They watched with cool detachment as, in the center of the battlefield, all of Keres's aspects merged into one. She beat her wings and raised her sword, having sucked down so many souls that her entire being gleamed the red of fresh blood. For a moment, she flapped in place above the field, the wind whipping her hair and robes. Her gaze locked on Del and Thanatos.

Then she dove.

Del did not wait to see the results. She grabbed Thanatos by the hand and ran, leading them through Sparta's war encampment. They wove through bedrolls and tents, the roar of the battle rising and falling depending on how the sound bounced off the tents. They darted through patches of light and shadow, feet pounding into the tortured grass. The sun seared Del's skin, and she broke into a sweat. Flags emblazoned with red pointed arches flapped overhead.

At last, they came to a stop behind a sprawling goatskin tent. "We have been dropped," Thanatos panted while Del collapsed against its walls of stiff leather, "into the middle of the Peloponnesian War." He gestured at the encampment. "Sparta and Athens have spent decades fighting each other. Athens is the brains of the Greek world, and Sparta is the brawn. They are always at each other's throats. I don't like it, but Keres was right—their fighting is natural. It helps uphold the balance of our world."

Del peeked out from behind the tent, where beyond the shoreline of bedrolls the battle raged even more forcefully than before. With a small shake of her head, she turned back to Thanatos. "If their fighting is natural, why does it pain you so?"

"Natural doesn't mean good. It is natural for us gods to uphold the balance, but we are merciless in doing it. Mortals get hurt in the process. Not only the mortals on the battlefield, but also those who live around it." Thanatos pointed behind them, in the direction of Athens. "The battle does not pain me so much as the city does. When this war began, many mortals who lived on this countryside took refuge within the city walls of Athens. They had been renowned winemakers, their vineyards blanketing these fields . . ." He gestured at a nearby firepit, which held the charred remains of a wooden grapevine trellis.

"The Athenian general had prepared for this. He stocked the grain stores well enough to feed the influx of people, but when the city received a bad grain shipment early on in the war, many citizens were overcome by illness. The plague is not so bad now, but for years I have spent days on end lulling those struck down into peaceful rest." His wings ruffled, then drooped against the tent. "Scores of them must have died violently since I left."

"I see." Del recalled what Keres had said about mortals no longer finding relief from illness. As she stared at the charred trellis, she imagined thousands of men, women, and children writhing in their beds. She saw angry blisters burst across their skin, rivulets of blood and pus trickling onto their mattresses. She heard their moans and coughs and bouts of vomit. She smelled their unwashed bodies. Excrement. Rotting flesh. She imagined the wails and sobs of their loved ones were audible even over the roar of battle.

Thanatos cocked his head, and she realized she was not imagining the wails and sobs. They were coming from farther into the encampment—from Sparta's wounded. When Del pictured them, she saw lacerated stomachs, split heads, limbs hanging on by sinuous threads. She saw scores of ravaged men being tended by medics unruffled by death.

If her mother belonged anywhere in a place like this, it was there.

With a tight smile, she gripped Thanatos's hand. "Let me go speak to my mother. But you go on to Athens. We need to see Zeus as quickly as possible, and . . ." She swallowed. "I have kept you from reaping souls long enough."

Thanatos cinched his eyebrows. "Are you sure? I might be able to smooth things over with Persephone. Do you not want my help?"

Del sighed. "The last time I spoke to my mother, I banished her from my Isle. So, yes, I would like your help." She chewed her lower lip. "But Yaya was right about her bewitchment. If she sees you, she will try to convince me to send you back to the underworld. She will focus on how much my father needs your help, and once my father is brought up, the conversation will devolve into a vicious argument—as it always does." She blew out a breath. "My mother never told you about my curse, so I think it will be easier for her to talk about it if you aren't there. Beyond that, I have lost my Isle. I know how it feels to be ripped away from the thing that makes you who you are. I won't do that to you anymore."

"Del." Thanatos lifted her hand and kissed it. "You don't have to worry." He smiled crookedly. "I vowed to help you, remember? I won't leave you here by yourself."

And then he was hugging her, and Del was breathing in his scent of earth and incense. She hated how good it felt to be held. It felt so natural. She wanted to collapse into his arms.

But she did not. She pulled away and said, "You promise you will stay in Athens, even if you are able to speak with Keres before I find you again?"

"I won't be able to talk to Keres until the battle has ended. She can't leave an active battlefield." When Del just kept looking at him, he shook his head. "But even if she could, and even if I spoke to her before seeing you again, I would stay in Athens." His expression softened. "I am here because I want to be, you know."

Del swallowed. Burying the flower that bloomed in her stomach, she nodded, then she turned and marched farther into the encampment before she could think better of it. Behind her, the flaps of his wings were deafening. The wind whipped her hair, and she glanced back in time to see him soar toward Athens. Her muscles tensed as his form shrank into the distance, but then the sounds of battle crashed back into her ears. The clash of swords and screams of men reminded her that preventing any more destruction was what was important, and Thanatos had to go to Athens to do that. He would stay there. He had promised.

She had to trust him.

Chapter Nineteen

The moans and wails of the wounded grew steadily louder while Del wove through the encampment. She braced herself for a sight to match her visions, but when she rounded the corner of a drab canvas tent, what she saw made her gasp.

While the rest of the vineyards surrounding Athens had been reduced to charred clumps of grass, here, grapevines still draped the trellises. Row upon row of them grew like a forest that shaded the bedrolls of wounded men. Medics in threadbare tunics rushed through them, carrying surgical knives, bandages, and platters of plump red and green grapes from the vineyard. As Del watched them work, a smile graced her lips. She applauded their diligence. But her smile faded when she saw one of Keres's aspects.

The aspect darted through the vineyard, invisible to all the mortals save her victims. She pounced on men who screamed when they saw her. In the few moments Del stood at the edge of the vineyard, she watched a man drown in blood filling his lungs, another bleed out from the stump of a missing leg, and a third fall limp while medics tried in vain to stitch a gash down the middle of his head.

While the aspect leaned over the man with the gash, Persephone emerged from the trellises. Wearing a white robe and a haunted expression, she waited for the aspect to suck out the man's soul. When the red smoke seeped into the aspect's wings, they flared red. The aspect darted off to her next victim, and Persephone spiraled her wrist.

A new trellis grew around the man, vines twining around it, ripe red grapes dangling like jewels from a necklace. The medics stumbled away from it, then fell forward, blessing Olympus for such a fine gift. Unseen by them, Persephone swept off to the other recently deceased men, where she grew two more trellises. Del gaped at her, realizing she must have grown the entire vineyard like this. She was pouring life into this sea of death, granting the small comforts of shade and fresh fruit to soldiers condemned to violent ends.

"Maytare!" Del strode into the vineyard. She forgot her anger, she was so inspired by her mother's craft.

Persephone startled, hair swinging as she turned her head this way and that. When she saw Del, her eyes widened. "Del?" She stepped away from her most recent trellis. "Why are you here? Your grandmother said you were keeping Than on your Isle."

"I was." Del schooled her face into cool detachment. "Until my father came there and told me the truth of Nyx's banishment."

Persephone shut her eyes and let out a breath. "Did he tell Than?"

Del crossed her arms over her chest. "He certainly did. Even when I free him, Thanatos will not rejoin your perfect family, I fear. His illusion of my father's goodness has been shattered. Though I get no satisfaction from the pain it brought him."

Persephone's expression reminded Del of her Isle after the storm Zeus had sent. Blinking back tears, her mother took a deep breath, then she exhaled and held out her hand. "Come away from here. We should let the medics keep about their business."

"It's not as though they can see us." Del watched her mother's hand.

"No." Persephone finally closed her hand and dropped it. "But we can see them, and if we are going to discuss this, I would rather do so without—" She pressed her lips into a firm line when a death scream went up from another man. "Distraction."

Del gestured at the encampment and led her mother back to the canvas tent.

"If Hades has told you about how he banished Nyx and imprisoned Erebos, you must know he is besieged by regret. He must have explained that this is the entire reason for the marriage alliance—"

"My father's reasons have never mattered. What matters are his actions. But there will be time enough later to discuss what he did. Right now, we have more pressing matters. Namely, the curse you put me under."

Persephone's eyebrows furrowed. "Your curse?"

"You see, once Thanatos heard about it, he vowed on the river Styx to help me break it. He will never marry me until I have fallen in love with him." She leaned against the tent. "I need to know everything about the day you cursed me, so that hopefully, Thanatos and I can find a way to break it. Otherwise, he will break his vow, and the mortals will forget he exists."

Persephone had listened to Del with horror creeping over her expression. Now she barked a laugh. "But your curse can't be broken. When I asked Cate about your betrothal—"

"You asked Cate about my betrothal?" Del stood from the tent.

"She has been my closest adviser ever since I moved to the underworld. I ask her about everything. Of course I spoke to her about it."

"And you didn't think to speak to me about it? Me, the person being betrothed?"

"She agreed with my plan to wait to tell you about it. She said the only way out of a curse is through it, and she assured me this betrothal would fulfill it."

Rage-red flowers filled Del's throat. "But why would you *want* to fulfill it? That's what I don't understand. You gave me that curse for my protection. I understand why my father would not care about it, but—"

"I didn't."

Del blinked. "What?"

Her mother took a deep breath. "Asphodel, I didn't curse you when you were born."

"No, what? Yes, you did. Yaya has told me the story since I was little."

Persephone shook her head. And as another death scream rose over the vineyard, Del buckled under the weight of the realization.

"No," she said, holding herself up against the side of the tent.

"Asphodel." Persephone reached toward her, but Del shoved her away. She disintegrated the vine of bindweed her mother sent twining around her wrist.

"*No.* That is not true. Yaya would not lie to me. She loves me. She always has. Yaya has always been there. She is the one who kissed my forehead at night and taught me how to make kykeon. She is the one who taught me how to fly a chariot and cultivate a field. She is the one who comforted me when I was scared my father would come steal me away, and she is the one who laughed and clapped with me on my birthdays." She lowered her voice, forcing Persephone to strain to hear her over the rising wind. "She has always remembered exactly what I need, while you have always strived to forget me. You barely know me, because from the moment I was born, you shoved me away."

Persephone shook her head, a tear falling down her cheek. "I did not. I did not have a choice, Asphodel. Listen. Listen to me say this now." Vines of ivy gripped Del's wrists, and the wind roared past her ears. "When your grandmother first found me pregnant in the underworld, she swore that you would not grow up in that realm."

"Stop." Del yanked her wrists, but the ivy was too strong. Her hair stung her face, but her eyes were tightly closed. "You're lying. Stop."

"I am telling you the *truth*. For the first time in your life, I am brave enough to risk ruining the relationship you and your grandmother have built. Asphodel, please be strong. She wants to keep you for herself. It was the same for me. She is scared to see us grow. She hates that we do not need her anymore. But, Asphodel, you must live for your*self.* Listen." The vines of bindweed thickened as Del tugged.

"When you were born, she convinced Cate to curse you never to fall in love with gods of the underworld. I don't know why Cate agreed with it—perhaps because she and your grandmother were already in love—but from that moment on, I have mourned that you will never truly be *my* little girl. You are hers, and I did not want to tell you all this because I wanted you to have a home. I wanted you to feel loved. When I came to your Isle, I wanted to tell you all this. Then I discovered that you had tried to dissolve my marriage vow, and I realized Yaya's hold on your heart is even stronger than I thought. I fear that by keeping this truth to myself for so long, I have made you afraid to do the very thing you must."

Her mother wrapped Del in her arms, her voice turning soft in the center of the maelstrom. "You must *grow.* You must learn how to be comfortable with constantly growing into new, better versions of yourself. You cannot expect to live your life standing still."

Del used this moment of closeness to slice the vines from her wrists one by one. She shoved out of the embrace and backed away.

"Wait," Persephone said. "Asphodel, please—"

"Get *away* from me."

Del turned to run, only to stumble into a field of asphodel that now extended through the encampment. She sliced her fingers through the air, trying to disintegrate it, but it was everywhere. The white flowers bowed against the wind, all pointing toward Athens.

Del followed them.

She moved as fast as she could, trying not to think about her mother's words. She knew they were true. That was why she had run. The truth had always been there. In the story Yaya had told her as a little girl. In all the moments her mother and Hades had professed their love. Her father was far from perfect, but her mother loved him. He loved her. They had wanted to raise her as their own. Yaya had never given them the chance.

Just as she had never given Del the chance to decide if she hated the underworld.

Yaya had always said she loved Del as her own beating heart. But a heart cannot be removed from the chest where it belongs. And Yaya would not be removed from Del.

Her mother cried her name, her voice chasing Del toward the battlefield. Her cheeks were wet. She struggled against the wind. Charred grapevines blew toward her, and her eyes stung with ash flung up from the firepits. The battle roared around her, but still she ran.

She ran to Athens.

Chapter Twenty

Del rushed to the edge of the battle. While she ran, she saw Ares and Athena toy with the men. Keres's aspects crashed through them. Rather than trying to find the city gates, she headed straight for the nearest wall and sent ropes of bindweed racing up its mud bricks. She took the vines in both hands and scaled it, her hair flying around her head. She nearly fell cresting the summit, blown backward by the wind, but she lassoed a vine around the opposite side of the guard lane and pulled herself onto it. Invisible to the guards who watched the battle grim faced, she snaked more bindweed onto the nearest rooftop and leaped.

She soared through the air, deafened by the wind screeching past her ears. When she clattered onto the rooftop, she loosened an orange clay tile and sent it shattering to the street with her footstep. A mortal shrieked, but though Del winced, she did not stop. Sending vines unfurling from the cuffs she wound around her wrists, she streaked from rooftop to rooftop, scanning the streets below. She had no idea how to find Thanatos.

She passed rows of empty market stalls. Faded rainbows of hanging clothes. A dog sharing a crust of bread with a child. She drew ever closer to the white temple on the hill, where the smoke of the braziers was swept into the bright-blue sky by the wind. The flames had been fanned into conflagrations. An acrid stench filled the air. Del sniffed, trying to place it, and realized it reminded her of the Fields of Punishment.

It smelled like burning flesh.

Fear sprouting in her stomach, she shot vines across the rooftops with renewed vigor. The wind filled her robe, which billowed around her hips and twisted through her legs. She glared down at the city, hoping for just one measly sign of Death—

There. At the base of the hill leading up to the temple, a man drew a cart filled with limp, lolling corpses. The horse that drew the cart hung its head, feet clopping a lonesome rhythm through the streets, which chorused with cries of grief.

Del slid down a vine of bindweed and stumbled onto the street. The sudden lack of wind made her eyes water and her ears ring. When she untwisted her robe, she saw the cart trundle down the street with a crowd stumbling after it. The mortals gripped the hands and arms of their dead loved ones, shooing flies away from the corpses. Some walked with solemn expressions, murmuring prayers. Others shouted and spat, cursing the name of Olympus. One man crawled after the cart, sobs shattering out of him until he collapsed, screaming into his knees while he rocked back and forth in the middle of the street.

Del was so struck by his emotion that she did not notice she had started walking toward him until someone gripped her shoulder. She whirled to see Thanatos. He gave her a small shake of his head. She opened her mouth, but he put a finger to her lips. His touch was soft. His skin was warm. It made her wish for another hug.

Her thoughts must have shown on her face, because Thanatos dropped his hand, sliding it down her arm before entwining her fingers with his. He walked her to where the cart had stopped at an open door and ushered her through it. Folding his wings tightly behind him, he led her into a dimly lit room that smelled of sour cloth and sweat.

At the opposite end of the room, a woman lay weeping over a thin bed, atop which lay a boy verging on adolescence. The woman clutched his hand, using a damp cloth to stroke his forehead. His eyes were closed, his skin sallow, and his hair matted with sweat. Every few moments, he let out a low, agonized moan.

Del swallowed while Thanatos drew them close. She looked up at him, her brow furrowed, but he only squeezed her hand and let go before sweeping toward the bed. There, he stood over the woman, wings folded around her and the boy on the bed. He reached out his hand and placed his palm on the boy's chest.

The boy fell silent. His muscles relaxed, his eyes taking on the appearance of one in peaceful rest. The woman began to shriek, to shake the boy's body and repeat his name, but the sound faded from Del's ears when Thanatos began to sing.

It was the same song he had sung to Cate. He began with the soaring notes, tracing his finger up the column of the boy's throat. His voice dipped low, but rather than call the boy by name, he sang, "Soul, oh soul of the traveler, are you weary and wishing for home?"

As his fingers stroked upward, a dim red light began to glow at the base of the boy's throat. Beyond the song, Del watched the man from the cart step into the darkness of the home. She saw the woman screaming, her head shaking as the man pulled her away from the boy's body, but she heard nothing, drifting peacefully on the notes of Thanatos's song.

"Soul, oh soul of the traveler," he sang while the red light followed his finger up the boy's throat, "you must tell me your story, for I am calling you home."

The light filled the boy's eyes, glowing behind his eyelids. Thanatos drew his hand down the boy's face, and it spilled from his lips in smoky tendrils. It curled toward Thanatos, twining around his arm like the tail of a cat.

"Soul, oh soul of the traveler," Thanatos sang as the light snaked across his wing tip, "you have tread a long journey, and now you are home."

With the last note of his song, the light seeped into one of his black feathers. The feather glowed red for a moment, the rays setting the room in sharp relief before paling, leaving the feather with a faint silver sheen. Many of his other feathers were sheened similarly, Del realized when he refolded his wings.

He stepped away from the bed, and all the sounds of the room rushed back in.

The woman sobbed like she was losing her own soul, hands pressed to her face while she watched the man from the cart carry the boy's body to the door. When the man laid the body alongside the others in the cart, she vomited into her own lap. Del shook her head, but Thanatos gripped her shoulder and tipped up her chin. Taking her face in both his hands, he wiped away the tears she had not realized were leaking down her cheeks. He kissed her forehead, then he led her back onto the sunny street.

Still holding her hand, he walked her into the next house where the cart stopped, and the next after that. As the cart trundled up the hill leading to the white temple, the houses became more grand. These mortals had courtyards, bathing pools, small temples of their own. But no matter how wealthy the mortals were, each time Death entered one of their homes, he sang the same song. The procession following the cart only lengthened, the chorus of grief echoing off the city walls, but Del began to find beauty in the moments when Thanatos called the souls home. His song gave her the most restful feeling she had ever known.

By the time they reached the top of the hill, Del understood what the braziers burned so hotly for. They burned the bodies of those the sickness had killed, lest the illness spread from their flesh to someone else. In the shadow of the great white temple, priestesses in fluttering robes placed a silver obol beneath the tongue of each dead mortal. Then they carried the bodies to the low bronze brazier bowls, where they tossed them into flames that roared. With each new corpse, the fires belched sparks and smoke. The crowd of people whimpered and sobbed, holding one another close.

On the steps of the temple, Del watched it all. Here in the shadows, the temple blocked the wind, but she saw its strength in the way the cypress and olive trees bent. Thanatos stood beside her, one wing curved around her while he squinted at the mortals gathered around the braziers.

"Why don't you help them?" Del asked. "Why don't you give their souls peace, as you did all these?" She gestured to his silvered wings.

Thanatos shook his head. "My help is not for them. I help the dead, and I leave the living to help their own. You see how they cling to one another? Even in times of such trouble, they hold each other up. They give each other hope."

Del swallowed. He had proven her wrong, she realized as she turned toward him, watching his eyebrows curve up at the grieving mortals. He was not deceptive, like her father was. He was good. He was good in the way of a fresh bloom. Lovely and open, generous with his kindness. Despite being raised by her father, despite his mother's banishment, he still looked out at the world and saw good in it.

He might be the purest person Del had ever met.

She squeezed his hand, and he turned from the mortals, a melancholy smile pulling at his lips. His brow furrowed. "What is it?"

Rather than answering him, Del drew him to the nearest olive tree, which grew in the center of the temple green. Its small white flowers bloomed like bunches of grapes. She reached for one of the branches and pulled it down to the crocus bracelet Thanatos wore. With a small twist of her wrist, the crocus grafted onto the branch. The stems hardened into intertwined twigs, flexible bark seeping across them. When delicate white flowers burst across the bracelet, Del spiraled her wrist, and the bracelet doubled in length. She snapped her fingers, and it split in half, allowing her to slip the new bracelet onto her own wrist.

"I trust you," she told Thanatos, tipping up her chin. "You had no reason to stay here in Athens, but you did. You did exactly as you said."

Thanatos smiled. He opened his mouth, but before he could speak, Del locked his lips with her own. She gripped his face with both hands, pulling herself tightly to him. She breathed him in. His arms tightened around her waist, and he deepened their kiss. Del melted into it. A garden of emotion bloomed through her chest. She couldn't think past it. She had taken lovers, but she had never felt like this.

She pushed Thanatos away with both hands. Breathing hard, she braced herself against the olive tree and scrubbed her face with her palms. She had no idea what had just happened. It terrified her, feeling all that. And for Thanatos, no less.

She startled when he placed a hand on her arm. "I apologize." His face burned red, and he dropped his hand. "I didn't know . . . I didn't think you wanted that."

"I didn't know either. I just—" She squeezed her eyes shut. She shouldn't have done that. She was just so overwhelmed with everything her mother had revealed. She needed an escape from it. She needed to feel like she was on solid ground again. Thanatos had been consistent ever since she had brought him to the Isle. Right now, that was all she needed.

Thanatos roved his gaze over her. She peered up at him, wondering if he would demand an explanation for the kiss. She almost yearned for it. But instead he asked, "Did something happen when you went to speak to your mother?"

Del shook her head.

"You weren't able to speak to her?"

"No, I did." Her hair thrashed in the wind. She didn't want to talk about this. She wasn't ready to make the truth of what Yaya had done real yet. She turned her attention to the priestesses, who were still tossing bodies into the braziers. Over the chorus of mortal grief, she asked, "What is all this wind?"

"It is the river Styx," Thanatos said after a few moments. "It arrives with each death, but it is rarely noticed. Often, mortals mistake it for a last breath. When a great many deaths occur at the same time and place, they sometimes call it the winds of fate. But as you can see . . ." He pointed at the horizon, where Del could barely make out a dark shape. "Charon and his boat are coming to spirit the dead away."

Del buried the fear that sprouted in her chest. Yaya had told her about Charon, the hooded riverman who sailed up and down the river Styx, ferrying mortal souls to the underworld. He lived on the seam of the living and dead realms. When Del was little, Yaya had warned her that if she ever saw him, she had ventured too close to her father's realm, and she should turn and run back the way she had come.

But Yaya had lied to her. She had lied to her about the things that mattered most, so she might have lied about this as well. Del did not need to run. She could trust Thanatos.

She turned to him and ran a hand lightly across his nearer wing, eliciting a violent twitch. "Sorry," she said as he folded them, teeth gritted. "But if the souls are in your wings"—she gestured at the black smudge that was Charon—"how do they get to him?"

"I will molt my feathers into his boat." Thanatos looked out on the sea of battle.

Del followed his gaze and tilted her head toward the two armies, which from this distance resembled rippling waves. "What about them?"

"Keres will molt as well. But she will not do so until the battle ends."

Del listened to the grief-stricken wind. There were still so many men, she doubted the battle would end for several days. Guilt constricted her chest. Perhaps this war was not her doing, but she had worsened it. In the days since she had taken Thanatos, she had condemned scores of sick, besieged mortals to violent deaths.

Confronted with it now, she could not abide it. She lifted her gaze to the vineyard that her mother had grown at the edge of the encampment. The sight of the grapevine trellises made her realize maybe she could do more than bring Thanatos to reap souls in Athens. Maybe she could prove to Zeus that she could bring the scales back into balance.

If she ended this.

Without giving herself more time to think about it, she spun toward Thanatos and wrapped her arms around his neck. "Take me to the battlefield," she said.

Thanatos stared, hands snapping around her waist when she hooked her legs around him. He flicked his eyes to the battle, and her cheeks pinked when she became aware of her body against his. Behind him, Charon had grown into a black blob on the horizon.

"Maybe you can't help the living," she said, "but I can."

Thanatos swallowed. His wings twitched as he unfurled them. He gave a sharp intake of breath, then he beat his wings and leaped into the air.

Chapter Twenty-One

Thanatos caught the wind easily, and before long they soared over the city. When they touched down at the edge of the battle, Del took him by the hand and waded into it. Recalling how her mother had grown the vineyard trellises from the bodies of wounded men, she looked out on the seabed of felled soldiers and held out her hands, planting her feet at shoulder width. While she concentrated on growing a dam large enough to stopper the violence, Thanatos curled his wings around her, shielding her from the pounding tide of horses and men.

Teeth gritted, Del spiraled her wrists. Around her and Thanatos, the battle still raged. Athena swooped toward them with a screech. Ares charged them with his spear. Keres's aspects dove toward them with a collective hiss. Del scarcely registered any of this. She was too focused on the ground beneath them.

Within the ground, the roots of the vineyards that used to grow here still languished. Del saw them as clearly as someone else might see the veins in their wrists. Around them, the roots of olive trees meandered. Eyebrows lowered, Del wound her will around them, creating a single taproot that bound them together. Then, with a guttural shriek, she wrenched her arms upward while splaying her hands in clawlike shapes.

Trees erupted from the bodies of felled soldiers from one end of the battlefield to the other. Horses reared and men screamed. Men who had been attacking each other moments ago now huddled together, shuddering in the newfound shade.

Del had grown a forest of fused grapevines and olive trees. Vines draped between the olive branches like festival garlands on city streets. In some places, they grew bunches of purple olives instead of grapes. Likewise, bundles of grapes sagged from the trees.

When the armies of Sparta and Athens realized they were safe, they blinked up at the canopy that now dappled them in sunlight and shade. Some of them gaped, blood drained from their faces. Others prostrated themselves, bellowing thanks to Olympus. The important thing was that they were no longer fighting, which meant no one else would die today.

The wind whistled through the trees, coalescing into a single stream. It carried small white flowers and leaves, and while Del watched, Charon and his boat emerged from the trees. Unseen by the mortal men who now wandered through the forest, eating olives and grapes, the hooded riverman plunged his oar into the wind stream. He sailed silently until he reached Del and Thanatos, where he came to a halt.

Thanatos squeezed her shoulder and stepped onto the boat. He lifted his wings, then he drooped them into the wind stream. The wind riffled through them as though it was unfurling a scroll. One by one, the silver-sheened feathers fell off, and Charon reached up to catch them in his palms. When the hooded riverman touched them, they gleamed like stars, then they morphed into silvery, translucent versions of their living selves. Dozens of souls sat shoulder to shoulder in the boat that somehow managed to fit all of them, distending without changing its shape.

"Where is Keres?" Del peered into the forest, but then the goddess of violent death stomped toward her twin. She threw Del a glare before taking up the same stance as him. When Charon caught her red-sheened white feathers, they grew into copper-tinted souls.

The moment the last soul was seated, the riverman lifted his oar, and the boat once again sailed silently down the Styx. Del watched, enraptured, until it vanished into the trees.

Then a fist collided with her stomach, and she fell to the ground.

"Keres!" Thanatos yelled.

Del looked up to find Keres leaning over her, face twisted into a snarl. "Why in the name of Olympus," seethed the goddess, "would you grow a forest in the middle of a Peloponnesian battlefield?"

She reached for the front of Del's robe, but Thanatos grabbed her arm. "Don't."

The Twins of Death unfurled their wings, facing off while Del reoriented herself. Her stomach throbbed, and she only managed to stand when Thanatos offered her his arm. "Are you all right?" he asked, and she nodded, though her head swam.

Athena and Ares stalked into the clearing, pointing at Del with their spear and shield. "What," demanded Ares, "is the goddess of flowers doing here?"

"She is putting a stop to our battle," Keres said, red-brown eyes boring into Del while she rested a hand on her sword hilt.

"Though I think that is rather obvious," Thanatos said as he drew Del close, "given the tranquil forest in which we are now standing." He gestured at the trees, through which Del could no longer see the mortal armies.

"Especially after all the trouble she has caused," Athena said, eyes flashing, though she kept her voice level, "she has no right to spoil—"

The goddess broke off when Persephone crashed through the trees, grapevines swinging wildly in her wake. Athena and Ares held up their weapons, but she rushed past them, knocking Keres into a nearby tree. Keres cursed and flapped her wings, but Persephone paid her no heed. Her white robe was stained with grape juice, and leaves were caught in her hair. "Asphodel," she panted, taking Del's hands, "this is too much magic for one goddess to manage . . ."

But Del could no longer hear her mother over the ringing in her ears. Her skin felt feverish, and she swayed on her feet. The forest seemed to be getting darker. Maybe that was because the wind had died down and the sun could not so easily filter through the leaves. She tried to blink the darkness away, but it only seeped farther into her vision like ink across a page. Her mother was gripping her shoulders. Athena and Ares had come closer, and Keres was watching her with narrowed eyes and crossed arms. She knew people were saying her name, but all their voices sounded far away. She opened her mouth to explain, but then her knees gave way.

Her mother tried to hold her up, but she could not manage Del's full weight. Del fell, but someone caught her around the waist. Strong hands tipped her horizontally, holding her beneath her back and knees, and she felt the brush of a wing. As she fell into a deep, dark sleep, the last thing she knew was that Thanatos held her in his arms like a babe.

Chapter Twenty-Two

When Del opened her eyes, she was still surrounded by foliage. But this was not the forest she had grown on the battlefield. No, these were cypresses, their needle tips stabbing the gloomy sky of the underworld. Del was walking through them, her feet scuffing along the road that led to her father's palace. Around her, snowflakes hung suspended. Narcissus swayed in their flower beds. Tartarus belched smoke in the distance.

Then the heavy black doors to the palace swung open, and as music spilled out of them, Del realized she was in her nightmare again.

With no other option, she strode into the palace. The sconces smeared the hall in blue fire and shadow. The funeral dirge enveloped her, and her footsteps echoed. Her family lamented how she did not belong, and when she floated into her mother's favorite meadow, she closed her eyes and felt tears trickle. Her mother's laughter drifted around her while she braided her hair, the summer sun warming the top of her head. Then the ground trembled, and without opening her eyes, Del tumbled back into the underworld.

She lay there in the hall, tear-streaked cheeks cold and wet against the black marble. Her father's voice boomed that she should marry Thanatos. Her mother agreed, wishing things could be so simple.

"They can," whispered a voice at Del's shoulder. It was a voice of secrets and shadow, soft as a moth fluttering past a moon netted with clouds. Del whirled, raising her hand to hit its owner, but no one was there. Instead, her momentum carried her fist into the wall. Pain blossomed through her fingers, and she gasped. Cold air swept through the hall.

"It would be so simple if you were to wed that darling boy, my dear," the voice said, snide as a star winking at the edge of dawn. "He would love you until the end of time and beyond it. You both would be happy down here."

The voice clattered off the walls, causing Del to look all around, filled with the fear of walking alone at night, terrified of what hides in the dark. "Down here, you will have a family unified, not divided, by love." Her gaze landed on the window as the voice wrapped around her like a hug. "You will have not merely an Isle, but a kingdom to rule." Beyond the window, Del saw the Isle of Elysium, the Fields of Punishment, and the Fields of Asphodel sprawl within the white poplar forest of the underworld.

"All you have to do is say yes to the marriage," the voice scraped past her ear, "and then you will be safe, for you will be queen. Imagine it. Total control." The voice settled like a crown of stars atop her head. "Queen Asphodel of the Underworld." Woody stems broke the floor of the hall, extending in all directions until Del stood in a field of asphodel. The white flowers bowed to her, blown forward by the force of the voice's echo.

"Queen Asphodel." It blew through her hair. "Queen Asphodel . . . Del . . ."

"Del!"

Del snapped awake, catching a flash of sunlight that beamed through a black wing. She squeezed her eyes shut against a gust of wind.

"Del, thank Tyche." Thanatos sounded strained, his voice coming from over the top of her head. "I'm sorry to wake you, but—"

Del realized he was holding her to his chest. The gusts of wind were his wing beats, and far below, she heard the crash of waves. She stiffened, clasping her hands behind his neck. He was holding her horizontally, her feet dangling while he cradled her back and legs.

Slowly, it all came back to her, the nightmare fading like night giving way to day. The battlefield. Athens. Growing the forest. Collapsing under her own weight.

"Where are we?" she asked through gritted teeth.

"Somewhere above the Aegean Sea." Thanatos gave another powerful beat of his wings. "I flew us as far as I could, but without your help, I can't find the Isle, and without your permission, I can't land on its shores. And you were squirming, and my wings are getting tired, and I didn't want you to fall . . ."

Del opened her eyes, squinting against the wind and sun. She caught glimpses of his pale face, the straining veins in his neck. His hair looked like a crow that had been run over by a chariot. "How long have we been flying?" she asked.

"A few hours?" Thanatos adjusted his hold on her, flexing his chest. At the way her body jolted away from him, Del felt wild panic and dug her fingernails into his neck. "Sorry," he said when she fell back against his chest. "But you were so exhausted from what you did in Athens. I wanted to let you sleep for as long as I could."

Del loosened her grip. "At the risk of exhausting yourself so much that you plunged us into the Aegean?"

He quirked his lips to one side. "Hey, I woke you up before that happened." When she only scowled at him, he shut his eyes. "Please tell me where to land."

Del looked down at the sea, craning her neck. An archipelago scattered the waves, rippling like stones across a bedsheet. It took a few moments of searching before the Isle of Flowers tumbled into place. "There, that's the Isle." She pointed. "The one with the . . . um . . ."

Thanatos didn't make her explain the destruction. "Ah, I see."

"I give you permission to land on the beach."

Squeezing her tightly, Thanatos descended, circling the Isle like a bird of prey. He jogged to a stop, flinging sand up in his wake.

"I'm sorry I didn't wake you sooner," he said when he set Del on the beach. In the fading light, the sand looked gray. He let go of her, but she swayed, and she allowed him to wrap his arm around her shoulders without complaint. "Your mother said using so much magic would make you sleep for a while." They hobbled up the beach. "She said your strength had to replenish. Like a flower bulb in winter, waiting for the summer sun to help it grow—"

"I know how my magic works," Del snapped as they navigated the ruined garden path. Thanatos lifted her over the gnarled white myrtle arches. He started to set her down, but then he shook his head and carried her the rest of the way to the door.

"Why did my mother tell you to fly me back to the Isle?" Del asked when they stepped into the cottage shadows.

"She didn't." Thanatos laid her on the sofa. "At least, not exactly. Keres tried to convince me to take you to Helios and Selene's palace. Ares and Athena wanted to take you to Olympus, and your mother just wanted you to get some good rest. So, when I said I was taking you back to the Isle, she explained how—"

"But why did she let you go? She wants you back in the underworld."

"It doesn't matter what she wants." Thanatos crouched next to her, running a hand across her forehead. "You kissed me. I'm certainly not leaving you now."

Cheeks burning, Del turned away from his hand. She flicked her wrist, unlatching the window screens so the evening breeze filtered in. It was scented with salt and wet grass.

"Why did you do it?" Thanatos asked. "And this, why give us matching bracelets?" He placed his arm next to hers, which was still lifted. In the breeze, the tiny olive blossoms danced. His pale face floated beside them, like the moon in a night filled with stars. He smiled, and muscles tightened in Del's gut. "Mistress, are you falling in love?"

Del dropped her arm to her stomach. "I did it because you proved me wrong."

His smile dropped. "How?" He sat on the sofa, her legs in his lap.

Del took a moment to respond. "When I brought you here, I thought you were as deceptive as my father. But you are not. Over these past few days, I have discovered you are kind. You are good. I can take you at your word. I don't need to trap you here, because as long as that cage exists, you will walk right back into it." She clenched her jaw and stood, waving her hand when Thanatos tried to help her to the kitchen. She leaned against the countertop, looking back at him. "You aren't like my father. Not at all. And I'm sorry I thought you were. I'm sorry for how I brought you here, and . . . for what he did."

Thanatos leaned his head on the sofa. "I'm sorry too. For what he did, and for how I still struggle to believe it. He has just always been so kind to me. Why would he do that, if he hated my mother so much? Why would he raise me and Keres as his own? I mean, he said it himself. He admitted it. I know it's true. I just don't *understand*."

Del grabbed one of the jars she had planned to take to the Spring Equinox Festival. "A few days ago, I would have told you evil needs no reason." She uncorked the jar and tipped three dried dates into her hand. "I would have told you it simply is. Yaya told me that, and I have always trusted whatever she says. But after speaking with my mother in Athens . . ." She ripped out a date pit and placed the dried fruit on her tongue, chewing the sweet, gummy flesh before swallowing it.

"What happened?" Thanatos asked.

Del ate another date before she answered him. Keeping her voice brusque, she told him about how Yaya had convinced Cate to curse her when she was born. "She wanted to keep me for herself. My parents never had a chance to raise me as their own. Not that it matters." She removed the pit from the third date, peeling the wrinkly brown fruit in half. "I wouldn't have wanted to grow up with my father. Even if he loves my mother, I could not abide what he did to Nyx. It's not all that surprising, I suppose. I've always known not to trust anyone but myself. Yaya taught me that when I was young. I just never thought . . ."

"You never thought it would apply to her."

She nodded before popping the last date into her mouth. As she chewed and swallowed, only the hoots of an owl, the crash of the waves, and the breeze filled the cottage. She stared out at her ruined garden, feeling her head throb. Nothing was simple. It was all gnarled and wilted and upside down. It all just went to show that Yaya had been right, and Del truly could not trust anyone but herself. That realization should have made her want to push everyone away more than she already had, but instead, it made her want to turn to the one person who had so far proven her grandmother wrong.

Thanatos startled when she took his hand, the olive-branch bracelet rustling when she lifted his palm and dumped some dates into it. "Eat those," she said. "You're exhausted. These provide energy, reinforced with my magic. They always sell out at the Olympian festivals."

While he ate them, she strode back into the kitchen. "Trusting others frightens me." She corked the jar and set it back on the counter. With a deep breath, she turned around, swallowing the tightness in her throat. He watched it bob. "If I trust you, it gives you the ability to hurt me when you let me down. It gives you the power to make me feel like I do now—sure of nothing, hollowed out."

"I know." Thanatos clasped his hands at his front. "I broke your trust at the Farewell Festival, when I failed to explain our betrothal before I made my announcement. I have been trying to mend it, and I only hope I have made some progress."

Del looked down to her feet, watching the gentle sway of her robe with her teeth clenched. Suddenly, she did not want him to be kind or gentle or patient. It wasn't helpful. It didn't make her feel good. It made her feel worse.

"Del? I'm sorry if I said something wrong—"

"No, you didn't say something wrong. You didn't *do* anything wrong. That's the point. That's why I just—"

"Look, I know you're tired. I'm sorry if—"

"Zeus's name, *stop it.*" She flung her gaze up to find him standing with his arms crossed in front of the cage. "Stop apologizing. Stop acting like you are the one in the wrong."

He cinched his eyebrows. "But you're upset—"

"It shouldn't matter that I am upset. In fact, it should make you glad."

Thanatos blinked. "What? Why would that—"

"Because I locked you up." Del marched toward him. She shoved him in the chest, tears blurring her vision. She knew she was being more than a little unfair to him, but she didn't know how to stop it. It was as though by proving he could be trusted, Thanatos had given her permission to lash out at him. "I stole you from your home," she said as he stumbled against the cage. "I locked you in my cottage." She pressed her palms to her cheeks. "Yet you still show me kindness. You have from the start. It makes no sense, Thanatos." She shoved him again, this time with both hands. "Have some respect for yourself."

Thanatos stumbled back again, now fully within the cage. The vines were drooping, half wilted. He could have easily stepped back out of them, but he didn't. He straightened, smoothing his tunic. With a flap of his wings, he looked at her with arched eyebrows, his voice cool. "You want me to hate you? Is that it?"

"Yes!" His calmness only infuriated Del further. She raised both hands and spiraled her wrists. "Yes, I do want you to hate me. I want you to be furious. I want you to try to escape at every chance you get. That would make me feel more justified in my choices. That would make me feel like I was protecting myself. Instead, you have made me feel like my father. Selfish. Evil. Choking on guilt—"

"If you were evil," Thanatos said dispassionately while the vines stiffened around him, the white flowers perking up, "you would not feel guilt."

"What is wrong with you?" Del gripped two of the cage vines and shook them. "Why won't you show some righteous anger? Why won't you hold something against me?" Her voice fell to a broken whisper that she spoke to the ground. "Why won't you at least yell?"

"Nothing is wrong with me," said Thanatos. Del did not look up, and a tear slipped from her cheek to the ground. "I am angry with you, but that does not mean I want you to hurt. I will not hold it against you that you want to live your life on your own terms. I will not yell because I have no need to prove myself dangerous. Everyone knows what I am."

Del narrowed her eyes at him. Her tears had dried on her cheeks, tightening her skin. She tasted salt on her upper lip. On the opposite side of the cage, he leaned against the wall, watching her watch him. His pale skin seemed to glow in the darkness, and the sharpness of his awareness shifted something in Del. Her anger ebbed, but she still wanted to draw a reaction out of him. Voice pitched lower, she said, "And what are you, then?"

Thanatos took a moment to respond. When he shifted against the wall, his wings twitched. "I am the ultimate inevitability," he said. His eyes met hers, the blue moons heavily lidded as he tilted his head. "Everyone knows that eventually I come for them."

Del slid her fingers down one of the cage vines. "But you take your time with it."

Thanatos shifted against the wall again. His wings gave a flap. "Yes."

Del pursed her lips. "Darling, why are you shifting around like that? Are you trying to free yourself?" She pressed her face between the vines, feeling their cool smoothness on either side of her head. "You had your chance to run from me back at the battlefield. I am afraid it is too late for that now."

Thanatos did not respond, only again shifted against the wall. Every muscle was clenched in his jaw. When she trailed her gaze down to his crotch, she smiled like a predator holding its prey in its mouth. "Ah, I see. Only *part* of you is trying to free itself." She let go of the vines and smoothed her robe down her front. "I'm flattered, but I do worry that you are enjoying this. Longing to lie with the woman who locked you up." She tsked. "It's depraved, darling Thanatos. It's wrong."

She paced the length of the cage, swinging her arms. Her movements were relaxed, but her mind was a river of rushing thoughts. Did he actually want this? Should she stop? Based on his body language, he was enjoying it well enough, and her skin was already sensitive and hot. It chafed against her robe. Outside the cottage, the waves crashed against the shore. She met his eyes through the vines, and he gave her an almost imperceptible nod. Del did the same. The dregs of sunlight were swallowed by the waves, and she curled her fingers around the vines of the cage.

"What we are about to do is probably not a good thing." She leaned forward, pressing her hips against the cage. Her gaze pinned him to the wall, her voice breathy and low. "But goodness has outgrown us both, and I am tired of being soft."

Thanatos swallowed. He removed his hands from his front, and at the sight of just how excited he was, Del buried her thoughts.

She arched her back, the vines brushing against her breasts. "Tell me," she said while she slid her hands through her hair and down her front, emphasizing her curves, "how often have you wondered what I look like without clothes?" When Thanatos merely watched her slide her palms over her breasts, lightly squeezing them, she gripped the nearest vine and pulled herself against it. "I asked you a question, Thanatos." She traced her opposite hand from her throat down to her navel, her voice dangerously soft. "After all your talk of deference, do you dare to defy me now?"

She rolled her hips against the vines, and Thanatos let out a low, pained sound. His wings flapped, but he still did not move from the wall. He spoke through gritted teeth. "No."

"Good." She leaned away from the cage, holding on to the vine with one hand while the other pulled her robe slowly up her legs. The fabric whispered against her skin, its touch wretchedly soft. "How do you think I look?" Holding her robe at the very top of her thighs, she leaned forward, feeling the vines press against her bare skin. "How do I look when you dream of me while I am sound asleep up in the loft?"

Tipping her chin toward the ceiling, she pulled her hair back from her neck to reveal the column of her throat. "You . . ." Thanatos began to respond, his voice thick with want, but then she swung herself away from the cage, and he stopped. Holding on to a vine, she pulled her robe up to her waistline. His eyes dropped to the space between her thighs, which was concealed by a thin white cloth.

Del danced her fingers along the top of it. "Would you like to find out how I feel?"

Thanatos nodded, just once, and at the sight of his knife-sharp attention, that space between her thighs throbbed. She slipped her fingers beneath the cloth, feeling how pleasured she already was, and Thanatos let out a small moan. The sound sent an electric thrill shooting through her blood.

She pulled her fingers out and held them up, examining how they glistened in the dark. "Yes, I am sure you would love to know how this feels." She traced her fingers along her hips, then she pressed herself against the vines again. "I am sure you would like me to cozy up with you behind these bars." She let silence fill the space between them before stepping away from the cage. "But I think I shall not so disadvantage myself."

She spiraled both wrists, and the cage vines wilted, tumbling to the floor. New vines split the ground around Thanatos's feet and crept along the limestone wall. They netted his wings, then they wrapped around his ankles and wrists, splaying his hands on either side of his head. As Del strode toward him, he was completely powerless. He could not stop her from tracing his arms with either hand, leaning her body against his. He could not keep her from running her hands down his chest toward the bulge between his legs. He could do nothing but moan when she leaned away at the last second, eliciting a buck of his hips.

"You are entirely at my mercy," she said as she walked away from him, swishing her hips. She stopped where the vines of the cage had wilted and turned back to him. He strained against the vines that bound him, his irises a thin blue ring around his blown-wide pupils. "You are so accustomed to choosing when you take someone, to waiting as little or as long as you like. But tonight, darling Thanatos, I will decide."

She started back toward him, pulling her robe slowly up her legs, over her hips, bearing her breasts. He made a guttural sound when she pulled it over her head. She swung her hair out of the fabric, dropping the robe to the floor when her hair draped across her arms and neck. Listening to the rough sounds of his breath, she circled her nipples with methodical slowness. She made sure he got a full view of how they pebbled before she started back toward him, slipping her hands down her bare torso to run them along the white cloth.

She leaned against him, their bodies separated only by the thin red fabric of his tunic. When she rolled her hips against his, they both let out a gasp. She shoved her fingers through his hair, her face inches from his, and dragged her finger up the column of his throat to his lips. "These," she said, "are my favorite." She traced her finger across them, eliciting another yank at the vines and roll of his hips. In a rush, she closed the distance between them.

He kissed her like a half-drowned man sucking in air, flicking his tongue across the seam of her lips. Pressing herself harder against him, she parted them, and his tongue quested into her mouth. She brushed it with hers, letting a small gasp escape into his mouth. He kissed her harder, and when she leaned back, he tried to follow her. The bindings held him against the wall, and he strained until Del rested her forehead on his.

"I have heard it said," she murmured against his lips, "that power is not a food fit for a little flower goddess." She smiled. "But I must disagree, because the power of death is mine now, and I like how he tastes in my mouth."

He kissed her again in response. Waves crashed beyond the cottage, and the two of them moved back and forth. The breeze danced through the air while their tongues chased each other through their mouths. When Del could not stand it anymore, she spiraled her wrists, disintegrating the vines that bound him to the wall. Instantly, his arms were around her, his hands squeezing her arms, her breasts, her waist. He gripped her hips and flipped them around, pinning her against the wall. Wings outstretched, he kissed her again. He tried to pull her arms over her head, but Del pressed her hands against his shoulders with a tsk.

"Darling, get on your knees for me," she said. He watched her, gently running his hands through her hair. When her hair fell against her chest, he ran his hands down her front until they reached her legs. He slipped two fingers between them, and she gasped, but he swallowed it with a kiss. As his fingers stroked her with painful slowness, he gave her another kiss on her chin, her throat, her chest. Circling the area where she was most sensitive, he kissed her stomach, either side of her hips. Del dug her fingers into his shoulders, watching him kneel before her. He spread her legs. Then his tongue was circling her entrance, and she let out a whimper, gripping his hair until he applied more pressure.

His tongue slipped in and out of her, and he continued stroking her with his fingers. Del rocked her hips back and forth in a gentle, then pounding rhythm. When his tongue and fingers moved faster, she whimpered and gasped, feeling like one of the waves drawing out from the shore, preparing to crash. She moaned, squeezing her eyes shut as pleasure rocked through her from end to end. He moved with her through it, draining the ocean within her down to the dregs. She was so totally lost in it, it was like a little death.

When she could think again, she tugged at his hair until he rose to stand. She gathered the fabric of his tunic with both hands, then she grew a single rose and used its thorns to slice through the tunic. Careful not to damage his wings, she dropped the tunic to the floor and pressed her hands to his chest. She kissed it, then kissed it again. As she sank lower, his wings twitched and flapped. She kissed either side of his hips. When she wrapped her hand around him, his whole body shivered. She leaned toward him, meeting his eyes while she licked his tip. He made a small, desperate sound and bucked against her mouth, but she leaned back again, stroking him with her hand.

"Beg," she said, watching him stare at her kneeling like this. She squeezed him, reminding him who had the power here, and at the added pressure, he shuddered, his mouth opening in a silent gasp. "Beg me, Thanatos." She smiled. "Beg me for release."

He fisted his hands against the wall above her, flapping his wings. His usually sonorous voice was a ragged, threadbare thing. "Please."

Del brought her lips toward him, tracing her tongue up his length before bringing her mouth away. He pounded his fist against the wall, gritting his teeth, and she let out a small, breathy laugh. She licked him again, drawing him partially into her mouth before pulling him out again.

His wings flapped as he leaned his head against the wall. "Please," he gasped while the wind gusted over them. "Please, Del. I'm begging."

"Darling Thanatos," she said before sliding his full length into her mouth. She slid back and forth, circling him with her tongue, her rhythm torturously slow. He hardened within her until she tasted salt. He was so close that he growled when she pulled out, trying to push her head forward until she finished him off.

"So hasty," she said, walking her fingers up his torso as she stood. She dug her nails into his back, whispering into his mouth, "I want you to take me now."

He shivered when she met his eyes. He kneed her legs apart, and she felt his hardened length against her inner thighs. "And in taking me," she said while he slid inside her, both of them letting out a shuddering breath, "you are going to lose yourself."

And he did, his uneven breaths filling the air as the waves crashed, his wings buffeting the wind in the cottage into a gale.

Chapter Twenty-Three

The next morning, Del rose from the sofa, where she and Thanatos had fallen asleep in each other's arms. Careful not to wake him, she poured water into a clay pot. In the quiet, the crash of the water was like a waterfall. She paused, ascertaining she could still hear his faint snores, then she set the pot on the edge of the oven to boil. She stood in front of the washbasin and hugged herself, looking out on the Isle.

Shrouded in sea mist, it looked like a dream world. Hazy and soft. Undefined. She could pretend it had not been destroyed by the storm. She could pretend nothing was real. Last night she had not danced for Thanatos. She had not gasped at his touch. She had not enjoyed the power singing through her blood quite so much. It was something best left in its moment, a way to regain control when she needed it. When Thanatos woke up, she would give him tea and breakfast, and she would tell him this. He would listen. He always did.

The thicket of panic loosened its hold on her stomach, and she rubbed her eyes and returned to the oven. She tossed sprigs of dried mint into the pot and stirred it, breathing in the bright, clean scent. The familiarity of it filled her with a surging desire to wake up in her bedroom on Yaya's farm. She wanted it to be summer, when she and her mother would gather mint leaves before Helios rose high enough for them to wilt. Then she and Yaya would brew mint tea in the farmhouse kitchen.

What she wanted, she thought as steam clouded her vision, was for someone else to make her decisions. That was how her whole life had been. She had never really had the control she sought. Yaya had decided she would grow up on the farm. Her mother had decided she would not know the truth about what had happened when she was born. Her father had decided she would marry Thanatos. The only choice she had made for herself was to feed her father the flower essence at the Farewell Festival, and she had done that only because of how Yaya had influenced her as a little girl.

She had no idea who she was on her own.

With a sniff, she ladled tea into one of her clay cups and took a sip, allowing it to wash away the tightness in her throat. Her lips still hummed from how Thanatos had kissed them the night before, and all along her body she could feel his phantom touch. When she leaned against the counter, the space between her legs stretched with slight soreness. The wilted remains of the cage served as a reminder that she was a grown woman. And the only thing she knew for certain was that she had thoroughly enjoyed last night's reckless abandon.

While she watched Thanatos on the sofa, she acknowledged that she was not going to be able to pretend last night had been meaningless. The daylight grew brighter, burning off the sea mist, and she forced herself to accept that she could not deny the one thing she knew for certain. She did not love Thanatos, but she liked the look and feel of him, and no matter how badly she wanted to believe last night had been a fit of exhaustion-induced delirium, she knew they had been progressing toward it long before Athens. She could not look him in the eye and tell him what a mistake last night had been, because she would be lying, and after all he had done to earn her trust, she found she did not want to lie to him.

Swallows sang outside the cottage, and Thanatos's wings twitched. When he rose from the sofa, Del smiled at him. But the smile was stiff, and he noticed it. Rather than stepping toward her and wrapping her in his arms, he stayed where he was, smoothing his hair. He was letting her take control of the situation, as he always did. She appreciated that. But she didn't know how to take control of it, so they watched each other in awkward silence. She drank more of her tea, giving herself time to figure out what to say, but the longer the silence stretched, the more inadequate each opening sounded in her head.

Finally, Thanatos said, "So. Have you ever . . . done that?"

Del blinked. "What? Yes, Thanatos. I've had sex."

"No. I mean, yes. Of course you have. We both . . . have."

Del slowly took another sip.

"What I mean is, have you ever had sex like *that*."

Del wondered what he meant. Did he mean good sex? It had been good. It had been great, even. If she was honest, it was probably the best she'd ever had. But surely he'd had good sex before this.

"Like, have you ever . . ." He gestured to the cage bars. "Like that."

"Ah." Del set down her cup. She gestured to the pot. "You want some?"

Thanatos nodded, and she talked while she poured him a cup. "I pretty much exclusively have sex like that. Never with a cage, I'll admit, but the vines, the bindings and such, yes."

"Always?" he said as she handed the cup to him.

Del nodded. It was surprisingly easy, talking about it like this. Removed from emotion, simply discussing why she did what she did. "I always knew I was like this. Or I always suspected. I tried having sex different ways the first couple times. Submissive, you know." She looked him up and down. "Gods are not typically excited about succumbing to the whims of the flower goddess they have decided to bed."

Thanatos cocked his head. "I was rather fond of it."

"Were you?" She could not keep the smile from her lips.

"I'd do it again."

Del's mouth went dry. Her cheeks heated. "Ahem." She picked up her cup. "Well, perhaps . . . we could arrange that."

"When?"

Del coughed. "When we are not in the middle of destroying the world. That's when."

"Mmm." Thanatos stood from the sofa. "Well. You were saying, you always knew you were like this. Why try submission, then?"

Del leaned against the counter while he walked toward her. Not breaking eye contact, she lifted her cup to her lips. Mint tea filled her mouth, and when she swallowed, he dipped his eyes to her throat. "I didn't want to be difficult. I knew they would reject me if I told them I didn't like being submissive. So I stopped trying with gods."

Thanatos stood right in front of her now. Gently, he took her cup and set it on the countertop. "Mortals? But I thought they didn't know you existed."

"They don't." Del placed a hand on his chest, fingers slowly spreading out. "I'm talking about nymphs, Thanatos. Most of them are more than willing to bend over backward for the goddess of flowers."

Thanatos leaned down, his voice a whisper against her lips. "You want me to bend over backward, then?"

Del wrapped an arm around his neck and sealed their lips. His body pressed against her hips. She felt a throb between her legs. A small sound climbed up her throat, and he swallowed it with his own. She leaned into him, grinding her hips against his. His hands were gripping her arms tightly enough to leave bruises, and she liked it. She loved it. Opening her mouth wider to him, she wrapped both hands behind his back and let her nails bite into his skin. Pushing against him, she walked forward with stumbling steps.

He collided with the sofa and sat down on the armrest. She hooked her legs around his waist and sat in his lap, and he let out a groan when she ran her hands through his hair. The sound sent lightning racing across her skin. She wanted him like this. Beneath her. Pliable beneath her hands. Drinking in her kisses with the same desperation with which plants devoured the sun. He circled her nipples with featherlight strokes, and she let out a gasp. The apex of her thighs throbbed again, and she bit his lip.

"You're so soft," he said, squeezing her breasts before running his hands across her collarbone, her shoulders, her arms.

Del whispered against his mouth. "Well, I can't say the same of you, darling, can I now?" She lowered a hand to his hardened length and guided it between her legs. His wings shuddered, and his grip tightened around her, but she did not slip him fully inside her yet. She circled his tip against the place where she was most sensitive.

"Do you want me to drop you?" he asked, breathless.

With a last brush of his lips, she moved him toward her entrance. She circled him there, denying both of them the pleasure of a full connection, and with a growl he moved his hand between her legs. He rubbed his palm against her while kissing her senseless. Both their kisses grew sloppy, and she pressed him inside her. She let him settle there. His wings splayed outward, and he panted, "You're so . . . small."

"I've always felt"—she broke into a moan when she lifted herself up—"the smaller the target"—she glided back down—"the greater the reward of hitting the mark."

She tilted her head back, losing the ability to form words as her movements became faster. Her heart fluttered, she gasped, she twisted her hands through his hair. Her eyes were squeezed shut, and the muscles in her stomach were coiling tighter and tighter. When he shifted his hips in a way that made him brush against her on his way out and in, a scream bubbled past her lips. He huffed a laugh, and release crashed through her again and again. Lips slingshotting into his wickedly soft mouth, she fell upward into the stars.

"Have I, then?" he asked, kissing her face while she floated back down. He brushed one of her braids out of her face with a smile. "Hit the mark?"

She blinked rapidly, still breathing hard.

He laughed. "I'll take that as a yes." He tossed sweaty strands of hair from his forehead, and Del slowly stood, sliding him out of her little by little. Purposely swaying her hips, she sprawled herself out on the sofa, legs spread.

Thanatos leaned over her, his hands on either side of the blue cushion. "This sofa is rather lovely." His wings fell over them, forming a curtain. His pupils were blown wide in the shadows, leaving his eyes black with the thinnest ring of blue at their edges. He lowered himself onto her, and she arched her back at the friction. A shiver ran through her when he whispered in her ear, "I would hate for us to break it."

"Beautiful things are not always delicate," Del said.

He lowered himself on top of her, and she ran her hand over his length. His mouth opened in a silent gasp, and she guided him into her. She walked her fingers over his stomach, watching gooseflesh prickle his skin. He bucked against her, but she splayed a hand across his chest. "Ah, ah, I'm in control here." She kept her hand pressed to his chest, holding him still, and his wings gave a strong flap. She ran her fingers along them, and he moaned. He shuddered, and his hands clawed at the sofa cushions.

"Please, Del," he panted.

She smirked at how undone such a small denial could make him. She loved taking him apart step by step. When she whispered her fingers over his wings again, stroking the inner feathers, his moan cracked into a whimper. His head fell forward, and he bit her collarbone, then her neck. As he sucked, Del arched into him, a small sound escaping her.

"Harder," she gasped. She increased the pressure on his feathers, and tight, welcome pain blossomed where he bit her neck. When she wrapped her legs around him, his wings gave a flap. Gusts of wind filled the cottage as he found his rhythm. He moved in and out of her, and her hair billowed in the wind.

When she soared into the sky again, his pleasure seeped into her core. Still panting, he rested on top of her, holding her close. For a short while, they lay there together, his heart thumping beneath her ear. Then he slid out of her and kissed the top of her head, squeezing her shoulder before striding into the kitchen. "Here, let me clean you up." He looked around. "Where do you keep your cloths?"

Del swayed into the kitchen. "Right here." She grabbed a cloth from one of the cabinets and let him dip it in the sun-warmed water in the washbasin. Gently, he cleaned her up, then she tossed the cloth into the wastebasket outside the window. They settled on the sofa, and he placed an arm around her shoulders. Still feeling loose and warm, she rested her head on his chest. "Have you always been like this?" she asked.

"What, submissive?"

She nodded against him and felt a hum vibrate through his chest. She looked up to find him scrunching his nose, emphasizing its slight crook. She tried not to stare and miserably failed. "No, I haven't. I mean, not consciously, I guess. I didn't *know* like you did. Generally, people see a god of death and just assume I must want to control the situation— Hey, is that it? Is that the reason you like dominance, to have control? Because I get that. That makes sense."

He was smiling at her, looking proud to have uncovered some hidden truth about her, but Del frowned. "I don't know." She moved away from him. "I don't think about why I like what I like. I just do it. I make myself feel good."

Thanatos pursed his lips. He nodded, then to her surprise, he pointed his thumb at the window and said, "About your Isle, I wanted to ask . . ."

Del raised her eyebrows, and he said, "I was thinking about it while flying us back here. When you turned the battlefield into a forest, it gave me an idea."

"If your idea is for me to regrow the Isle in one fell swoop, I'm afraid I can't do that. You saw what happened to me in Athens. If I tried to regrow the whole Isle . . ." She shook her head. "Even if I could regrow it all at once, I'm not sure I would. I took time perfecting it. That's where I find joy in my work. The process."

"Oh, no." Thanatos shook his head. "I wasn't going to tell you to regrow it all at once. I was thinking, I might be able to help you get it ready to be regrown. Little by little." He gestured at the window. "I might be able to help . . . clear everything up."

"Hmm." Del stood from the sofa. "Well, let me find us some clothes, then we will go out there and see what you can do." She hurried up to the loft, where she found a white robe for herself and a black one for him. She kept the black robe for cold days in winter, when she wanted to wrap herself in multiple layers. It was the only thing that looked large enough to fit him, but when she came back downstairs and handed it to him, she realized her error. "How do you put things on without damaging your wings?" she asked.

"Ah." Thanatos took the robe from her. "I have my clothes bespelled so that my wings can fit through them."

"Well, I don't know how to do that, but I might have an alternative." She grew a rose thorn and told him to hold still, then she sliced two long slits down the back of the robe. She fitted it around his wings and spiraled one of her fingers so a thin vine wove through both slits, cinching them together. The robe was embroidered with a garden at the hem and shoulders, so the vines looked like extensions of it. She stepped back and admired her handiwork.

"That suits you," she said.

"Why, thank you, mistress."

She tried to ignore how his smile made her stomach flip. She strode to the door, and he followed her into the garden, where the air felt like a damp cloth. Soothing yet heavy, scented with florals. The sea was calm, the waves lapping against the shore. Before Del could ask what he had planned, Thanatos cleared his throat. Then he opened his mouth and began to sing his song. He started with the high notes, and the birds in the broken woodland joined in, forming a chorus as they soared into the air, sending shadows cascading over the land.

She watched in amazement when the Isle began to glow. At first, the glow was so subtle that she convinced herself it was merely the sunlight reflecting off the grass. But as the green light grew stronger, she could no longer deny it was real. Like a sun rising from the soil, its rays enveloped the gnarled arches of white myrtle, then the upturned rosebushes and white lilies that scattered the ground.

Thanatos sang louder, his voice echoing across the Isle, and the green light shrouded the woodland. It hung from the limbs of the orchard like a veil. All the light bent toward Del, until it appeared the Isle was a great green eye with her as its pupil.

Still singing, Thanatos placed a hand on her back, giving her a reassuring nod. Cheeks wet with tears, Del closed her eyes, imagining the roots of all the plants on the Isle curling back into themselves. She imagined them letting go of the soil, and when her eyes fluttered open, she saw each and every plant hovering just above the ground. As Thanatos's song crescendoed, their roots and limbs and leaves crumbled, raining back onto the ground as soil. When the green light faded along with the song, the Isle was rendered a freshly tilled field, ready and waiting for whatever new world Del wanted to grow.

She gazed at the rolling hills, only the cottage interrupting the gentle slide toward the Aegean Sea lapping at the Isle. Birds sloughed over the waves in dark clouds, off to find new homes. Rabbits and deer and other woodland animals scampered through the soil, and Del resolved to first regrow some of the trees, giving them a place to call home.

"Is this okay?" asked Thanatos. "I thought it might make it easier, having a fresh place to start. Your mother has told me it helps to have old plants decompose in the soil. She says it makes the ground more fertile—"

"It's perfect," said Del. She wrapped her arms around him and inhaled the scent of fresh soil. "I can't wait to start. When all this is done, whenever we have figured out what to do about all these vows and curses and betrothals," she said, looking up at him, "I would not mind if you helped me regrow the Isle."

"I would like that very much." His smile was as soft as the dawn, but it faded when he said, "Speaking of, I talked to Keres while we were in Athens—after you fainted."

"About your mother?" Del asked.

He nodded. "That was why she wanted me to take you to Helios and Selene's palace. She said our mother would want to see us as soon as possible."

"So why not take us there?"

He huffed a laugh. "I didn't think you would take kindly to waking up in an unfamiliar place." He shook his head. "And even though I want to see my mother, the knowledge that I have been wrong for all these years . . ."

"It makes the idea of facing her difficult," Del said.

"Yes."

She sighed. "I understand. Now that I know Yaya has been lying to me, and my mother was in love with my father when she ran away with him, I don't know what I will say when I see my mother again." She closed her eyes. "I tried to dissolve their marriage vow. I tried to rip her away from the man she loves."

"But your grandmother was not lying about who Hades is."

Del opened her eyes, and Thanatos scratched the back of his head. "I mean, she was wrong about how your mother felt about him, but she wasn't wrong about him being a bad person." His wings twitched. "I'm not sure how I feel about both your parents. Yes, Hades was the one who banished my mother, but Persephone still forgave him. She hid the truth from me for all these years."

"She hid the truth from me too," Del said.

"I just don't understand why she would help him like that."

"She thought it would be better, I think, for us to have happy childhoods. For us to know we belonged somewhere."

"Is it better? To grow up thinking you know your place in the world, only to realize later that you never belonged there at all?"

"I'm not saying I forgive my parents for what they did, but I think I understand it. Think of the triplets. Can you imagine going up to them and telling them my father is a terrible person? It won't change anything about where they live. They have to live in the underworld to practice their magic before they are sent to the mortals—just like you and Keres did. I had to live with Yaya to practice my magic, and despite everything, my childhood was still good. I will always cherish the memories I made on Yaya's farm."

Thanatos looked out at the waves. "I suppose Hades treats the triplets well."

"According to my mother, you are a large part of why they love the underworld." Jealousy crawled up her throat, but she chopped it down. There was no reason to be jealous of Thanatos. He might spend more time with the triplets than she did, but they had both lost the homes they thought they had. "Think of all the good memories you have made with them. When I first brought you here, my mother said Mak thinks you are the best teacher in the world."

Thanatos tried to smile, but it came out as a grimace. "We do have good memories together, but most of them involve their magic lessons. Which might be how Hades controls them. Just as he controlled me for all these years." He crossed his arms and blew out a breath. "He only lets Mel practice her nightmares on him, me, and Persephone. Zag practices his magic on the old hellhounds. And Mak, well . . . Mak is who I help the most."

He looked out at the Aegean. "Hades and I take Mak to the Isle of Elysium, where she speaks to the souls of mortal heroes. She learns how they died, why they gave up their lives, and how they felt while making that sacrifice. Hades explains why he felt the soul deserved Elysium, and the three of us discuss the merits of the war in which they perished. It would be helpful if Keres was still in the underworld. When Mak goes to the mortals, the souls she reaps will die in battle. She will be taking some of the burden from Keres, not from me. But I am all she has." He flexed his jaw. "Unless I also decide to leave."

Del looked up at him. She was also angry at her parents, but she supposed the difference between her and Thanatos was that she had always been furious. She had hated her parents for so long, had resented that they did not want her in the underworld, that knowing their reasons was a relief. She could not yet forgive them for what they had done, but she understood them now. Having that certainty made her feel calm.

Thanatos, on the other hand, had grown up adoring her parents. He felt as betrayed by them as she felt by Yaya. Perhaps even more so. Because while Yaya had at least admitted to her hatred for Hades ever since Del was small, Hades had never mentioned that he felt anything for Nyx and Erebos at all. It would likely take Thanatos a long time before he could so much as consider forgiveness. His anger was more than justified, but Del wanted to help him take the first step toward healing.

"We still need to tell Zeus about our trip to Athens," she said. "On our way up Mount Olympus, why don't we stop at Helios and Selene's palace? We can go to the farm and ask Cate and Yaya how to find it, then we can go meet your mother." She took his hand and squeezed it, feeling the rustle of their olive-branch bracelets. "Together."

Thanatos met her eyes. "You would do that? Go to the farm so soon after learning how your grandmother has lied to you for all these years?"

Del turned to the Aegean, watching its waves spread in all directions. She remembered how, just a few days ago, she had sent her mother floating into this endless expanse. Tears pricked her eyes.

"I know how it feels to lose your mother," she said.

A moment of lapping waves and wind. Then Thanatos nodded, and they walked across the freshly tilled soil to the beach. Their feet sank into the sand, and as cool water filled the space between her toes, Del realized she had no way to get them off the Isle.

"I suppose," Thanatos said with a smile, "I need to fly us to the farm."

Chapter Twenty-Four

As the flight began, Del could not focus on anything but her closeness to the god of peaceful death. She was keenly aware of his hands on her waist. Her cheek on his chest. When he beat his wings, the wind roared in her ears. Her stomach plummeted with each bob and dip. Her eyes stung, and her hair whipped her face. She was entirely at his mercy.

She focused on the sea glittering beneath them. Land would soon split it, and she would be on solid ground again. She breathed more easily—

Thanatos tucked in his wings and dove toward the waves. Del shrieked, watching the sea rise to meet them, but he snapped out his wings at the last moment. They soared on the updraft created by the waves, and as they glided peacefully, Del found herself marveling at their reflection in the sea.

With a gasp, she realized a pod of dolphins swam alongside them. They leaped out of the sea, chirping while Thanatos's wings skimmed the waves. Hesitantly, Del reached out her hand and ran it across one of their cool, slick bodies. She laughed, light and free, and skimmed her hand over the sea. Losing herself in the sea mist and salt breeze, she grew accustomed to his rhythmic wingbeats.

Before long, they abandoned the sea for the valley, sweeping over fields in streaks of gold and green. They touched down by the stables in the shadow of Mount Olympus, and she found herself regretting that the flight had already ended.

"That was rather beautiful," she said while she straightened her robe.

Thanatos smiled, his hair sticking up at odd angles. "I'm glad you think so. We will have to do it again once all this is over."

"Perhaps we will." They started down one of the poppy-lined aisles between the fields. When they neared the farmhouse, the thicket of panic crawled up Del's throat.

"Are you sure you want to do this?" Thanatos asked, gently tugging on her wrist to bring her to a stop. "If you aren't ready to see her, we can go on to Zeus's palace right now."

Del met his eyes, letting out a breath while he rubbed the space between her forefinger and thumb. "I'm sure. Your mother might be able to help break my curse, but more than that, you both deserve to see each other. Whatever my feelings for Yaya, I won't let the two of you be kept apart any longer than you already have."

He swallowed, his eyes searching hers, before he gave her a nod. "I'll be right here the whole time. You won't be facing your grandmother alone."

He placed a hand on her back, steadying her as they walked to the farmhouse. They passed the yew that shaded the front and saw the spell room sat in its usual spot, surrounded by Cate's garden of herbs. The low-hanging yew branches cast deep shadows around its ebony walls.

A trio of voices shattered the silence when they entered the courtyard.

The triplets tumbled off an overturned amphora, where they had perched to peek through a window. They dashed across the grass and plowed into Del and Thanatos.

"Than!" Zag said, face split in a toothy smile.

"Del!" Mak crushed Del in an embrace, and with a delighted shriek, Zag latched his legs around Thanatos's waist.

"Are you coming home?" He swung his legs so they brushed Thanatos's wings.

"He can't," Mel said when she joined them. "Remember?" She peered up at Del, her black eyes absorbing the sun. "Pater said Than made a vow to help Del. He has to stay with her now."

Mak looked up at Del and let go of her waist. "Maytare wrote him a letter last night. She said she saw you in Athens."

"Is it true you turned the battlefield into a forest?" Zag asked.

Thanatos smiled at the boy with giddy fondness. "It certainly is."

"How did you find out about this letter?" Del cut in before Zag could interrogate Thanatos further. "Did you sneak into Pater and Maytare's room to read it?"

"No, he told us," Mel answered. They started toward the kitchen door, and perhaps it was paranoia, but Del swore the sky was filled with more clouds than usual. "Pater sent us here while he deals with all the mortal souls pouring into the underworld."

Zag nodded. "All of them are red—because they died violent deaths. It looks like the underworld is on fire, there are so many of them down there. The Furies keep watch over them."

Mak looked up at Thanatos. "Than taught me that trials for violent deaths take longer than peaceful ones. Pater doesn't have enough time for them."

"He sent Zeus a message about it," Zag said when they reached the door. "That's why Zeus is here now."

Del blinked. "Zeus is here?"

"He's talking to Cate and Yaya," Mel said.

"We were watching them." Mak pointed at the window. "He brought an eagle."

Zag whispered, "We heard him say something about Mak when he got here. That's why we were trying to listen."

Del flicked her eyes to Thanatos, whose mouth was pinched in a frown.

"Come on." Mel pulled them toward the door. "You're both old enough. You can go in there and tell us what they are talking about." She reached out to open the door, but then it swung open of its own accord, and Yaya stood on the threshold.

"Seedling!" She smiled at Del, who blinked, experiencing emotional vertigo. It seemed impossible that, despite how her perception of Yaya had changed, her grandmother looked and sounded exactly the same. "I was just about to send you a message." Her smile faded when she saw Thanatos. "Zeus wants to speak with you about your betrothal."

"We were on our way to see him," said Del. "We handled things in Athens."

"Better than we expected," said Thanatos.

Yaya made a small hum. "Yes, that's why Zeus is here. He . . ." She looked down at the triplets. "Well, you will understand when you talk to him." She stepped back from the door, waving them into the kitchen. "Come in."

"Tell us what you hear," Mel whispered to Thanatos.

"Maybe," Zag said, "he wants Mak to go to one of the Olympian festivals."

Mak smiled. "I hope so."

"You can come back and tell us," said Mel. "Then you can fly us around the farm."

While Thanatos hugged the triplets and promised to fly them around the farm as soon as possible, Del stepped into the kitchen, her footfalls echoing off the blue tile. The table was littered with breakfast dishes, and Askalabos sunbathed on the Cornucopia of Life, which hung beside the washbasin window. The wicker horn gleamed rich brown.

"So." Yaya strode toward the gecko. "Did you find your mother in Athens?"

Del nodded. "We did."

"And what did she tell you?"

Del hesitated. She hated how stiff she sounded. The air was heavy with the unsaid truths hanging between them. It was incredible. A handful of days ago, she had run to Yaya for comfort from Thanatos, and now she did not trust her at all. She wanted to sob. This was worse than losing the Isle. She felt like she had lost her truest home. She could not bring herself to confront Yaya about the curse just now.

"She said Cate told her my betrothal would not break my curse, but fulfill it. And she said Cate agreed it would be best to keep it a secret."

"Well." Yaya visibly relaxed. She pulled the Cornucopia of Life away from the wall with one hand, holding up the other for Askalabos to grip. "I am none too pleased that Cate kept the secret, but after seeing what the Fates tried to do to her . . ." She shook her head. "I understand why she could not tell us about it."

"Why is Zeus here?" Del asked. "Is he succumbing to the madness?"

"Zeus has always been a bit mad." The gecko skittered into Yaya's palm, his yellow-and-black-speckled body vibrant in the sun. "Think of how he let Hades kidnap your mother from the farm. But yes, it is worse now. I don't know . . ." She shook her head when Thanatos joined them. "He is through here. Come along."

She led them into the living area, where the king of the gods sprawled across the sofa from end to end. One of his hands propped up his head. The other stroked a brown, yellow-eyed eagle that plucked red grapes from a clump, lifting them to his lips one by one. Cate sat in the chair across from him, Gale curled around her neck. When the polecat spotted Askalabos, she perked up. Askalabos screeched and darted down Yaya's arm.

"Del," Zeus said while the polecat chased the gecko down the hall. The eagle dropped one of the grapes toward his mouth, but it bounced off his nose. It vanished into his beard, which was the color of storm clouds.

"Your Majesty." Del sat on the chair beside Cate while Zeus raked his fingers through his beard. It was threaded with lightning-white strands. "A pleasure to see you again."

"And what of the storm I sent to your Isle, was that a pleasure as well?" Zeus held up the grape before popping it into his mouth. The eagle flared its wings. "I was just telling your grandmother. We missed you at this year's Spring Equinox Festival. Helios in particular was rather upset about not getting first pick of the yearling drakones."

"I'm sure he could come by the farm anytime he wants." Del shared a look with Thanatos. He stood behind her chair, his wings curved around both of them. She turned back to Zeus, folding her hands in her lap. "Though I do wish I had been able to attend."

"Ah." Zeus grinned. "But not badly enough to cooperate with the hand the Fates have dealt you with."

"The Fates did not deal her this hand," Yaya said from where she perched on Cate's armrest. "Last I checked, that was Hades and Nyx."

"The Fates pull all our strings." Zeus raised his eyebrows at Cate. "Isn't that what you always say?" Yaya gritted her teeth, her hair shedding seeds of barley and wheat, but even she would not interrupt the king of the gods. He was too powerful. And unpredictable. His affability unsettled Del.

"The mortal world is in turmoil." His eyes darkened as he addressed her now. "I understand the way you learned of your betrothal was less than ideal, but by now you have had ample time to acquaint yourself." He splayed both hands at Thanatos. "This is a fine young god. Your differences balance each other well. You will live in a palace, with a loving husband and your family in the same walls. Let us stop the dramatics and be realistic, now."

Del clenched her hands. "I have seen the mortal wars—"

"Yes, Ares and Athena told me you made quite the spectacle of yourself. I must say, I had a good laugh when Athena screamed that you had lost her the Peloponnesian War. Sparta beats Athens. Ha!" Zeus held out his hands as though sizing Del up. "Such great power in such a small girl. I should like to test out the theory on those even smaller than yourself." He grinned. "See if I get the same result."

Del swallowed the rage-red flowers that threatened to bloom from her mouth. "As I was saying, we went to Athens because—"

Zeus waggled his finger. "You must not go meddling about like that anymore, though. I might be glad to see an end to the Peloponnesian War, but the goddess of flowers does not belong on a battlefield. It will confuse the mortals." He flicked his finger between Del and Thanatos. "The best way for you to stop the chaos you have caused is to wed one another. Let Athena and Ares handle the wars on their own."

Del scowled. "They can be angry with me if they want. Thanatos and I went to Athens so he could reap souls, and all I did at the battle was even the scales. Over the past few days, I have kept mortals from dying peaceful deaths, so I gave all those men who ought to have died in battle the chance to live long lives and die peacefully in their beds. You want me to fix the damage I have caused, so there—I have balanced things out."

"Silly child." The eagle dropped another grape into Zeus's mouth, and he bit down with a juicy pop. "That is not how we balance the scales. Mortal deaths are fated from the moment they are born. By robbing more mortals of the deaths they should have been dealt, you have worsened the imbalance, not canceled it out." He smiled. "You see why we are all so angry at you now? The damage you have done cannot be reversed. All you can do is change your course. So," he said with a nod at Thanatos, "you will marry this god."

"She will not." Thanatos squeezed Del's shoulder, his voice as cold as the underworld. "I vowed not to marry Del until we fell in love. I have no interest in marrying her unless it is of her own free will."

"Ah, yes, this pesky vow." Zeus nodded. "I know, I know. A fine statement for a god whose sole purpose is to take the lives of mortals."

Thanatos curved his wings tighter around Del. "The deaths I dole out are peaceful. I force no one to leave their lives behind them, and I will not force Del." He paused, letting out a breath through his nose. His wings relaxed on either side of the chair. "Until she is free of the curse she was shackled with at birth, I will not marry her. If, after her curse is lifted, she still does not fall in love with me, I will never marry her at all."

Zeus smoothed a finger down the beak of his eagle. "What do you think, Aitos? Isn't that rather sweet?" Aitos snapped his beak, his yellow eyes boring into Thanatos's face. Beyond the windows, the clouds filling the sky deepened to gray.

Zeus looked up at Del and Thanatos, his eyes sparking with glee. "You see, I do not care about this little vow you have made. I do not care if the two of you do not want to get married. You have made a mess of our world, and if you will not clean it *up*"—his voice crescendoed as lightning flashed beyond the windows—"I will be forced to use little Makaria. Makaria!" Aitos leaped into the air, stirring up a gust of wind that threw open the door.

Mak peeked inside, eyes darting from Yaya to Del, and Zeus smiled. "Come in, come in, little one. Don't be shy."

With a nervous smile, Mak tucked her black curls behind her ears only for them to pop right back out again. Zag and Mel appeared in the doorway behind her, but the wind snapped the door shut before they could step into the living area.

"Zeus!" Yaya squawked. "Do not slam doors in the faces of my grandchildren."

The king of the gods ignored her. He placed a hand on Mak's shoulder, and the little girl folded her hands at her front.

"What are you doing with her?" Del demanded, heart pounding in her throat.

"Makaria here," Zeus said with a smile, "is a very important god. Her magic is quite similar to yours, Thanatos. She says you help her practice in the underworld."

"I do . . ." Thanatos leaned forward. "But she won't be able to reveal herself to the mortals for many years to come."

"Oh, I don't know." Mak winced when Zeus tightened his grip on her shoulder. "Makaria is the goddess of blessed death. Perhaps that is not the same as peaceful death, but it is close to it. I am sure you have trained her well. She is probably very ahead of most young gods. When she goes to the mortals, she can follow Keres around on battlefields.

She will reap the souls of heroes, who will earn praise from their fellow mortals. This will not balance the scales forever, but for now it will keep the mortals happy enough to give us their worship." His stormy gaze settled on Del and Thanatos. "If the two of you are determined not to marry each other until you have fallen in love, she will work until then."

Del blanched. "You are *mad*!"

Zeus laughed. "Well, thanks to you, yes."

Del stared at Mak, who stood utterly still, even paler than usual. She understood the danger of going to the mortals too young. If she followed Keres to the battlefields, she would be exposed to the drug of mortal worship. She would start to believe her power was all she was, and she would lose her soul in the space between realms.

Del stared at Zeus from within the field of asphodel that had grown through the cracks in the floor. "You cannot force her to go to the mortals this young."

"I assure you," Zeus said, "I can do whatever I want."

"I will not allow it." The asphodel grew thick and tall.

"You will not allow it?" Zeus laughed. He let go of Mak, who ran to Yaya. Yaya enveloped her in a hug. Thunder rattled the living area with such force that Del feared it would bring down the farmhouse. Zeus stood, and lightning flashed so brightly that the world snapped into a blank sheet of whiteness. When it faded, Del was no longer in the living area. She was in the midst of a mortal city devoured by flames.

"You see this?" Zeus's voice thundered through her head. Mortals ran screaming through a city that looked like it had been dropped in a brazier. The roof of a temple concaved, and flames poured onto the streets. In the blast of heat, a woman stumbled, clutching a wailing infant to her chest. The woman fell, and the baby hit the street, falling abruptly silent. Blood poured from their head. Del retched as lightning struck again.

"And this?" Zeus demanded. When the white lightning faded, Del stood not in a city but in a field of black ash. The ground was littered with sooty roof tiles and singed stuffed dolls. The occasional bracelet of gold or necklace of jewels glittered in the dark. This was a city once. Perhaps the same city where the woman and her baby had just run. Now it was desolate. The screams had turned to silence. The silence was worse.

"You see what your stubbornness has wrought?" Zeus's voice rumbled while Del reached down to pluck up one of the singed dolls. The second her fingers touched it, it crumbled apart, the ash on her fingers liquefying into blood. Del tried to scream, but the sound caught in her throat. She was choking on her own tongue. She pressed her bloody hands to her throat, looking up at the cruel blue sky in the hope that Thanatos would fly down and help. Instead, another bolt of lightning shook the world.

"Thanks to you," Zeus said while white-hot electric current shattered the ground, flinging her backward with ozone on her tongue, "this is reality across the Greek world. Burning cities. Crumbling temples. Hatred for us gods."

Del tumbled head over foot through the current, Zeus's voice rattling her skull. She scrabbled for a shoreline, an outstretched hand, but there was only her body and the blinding white world. She accelerated, catching glimpses of burning towns, gutted mortals, seas of funeral pyres sending souls into Keres's arms. Her skin buzzed, stretched so thin she felt it might wear off her bones. Eyes shut, she imagined her skeleton clattering into her father's throne. It would adhere to the conglomeration of bone. For eternity, she would watch her father sentence mortals to the Fields of Punishment, the Isle of Elysium, the Fields of Asphodel. She would be trapped within the throne, forced to witness their trials—

"Your stubbornness did all this," Zeus said when Del snapped back into her chair in the farmhouse. Thanatos clung to her upper arms. He gripped them hard enough to leave marks, but instead of telling him to stop, she latched her hands around his wrists. They stayed like that, breathing hard while Zeus swaggered away from them.

"You are threatening the survival of the gods," he said. "In my palace, I have a scale representing the principle of balance." He snapped his fingers, sending a web of electricity spidering into the air. The white-blue threads wove together, creating the crackling image of a giant oak. It rose from the throne, its limbs arranged in the shape of a scale. Del had seen it on her trips to Olympus for festivals, but now the branches were off kilter. Some hung so low that they brushed the marble floor, while others scraped the skylights far above.

"This imbalance has occurred mere days after you captured Thanatos," Zeus said while everyone watched the oak. "That is the precarious nature of our world. As the king of the gods, I cannot allow it to become worse. Perhaps if you had not stolen Thanatos, keeping him from his work, this could have been avoided. Now, the only way to counteract the damage you have done is by marrying him. By sharing the story of your marriage with the mortals, you will restore the balance." He wriggled his hand, and the image of the oak grew more and more gnarled until it uprooted and fell, crumbling into soundless white-blue sparks.

He stood, smiling down at Del and Thanatos. "You have three days to marry each other. After that," he said as he ruffled Mak's hair, "I take little Makaria to the mortals."

With that, he strode into the courtyard, Aitos soaring after him.

Chapter Twenty-Five

Mel and Zag dashed into the living area, while Mak looked up at Yaya in tears. "Did he mean that? Will he really make me go into battles if Del doesn't marry Than?"

"What do you mean, go into battles?" Mel's gaze darted from Del to Yaya. "Mak can't go to battles. Pater said we can't reveal ourselves to the mortals until we are one hundred and twenty years old."

"He said if we try, we will lose our souls," Zag yelped. "We will be caught in the space between realms." He turned to Del. "You wouldn't trap Mak there, would you, Del? Just marry Than and everything will be all right. He's nice. He likes you a lot."

Del stared at her siblings, who were all waiting for an answer. Zag, with a smile. Mel, with her eyes narrowed. Mak, with tear-stained cheeks and eyes full of hope.

It was Mak who did her in. She backed away, unable to answer them. She deserved Tartarus for this. She imagined it: fire, darkness, flashes of leather and talons. Screams and the hiss of flame on skin. The groaning of rock falling into oblivion.

It would hurt less.

Thanatos took her by the shoulders. "Come with me," he said. She disintegrated the field of asphodel in the living area, and he led her into the courtyard, where the sun warmed the top of her head. Birds chirped in the cloudless sky overhead. A crane bugled in the forest.

The world should not be so beautiful on a day like this.

"Del." Thanatos rubbed the space between her forefinger and thumb. "Del, look at me. Remember? Take deep breaths." He breathed in, and she mimicked him.

"Mak," she said, feeling like the sound came from someone else. "She will be lost. Forever. And it's all my fault."

"It is not." Thanatos held her face in his hands, his eyes meeting hers. "Listen to me. It is not your fault. If anything, it's my fault for making the vow. Now, listen." Del focused on his eyes, which in the sun looked like twin blue flowers. "Mak is like a little sister to me as well. I won't let anything happen to her. We came here to find my mother, and we still need to do that. If she will open the door to where the Fates live, they might give us a way to break your curse. Mak will be safe from Zeus's threat."

Del sucked in a breath. "Okay, all right. Yes." She turned back to the farmhouse, but Cate and Yaya were already running into the courtyard, the triplets following them.

"We need to see Nyx," Del said. "Cate, I know you said visiting the Fates is dangerous, but we have to risk it. Can you tell us where to find Helios and Selene's palace?" She beseeched Yaya. "I don't want to live in the underworld, but breaking my curse is our only chance."

Cate took Yaya's hand. "What I cannot do for Del, Nyx can."

Yaya squeezed her eyes shut, but she nodded. "Come with me to the stables." She spoke while she walked. Cate remained with the triplets in the courtyard. "The drakones I flew to Helios and Selene's palace when your mother was stolen are much older now, but they still know how to get there. Tell them where to go, and they will not need any direction."

They stepped into the dimness of the stables, surrounded by the scent of hay and reptiles. Yaya led two of the largest drakones out of their stalls. Their green scales were nicked with scars, and their claws clacked against the floor. They flapped their white-feathered wings while Del helped harness them to the chariot.

When she led them outside, Cate was there holding a jar of yew-berry paste. Gale was wrapped around her throat, and the triplets clung to her robe. "If you are going to see the Fates," she said, handing the jar to Del, "this will help."

"Thank you." Del took the jar and stepped into the chariot. Thanatos climbed in behind her, and she passed him the jar before she took the reins and looked down at Mak. "I promise, I am going to keep you safe. No matter what it takes."

Mak gave her a trembling smile, and Cate and Yaya backed the triplets away.

Del snapped the reins. "Take us to the palace of Helios and Selene," she said, and the drakones gave a reptilian screech. They soared into the sky, pumping their wings.

Chapter Twenty-Six

Thanatos latched on to her waist. He yelled over the wind, "You could have given me some warning before taking off!"

Del leaned forward in the chariot. The drakones veered to the left, climbing up Mount Olympus. "What, are you scared of heights, darling Thanatos?"

"I prefer to be in control when I fly, if you must know."

"Relax. I have been flying chariots since I was a little girl."

"If I were to race you, do you think you could win?"

"I know so."

His lips tickled her ear. "We will see about that."

Without further warning, he leaped from the chariot. Del shrieked, but he spread his wings and flew alongside her. The drakones bucked and flicked their tongues through the air, straining their necks. In the afternoon sunlight, their white feathers turned gold. They soared through a sky streaked with blue and yellow, lavender and orange clouds. Despite how desperate Del was to save Mak, it was impossible not to enjoy a flight with Thanatos.

They spiraled around the mountain, him tucking in his wings to take corkscrew dives before snapping out his wings to whoosh upward far higher than Del. At one point, he placed his hands on her shoulders and flew directly above her, pushing the chariot through the clouds. "I thought you could use the encouragement," he yelled. "Plodding along as you are."

Del tugged on the reins, turning the chariot on its side, and Thanatos let go. "You will regret that," she called out. She straightened the chariot and leaned forward, the Olympic forest whisking below in a sea of pines and oaks. The trees thinned until they reached a rocky section of the mountain, and Del slowed. She worried the drakones had forgotten the way to the palace after all, but then Thanatos shot past her with a whoop, and she looked down.

The palace was carved into the side of the mountains, the rock around it gilded in silver and gold. It glinted in the sun, reflecting the sky around it so that it nearly vanished into the clouds. Golden light speared the air, and a towering heliotrope plant clung to the sheer cliff, forming a rustling canopy that shaded the front steps. Its clusters of purple blossoms looked like clouds, their scent reminiscent of warm sugar and home.

This was the plant that held the soul of Eos, the goddess of dawn.

A shelf of rock jutted out from the front doors, where Thanatos landed just before the drakones. "I guess," he said, not even winded, "I won't regret anything, after all."

He grinned and gave Del a bow. He held out his hand to help her from the chariot, but she smacked it away. "You are such a show-off."

"Oh, and you wouldn't know anything about that. You would never, say, announce you are kidnapping someone and trap them in a laurel."

"Only for you, darling Thanatos." Del scratched the drakones under their chins, and the reality of their situation settled on her shoulders again. They were here to save her little sister by speaking to Thanatos's mother, whom he had not seen since he was younger than the triplets were now. Wiping sweat from her brow, she turned to the carved double doors. One depicted the night sky in silver. The other displayed a sunrise in gold.

"Well," she said, "here we are."

Thanatos let out a breath. "Here we are."

"She won't resent you. Not for the marriage vow you gave her and Erebos, and not for loving the man who raised you—just as my mother would never blame me for loving Yaya."

"No, but she might not take kindly to me only coming to visit when I have a request."

"That is not the only reason you're here. And she did not want to leave you. She will be thrilled to see you again." Del tried to sound confident, though she was reassuring herself as much as him. "When we explain Mak's situation, she will understand."

Thanatos swallowed. He nodded, and they stepped up to the doors. They knocked, and the sound echoed, reverberating across the cliff face with a rippling sheen. Footsteps filtered through the other side of the door, and Thanatos squeezed her hand when they saw the turn of the door handle. Del held her breath.

The doors opened, and there stood a tall, pale woman with lapping waves of black hair. Streaks of gray like shooting stars ran through it, and her cape hung heavy, soaked with purest darkness. Her eyes twinkled indigo and violet, which widened when she saw Thanatos.

"Thanatos," she said, and Del recognized the voice from her nightmares. Sharp and deep. Demanding attention like the brightest star in the night sky.

"Mother." Thanatos glanced up at Nyx before lowering his eyes to the front steps. "I—I don't know what to say. I was wrong. All these years. I have finally learned—I mean, yesterday. I finally learned what Hades did to you and Erebos when Keres and I were children." He gave Nyx the same earnest expression he had used on Del when she kidnapped him. "I am so sorry, though I do not think sorry is a large enough word for what I feel."

Nyx came forward. Slowly at first, as though she was not sure he was really there. The wind blew past them, billowing her hair. She stopped in front of him and lifted shaking hands. She touched both sides of his face, eyes rimmed with tears.

"My son," she said.

She threw her arms around him, wrapping him in deepest night. She clutched him tightly, and his wings encircled them both. Del smiled, but in the back of her mind she wished she could have had such a moment with her mother. Instead, when Persephone told her the truth about her childhood, she had run. She wished she could go back and change it. She should have stayed in the encampment and held her mother close.

"You do not need to apologize," Nyx said to her son. "You were lied to as a child."

"He banished you," said Thanatos. "He caged the man you loved and banished you from your home, just because he was jealous. And I was complicit. Not just in the marriage vow I gave to you and Erebos, but also in loving him for all these years."

"Erebos and I wanted you to bind our souls in marriage. That was a great day for us, and one I shall never regret. All that matters now is that you know the truth of who Hades is. I have loved you since the day you were born, and I will love you to the end of time and beyond it. My son." She turned to Del. "Thank you for bringing him home."

"No thanks are necessary," said Del. "My father told us the truth, and—"

"Do not give him any credit."

"I'm not. I'm merely saying that as soon as Thanatos learned the truth, he wanted to tell Keres about it. He wanted to see you." She glanced at Thanatos, who was wiping tears from his cheeks. "We would have come here sooner, but—"

"You are trying to break off your engagement. Yes, Keres told me about this curse you have." Nyx held open the doors of the palace. "Come inside and we will talk through it."

Del grabbed the jar of yewberry paste from the chariot, then she followed Nyx and Thanatos into the palace. Windows were cut out of the rock to let in the breeze off the mountain, and purple blooms of heliotrope lined every sill. Between the windows, the walls were carved with intricate friezes of the sunrise and sunset. One entire wall depicted a scene of Helios tending to a herd of horned cattle. Another showed Selene flying her moon chariot while maidens chased a sleek doe through a forest far below.

Del glanced at Thanatos and cleared her throat. "Nyx. As we said before, we came here because Thanatos wanted to see you, but we also—"

The frieze of Selene sprang open. Del startled, and Thanatos flared his wings, pulling her close. The woman who stepped into the hall had lily-white skin and silver hair that matched her robe. Her eyes were almost as pale as Cate's, but instead of white, they were moon gray.

"I didn't mean to startle you." She smiled. "I was only curious. I heard voices I didn't know." She turned to Nyx with raised eyebrows.

"Selene." Nyx gestured at Del. "Meet the eldest daughter of Hades and Persephone."

"Ah, I recognize you from Cate's stories." Selene winked at Del. "And from when you pulled that laurel through the sky a few nights ago." She turned to Thanatos. "And I take that to mean you are . . . ?"

He dipped his head. "Thanatos."

Selene clapped, and her smile was like a moonbow. "At long last!"

"Indeed," Nyx said. "But it is not time for celebration just yet." She turned her attention to Del. "I believe they were about to ask for my help."

"Mother, we need to see the Fates," said Thanatos.

Nyx arched an eyebrow. "The Fates might be my children, but they are forces unto themselves. I'm not sure I can convince them of anything they wouldn't do on their own."

"We aren't asking for certainty," Del said. "We just need a chance."

"You see . . ." Thanatos explained his vow not to marry Del until they fell in love, then Del reiterated Zeus's threat to send Mak to the mortals.

"We have this from Hecate." Del held up the jar of yewberry paste. "She says you have a door that leads straight to the Fates' home. If you can open it for us, we think they might be able to help me break my curse. If I can fall in love with Thanatos, I can save Mak." She paused. "And I will live in the underworld. You will get the alliance you want."

Thanatos turned to her, eyes searching hers. "You would live in the underworld?"

She set her jaw. "If it means saving my little sister, then yes, I will."

Thanatos opened his mouth, but Selene stepped forward, hands clasped at her front. "Oh, Nyx, let them go. You recall what happened to Eos when you first came to live with us." The goddess of the moon addressed Del and Thanatos. "Nyx barely had the chance to meet Eos before . . ." She gestured at the heliotrope plants creeping through the windows. "I cannot bear to see another young goddess lose herself."

Nyx sighed. "I will open the door, but you must understand. The Fates are different from the rest of us gods. They exist outside of time, weaving the great story of the world. You might be their little brother," she said to Thanatos, "but that will not grant you any favors. They will speak in riddles. Even if they do give you an answer, you will have to dissect its meaning. And with only three days to do so, I am not sure you will succeed."

Del nodded. "I understand."

"We would still be grateful for the opportunity," Thanatos said.

"Very well." Nyx turned to Del. "But when you return, we have much to discuss. I did not mean to trap you in a loveless marriage, and I would like the chance to explain myself."

"As soon as we have saved Mak," said Thanatos, "we can talk about the alliance in detail. But Mak has to come first."

Del smiled at him, and Selene placed a hand on her heart. "I must go rest before my flight tonight," she told Del, "but I truly hope you can save your sister. Helios and I are forever indebted to your grandmother. It is only thanks to her that we have anything of Eos left in our home. If you need any assistance from me, I will give it freely."

"Thank you," Del said, and the goddess gave a final nod before stepping back into the wall. The frieze closed, leaving no proof of a door. Nyx led them deeper into the palace, where the windows gave way to sconces of red fire. She told them to take great scoops of the yewberry paste into their mouths. "It will help keep your souls firmly planted within your physical forms while you travel. Without it, you may slip out of yourselves."

Del recalled what had happened to Cate yesterday morning, when Thanatos had brought her soul back to her body. At the thought of the same thing happening to her and Thanatos, the thicket of panic flourished through her limbs. But there was no other option.

It was this or lose Mak forever.

"Something else you should know," Nyx said, "is that the Fates live in the space before, after, and between realms. Time passes differently there. What may seem like only minutes for you will be hours here, or perhaps even longer. By the time you return, the three days Zeus has allotted you to save your sister may have already elapsed."

This only worsened the thicket of panic, but Del said, "If we don't go, we have no chance." She scooped some of the yewberry paste into her hand, then she handed the jar to Thanatos. While he removed some paste for himself, they turned a corner into a hallway devoid of any torches or windows. The only light came from a door at the end of the hall, which was outlined in gold. The hall was eerily silent. Their footsteps echoed.

"I will stand watch until you return," Nyx said. "If you are still with the Fates come nightfall, I will leave Keres to watch over you while I bring night to the world. Helios will also be here, but he will need to rest like Selene is now."

"What about Hemera?" asked Thanatos. "Will she be resting as well?"

"She will, but . . . Hemera is not well. I have never seen her for myself, but Keres tells me it is all she can do to bring day to the world. Helios is very protective of her. Ever since Eos— Well, the days get longer each year, for Hemera is overextending herself. If you see her, please do not try to speak with her much." Her expression was pained when she gestured for them to eat the yewberry paste.

Del took a deep breath and locked eyes with Thanatos. She held out her hand filled with yewberry paste and gave him a tight smile. "Together?"

He tapped his hand against hers. "Always, mistress."

As they lifted their hands to their mouths, Nyx said, "Do not let go of each other while you are there. Where the Fates live, it is very easy to . . . slip."

Perhaps this should have prompted some hesitation, but they were past that. Thanatos took Del's empty hand, interlocking her fingers with his. At the same time, they ate the yewberry paste from their opposite hands. Del grimaced at the sickly sweetness. Then Nyx opened the door, and hands held, eyes shut, they leaped into a golden world.

Chapter Twenty-Seven

Time unrolled beneath Del in the form of wide, carpeted stairs. That was the only way she could describe the series of reflections staring back at her, descending in age. On the step directly beneath her frowned her current face, while the one beyond it bore the image of her scowling at the Farewell Festival last year. The step after it showed her as a child, glowering at her mother on Yaya's farm, while the next showed her grinning as she stepped onto her Isle for the first time. The stairs extended like that, down and down, until they curved in on themselves. The last visible reflection was of her laughing toddler self.

Staring at that wild-haired child now, she swallowed, the saccharine yewberry paste still lingering in her mouth. "Do you see yourself," she said to Thanatos without looking up, "every past version of yourself, when you look down?"

"I do." He squeezed her hand, his wings folding her body close to his. "And when I look up, I see every version of myself I might still become."

At the reminder that the past was not all there was, Del peeled her eyes away from her younger selves. Blinking rapidly, she looked up, and her hand flew to her mouth. All around them churned interlocking woven wheels, each composed of the same mirrored stairs as the one where they stood now. Some of the wheels were relatively small, about the height and width of a fully grown oak. Others were as large as the mountain that filled the underworld. Despite their variances in size, every last wheel interlocked, fitting together so well it appeared there was no way out. This omnipresence gave the wheels the impression of sound, but they moved in silence, with the looming inevitability of an enemy ship approaching a defenseless shore. They shone with the brightness of dawn.

Del pressed her hand to her mouth when she realized every stair in every wheel reflected some version of herself. She looked up and glimpsed herself swimming through the river Styx into the underworld. She saw herself hugging the triplets on the Isle. She saw herself leaning over the pit of Tartarus, her eyes full of flames and her wrists bound. The wheels showed her infinite possibilities for what she might do and whom she might become.

Tears pricked her eyes. "It's incredible," she gasped out. And it was, but as the wheels continued their slow churn with no intention of letting them out, she realized it was also dangerous. She was immortal, as was Thanatos. If this was a realm composed of all their possible selves, it was endless. Which meant they were trapped, with no idea how to find the three women who called this place home.

"We're moving down," Thanatos warned. Del lowered her dazzled eyes and saw with a surge of panic that he was right. Before, the last visible reflection of herself had been a toddler. Now it was her on the farm, red-faced and yelling at her mother when Persephone told her she was going to raise the triplets in the underworld. Ignoring how her heart seized at the reminder of that moment, she forced herself to focus on finding a way out. A quick scan revealed that if they didn't move soon, they would be crushed by the steps of the nearest wheel. Already, its own stairs were interlocking with the image of her on the farm.

Burying her panic with a shovelful of calm, Del danced her gaze across the wheels. The closer she looked, the more she risked being dazzled by the light that shone through them. Not willing to risk that, she looked at the images of herself out of the corners of her eyes, discarding each one. What she needed was a gap, a hole in this woven world—

"There," Thanatos said, pointing down. Del followed his hand and glimpsed what appeared to be a solid gold spiral nestled in the very center of the wheels. It was gleaming and thick, like it was the trunk of a tree, and its branches were the wheels. Most important, in this altogether moving realm, it alone stood still.

Del could have collapsed with relief. "Can you fly us down?" She glanced at the wheel nearest them to see it interlock with the image of her frowning down at the swaddled triplets the summer after they were born. As the image vanished beneath the other wheel, Thanatos spread his wings. But before he could flap them, they splayed outward, filled with the up and down drafts the wheels created with their hulking, incessant spins.

"I can't." He refolded them, shaking his head. "It will be nearly impossible to lift off, and if I do, I don't trust that we won't end up being sucked into one of the other wheels."

Del swallowed. The nearest wheel had now interlocked with all the reflections leading up to the image of her staring at Thanatos when he announced their betrothal. "So we will have to climb and jump and walk."

He nodded, locking his eyes with hers. "Don't look up. Don't look down. Focus only on the now."

Del repeated this refrain to herself as they leaped off the wheel, the interlocking stairs nipping their heels. She repeated it again while they sailed through the air, her hair whipping around her head, and again when they landed on a step that showed her sitting on her father's throne of bone, Coronis's beak clacking as she stroked his head. Side by side with Thanatos, she forced herself to ignore every teasing possibility for her future and focus only on the warmth of his hand. If she stopped to consider either her future or her past, the wheels would interlock, and she would be squashed between them, forever lost.

When they finally leaped onto the gold spiral, they both almost tumbled off, for it was not nearly as solid as Del had thought. Instead of a pure gold spiral, it was a skein of yarn. Its individual strands shifted about like hair billowing in the wind created by the wheels. Clinging to one another's hands, they both dropped down, shimmying across the skein like caterpillars across a leaf. They kept their heads low, Thanatos's wings drooping over them as the wheels churned perilously close. Sweat dripped from her brow while Del crawled with him beneath one of the giant wheels, ducking her head low. When she looked up, still clutching the skein of yarn, she saw they were suddenly outside the woven realm.

Rather than the infinite interlocking wheels, oblivion surrounded the golden skein now. It was not darkness, Del thought as she blinked at it, trying to convince her eyes to focus. Darkness implied shadows, which implied shape. This blackness stretched interminably, sucking in all the golden light glancing off the skein. The skein itself had begun to ripple like a lyre being played, its individual strands twanging against Del's body.

"It's them," Thanatos said, lifting one hand and pointing. "They're weaving."

Giving up on making sense of the oblivion, Del looked to where he pointed at the end of the skein. There, three women sat in a circle weaving. As Del and Thanatos crawled closer, the twanging of the yarn beneath them increasing, Del watched their fingers loop the golden strands into impossibly complex braids. They embarked on their task seamlessly, reaching over and under to complete each other's weavings.

"So," one of them said when Del and Thanatos reached the end of the skein, her ageless face framed by waves of black hair that descended endlessly, "you have walked through every possibility . . ."

". . . for your lives without getting lost." The one with gray hair finished the thought, yanking a golden strand from her black-haired counterpart and tying a knot. "We congratulate you on succeeding . . ."

The one with white hair leaned forward and bit off the knot. She chewed and swallowed before finishing off, ". . . where many would have failed."

Kneeling at the edge of their perch, Thanatos intoned, "Sisters, what is this place you call home?"

"Little brother . . ." The white-haired one licked her lips with a bloodred tongue.

The gray-haired one chuckled. "Mother Nyx is very pleased with your decision regarding the king of the underworld."

Eyes wide, Thanatos glanced at Del. Del's brow furrowed, but she turned back to the sisters when the black-haired one sighed down at her work. "Mother Nyx did not see fit to include us in her plans . . ."

The white-haired one tossed another golden knot into her mouth. ". . . perhaps because we must always remain here . . ."

The gray-haired one looped three golden strands into a thick knot, her expression morose. ". . . everywhere and nowhere, all at once and never at all . . ."

". . . tethered to our world without being tied down." The black-haired one settled her milk-white gaze on Del. "As you are by the knot around your heart." With her words, she lifted one hand, making a quick, cutting motion, and Del gasped, looking down to find herself wrapped in glowing red threads.

"Ah . . ." The gray-haired one tied a single strand into a trio of knots, then connected it to another held in her black-haired sister's hand. "Hecate has done well." She nodded at the threads binding Del, which felt like warm bands against her skin.

"To unravel a net so well woven . . ." the white-haired one said around a mouthful of yarn.

The black-haired one braided eight golden strands together at once. ". . . you will require meticulous skill."

"To practice," all three sisters said as one, their voices taking on an echo that blew through Del's soul, "first you must enable the embrace of night and day."

Del locked this task away in her mind, too cold to think about what it meant just now. In the same moment, Thanatos wrapped his wings around her as though trying to lend her some of his warmth. Not that he had much to spare, for his own teeth had begun to chatter, rosiness blooming across his pale skin.

Unmoved by the effect their combined voices had on their guests, the Fates continued to speak as one. "To further enhance your skills," they said, their black, gray, and white hair flowing beneath them while their faces glowed in the light of their yarn, "you must heal the rift between the four seasons of the world."

Mentally repeating her two tasks over and over again, Del huddled into Thanatos, whose skin was like cold stone. Hers was the same, she knew, because her fingertips were blue and going numb. "Finally," the Fates said as the red threads wrapping her body grew searing hot, "you will have the skill to break your bonds. In order to do so"—they leaned forward—"you must send life into death to save what is already lost."

The final task echoed through the woven realm, and the golden strands lashed toward Del and Thanatos. Blinded by their glow, Del reeled backward, tumbling off the skein of yarn.

Chapter Twenty-Eight

Too cold to scream, Del fell through the oblivion. She held tight to Thanatos, but he shoved her back toward the skein of yarn. She grabbed at his wings, but he fell farther away. His blue eyes met hers, his wings wrapping around him as he vanished into the dark. Del was all alone. She felt like she was back in her nightmare, descending into the underworld. But when something smacked her face, it was not cold marble.

It was the thwap of a hand. "Wake *up*," someone growled. Her eyes fluttered open, and she saw Keres glowering at her, her face framed by her mane of white hair.

"You almost lost your soul, little flower girl." The goddess leaned back and reached out a hand, shutting the door to the space between realms. Without the golden light, the hall descended into shadow.

Del sat up. Her entire body was sore. "How long have we been out there?" Her eyes widened when she realized what it meant that Keres was here instead of Nyx. "How many days has it been? Do we still have time to save Mak?"

"It has been a day and a half. I watched for you last night, but you didn't return. My mother came back this morning, but about an hour ago she left to bring night to the world."

"A whole day and a half?" Del's head throbbed, and her stomach was icy with dread. That left them with less than two days to save Mak. She stared at the door at the end of the hall, which was limned in gold. She knew losing time had been a risk, but—

"Stop glaring at the door and help me with Than," Keres said. Del turned and saw she had moved to lean over Thanatos. He was still prostrate on the floor, his eyes darting back and forth while they were still closed. He looked like Cate in her spell room when the Fates tried to take her soul. The image of him disappearing into the darkness came back to Del, and she scrambled toward him. She would worry about Mak later. Right now, Thanatos was in peril.

"Is he still caught out there?" She knelt beside Keres, eyes searching Thanatos with no idea how to help. Her fear made her angry, and she demanded, "Why did you shut the door?"

"Shut up." Keres held up a clay jar and opened her brother's mouth. Del winced at the slackness of his jaw. The goddess tipped a drop of blue water onto his tongue and snapped his mouth shut. "Than!" She slapped him across the face, but his head only lolled.

Del took his limp hand. "When the Fates pushed us away, he tried to throw me back toward them. He fell into the nothingness all around them."

Keres growled. "He was trying to save you. He put your soul before his own." She rocked back on her heels and covered her face with both palms. "I cannot do what he does. I can't coax out souls. All I have is this." She held up the jar. It was just like the jar of Styx water that Thanatos always kept on his person. Except for right now, because it was back in the pocket of his tunic at the cottage.

"Water from the Lake of Mnemosyne," Keres said. "It helps the souls of mortal heroes remember who they were before they came to the underworld. It helped call back your soul well enough, but . . ." She stared at her twin brother, who lay unresponsive.

The thicket of panic twined through Del's limbs. She had never seen Keres like this. The goddess always seemed to be as strong as Del wished she was. But perhaps both of them were only putting on a show while, in truth, they were both terrified of their own weakness.

Del could not let Keres feel that way about herself. She could not lose Thanatos.

Hesitantly, she reached out and placed her hand on Keres's upper arm. The goddess startled. She glared at Del, her red-brown eyes promising violence, but Del managed a smile. She adopted the same calm tone Thanatos used on her when she was overwhelmed. "You can do this. You're his twin. If anyone can call back his soul, you can."

Keres closed her eyes and sucked in a breath. She swiped her palms down her face and turned to her brother again. "I think it might help if you call out to him."

Del nodded. Keres tipped another droplet of water into his mouth, and Del shook him. "Than!" she called out. She took his hand and rubbed small circles in the space between his forefinger and thumb. "Than, deep breaths. Remember? Focus on being here."

Nothing. Nothing. Then—

He gave a violent inhale and groaned, holding his head. "Than!" Del threw her arms around him, and Keres let out a breath.

"You were gone." Del held his face in her hands, looking into those pale blue eyes of his. She had never been so thankful to see his soul looking out of them.

He smiled at her. "So, now you're calling me Than?"

"Thanatos," Del corrected herself.

"No, keep doing it. I think we are more than close enough for that."

"Ahem." Keres took two cups of tea from the floor. "You should drink this." She handed one to Del and the other to Than. "It's a blend of heliotrope and the yewberry paste you brought here. Helios makes a similar brew each night for Hemera. He says it should help you come back to yourselves." She scowled at Than. "I hope that visit was worth almost losing your soul. Did you at least receive the answers you sought?"

"Sort of." Del watched Than bring his cup to his lips. She glanced at Keres, admiring how quickly the goddess had gathered herself. "They gave us three riddles. And they said something odd. They said Nyx is pleased with Than's decision about—"

"What are you wearing?" Keres wrinkled her nose, looking Than up and down. "Are those live vines on your robe?"

He lifted his arms. "Del grew them," he said, watching the sleeves billow.

"What, you couldn't leave the cage back on her Isle?"

"It was a nice gesture!" He grimaced and lifted a hand to his temple. "Ah, my head."

"Serves you right for almost losing your soul to save the woman who kidnapped you from your home." Keres turned to Del. "So, you like a masochistic lapdog?"

Del spiraled her wrist, and one of the vines on Than's robe grew into a leash that she looped through her fingers. "We have to solve the three riddles—complete the three tasks—to break my curse. And we have less than two days to do it." At Than's shocked expression, she explained how long they had been in the space between realms.

Than's eyes were worried, but he held her close. "We will save Mak," he swore. "Now that we have the tasks, we know how. And besides . . ." His lips quirked up. "We have your stubbornness on our side, which I, for one, know to be unstoppable."

Del returned his smile, and Keres cleared her throat. The goddess was still studying the vine leash Del had grown. With a slice of her finger, Del disintegrated it, and Keres shook her head. "All right, then. What are these tasks?"

Del took another swig of tea. The rich nuttiness of the heliotrope offset the sweetness of the yewberry, and with each drink, she felt more grounded in this world. The woven realm of the Fates felt like a dream she had had long ago. Nevertheless, their words were so vital that she knew them by heart.

First, enable the embrace of night and day.

Second, heal the rift between the four seasons of the world.

Third, send life into death to save what is already lost.

She drained the last of her tea, turning the riddles over in her mind, and realized they were not as confusing as she had thought. The third seemed to refer to her and Than. She did not know exactly how, but they had almost two days to figure it out. The second referred to her family, she was sure of it. And the first, well, that could only refer to—

"We have to break my mother's banishment." Than set his empty cup on the floor, the sound of the clay hitting the stone echoing through the hall.

Chapter Twenty-Nine

Keres laughed, the sound harsh. "Mother and I have been trying to break her banishment for years. You think you can receive one message from the Fates and solve all our problems with a wave of your hand?" Her eyes blazed at Than. "You don't get to hate our mother our whole lives, then fly in and rescue her the moment you realize you were wrong."

"I was not trying to rescue our mother. We," Than said with a gesture between himself and Del, "are trying to save her little sister. Breaking our mother's banishment is part of that. You should be glad. It isn't as though you tried to tell me the truth for all these years. You left!"

"Do you remember my last Farewell Festival?" Keres asked.

"You slapped me across the face. It is difficult to forget."

"I was trying to tell you then. Or, I was trying to convince you to come visit, so Mother could tell you what happened. I thought she deserved that. And I thought if I could get you away from Hades, you would be more apt to listen. But you refused to even give me a chance. You wanted to stay down in the underworld with *him.* Blissfully ignorant. For nearly two hundred years, I have been trying to get you out of his grip, and you have defended him at every chance. You have no idea how infuriating it is—" Keres shut her eyes, her form shimmering at the edges, threatening to split into multiple aspects.

Than opened his mouth, but Del said, "I think I understand."

"Your mother abandoned you," Keres spat. "Mine was *banished*."

"Yes, but I have spent my life thinking my mother was bewitched. I understand how it feels to wish you could free your mother from a terrible situation. I won't pretend our lives have been the same, but I understand loneliness. You learn so quickly no one can be trusted. When you look out at the world, you see betrayal, cruelty, violence. So you harden yourself. You become a reflection of what you see in the world."

Keres narrowed her eyes, but she had returned to one aspect of herself. "What exactly is your point, little flower girl?"

Del blew out a breath, watching the red flames quiver in the wall sconces. "I think the time for our loneliness is over. I have never known how it feels to have friends, but I think the two of us could be good for one another." Keres looked as if she had been slapped. Del glanced at Than. His eyes shone, and he took her hand. "After we have saved Mak, I would love for us to spend more time together. You are always welcome on my Isle. Maybe I can teach you how to grow flowers, and you can show me how to use a sword."

Keres looked her up and down. A moment of silence passed. Then her face softened into the smallest of smiles. "So long as you don't mind me knocking you to the ground. I won't go easy on you just because you have never held a sword."

Del smiled. "I hope you won't."

"Maybe you aren't as infuriating as I thought." Keres turned back to her twin. "But that does not mean you are forgiven for leaving Mother all alone up here. It hurt, Than. All those years of us in our palace beds, wondering why she left, and then I find out the reason, and you will not accept it."

Than took her hand. "I know. You were right all along. I wanted you to be wrong, because I didn't want to lose the family I had always known."

"I know you didn't, but I didn't either. I lost my family in the underworld, but I lost you too. I lost my twin brother. That hurt the most."

"I'm sorry." Than pulled Keres close. At first she was rigid, but then she melted into his arms. Their black and white wings folded around each other, and when they parted, Keres batted Than's shoulder. "You are an idiot."

"I am." Than smiled gently. "From now on, I will listen."

She sniffed. "You better." She turned her attention to Del, gathering herself. "As for saving your little sister, Selene told Helios about Zeus's threat, and he has offered to help in any way he can. He has seen the exploits of many gods and heroes on his flights across the Greek world. If anyone knows a place to start, it will be him."

She led them back through the palace until they reached a large, circular sitting room lined with windows. Heliotrope burst over the sills, and the white sofas were cushioned with sunset-colored pillows, where a man sat with golden skin and hair. Helios gave Del and Than a wave of welcome, but Del was focused on the woman cuddled into him.

"Hemera?" Than asked.

The woman gave him a trembling smile. "Brother," she said, and her voice rasped. The goddess of day held a cup of steaming tea between her hands. Her hair, which should have been luscious gold, was dry and limp. Her skin bore a gray tinge. Her eyes were sunken in their sockets, reminding Del of the mortal boy whose soul Than had taken in Athens. The goddess looked like a mortal hollowed out by illness.

Gods were not supposed to look like this.

"It's a pleasure to see you," Than said, though his gaze roved over his older sister in the same way Del's did, "after all these years."

"Sit down, sit down." Helios gestured to the sofa opposite him and Hemera. "The wayward son visits at last. I know Keres brought each of you a cup of tea, but help yourself to another." He waved at the steaming pot and stack of cups that adorned the table between the sofas. When Del reached for them, he gestured at her wrist. "What's that?"

She held up her wrist, and Helios smiled. "Ah, matching bracelets."

"Olive branches," Than said.

"Young love." Helios tucked a strand of hair behind Hemera's ear. "Remember that?"

"We are not in love," Del said.

Helios waved her away. "Because of your curse. Yes, Keres told me all about it. I know."

The three of them sat down, and Than cleared his throat. "Forgive me for asking, but—what happened?" He looked at Hemera. "How did you get sick?"

"She has been sick for years," Helios said.

Keres nodded. "Ever since Eos disappeared."

Hemera patted one of Helios's perfectly tanned hands. "Talk about it," she said.

Than poured Del a cup of tea, and she took it. "Eos vanished when my mother went to live in the underworld." Her eyebrows furrowed at Hemera. "You've been sick ever since then?"

"Indeed." Helios squeezed Hemera's hand. "I apologize for speaking for her, but too much talking is difficult in Hemera's condition."

Hemera lifted his hand and kissed it, and with a sigh, he said, "Selene and I don't know how Eos left the palace. We were both in the stables. Selene was feeding her horses after arriving home, and I was saddling my own. Eos should have been inside with Hemera, but when Selene walked in to see her, Hemera had fallen asleep. Nyx had not seen Eos for hours, and we searched the palace to no avail. Eos was so young, we thought she could not have gone far. For the next few days, we scoured Mount Olympus. Then . . ." He swallowed, and Hemera rested her head on his shoulder. "On one of my trips across the Greek world, I saw her first mortal temple. She had just learned to fly. She must have flown off to the mortals on her own."

"I apologize," Del said. "You need not relive such an awful experience."

"No," Helios said. "Hemera thinks it might help to share the tale, and I do not wish what happened to Eos to befall anyone else." He took a gulp of tea and leaned back on the sofa. "Eos was there that day—at the temple. She was gazing at it, amazed by it, but she was fading before my eyes. She was almost transparent by the time I found her. I did what I could. I scooped her up and brought her back to the palace, but were it not for Demeter, she would have vanished. All that remains of her resides in these flowers."

He gestured at the heliotrope that crept through the windows. "Ever since then, Hemera has had to make up for the loss. Eos should be old enough to bring dawn to the world by now. If she were still here, she would leave the palace first, then Hemera would follow her. Instead, Hemera is forced to leave earlier. I was hoping to make her journeys faster by purchasing a pair of drakones at this year's Spring Equinox Festival. Demeter has always said they are the fastest flying creatures in the Greek world."

"She would be thrilled for you to buy a pair of them." Del smiled. "I flew some of them here. They're on the front steps. If you want, you can go see them."

"Thank you for the offer." Helios stood and stretched. "But I am afraid I must take Hemera to bed. She needs her rest, but I will come visit the farm soon enough. Something must change." He helped Hemera up from the sofa. "This cannot go on. It's too much for Hemera."

"It would be too much for anyone," Than said.

Helios led Hemera out of the room while her light flickered and dimmed. When the doors closed behind them, Than turned to Keres. "Has she really been like that for all these years?"

"That's what Helios says."

He sighed, laying his head on the back of the sofa. "Just another way Hades has ruined us. Turning our sister into a husk of who she once was."

"My father did not do that," Del said.

Than cinched his eyebrows. "What?"

"Why do you defend him?" Keres's eyes were sheened red in the sun. "Helios has seen you all your life on his trips in the sun chariot. He says you hate Hades as much as the rest of us. He saw you grow a flower to *poison* him before the Farewell Festival this year."

"I have always hated him," Del said. "And I did grow a flower to hurt him, but I don't think he is responsible for what happened to Hemera. If he was, my grandmother would have told me about it. She hates him more than anyone. But she—like Helios and Selene—has always told me that Eos went to the mortals by herself."

Than sat up. He set his cup on the table. "But you don't think so."

"No, I don't. She was too young—younger even than the triplets, and they would never be able to make it to the mortals on their own. It doesn't make sense for her to go alone. I think . . . Well, I don't think you want to know."

The Twins of Death were silent, and Del watched the purple clouds of heliotrope bob in the windows. Finally, Than said, "You think our mother did it."

Del opened her mouth, but Keres slammed her fist on the sofa arm. "She did not. She wouldn't. Not after knowing how it feels to be banished." She stared daggers at Than. "You have no idea what you have missed over the years. Sometimes Mother will be doing something totally normal, like washing a dish, and she breaks down in tears. She apologizes for falling in love with Erebos, because it led to her banishment. She sings just as well—if not better—as you can. Her favorite snacks are cucumbers in vinegar and honey-drizzled pears. She is a person. A person who has been wronged, but who continues to live. Do you honestly think she could kidnap a child and send her to the mortals, knowing Eos would lose her soul?"

"I think those who are wronged often wrong others in an attempt to right the wrongs done to them." Del turned to Than. "I have certainly done that."

"I cannot believe . . ." Keres blinked back tears, and Del's stomach flipped like the barley bread discs she used to make in Yaya's kitchen. She hated seeing the goddess upset. "Even if my mother did do it, how would we fix it? Regardless, Eos has vanished."

"Perhaps she hasn't," Del said. Eyes narrowed at the heliotrope, she explained how she had hoped to dissolve her parents' marriage vow with the flower essence. "Than said it would not work, but I wonder . . ." She gestured at Keres. "That jar you used when we were trying to bring him back from the space between realms. You said it helps mortal souls remember who they are. It called back both our souls—Than's just needed a little extra help."

Keres took out the jar. It fit in the palm of her hand, painted black with an orange cork. "I see what you're getting at, little flower girl."

Than grinned at Del. "What's your plan?"

Chapter Thirty

When Hemera told them that Nyx and Selene were approaching with the moon chariot, they followed the goddess of day onto the front steps, where they rejoined Helios and explained the plan. Helios was ecstatic in his agreement to help with it. He practically skipped to the stables on his way to harness the sun chariot.

When he returned, they all watched the silver speck of the moon chariot zip toward the palace, followed by a wall of darkness. The towering heliotrope plant wafted its warm, sugary fragrance. One of its leafy branches brushed against the sun chariot, and the horses bobbed their heads. The drakones flicked their tongues at the night air.

"Even if this works," Helios said, "I still might buy a pair of them. They look more impressive than the horses. What do you think, Hemera?"

Hemera reached toward one of the drakones, and it nuzzled her palm. "I like them."

Del examined the heliotrope plant, fingers running over her olive-branch bracelet. Than had his hand on her back, his wings wrapped around both of them. "You might like them less when you have to feed them live doves and serpents—but once you tell them something, they never forget it. This is the same pair Yaya flew here."

"How fitting," Helios said.

They shielded their faces when the silver gleam of the moon chariot swamped the front steps. "Ready?" Del asked, and the rest of them called back the word in assent. She stepped forward, and three things happened in rapid succession.

One, Del spiraled her wrists.

Two, Keres emptied the jar of Mnemosyne water onto the heliotrope plant.

Three, the heliotrope plant collapsed atop Helios, cocooning him in a purple blanket.

"Eos!" he called out while Than knelt in front of him and sang his song. "Eos, come back, darling girl. It has been too long."

Time seemed to stop when Selene stepped out of the moon chariot. Cheeks wet with tears, the moon goddess lifted a hand to her mouth. Silver light undulated across the face of the mountain while Than sang his song. Hands held in front of her, Del gritted her teeth, willing the soul caught within the heliotrope to bloom out of it. She could feel it growing stronger each time Helios called the name of his sister. The heliotrope was wrapped around it like a weed in a garden. Unraveling them drained her energy, but she refused to give up.

"Hemera, now!" Keres said when Nyx swept onto the front steps. Her Cloak of Darkness spangled the night sky behind her, and with Helios blanketed in the heliotrope, nothing alleviated the shadows. An eclipse spread across the Greek world, no doubt terrifying the mortals, but if this plan worked, it would not last long.

Nyx turned her gaze to Hemera, who ran across the front steps. She flung herself at her mother, and Nyx let out a shocked, breathless laugh. When the two goddesses embraced, golden light shimmered between them. The rays were pink and orange and red, cutting through the silver light from the moon chariot.

Sweat poured down Del's face, but the heliotrope plant shrank while Than's song came to an end. The radiant light grew brighter and brighter, forming an orb between the two women. It pushed them away from each other, and they panicked. They clawed at each other's wrists, but then the ball of dawn-colored light lengthened. It stretched into the gauzy image of a young woman with a Cloth of Gold mantle draping her shoulders. She collapsed onto the front steps, breathing heavily between Hemera and Nyx. Her pale face was sheened with sweat, darkening her waist-length curls of red hair.

"Eos!" Selene and Helios wrapped their arms around their little sister. The heliotrope plant had vanished, and spots danced in front of Del's vision. She swayed on her feet, and Than and Keres grabbed her arms before she could collapse.

"You did it." Than grinned.

Del exchanged a tired smile with both of them. "We did it together."

"How . . . ?" Selene wiped her eyes, turning toward them. She looked back at her little sister. "How did this happen?"

"I was trapped," Eos said. Her voice was like a bird singing for the rising sun, and her face was delicate and round. She had eyes so light blue they bordered on white, and her red-feathered wings fanned across the front steps. "I was lost in all these wheels, which were filled with endless versions of myself." Her gaze pinned Nyx, who held Hemera to her chest. "You tricked me into going to the mortals too young."

Selene gasped. "Nyx told us you flew to them on your own."

Eos shook her head. "No."

"Mother." Keres was aghast. She let go of Del, and Than took her in both his arms. "Del said you had done it, but I never thought—I didn't believe you could be so cruel. How could you do that to a child?"

Nyx closed her eyes and swallowed. "When I first came here, I spent lots of time with Eos. I taught her how to fly, and I realized if she went to the mortals, it might give me a few moments with Hemera. I thought if Eos could bring dawn to the world just once, I could end my banishment. I could free Erebos." She shook her head. "I told her going to the mortals would be a fun challenge, but she must fly back to me as fast as she could. When she didn't return, Hemera still had to leave the palace before I could see her. I solved nothing. I made everything worse." She turned to Del. "Thank you for bringing her back to her brother and sister."

"We took you in!" Selene's voice echoed off the mountain. "We let you live with us when you had nowhere else to go. And this is how you repay us—by trapping our innocent sister in the space between realms."

"And lying about it," said Helios. "We thought you were mourning her along with us." He turned to Hemera, his face shattered. "Did you know?"

Hemera shook her head. She ran toward him, clinging to his hands. Her color was already coming back to her, making it difficult to see where he ended and she began.

"Hemera had no idea," Nyx said. "Please, do not blame her for my actions."

"Why would you do this?" Keres's form was shimmering, threatening to split into multiple aspects. She gave a mirthless laugh. "Here I thought you were a victim in all this. But all along, you have been as awful as Hades is."

"I'm so sorry," Nyx beseeched Eos. "I don't expect forgiveness. Now that my banishment has ended, I need no longer live here. You will never have to see me again."

"But I will," Eos said. "Each day, I will see you in night's fingertips that try to reach out and take me, but from now on I will be too fast to catch." She surveyed the world beyond Mount Olympus. It was still twilit, though the sun should already be streaming over the cliffs. "The world needs to feel the dawn, and I am old enough for mortal worship now."

She stood on shaky legs, but Selene wrapped her in her arms. "Surely you can take the day to rest." She looked at her brother. "Hemera has been managing on her own for so long."

Hemera's eyes widened. She clutched Helios, who said, "I will not force Hemera into doing that ever again."

"It's all right, sister." Eos gently extricated herself from Selene and walked to the edge of the front steps. "Hemera did nothing wrong. She need not suffer, and I want to see the world again." She breathed in the clean night air, smiling down at the flickering lights of the mortal cities that speckled the land.

She turned back to Del while her wings unfurled. "Thank you for bringing me home. If you ever need to know anything that happens, anywhere during the dawn, you need only ask, and I will tell you all I know."

Del dipped her head, and Eos spread her arms. She flapped her wings once, twice, then like a songbird, she fluttered off the front steps, spreading tendrils of soft light into the darkness with each wing flap.

Chapter Thirty-One

Selene stabbed a finger at Nyx. "You. Leave my palace. I never want to speak to you again."

She stormed toward the stables with her moon chariot, and Hemera turned to Helios, eyes wide with terror. He scrubbed a hand down his face. "I will talk to her." He glared at Nyx. "Not for your sake. For Hemera's. I will not have her separated from her mother again."

Hemera planted a kiss on his lips. He returned the kiss, hands on her waist. "Okay, okay." He smiled and pulled away. "I need to speak with Selene before we follow Eos into the day." He addressed Del. "Thank you for saving Eos. What she said about the dawn applies to me and Selene as well. Ask us anything, and we will tell you all we know."

With that, he snapped the reins of the sun chariot and followed Selene to the stables. Left alone with Than's family, Del felt distinctly uncomfortable. She took the reins of the drakones and looked up at him. "We need to go back to the farm. Yaya has some of my dried dates, which will help me regain my energy. And"—she blew out a breath—"I think I need to confront her to complete the second task."

"I think you're right about that."

Than helped her into the chariot, but before they could take off, Nyx said, "I know you remain none too pleased with this alliance. And now that you have seen what kind of person I am, I completely understand. But now, more than ever, I would be honored to count you as a family member. I wish you all the best in saving your little sister, and I hope you will join my son in marriage."

"I appreciate the well-wishes," Del said, "but you trapped a young girl in the space between realms. You have been giving me nightmares ever since I took Than from the underworld. You say you want me to be queen, but my father has no intention of stepping down. And beyond that, I don't understand why you want this alliance at all. In the past few days, I have wearied of lies. Be honest with me about what you want."

Nyx pursed her lips. "What I did to Eos was terrible. I regret it with all my heart. But Hades is different. He has ruined entire families multiple times over. He makes mistakes and does not learn from them. He is a wicked man."

"I . . ." Del struggled to find the right words. A few days ago, she would have agreed with Nyx. Part of her still did. But it was more complicated than that. It was true that she had wearied of lies in the past few days, but new truths were piling up too fast. She plucked these truths from her memories like she might pick fruit from a tree, and she found they were too heavy to carry. She buckled under their weight, and Than caught her, holding her against him so she felt his angry words rumble through his chest.

"Del needs time to think things over," he said. "She just expended far too much magic to right the wrong you did, and we have to complete the other tasks the Fates set. Everything else comes second."

"Thank you." Del stood and handed the reins to him. "You said you like to be in control when you're in the air. Well, I'm too tired to fly the chariot." His eyes widened, and she gave him a reassuring smile, placing a hand on his bicep. "You will be fine. The drakones know how to find their way home. Just hold tight to the reins and don't pull too hard."

Nyx scrutinized Than. "You know where to find me," she said.

Chapter Thirty-Two

Yaya leaped up from the table when they entered the farmhouse.

"Seedling!" She rushed to Del, whom Than carried under both arms. "What happened?" She glared at Than. "What did you do to her?"

"He didn't do anything," Del said. Around them, the triplets stood from where they had been drawing at the table. It was covered in pieces of papyrus and charcoal. "I used too much magic all at once. Do you have any of my dried dates left?"

Yaya rushed to one of the jars on the counter. She pulled out some dates and handed them to Del, who chewed and swallowed. Than sat her down at the table. She rubbed her eyes, feeling the ache leave her muscles.

"You must stop overextending yourself." This came from Persephone, who sat beside Cate at the table. "You know better than this, Asphodel."

"Were you able to figure out what to do?" The hope in Mak's eyes made Del want to crumble, but Than steadied her with a hand on her shoulder.

"We did," she said, and Persephone broke into a smile. She rose from the table and wrapped Del in a hug. Yaya must have filled her in while they were gone.

"The Fates gave us three riddles." Del pulled away from her mother. "We already solved one of them."

"We broke my mother's banishment," said Than.

Persephone beamed, hands clasped beneath her chin. "Oh, Than, that is wonderful." When he said nothing, her smile faded. "I'm so sorry Hades and I did not tell you the truth sooner. We wanted you to have a good childhood—"

"I understand why you did it," Than said. "That does not mean I forgive you for it."

His tone kept Persephone from reaching out to him. She sat back in her chair while Del said, "The second riddle says I must heal the rift between the four seasons of the world. I believe that refers to us." She turned to Than. "I know you won't want to do this, but the fastest way to get my father here is by using the mind-to-mind conduit the two of you share. I need him to bring water from the river Styx and his Cornucopia of Death."

Than flexed his jaw, but he didn't argue with her. "Can I use the sitting room?" he asked Yaya. "Silence helps ease the communication."

Yaya waved her hand. While he was gone, Del reiterated what had happened in Helios and Selene's palace. The triplets gasped and clapped at all the right moments, but when they reached the part about Eos, Mak sobered.

"If you can't stop Zeus from sending me to the mortals, could you put part of me in a flower? What about aconite? I love how Cerberus grows it when he slobbers. It makes me laugh. You can put me in that."

Persephone made a small sound of despair. Del's heart shattered, but she leaned down to her little sister. "We will not be putting you in a flower. Anytime you see aconite, it means you are safe and loved. It means everyone will be staying right where they should." She hugged Mak, and Than came back into the kitchen.

"Hades is coming here using his path under the white willow." His voice was stiff. "When I told him about Mak, he was very distressed. He said we should go meet him there."

Yaya opened her mouth, but Del said, "I know you hate him, Yaya, but we need to solve this riddle as soon as possible." She pointed at the Cornucopia of Life, which hung in its usual place beside the window. "Bring the Cornucopia."

After a moment of hesitation, Yaya took the wicker horn. "I hope you know what you are doing, seedling," she said while everyone walked into the courtyard. Than was bombarded by the triplets, who tugged at his robe.

"Than, will you fly us to the meadow?" Mak asked.

Than glanced at Del. "I don't think I should leave Del—"

"It's okay," Del said. The triplets cheered. "You can fly them. It's not far, and I think they deserve some fun with everything going on right now."

"Are you sure?" Than asked, but the triplets were already climbing into his arms. Zag clung to his neck, legs wrapped around his middle, and he situated Mel and Mak in either arm. They clung to him like he was one of the poplars in the underworld. Del waved off his concern with a smile, and he pumped his wings, the gust of wind flattening the grass in the courtyard. He soared into the sky with a trailing whoop from Zag, leaving Del to follow the rest of her family into the meadow.

When she slipped into the forest shadows, she took a deep breath, taking comfort in the familiar melody of birdcalls and the green scent of foliage. On either side of the overgrown path scampered small animals. Everything had changed so swiftly in the few days since she had brought Than to the Isle, and her life would never go back to how it had been before. In the face of such change, it was nice to know the forest would remain the same.

Steadied, she pushed aside a tree branch and emerged into the meadow. Her mother, Cate, and Yaya already stood near the white willow. They were looking up, pointing and shielding their foreheads while

Than circled, his shadow growing larger and larger until he touched down. The triplets tumbled into the narcissus that filled the meadow, laughing and squealing about how amazing it was to fly with him again.

They splashed into the lake shallows, filling the air with giddy shouts, and Del felt herself being pulled back into the memories of her time here as a little girl. Life had been so simple. She had only wanted the sun and her mother and Yaya.

Now she had to convince them that they loved each other with their whole hearts.

The ground began to rumble, and Than drew her close. Everyone stumbled back from the white willow. The tree shook, and the ground around it crumbled. The tree became an island in a sea of darkness from which Hades emerged. His cloak glittered with onyx, and he held the Cornucopia of Death under one arm and a small jar in his hand. He lifted his scepter, and Coronis landed atop it, becoming stone again.

"What is this about Zeus taking Mak to the mortals?" He swept toward them while the ground resealed. Mak ran to meet him, and he picked her up. She nuzzled into his shoulder, and Persephone went to stand at his side with Mel and Zag.

"I know how to save her," Del said. "That's why I asked you and Yaya to bring the Cornucopias." She addressed Persephone. "Mother, when Hades first stole you—" At the cloud that passed over Persephone's face, she let out a breath and reworded. "When you first went to the underworld, why did you only eat half the pomegranate Hades offered? If you wanted to make sure you could stay there, why not eat all of it?"

Her tone was not accusatory, but Hades scowled. His eyes darkened, and he gripped his wife tightly. "Talking about this time is difficult for Persephone—"

"No." Persephone squeezed his hand before lowering it from her arm. "Hades, it's okay." She sighed, fingertips drumming her sternum. "Half the pomegranate was all I could stomach. It was enough to make the underworld hospitable, but the living world still holds my soul. When I tried to eat more of it, I could not keep it down. Remember,

Hades?" A spark of mirth returned to her face. "I was sick in bed for days."

"You were?" Yaya reached for her daughter. "You never told me about that."

Persephone closed her eyes briefly. "He cared for me, Mother. He fed me, bathed me, read me all my favorite stories." She smiled up at Hades. "To tell the truth, it was a bit annoying."

Hades wrapped his arm around her shoulders so she nearly vanished beneath his cloak. He tipped her chin toward his face. "Oh, you enjoyed the pampering."

"Well, I have a theory." Del's hands shook as she turned to Yaya. "The reason my mother remains trapped in the underworld for half of each year is not her marriage vow. It is because you do not want her back on the farm with your whole heart. You only want the parts of her that existed before she went to live in the underworld."

She pointed at Yaya's Cornucopia. "When she ate from the Cornucopia of Life all those years ago, the rest of her soul remained trapped in the pomegranate from the underworld. The only way she can move freely between realms is if she eats all of both pomegranates, making her soul whole. And she can't do that until you stop believing the only way she can have her family and true love is to lose part of herself."

"That is not true." The words burst from Yaya like juice from an overripe fruit. She stalked toward Hades, stabbing a finger at his Cornucopia of Death. "She is trapped in the underworld because he poisoned her mind and soul with his marriage vow."

Persephone grabbed her mother's wrist. "Hades did not—"

"Look at her!" Yaya freed her hand and splayed it as though it was evidence. The triplets ran from their parents. They tucked themselves against Del and Than, and Yaya barked a laugh. "Look how your mother defends the man who stole her, how she clings to him even as her children cower in fear."

"They are afraid of *you*," Persephone hissed, "of you and your arguing, not him."

"My daughter." As soon as the rage had burst from Yaya, it fled. She wrapped her arms around her middle, beseeching her daughter. "I am so sorry for failing you that day. You know I will never forgive myself for letting you wander off into this meadow alone." Her voice thinned to a barely audible whisper. "It is all my fault."

"How many times do I have to tell you," Persephone lashed out, "that Hades did not kidnap me from this meadow. I ran away of my own free will. All our prim little meetings in the sitting room, with Hades on the sofa and the two of us in those chairs." She waved a hand in the direction of the farmhouse, and the narcissus tilted as though in a strong wind. "All our strolls in the courtyard with you watching us from the windows. Finally I had enough." She made a slicing motion with her finger, and the narcissus around her crumbled. "Hades didn't even want to take me to the underworld. I had to convince him to do so. Whatever story you have fed the mortals, you know I wasn't stolen. I *sneaked out*."

Del held up a hand when Yaya opened her mouth. "It pains me to say this, Yaya. It pains me more than you know, but the fact is you like to keep things for yourself. You can't have my mother all to yourself anymore, so you don't want her at all. You want me instead." She locked eyes with her grandmother. "Which is why you have kept me from revealing myself to the mortals—and why you convinced Cate to curse me when I was born."

Yaya blinked rapidly. "Seedling." She stepped toward Del, but Than flared his wings, and she stopped. Wheat and barley fell from her hair, and she rubbed her chin. "I did curse you," she said at last. She pointed at Hades. "But I was trying to protect you from that man. Whatever your mother has tried to tell you, you must not be swayed by him."

"I am not being swayed by anyone. Not by Hades, not by my mother, and—for the first time in my life—not by you. I am not yours anymore. I am living for myself."

For a long moment, silence reigned. The sun shone down and the narcissus swayed. Yaya looked like she might break down in tears.

Then Hades took Persephone's hand, and Yaya's eyes flitted down to the movement. A crane bugled, spraying water from the lake while her face twisted into a snarl.

"Is it so awful," she said to Persephone, "that I wanted to protect your daughter as I protected you until you would not let me anymore?"

"So you admit I wouldn't let you," Persephone said. "You admit it was my choice to leave. You admit I am not bewitched and never have been. You admit, here and now, that you cursed my daughter for selfish reasons."

"It was not selfish. It was an act of protection."

"And hiding her away from the mortals, was that protection as well?"

"It was to protect her from the temptation all of us gods feel! When you were growing up, you never cared for the opinions of others. You were happy with your small life on the farm. Then you met him"—she gestured at Hades—"and suddenly you wanted a throne. You wanted to be married to a man the mortals feared—who they worshipped. You wanted to be known and loved. It is poison to live for someone else. It is a drug."

"I am my own person." Persephone dropped her husband's hand and spiraled her wrists. Needlelike juniper trees stabbed the air, her voice as cold as their crisp pine scent. The triplets shrieked and hid behind Than's wings as she said, "I have *changed*."

"Yaya." Del stepped toward her grandmother, who was surrounded by the small trees. "I know you cursed me out of love." She entered the circle of junipers and stopped beside Yaya. Her mother was next to her, her eyes the frosted brown of winter soil. "But how is what you did to me any different from what you told me Hades did to Maytare? You decided where I should live. You took me from what would have been my home. You kept me locked on your farm, never letting me learn the world for myself. I always trusted you," she said with tears in her eyes, "and it hurts that I was wrong. I wish I could hate you. I wish I could scream and curse you and never want to see you again, but that is not what I want. I still love you, despite how you have made me hurt."

She turned to Than, who sheltered the triplets. "When someone raises you, even when you discover how many mistakes they made once you have grown up, you are still grateful for the safety they gave you when you were small. For better or worse, they make you who you are. To despise them is to despise part of yourself. You have to forgive in order to move on." She looked back at Yaya. "I forgive you for your lies, but my relationship with you will look different from now on."

"Not you too, seedling." Yaya croaked out a laugh. "Is it you?" She shot her gaze to Than and stepped out of the juniper circle, heedless of the triplets' frightened squeals. "Did you poison her mind the way Hades poisoned my daughter's? Will you deathmongers ever leave my family alone?"

She was halfway to Than before Del shot out a vine that pulled her back into the juniper circle. Yaya looked aghast, but Del kept her voice calm. "No, they won't. Because we are their life-giving counterparts. It's like Zeus told you all those years ago. Maytare and Hades's love brings balance to the world." She intertwined her grandmother's fingers with her own. "I understand why you hate change, Yaya. I do as well. But growing up is only natural, and if we never changed how we saw the world, eternity would be rather dull."

With a small smile, she squeezed Yaya's hand and let go. Songbirds trilled in the canopy, and the sun danced across the lake. Yaya and Persephone watched one another from within the circle of juniper trees. Yaya flicked her eyes from Del to Hades, then back to Persephone. "You left me all alone," she whispered brokenly.

"You pushed me away," Persephone said, tears trickling down her face.

"For three centuries . . ." Yaya's voice trailed into the air that rippled her robe, and Del imagined her words traveling back through time. Back to the day Yaya had run to this meadow to find Persephone gone. Back to her mad dash up Mount Olympus to find out what went wrong. Back to her trek through the underworld, begging Cate to stay with her daughter until she found a way to bring her home. Back to the day Persephone ate from the Cornucopia of Life and, months later, gave birth to Del.

Yaya's first tear hit the ground, and from it grew a fat, vibrant poppy, its red petals stark against the sea of yellow narcissus. "I'm sorry," she said as it opened, its delicate face turned toward the sun.

Persephone made a slicing motion, disintegrating the juniper trees that grew around them, then she crushed her mother in a hug. "It's okay," she said, burrowing her face in the crook of Yaya's neck. Both women shook with sobs. Yaya held out her hand, and when Del took it, she pulled Del into the hug. More poppies grew around them, forming a red circle that extended in a spiral. Red for change. Red like the threads of Del's curse that had brought them here today.

Red like the pomegranates her mother needed to eat.

"Mother." Del pulled away, wiping the tears that had begun falling down her cheeks. She waved at Hades, who joined them in the circle of poppies and reached into his Cornucopia of Death. Persephone let go of Yaya as he pulled out half a pomegranate. In the sun, its red seeds glittered like rubies. When Del turned to Yaya, her grandmother stuffed her hand into the Cornucopia of Life and took out another pomegranate half.

"I need the jar of Styx water," Del told Hades. He handed it to her, and she waved Than forward. "I think this will be similar to the vow renewals at the Farewell Festivals, only stronger." She lifted her hands. "And I will help—like I did with Eos."

With a nod, Than uncorked the jar. Hades and Yaya held out the pomegranate halves, and he poured the black water onto them. They flared with red light, and Persephone took both of them with trembling hands. When he started to sing, Del held her hands over the pomegranates and willed her mother's soul forward. "Try eating them," she said.

First, Persephone swallowed the seeds from the Cornucopia of Death. The light of its seeds grew brighter, and a cool stream of air blew through the meadow. She scooped out a handful of seeds from the Cornucopia of Life's pomegranate, and as she chewed and swallowed, the sun shining down on the meadow grew hotter. When Than's song came to an end, Del dropped her hands, and Persephone took to the pomegranates like a woman starved.

She ate them by savage handfuls, juice dribbling down her chin. With each bite from the Cornucopia of Death, colder winds blew in from the forest, swirling with the hot air that seeped down from the sun each time she took a bite from the other pomegranate. By the time she had finished both halves, impossible snow dusted the meadow. The poppies and narcissus looked like crystals, and snowflakes glinted in the air, dancing on the streams of wind.

In this four-season world, Persephone took both Yaya's hands in hers. With her pink-tipped nose and eyes like freshly tilled soil, she looked like the version of herself Yaya had always spoken of when Del was a little girl. Happy. Full. In love with and loved by the world. Smiling wide, she squeezed her mother's hands. "I love you, Maytare."

"I love you," Yaya said. In the streams of hot and cold air, her hair had fallen from its usual chignon. It fluttered around her shoulders, her features softened by the dark, curly mass. "You might have changed, but you are still my daughter."

"I always will be," Persephone said. She pulled Hades toward them, and Yaya stiffened, but then she pulled both of them into a hug. The three of them stood in the center of the red and yellow spiral, beams of sunlight causing rainbows to leap out of the snow. The triplets dashed through the meadow, shrieking with laughter when they slid across the frozen lake. The rest of Del's family followed them, but Del and Than stayed where they were, listening to the ice-covered branches clink against one another.

"That was beautiful." Than kissed the top of her head. "I'm proud of you," he said, but Del leaned away from him. As she looked out at her family, all she could think about was how different things would be if she couldn't solve the third riddle. She had hoped to figure out the answer during the process of completing the first two tasks, but now she still didn't know where to start, and there were less than two days to save Mak.

"What's wrong?" Than took her shoulder. "Are you feeling tired again? I should have brought the dates with us. I can fly you back to the farmhouse to get them."

"No, I'm not tired," Del said, but her breaths were coming faster, and asphodel had begun to creep through the poppies and narcissus. "I just don't know what to do next."

"We'll figure it out. You've done so well."

"Not well enough."

Than rubbed the place between her thumb and forefinger. "Hey, focus on being here."

"I can't." She could barely get the words out. "I can't rest until—"

"Del!" the triplets called. "Come skate on the lake with us. Bring Than!"

Del shut her eyes tightly, and Than pulled her against him. "Do you want to go back to the Isle?" She nodded, and he picked her up.

"We have to solve the third riddle," he called back to the triplets. He gave a powerful wing flap, and Del's family waved to them. He flew her through the icy leaves, and Del tucked her face into his shoulder, hiding her tears.

The last thing she heard was the triplets yell, "We believe in you, Del!"

Chapter Thirty-Three

By the time Than touched down on the Isle, Del could not catch her breath. Her legs were still wrapped around him while he sank onto the beach, cradling her in his lap. "Hey, hey." He lifted her chin. She felt the gritty sand grains on his hand. Behind her, the waves crashed. The wind kicked up sand, and golden light speared across the Aegean. As asphodel bloomed around them, Than smoothed back her hair. "We're going to save Mak. I promise."

Del stared at him. The crease between his eyebrows. The way his eyebrow hairs feathered out at the ends. The dark circles bordering his nose with a slight crook in it. She tried to breathe evenly. She could not solve the last riddle unless she calmed down. But even if she did solve the riddle, she still had to complete the last task. And even if she did complete the last task, she still had to fall in love with Than. And even if she did fall in love with Than, she still had to live in the underworld with him. There was no good end to any of this. All her attempts to maintain freedom had been useless.

"I wish I had just married you when I had the chance." She realized with removed mortification that she was dripping tears all over his lap. The beach around them had become a field of star-shaped white flowers bobbing on woody stems. "I might not have loved you, and I might have hated the underworld, but at least I could have avoided all this. Mak would not be in danger. The gods would not be succumbing to madness."

"But my mother would still be banished," Than said. "Your mother would still be trapped in the underworld for half of each year. Eos would still be lost in the space between realms, and I would still follow Hades anywhere." He rubbed her back, and she sniffed. She pressed the heels of her hands to her eyes, hoping to staunch her tears, but this only resulted in more intense puffs of air. It felt like her lungs were trying to escape from her chest.

"It's too much," she said.

"It's the truth." Than's voice was so earnest, Del blubbered another puff of air. She tasted salt, seeing spots of color behind her eyelids when she added pressure to the heels of her hands. He gripped her wrists, gently moving her off his lap. "Come here," he said, and wiped her tears with his gritty hands.

"You've gotten sand on my cheeks," she said, but she could breathe again.

He laughed. "Well, we can't have that." He leaned down and kissed the grains of sand from her skin. The kisses were soft as the flutter of butterfly wings, sweet as the scent of the asphodel flowers carrying on the sea air.

She disintegrated the flowers, and he pulled her up by both hands. She made a face, gesturing at the tear blotches on his chest. "Thank you for . . . that."

"Always, mistress," he said, and they started through the freshly tilled land. Seabirds cawed overhead. Everything was exactly as they had left it. Empty. Quiet. But never before had Del been so aware of the Isle's smallness. It was just the beach, a short stretch of land, and the cottage. Just small enough, Del thought, to be maintained by one person.

They stepped through the remains of the crocus lawn, and Than led her to what had been the woodland. Deer and rabbits and other small animals bounded after them. "I remember you saying gardening helps you when you're upset. I thought, perhaps, we could grow something together. I could sing while you work your magic."

Del looked up at him. "I would love that." She squeezed his hand and closed her eyes, and when he began to sing, she imagined vast roots extending beneath them. The ground shook, and his voice faltered while he pulled her to his chest, but she opened her eyes with a bright laugh. She wrenched up her hands, and a trio of elms shot out of the ground. Their canopies bloomed like flowers, rustling far above their heads. In the dappled light and shadow, deer pranced. The few swallows that had remained on the Isle alighted on the branches.

His song sent green light shining across the Isle, emanating from Del. The words, which were all about regrowing what had been cut down, gave her the strength to work her magic faster than usual. Lifting her hands again, she spiraled her wrists and flung her arms forward, creating a pathway lined with pink-blooming lotus trees where her orchard had been.

While the last notes of his song drifted across the Isle, she led Than down the path, surrounded by the fading green light and the lotus flowers' sweet scent. Blooms caught in the breeze and drifted into their hair. She plucked one of them and popped it into her mouth. It melted on her tongue, and she swallowed. She handed a bloom to Than, and he held it up, examining its magenta veins in the sun. "Aren't these addictive?"

Del plucked one of the petals from the lotus and slipped it into his mouth. "They are addictive for mortals. For gods, they merely promote relaxation. I have met a few nymphs who grow overly fond of how carefree the lotus petals make them, but I think right now we could both use some of that." She fed him another lotus petal, and he kissed her hand. Then he pulled her toward him and kissed her on the lips.

It was different from their previous kisses. Those had been hard and fast, as though they were stealing time they did not have. This was soft and slow, as though they had all the time in the world. When they paused for breath, he gave her a sleepy smile that made her heart swell. She wanted to wake up with him looking at her like that.

She had never wanted to wake up next to anyone before this.

"Come with me," she said, and held out her hand. She led him to the cottage, sending a sea of pink rosebushes lining the path. The flowers bloomed all around them, but when they entered the cottage, it had the air of a building abandoned. Dimly lit. The wilted remains of the bindweed cage draped across the kitchen. The windows were open, and a swallow hopped around the empty washbasin. The goods Del had planned to take to the Spring Equinox Festival had been pecked open and scattered throughout the kitchen.

Del shooed the bird, running at it. Than laughed, but when her foot caught on one of the cage vines, he caught her before she could trip. While the bird flew out the window in a flash of black and white and red, he flipped her toward him. They kissed, harder this time, more passionate. Del took him by the front of the black robe she had given him.

Between kisses, she led him up the stairs. She pushed aside the vine curtain and flopped onto her bed. Than lay beside her, wings splayed across the wall as he held her to his chest. He kissed her neck, and she whimpered. He sucked it, and she moaned. He made a small sound of his own, then he wrapped his arm around her waist and pulled her close. "Send life into death to save what is already lost," he said, voice thick with want. "It *could* mean . . ."

"No." With a sigh, she moved away from him. "It isn't as simple as us being together like this. If my curse had been broken, I would have felt it. We still have to figure out the last task." She looked out at the waves that crashed against the Isle. The sun had reached the horizon, its red light painting the ocean in gold. "We have so little time left."

"Hey." He pulled her back toward him. "Everything will be fine, I promise."

Del huffed. "I'm glad everyone else seems confident."

"I have no doubts in you."

"How could you not? Since I met you, we have discovered everything I ever believed was wrong. I thought my grandmother always told the truth. I thought my mother was bewitched. I thought my father stole her away to the underworld."

"I was wrong about many things as well. I thought my mother abandoned me. I thought Hades could do no wrong. Now we both know your mother might love him, but Demeter was right about him being terrible."

"Even so." Del shook her head. "I don't think he is as awful as I always imagined. If I can be wrong about all of that, how can you believe I will be able to complete these tasks? I mean, you barely know me, Than."

"I know you are the most determined person I've ever met." He kissed one side of her face, then the other. "If you want to achieve something, you will achieve it." He kissed her forehead. "If I could go back to the night I vowed never to marry you until we fell in love, I would do the same thing all over again. The one thing I do regret is that our marriage is a sacrifice you are making to save Mak. I admire that, and I, too, want to save her above all else, but—if you were going to marry me, I wanted you to do it of your own accord."

"Even if we do break my curse, I will still have to fall in love."

He met her eyes. "Do you think you could?"

"I don't like to think that you could change my mind in so little time, but . . ."

His lips curled into a smile. "But?"

"I feel open to the possibility of love. This betrothal has destroyed my old life in every way possible, but maybe that life was meant to end. I was rootless. Perhaps you will be the first person to tie me down."

"I would never," said Than. "I want to see you rise higher than ever before."

Del felt a flower bloom in her stomach, but at the same time, she wondered if he was only saying all this because of the lotus. "You must stop being kind," she said.

That surprised him. "I must . . . What? Would you rather I was cruel?" He leaned back, loosening his grip on her hand.

"No, but—" Del sighed. "*Yes.* I do wish you were cruel. I wish you would prove to me that this—whatever this is between us—isn't real. That something can't be this good. That someone can't be as strong and as soft as you are. Because the longer you go on acting good, the more I believe you actually are. And when I find out you aren't, the greater the loss will feel." She squeezed her eyes shut. Her voice shook. "I'm strong. I've always gotten along very well on my own. But now I am afraid. I am so *afraid* that this, getting so close to someone else only to have them slip through my fingers, is what will finally break me."

There. She had said it. A truth she had not even known grew inside her until it had bloomed from her lips. She wasn't just scared that she would not have enough time to complete the last task. She wasn't just overwhelmed that her father was such a complicated man. She wasn't just panicked that her life was changing forever at last. She was terrified that, after all the fuss she had made over her marriage, once her curse was broken, she might actually find herself falling in love with the god of peaceful death.

Her words hung in the air between them. Then the light shifted beyond her eyelids, and Than cradled her against his chest. She lay there, listening to his heartbeat while he kissed the top of her head. "I'm sorry, Del," he murmured into her hair. "I'm sorry your life has given you that fear. And you're right. It is safer to be alone. There is cruelness in the world, but there is kindness too. There is gentleness, and sweetness, and great sadness when someone you love forgets how much they deserve."

He lifted her chin, his face taking up her whole field of vision. In the golden light shining upon them, his pupils were tiny black cores in the centers of his blue irises. "I can be firm with you," he told her. "I can be angry, and at times I will say and do things I will regret later. If you wish, today I can be rough with you. I can make you feel powerful until you are ready to let vulnerability in. That would be my privilege."

He leaned forward, resting his forehead against hers. Their mouths were so close, she felt his lips form the words, "But I will not permit you to forget your worth."

Del lay there against him, feeling his breath mix with hers, weighing the truth of his words. She thought back to their days together. His acquiescence to his capture. His lack of anger. His vow not to marry her until they loved one another. He had always been swift to protect her, support her, defend her. Maybe, she thought as his nose brushed back and forth against hers, she would enjoy loving him. Maybe life could be good in the underworld.

"If I marry you," she said, pulling slightly away to look up at him, "and I live in the underworld, perhaps we could do what my mother suggested. Maybe we could improve the Fields of Asphodel together."

"You would want to do that?" His face broke into a grin.

"Seeing what Keres did with the water from the Lake of Mnemosyne gave me an idea. The mortal souls who enter the Fields of Asphodel drink from the river Lethe beforehand. Isn't that what you said?"

He nodded. "They forget who they were before death."

"Well, what if we convinced my father to let all of them drink from the Lake of Mnemosyne from now on? They could remember who they are, and I could regrow the Fields. We could show them that living a small life is beautiful."

"That would be the perfect tale for you to take to the mortals. They will love you for it, and you could finally reveal yourself to them."

"I will have to reveal myself to them. Zeus said telling the mortals our story is the only way to bring the world back into balance." She shifted on the bed. "I always told myself I would never become my mother." She scoffed down at her hands. "Now I am to be the goddess of flowers, who went to the underworld to marry the god of death."

After a moment, Than took her hand. "You need not tell it in that manner. When the mortals learn that their loved ones are spending eternity in a place so beautiful, they will be grateful. They will go back to worshipping us. You need not mention me at all. The mortals won't notice. I barely feature in the stories they write about the gods."

"But you are the god of death. Mortals know you better than any of us. They are obsessed with what happens when they die."

Than tilted his head, his face scrunched. "Mortals write around death. They write about what happens before and what comes after, but rarely—if ever—do they write about the moment itself. They strive not to think about it, because it strikes terror in their hearts. They want to understand it, but they cannot. They call death the end, then they say every end is where a new story begins. This is a comforting notion, perhaps, but it is not death."

Del watched him. She thought about how he had spent his life feeling unwanted. Trying to prove he deserved his place in her father's palace. He seemed to believe he was the enemy of all mortals. Even to her, it seemed like a lonely existence.

"What is death, then?" she asked.

He smiled down at her. "Death is the released breath after a good story ends. It is the feeling of completeness when one places a book back on the shelf, and it is the anticipation of cracking open the next book."

In the golden evening, everything looked soft and shimmering. Del leaned forward and kissed him. He lifted her onto his lap and took her face in both hands, but his kiss was slow, sweet, with reverence.

"No," Del said. She sprang away from him.

He reached halfway toward her before curling his hands into fists and dropping them into his lap. "It's not good?"

"No." His wounded expression sent panic snarling through her chest, and she shook her head. "I mean, yes. It is. It's very good." She let out a hopeless laugh. "It's just— I don't feel . . ." She searched the room, trying to find the right words. Her eyes caught on the flowers that dangled from the ceiling. The curtain of vines. The rumpled bed. She pressed her face to her hands. "I guess you're right. I like control, and I don't feel in control when it's like this."

Than remained silent for so long that, inexplicably, she worried he might be angry at her reaction. But when she met his eyes through her fingers, she found him watching her with a tender expression. She lowered her hands and gestured between them. "That's what this has all been about it, isn't it? It's all about power, and I can't stand not to have it."

Than did not try to reach for her. He kept his hands in his lap. "Maybe sex is about power," he said, his voice as soft as his lips, "but lovemaking isn't. Lovemaking is about vulnerability and trust."

Del's eyes searched his. "Lovemaking?"

Than took her face in his hands. "Yes."

He brushed his thumbs on her cheeks, and after a moment, Del nodded. With a smile, he kissed the top of her head. His fingers were impossibly soothing when he tucked her hair behind her ears. He cupped her chin. Then he paused and just looked at her. He ran a finger across each of her eyebrows and down her nose. He traced her lips and her jaw. Del trembled, and he studied her with awe. "You only ever grow more beautiful."

He locked his lips with hers. It was slow and luxurious. Encouraging dips of his head, featherlight brushes of his tongue. It was so filled with loveliness that Del felt she might sob. The sense of peace she felt was the same as when she looked out at her garden on a late day in spring, when all the flowers were blooming, and birds and butterflies flitted through the rainbow sea. It was the simplest, most natural form of magic, and when Than deepened their kiss, she realized she could have it forever—if she let herself fall in love with him.

He pulled her robe over her head. He looked down at her, drinking her in, and by the wonder in his expression, she knew he felt the same magic she did. She spiraled her finger through the air, unwinding the strand of vines that held his robe together. He slipped his wings out of it, then his eyes flitted up to hers. His face was framed by the golden light that streamed through the window behind him. "Is this okay, then?"

Del nodded, her hair rustling against the bed, and he lowered his lips to her chest. He adorned her with a slow kiss, then he peered up at her through his mussed hair. "Is this?" She nodded again, and he kissed her lower, on her stomach. Lower, her hips. Lower, she gasped. He peered up again, and this time his smile reflected the curl of her pleasure. "Is this?"

"Yes," Del said, breathless. "All of it is."

He spread her legs with his slim, gentle fingers, and as the air shimmered gold between them, she thought that she could spend the rest of her life like this.

Chapter Thirty-Four

Del woke up alone. Gasping, she scrabbled at the blankets with splayed palms. She had endured another nightmare. Walking through the palace. Her family wishing she would marry Than. Watching her mother vanish beneath the white willow. Only this time, when she landed in the palace after sinking into the lake, her family began to scream.

And scream.

And scream.

She thrashed at the blankets and realized Than was gone. Rubbing her eyes, she scanned the loft. Soft morning light pooled through the windows. Swallows and seabirds called to one another across the Isle. The white sheets were tangled around her ankles. Everything was peaceful, but Than was nowhere to be found.

Curling her knees up to her chin, Del shut her eyes tightly and expelled the dregs of the nightmare. There had been fire and smoke curling in from the palace windows, as though the pit of Tartarus had swallowed it whole. Blinking at the close darkness between her knees and torso, she forced herself to be rational. Than would not have left her alone. Not after all his soft touches and kind words.

Chin rested on her knees, she squinted out the window. It was barely past dawn. He had probably crept downstairs for some reason. Perhaps he was making breakfast. That seemed like him. No, she couldn't hear him, but he was good at being quiet. Or he might have gone out to the garden. Maybe he was gathering more of the lotus flowers from the orchard.

Reassured, she pulled on her robe. She crawled to the edge of the bed and slipped through the vine curtain, then down the stairs. Than was not in the kitchen, but she blew out a breath and reminded herself not to leap to the worst-case scenario. She strode down the garden path, breathing in the floral scent of the new rosebushes. When she curved off the main path to the lotus trees, birds flapped overhead. Deer pranced among the nearby elms.

Other than that, the Isle was still.

Hugging herself, Del trudged down the path through the lotus trees. It was eerie how well she recalled walking through it with Than yesterday. She swore she could still hear their voices swirling through the air. Pink flowers loosed themselves from the branches and landed in her hair. When she reached the trio of elms, she leaned against one of the trunks. She looked out at the waves crashing against the shore and admitted it—Than was gone.

She didn't know why, but he had left her here alone.

She pushed off from the elm. Oddly, she didn't feel panicked. She did not buckle under the weight of her grief. She only felt a resounding numbness. A hollow tree.

She walked aimlessly down the beach, circling all the way back to the cottage before remembering she knew someone who could tell her why he had left. Squinting up from the rosebushes, she raised a hand to her forehead. The sky was clear, the morning sun having already burned off the mist. Eos would be heading back to Helios and Selene's palace. Del hated to call on her so soon, but she doubted she would ever need to know anything that had occurred during the dawn more than she needed to know this right now.

"Eos!" she called up at the sun. Seabirds flocked from the beach in response. "Eos!" she yelled even louder to be heard over the chorus of squawks. Their wings cast wild shadows, and she tried not to think about Than flying back down to the Isle. She failed. Her heart leaped when she saw a winged figure gliding down, rendered a silhouette by the sun, but it was much too small to be the god of peaceful death.

Eos alighted on what used to be the crocus lawn. She folded her red-feathered wings and gave Del a friendly wave. "You called?"

"Eos." Del tried to sound grateful rather than disappointed as she approached the goddess of dawn. "Will you tell me what happened on my Isle this dawn?"

The girl nodded, radiant in her Cloth of Gold mantle. With her eyes closed, she recounted in vivid detail how Keres had touched down on the Isle with the first tendrils of dawn. Fluttering her white wings, the goddess of violent death had leaned through the window of Del's loft. A few minutes later, the door had opened, and Keres had vanished into the cottage. Unable to see through the roof tiles, Eos did not know what had happened within its walls, but before long, Keres was dragging Than out the door.

"He did not look happy," said the goddess of dawn. "I knew this was where you lived, so I listened. I heard Keres say something about needing his help in the underworld. They mentioned Hades as well. Then they both took off, and I had to move on."

So, Del thought, Than had left the Isle not long before she awoke. She nodded, thanking Eos for the information, and said she could go. Eos hesitated, but Del barely noticed when the girl winged over the Aegean. She was too lost in thought. Staring at the rosebushes, she wondered what Keres could have said to make Than leave without so much as a farewell. Maybe she had thought of some way to solve the third riddle. But if that was so, surely Than would have woken Del. He would not have gone to the underworld—

The realization hit her like a stone.

Send life into death to save what is already lost. The answer to the third riddle had to be saving Erebos from Tartarus. The other two riddles had centered around problems with their families. It only made sense that the third would follow the same pattern. Yesterday morning, they had left Helios and Selene's palace so quickly that Nyx barely had the chance to speak with them. Keres must have come to the Isle this morning and told Than that she and Nyx were going to the underworld to free Erebos. Of course he would have wanted to join them. But Eos had said he did not look happy when they left.

Surely, he would have been happy about freeing Erebos. And what was the reason for giving Del another nightmare? Nyx's banishment had been ended. As soon as the third task was completed, Del would marry Than and live in the underworld alongside him. Nyx would get exactly what she wanted. There was no reason for further pressure.

Del rubbed one of the rose blooms between her fingers. Something was not right here. She believed Than would go to Nyx if she needed him, but the rest of it didn't make sense. Unless Than had left because he had finally seen his chance. Maybe Del had been wrong to trust him, and this whole time he had merely been finding ways to keep her content. Then, when he found the right moment, he had fled.

No. Del crushed the rose petals between her fingers, breathing in their heavy scent. She would not believe that. Than would not hurt her like that. He had never done anything to suggest untrustworthiness, so she had to do what he always did.

She had to believe the best in him.

That meant, somehow, Nyx was using him. Del could think of no other reason why he would have left. He had been through turmoil since Del brought him here. He was vulnerable right now. She could not stand the thought of him facing anything else on his own.

What was more, she had to complete the third task by the time the sun set or Zeus would send Mak to the mortal battlefields. Del could not let that happen. Which meant she had only one option.

She had to follow Than to the underworld.

Chapter Thirty-Five

Del marched to the shore. She had no chariot, which meant she had to weave a raft very similar to the one she had used to banish her mother from the Isle. She clambered onto it and spiraled both wrists, sending two vines shooting into the sparkling waves of the Aegean. A few moments later, they caught a rip current. With sudden force that snapped back her head, she swerved into the open water.

Dropping old vines and shooting out new ones, she navigated the network of currents until she reached the shoreline near the base of Mount Olympus. She hopped off the raft and ran toward the mountain, bent double by the time the Olympic forest enclosed her in its leafy arms. The entire trek to the farm was downhill, and by the time the sun had reached its zenith, she was tumbling past the stables. Panting, she trudged through the fields, the red poppy aisles guiding her to the farmhouse.

Once inside, it took her a few moments to adjust to the shadows. Everything was green until she rubbed her eyes and blinked them a few times. She poured herself a glass of water, chugging it down, and it wasn't until she had eaten one of her dried dates that she noticed the silence of the house. No squealing triplets. No bustling Yaya. Not even the clattering of Gale's claws as the polecat chased Askalabos.

With a frown, she turned to the kitchen table. On it lay two notes, beside which rested a golden head of giant fennel. Del stepped toward it and looked down. In Yaya's tight, precise letters, the first note said Cate had taken her to visit a mortal temple, where she would begin telling the truth about Persephone's marriage. She hoped this would result in more worship from the mortals, and Zeus would rescind his threat to send Mak to the battlefields. The note ended by saying they would be back before nightfall.

The second note was on a small slip of parchment, written in the same long, slanted hand Cate used in her spell scrolls. When Del picked it up, it read simply:

Some mountains
must be climbed alone.

It was all the direction she needed to pluck up the head of giant fennel. Still connected to a thick length of stalk, it would serve well as a torch. She tucked Cate's note into the pocket of her robe and exited the house.

After trudging through the courtyard, the fields, and the forest, she emerged into the meadow. The wind flung up blooms of poppy and narcissus, along with diamond flecks of snow. Kneeling beside the frozen lake, she held the head of giant fennel in a direct ray of sun. Helios must have been watching and made good on his promise to help, because before long, the fennel began to smoke. Del whooped when a tongue of flame lapped at the snow. She held the fennel above the lake for a bit longer, blanketing it in flame before she held it aloft.

She slipped beneath the canopy of the white willow. For a moment, she stared at the trunk, realizing she did not know how to open her father's pathway to the underworld. She scanned the tree until she saw a knot that looked suspiciously like a door handle. She pushed it inward with all the force she could muster, but nothing happened. Then the snow swirled in front of it, and she gripped the knot before turning her wrist. The knot turned with it, and slowly but surely the ground fell away, revealing a set of spiraling stairs.

With a sharp intake of breath, Del watched the black hole deepen, turning the knot in the trunk until it came to a stop. The white willow trunk rose from the center of the stairs, an island with darkness surrounding it. Darkness in which Del would have to swim.

She stared into it. It was as dark as death, but she had bent death to her will before. Behind her, a gust of wind blew through the meadow, and the air came alive with the musical tinkling of leaves covered with ice and snow. Del resituated her sweating hand on the torch. She sucked in a breath.

Then she took her first step down the stairs.

Chapter Thirty-Six

Del waded into the darkness. Round and round, deeper and deeper she went, dragging her hand along the inner wall of the stairs. Before long, the light above faded into a pinprick. Not long after that, it vanished, leaving her wrapped in syrupy darkness. It was not as disorienting as the nothingness where the Fates lived, but only because she could hear the scratch of earth beneath her feet and feel the smooth stalk of the torch in her hand. Its heat wafted onto her forearm and cheek, though the orange orb of its light barely extended beyond her face. Still, her stomach knotted at the thought of it winking out her entire way down the stairs.

This fear became a very real possibility when the stairs evened into a winding path. Based on the way her footfalls echoed here, she could tell the ceiling extended quite a way above her head. Which would have been comforting, had it not made room for the steadily strengthening streams of wind. They whistled past her head, sending her hair rearing outward like a mane. They tugged at her robe, causing her to stumble by shoving her forward too quickly. They accentuated the musty scent of earth by flinging dirt that pinged off her skin.

Hand splayed over her torch, she held the giant fennel as close as she could without burning her robe. Even so, when the streams of wind strengthened, the flames guttered to embers. She was working up the courage to admit it was hopeless, but just before she dropped the torch and continued in darkness, she felt a shift in the wind. Its braided hands slid down her back and calves before wrapping her ankles in icy manacles. The roar of the air became a crash. Pushed forward by the current, she squinted down and gasped.

The wind had become a river, which deepened the farther she went. Its current became stronger, and soon she was moving forward with scarcely any effort, holding the torch aloft as she was buoyed along in the cold water. Moving through the tunnel like this was much easier, but it couldn't last. Her arms and legs were already succumbing to numbness. She started sweeping her legs in wide arcs beneath the surface, searching for an embankment, but the river only grew deeper. Her skin prickled with gooseflesh. Her teeth chattered. The base of the torch was already submerged in the river—

She shouted when her nose filled with the scent of balsam. She kicked her legs, swimming with renewed vigor as the rushing river lapped at her lips and the tunnel opened into the underworld at last. There was the snow suspended in the air. The mists swirling overhead. The clouds of black smoke from Tartarus in the distance. Before her, the white poplar forest extended up the mountain, sending its heady scent of balsam through the air. She kicked harder for the cypress-lined embankment and glimpsed a narrow black boat far in front of her. It was filled with flickering red shadows and a hooded black figure.

It was Charon, she realized when the current pushed her closer. She spluttered, icy water filling her mouth and nose. Finally, she managed to get a handhold. Hands squelching in the mud, she dragged herself out of the river, coughing into the sparse grass. She lay there, forehead against the ground, more grateful than ever to be on dry land. Then she forced herself up, planting the torch in the dirt while she wrung out her robe. The white fabric was stained gray from the Styx. Looking around, she saw Charon hook his oar around a cypress trunk a short way down the embankment. He pointed, the winglike sleeve of his robe falling to his hip, and the flickering red souls disembarked.

They were all Keres's victims. Their faces were frozen in their final living moments, eyes wide and mouths open in terror. In silence, they drifted down the banks of the Styx, which ringed the base of the mountain. Shoving herself up, Del followed them, knowing they would lead her to the road of smooth black pebbles that led to the palace. They would all have to face her father for trial, but as she trudged behind them, she realized they were not continuing up the mountain. Instead, they gathered among the white poplars on either side of the path, making the forest appear caught in an eerily silent inferno.

Tiptoeing around them, Del started up the path. The smooth black pebbles clattered beneath her feet. The inexplicable crowd of souls vanished behind the white poplar trees, but when she reached the first fork in the pathway, she found her way blocked by another large group of them. These souls were a mix of blue and red, all of them waiting in lines that extended down either fork in the path. These must be the souls from Athens, having completed their trials and now on their way to where they would rest.

Del hurried past them, nearly choking on the thick scent of balsam. The higher she went, the more snowflakes dazzled her eyes, and she struggled to breathe through the fragrant air. She was almost grateful for the break in the foliage that marked the Fields of Punishment.

Almost, but then the screams filled her ears. The Fields of Punishment rolled down the mountain before spilling into Tartarus, the charred, blackened ground lacerated with the fiery whip of the Phlegethon. The river Acheron wove parallel, from which a line of souls waited to sip. Usually, the Furies would have been here, herding the souls who had spent their lives hurting others toward the wine-red waters. Now the souls simply stood, drifting along it, unwilling to take a gulp of their own accord.

Del could not blame them, for though these souls had earned their punishment, drinking from the Acheron would cause them to recall only their horrible moments. For eternity, their minds would be tortured by their failures and regrets, while their bodies would be subjected to whatever horrors her father came up with. She caught a glimpse of the Acheron inlet where Tantalus sat surrounded by fruit trees always heavy with harvest. The skeletal soul reached for one of the shining red prizes, but just when his fingers brushed it, the fruit flung itself from the branch. He wailed as it tumbled down the mountain. He cursed the water surrounding him, which lapped just out of reach of his lips.

Countless other souls screamed and wailed across the Fields, begging to be given another chance. This would never happen, so Del gritted her teeth and pushed through it, letting out a long, relieved breath when she reentered the poplar forest. This time, she had no qualms with breathing in the thick, heady air. She shifted the torch to her other hand and wiped sweat on her robe, which was still damp and now hemmed with ash.

When the poplars grew sparse again, she stepped into the Fields of Asphodel. Rather than charred and blackened, here, the ground was totally obscured by a sea of star-shaped white flowers. While Del trod through them, gray souls emerged from the foliage. She tried and failed not to look at their faces, which were wiped not only of expression, but also of facial features. The river Lethe gurgled through the colorless land, where blue, slack-mouthed souls waited in line to drink from its cloudy white water.

Del hated it. It was a reminder that this was all one deserved for being decent, and she was named after it. These mortals would be forgotten. Not only by those who went on living, who would forget the names of their fellows who did not earn hero tales, but also by themselves. They would go on forever, faceless and silent, as they did now, making Del jump each time one of them bloomed from the asphodel. They might as well have never existed, and she was no better. Forgotten on her Isle, unneeded in the great story of the world.

She wove through them as swiftly as possible. When the Fields of Asphodel thinned, she glimpsed the Lake of Mnemosyne lapping on the side of the path. Only a handful of red souls waited to drink from it, for very few souls were deemed worthy of Elysium, the Isle in the center of it. Del watched the soul at the front of the line kneel before the crystal-blue water and drink from it. From head to foot, the flickering red coloring fled their body in favor of white, like the soul of a god. Stepping across the water, the soul headed toward the verdant Isle of Elysium, where they would spend eternity.

The path widened, and through the poplar forest, Del saw the black marble walls of the palace. They glinted in the mists. Cypresses stood sentry on either side of the path, and the flower beds beneath them burst with red pomegranates. The silence and the snowflakes, combined with the hulking doors rising before her, were all exactly the same as her nightmares. Except for one thing.

When the doors opened, she heard Than calling her name.

Chapter Thirty-Seven

Del charged into the palace. The doors closed silently behind her, but she focused solely on finding Than. His voice had been tattered, as though he had been calling her name for hours. It bounced off the black marble walls, which mirrored her mad dash through the halls. She saw her own wild face reflected back at her again and again. Once, she screamed when she thought it was someone else coming around a bend.

It was strange, the silence of the palace. Yaya had not mentioned the triplets in her letter, which meant they must be here. Yet Del heard no sign of them. Her father should be in the throne room putting mortal souls on trial, but all those new souls had been standing at the base of the mountain.

Something was very wrong here.

Than called her name again, and when she neared the throne room, a hysterical laugh bubbled from her lips. How different her desires had been the last time she had made this trek. Now, as she turned the talonlike handle, her only plan was to save the god of peaceful death. But all thoughts fled her mind when the doors opened and she saw him chained to the throne of bone with pitch-black manacles.

"Del!" He lifted his head, and she ran toward him, past the pillars carved with scenes of torture. "What . . . ? How did you know I was here?"

"Than!" Del fell to a crouch in front of him, dropping her torch to hold his face in her hands. He looked exhausted, his cheeks streaked with tears, but otherwise nothing seemed to have harmed him. His chains looped through both of the throne's bony hands, holding his arms out on either side of him. His wings drooped in front of the seat behind him. His appearance sent rage-red flowers blooming through Del's chest.

She gave him a quick kiss. "Are you all right? What happened? Eos told me Keres came to the Isle this morning. She said she heard something about Keres and your mother going to the underworld. Why did you leave without me? Is it about the last task? I think the answer might be freeing Erebos. What *happened*?"

Than clenched his eyes shut, the fight going out of him. "Del, listen—"

"Because you could have brought me with you," she said, directing her attention to the thick cords of blackness that bound him. "I know the past few days have been more than stressful, but we're in this together. We need to help each other. Waking up alone was . . . *What* are these manacles?" She ran her fingers over one of the cords and hissed. Her hand was colder than it had been in the Styx, and when she looked at it, it shimmered. Stardust. Nyx had done this. Her gaze snapped to him. "Why are you trapped?"

His eyes were still shut when he let out a bitter laugh. "Because—"

"Because," said the voice from Del's nightmares, "he was trying to run back to your Isle and tell you everything that had happened here."

Than's eyes flew open, and Del whipped around to see the goddess of night striding toward them. Her hair waterfalled down her back, becoming lost in her Cloak of Darkness. "You see, Than?" she said. "I told you she would come to us."

Del stared at the goddess, who carried her father's scepter to the throne. While she tried to make sense of the scene before her, Than scoffed. "You couldn't have possibly known Del would follow me here."

Nyx smiled. "I gave her the right nightmare." She stepped straight through one of the cords entrapping her son and sat on the throne, crossing her legs beneath her shimmering gown.

"Where is my father?" Del snapped. "What's going on?"

Than saw something behind her, and his eyes widened. "Del—"

Before he could finish, a pair of strong arms yanked Del backward. With a gasp, she stumbled down the stairs, only to be buffeted into an upright position by a powerful gust of wind. "I'm sorry about this," Keres said in her ear. "I truly am."

Del struggled against her captor. She tried to spiral her wrists, but the goddess of violent death was accustomed to her methods. She gripped Del's wrists, and Del screamed when biting cold snaked around her arms.

"Mother, stop!" Than yelled, but Nyx did not acknowledge him.

"I tried to tell you," she said to Del, "in all the nightmares I sent. I offered you a kingdom, and still you rejected my alliance."

"This is my father's kingdom," Del spat. Rather than struggle, which she had realized was pointless, she stood straight and tall, modeling herself after how her mother cut through this realm. When she next spoke, her voice was as cold as her manacles. "Where is he? Where is my mother, the triplets? Why aren't the Furies guarding the palace?"

"Mother," Keres said, "maybe you should let Than explain it."

Del would have crumpled to the floor had Keres not held her arms. Even so, her heart plummeted to her feet when her eyes dropped to Than. She spoke her next words through numb lips. "You knew about this?"

Than kept his gaze on the floor.

"Del," Nyx said, her tone telling Del to be reasonable, "you know your father is an evil man. Keres told me that just recently, you tried to dissolve his and Persephone's marriage vow. You could not have believed I would actually want an alliance with him."

Del stared at Than. "You—"

"Keres knew Than was infatuated with you," Nyx said.

Del's eyes snapped back to Nyx. The goddess lounged on the throne as though she had sat there for years, her torso embraced by the rows of ribs. At Del's expression, she barked a laugh. "Surely he told you. He has been for years. So, I negotiated a marriage alliance, knowing he would say yes."

She twirled the black-and-gold scepter, watching the stone body of Coronis.

"I will admit, I did not account for you kidnapping him. Keres and I knew how much you hated your father, but we did not realize how much you hated the underworld. I didn't intend to trap you in a place you feel is so incompatible with who you are, but once the plan was in motion, it could not be stopped. And in the end, all things worked out for the best. I thought it would take years to convince Than to help overthrow Hades. Thanks to you"—she pointed at Del with the scepter—"he learned the truth of my banishment and told Keres he wanted to right the wrong mere days after you took him to your cottage."

"What?" Del's eyes darted from Nyx to Than. "When . . . ?"

"After you and Than left the battle in Athens." Keres's voice was horribly monotone. "You had fainted, so I flew with him over the Aegean. I tried to convince him to come to Helios and Selene's palace, where all of us could discuss the plan, but he said he was not certain you would agree to it yet."

"And I was right," Than said. He beseeched Del, eyes rimmed with tears. "Please understand. You helped me realize I was wrong to let Hades control me for long. I didn't agree to this plan out of anger. I agreed to it because I don't want to give him the chance to control anyone else. Please, Del. I know you can understand that."

Del fought back a wave of nausea. Than had been so kind to her. Supporting her while she tried to complete the three tasks. Holding her up with his arms and his encouraging words. And ever since Athens, he had been keeping this from her.

"I trusted you," she told him. Her voice broke on the words.

He strained against his manacles. "Del—"

"Dear girl, this cannot come as a shock." Nyx spared Del from whatever new lie he had planned to spout. "I need you to marry my son to maintain the principle of balance. You see, when I overthrow your parents, I will need someone to replace them as the underworld's rulers. You and Than will sit on the throne, while I make the decisions from the shadows. Zeus will not care who rules—not so long as he gets worship from mortals."

Del scowled up at the goddess, but Nyx only laughed. "In fact, I never even expected to come back here. I thought I would spend the rest of eternity banished. Then you marched right up to Helios and Selene's palace and caused an eclipse." She drummed her fingers on her chin. "I suppose I will have to reward those Fates of mine for those tasks."

She shifted her gaze back to Del, and her voice brightened. "Well, after that, I decided we would have the best chance of success if we acted while Hades is still distracted. Right now, he has the spike in violent deaths to contend with, not to mention his fear for your little sister. Plus, since Persephone can now travel between realms whenever she wishes, it was much easier to capture all five of your family members. Really, Del." Nyx pressed her palm to her chest. "I cannot overstate how grateful I am."

Del used all her willpower to glare at Nyx instead of Than. He was still watching her, trying to free himself, and she wanted to attack him with every last drop of her magic. But Nyx had captured her family. Right now, they were what mattered.

"What have you done with them?" she asked.

Nyx roved the scepter lazily through the air. "Oh, they are locked up somewhere. I am not telling you their location, but don't fret. They are being well treated. Food, water, blankets." She frowned. "Well, except for your father. He is getting a taste of what he will experience for the rest of his existence in Tartarus."

Del heard herself whisper, "Tartarus?"

Nyx brought the scepter to the floor with a rap. "A fate worse than death. Just as he granted Erebos." When Del opened her mouth, she lifted a finger. "Only Hades can free him, which will never happen unless I have leverage."

Del rocked back on her heels. "My mother and the triplets."

Nyx nodded. "Of course, after Hades has freed Erebos, I will still lock the lot of them in Tartarus. A fair trade, considering how he has treated me all these years."

Del spluttered, "The triplets are *children*."

Than glanced wildly from Keres to his mother. "You never told me you wanted to throw the triplets into Tartarus." He looked at Del, eyes widened. "I promise, I had no idea. The triplets are like siblings to me. I adore them. You know that."

"How can I believe anything you tell me?" Del asked. The depth of his deception was unbelievable. It felt like her heart was being carved out of her chest.

"The triplets are your father's heirs." Nyx drummed the armrest. "I truly am sorry that they must pay for your father's actions, but I cannot risk their retaliation. That little Mel . . ." She shook her head. "She reminds me of myself. I have no desire for revenge to be enacted upon me when she is full grown. But their cells will be much nicer than your father's, and your mother will stay with them. Now—"

"You are no better than my father," Del said. She tried to look back at Keres, who held her in a viselike grip. "I thought you were furious with her for trapping Eos in the space between realms. Now you are fine with throwing children into prison cells?"

"I said I was sorry," Keres growled, "but this is what has to be done."

"I understand why you're angry." Nyx petted Coronis's head. "But I hope someday you can come to enjoy your place in my household. Ever since you stole Than from the underworld, you have proven yourself to be strong and resourceful. Hate me if you must, but you will want for nothing here. You will always be in control."

She lounged on the throne wearing a fat smile. Behind her, the wall gleamed with gemstone flowers. For a moment, Del imagined herself in that position. She saw herself listening to the lives of mortal souls and dictating where they should go. She saw Than at her side, holding her hand in the day and at night sharing her bed. She would walk these halls with all the cutting confidence her mother did.

But in this future, her mother would no longer be here. Del would live as Than always had, in a palace with a family that was not her own, always trying to prove she deserved their love. No matter what Nyx said, she would live in constant fear of disappointing her and being thrown into Tartarus with the rest of her family members. Del had no desire for any of that. She no longer wanted to feel alone. She wanted to share her life with someone else.

The someone else she wanted to share it with, however, currently knelt in front of his mother's throne, no longer daring to meet the eyes of the woman he claimed to love. No, she had lost Than. She had lost her Isle.

She would not lose herself.

"I will never marry you, Thanatos." She glared at her betrothed, her voice as black as the river Styx itself. "If you are determined to throw my family into Tartarus, I have no reason to complete the Fates' last task." She lifted her chin to Nyx. "There is nothing you can give me that you have not already taken away. I will not help you destroy my family."

Nyx sighed. With a wave of the scepter, she told Keres to take Del to one of the palace bedrooms and hold her there until she came to her senses. Del refused to look at Than's expression. She did not want to know what she would find there. Shock, relief, anger. It was best for her to imagine him shattered.

Instead, she watched her own reflection in the marble floor. Her face was devoid of tears as Keres yanked her into the palace halls.

Chapter Thirty-Eight

Del lay on a plush bed deep in the palace. It was swathed in black linens, pressed against the wall between two black marble columns. More columns ringed the room, which was filled with jewel-toned furniture. Mists swirled through the windows, and the only light came from the network of roots that snaked across the ceiling, casting a faint green glow. The light glanced off the field of asphodel that swayed over Del, making the white blooms look ill.

It was fitting. For as Del lay on her back, staring at the star-shaped flowers, she admitted she had never felt sicker than she did right now. The moment she discovered her betrothal, her life had shriveled up like a plucked flower left to dry in the sun. She had been trying to preserve it, but lying here, she acknowledged it could never be what it once was. Her life had been a living thing, soft and sweet smelling, bobbing in the sun. Now it was pinched and hard. At the slightest touch, it would crumble to dust.

Seeing Than side with Nyx was that touch.

She felt complete numbness. For the first time in her life, she had put her trust in someone else, and he had broken it. She had told him she feared he was not as good as he said he was, and he had proven to be even worse.

Behind her back, she tightened her hands into fists. She could still feel his hands in her hair. She could still hear his heartbeat against her ear. He had comforted her while knowing he was going to throw her family into Tartarus. He had helped her try to save Mak while knowing her little sister was doomed no matter what. Yes, he had said he hadn't known about that part of his mother's plan, but she couldn't bring herself to believe him. Not when her instincts that very first day with him had been correct. Death had waited, quiet against the wall, until she let down her guard. His freedom had always been an inevitability.

She had just been foolish enough to believe he would stay.

All at once, the field of asphodel buffeted with her heaving breaths. Tears streaked down her cheeks, and she rolled onto her side, pulling her knees up to her chin. She shut her eyes and screamed through clenched teeth. Her muscles were so tense that her limbs shook, and her face was slick with tears. They trailed down her cheeks before reaching her neck, encircling it like the rose-bloom necklace she had received from Than.

It seemed impossible that she could look the same as she always had. There should be some outward representation of the destruction beyond her tears. The tears would ebb, but for the rest of her life, she would feel a gaping bright-red wound in her chest.

The thought sent her into panic. Her breaths came faster. Faster. Her lungs weren't holding any air. She shoved her face into the bed. It felt like she was leaning forward off the edge of a cliff, reaching out for something to grab, but no matter how far she stretched, her fingers caught only empty air. Nothing was there. Nothing, nothing, but she would keep reaching outward until she fell into the pit—

The pit of Tartarus, where Nyx would toss her family if she did not pull herself together and find a way to stop it.

She shot into a sitting position. Suddenly, she understood the third task. Send life into death to save what is already lost. It was not about freeing Erebos. It was about her family. She had to save her family from Nyx.

The Fates were not on Nyx's side. Their plan was for Del to win.

She just had to be strong, brave, and smart enough to do it.

Her tears stopped, and she scrambled up from the bed. There would be time for anguish later. Right now, she had to focus on rescuing her family from a fate worse than death. And thanks to Than's betrayal, she knew just how to do it. Because while yes, Nyx was filled with anger and revenge, these were paltry motivators when pitted against love and passion. Her love for Erebos was the real reason she was here.

All Del had to do was exploit it, and the best way to do that was to shrink into the version of herself Nyx would expect. Beaten. Broken. It would not be difficult. Beaten and broken was exactly how she felt.

All the best lies have a seed of truth at their core.

Leaving her face stained with tears, she padded through the field of asphodel. When she reached the door, she made her voice sound brittle. "I would like to see Nyx."

Chapter Thirty-Nine

Footsteps sounded in the hall, and Keres opened the door.

"You changed your mind quite quickly, little flower girl."

Del sniffled. "I really would have enjoyed spending time with you on the Isle, you know."

"We still can." Keres grabbed her bound wrists and led her into the hall. "Living in the underworld doesn't mean you can never visit the Isle again. And if you are willing to help us, I would still love to be friends. Kidnapping my brother took guts. I admire that."

Del resisted the urge to shake herself out of Keres's grip. "Perhaps."

The goddess opened the door to the throne room, where Nyx still sat. Unbidden, Del scanned the room for Than, but he was not there. Tucking her chin toward her chest, she flitted her gaze up at the goddess of night and said, "You were right. After learning what my father did to you and Erebos, I hate him more than I ever have. He deserves to spend the rest of his life in Tartarus, but please, don't give my mother and the triplets his punishment. If you do, you are no better than he is. I stand by that."

Nyx glanced at Keres and gestured to the door with the scepter. When Keres had left, she rolled her hand at Del, who blew out a breath.

"The final riddle the Fates gave me is to send life into death to save what is already lost. While I was lying in that bedroom," she said with a tilt of her head toward the door, "I realized it must mean Erebos. To break my curse, I must free him from Tartarus—which means if I don't help you, I can never marry Than, and you can never throw my father into the pit."

"And the only way you will help me is if I free your mother and the triplets."

Del nodded. "When my father is thrown into Tartarus, my mother will be banished from the underworld. She and the triplets can live with my grandmother on the farm—free from my father's clutches, just as I have always hoped to accomplish."

She swallowed. This next part was the most difficult. It was the seed of truth at the core of her lie, which made everything that grew around it more believable. "When my curse is broken, I will marry Than and rule the underworld alongside him. I will share our story with the mortals, and the principle of balance will be restored."

Nyx's lips slowly stretched into a grin. "I knew you would come to your senses." She flicked her wrist, snapping the cords of night that bound Del's wrists. Del gasped as warmth flooded into her hands, holding them to her stomach.

"Yes, I will spare Persephone and the triplets. That was always my intention. I just needed your loyalty." At Del's shocked expression, the goddess barked a laugh. "You didn't honestly think I would throw innocent children into Tartarus?" She sobered. "No. After Eos, I have learned that lesson. I have no desire to hurt anyone other than Hades." She twirled the black-and-gold scepter, stroking Coronis. "Now, tell me how you plan to do that."

Chapter Forty

Of course Nyx loved the idea. When Del finished explaining it, the goddess sent her to collect what she needed to enact it. The only trouble was that she sent Than with her, claiming they should take this time for reconciliation. Del ground her teeth as he accompanied her to the gardens in the central courtyard of the palace.

"I'm so sorry," he said as soon as the door shut behind them. "I was going to tell you everything. I swear it." While he kept talking, Del scanned the flower beds. "I was just nervous. Especially after completing the second task, you seemed to have this new . . . understanding for your father. This softness. Like you were on your way to forgiving him. And I understand. Trust me, more than anyone else, I understand that. So I didn't want to rush you. I didn't want to confuse all the emotions swirling through your head."

They reached the far end of the gardens, where cords of night chained Cerberus to the trunk of a honey-sweet linden. He had been lying with his paws forming a cushion for his three heads, but he perked up when Del and Than stepped beneath the branches. His tail thumped while Del knelt beside him, and he snuffled her hand. Purple aconite blooms grew around his heads. Del searched for a suitable one and heard Than's wings twitch. She knew he was anxious. She could have turned around and pointed out that she had already trusted him, and he had ruined it. But it was easier to let him talk himself into oblivion.

"I wanted you to work out for yourself that Hades deserves to pay for the horrible things he has done to us—regardless of how much we still love him. And on top of that, I know how much you value control. I didn't want to rob you of it again."

Del found an aconite bloom that was large enough and gripped the base of its stem. Cerberus shoved his heads toward it, and she grimaced when his saliva coated her hand. She wiped it on the ground, and more aconite grew there. "As though you have not forced my hand by withholding information."

"I have." Than sounded desperately thrilled that she had spoken to him. "But you must understand. Keres told me about the plan when we left Athens, but she said it would not be executed for several years. When she came to the Isle this morning, I only went with her to explain why I thought now was not the right time for it. They chained me up because I wanted to go back to the Isle and help you complete the last task."

"Which you only cared about because you needed to break my curse." Del snipped the aconite stem. "You never cared about saving Mak from the mortals."

"Of course I care about saving Mak. What are you talking about?"

"Your mother threatened to throw her into Tartarus. Don't lie to me now."

"I told you, my mother never mentioned that before you came down here. Zeus's name, do you really think I would be capable of throwing the triplets into Tartarus?"

Del looked up at him. "I have no idea what you're capable of anymore."

Than's expression crumpled. "Del."

She petted each of Cerberus's heads, then she stood and held out her hand. She met Than's eyes. "Give me your hand."

His face brightened, and pain stabbed outward from the wound in her heart. But she kept her face expressionless as she hooked her finger beneath the olive-branch bracelet she had given him. She yanked her finger upward, and the brittle braids snapped. She snapped off her own bracelet, and together, they watched them drift into the flower beds.

Than remained silent after that.

They strode down to the docks, where all five rivers of the underworld burbled out of the mountain. She knelt at the spring of the river Lethe, and Than sucked in a breath. When his hands grazed her arms, she snapped, "Don't touch me. I'm not going to fall in."

She dipped the aconite into the cloudy water. The current tried to yank it from her hand, but she held tight to the base of the stem. The water swirled around the hood-shaped blooms, rippling them like a great wind until she lifted the plant. She held it over the spring, waiting until water had stopped dripping from it before she led Than back into the palace.

When they reached the throne room, Nyx clapped. "Did the two of you resolve your differences?" Del only stiffened, and Than shook his head. "Well"—Nyx's smile dimmed—"I suppose there will be time enough later for that." She handed Del a black jar. "I hope this is large enough. The mouth is a bit small. Be careful slipping the plant inside it."

With some effort, Del finagled the aconite into the jar and corked it. Than tried to take it from her, but she held it close, carrying it as they headed back down to the docks.

No sooner had the three of them stepped into the long black boat floating atop the Phlegethon than Keres emerged from the palace. She had split herself into five aspects, each of which held one of Del's family members.

The sight made Del's heart seize up. All of them had cords of night binding their ankles, wrists, and hands. When the triplets saw Del, they screamed through their cords. They squirmed, trying to run to their big sister, but Keres's aspects tightened their grip. Persephone yelped Del's name through her cord, but the triplets stole her attention when they huddled around her in the boat.

Hades alone remained calm. In the way he flicked his eyes toward the rest of the family, Del saw him pleading for their survival. She could have nodded. She could have given him some inkling that they would be okay.

Instead, when Keres returned to one aspect of herself and pushed the boat into the fiery river, she turned away.

Chapter Forty-One

The journey down the Phlegethon was terrible.

The whole way through the Fields of Punishment, the triplets screamed and whimpered. This was their first time seeing mortal souls suffer. Del faced the prow, watching Nyx's Cloak of Darkness swing back and forth in the fiery current, but she could feel her parents watching the back of her head. Her skin prickled at the sensation.

She held the black jar to her chest. Her hands were slick with sweat. Her heart pounded, and she licked her dry lips. Than sat beside her on the wooden bench, but she did not speak to him. When they at last reached the alcove at the edge of Tartarus, she did not take his proffered hand. Nor did she allow him to lift the jar from her hands.

Instead, she heaved herself onto the ledge. This close to the pit, she could barely see through the black smoke. It felt like she was breathing in dirt. Taking shallow breaths, she squinted at the waterfall of fire descending into the pit. Her eyes watered and felt dry all at once. Each blink stung. The hot air from the waterfall swirled with embers, and one of them landed on her arm, searing her skin.

With a grimace, she made her way toward the edge of the cliff. A lip of black rock curled over it like a cloak hood, and she leaned against it, staring into the sea of fire below. The triplets yelped when Keres lugged them out of the boat, and Del tightened her grip on the jar. She hated to think of the triplets enduring this for even a moment.

Keres cornered Persephone and the triplets against the shelf of rock, and Nyx swept Hades to the lip of the alcove. The triplets shrieked, and Persephone lunged for him, but Nyx paid them no attention. As her Cloak of Darkness fanned out behind her, she sliced her finger through the air.

The cord of night evaporated from Hades's lips. He looked up at her, showing the whites of his eyes. "Please, spare them," he said in a hoarse voice.

"Hades, Hades," Nyx singsonged, smoothing two fingers along the top of his head. Del shuddered at how similar she sounded to Than. "I will. You did not honestly think I would toss an innocent woman and her children into Tartarus, did you, now? No, I have other methods of persuasion. Or . . ." She turned to Del with a smile that flashed like starlight in the smoky dark. "I suppose that honor goes to the new queen of the underworld. Del, why don't you tell your father the fate you have woven for him?"

Under the weight of her family's attention, Del wanted to shrivel. Mak darted her gaze from her big sister to Nyx as though trying to make sense of what the goddess of night had just said. Zag was crying so hard that his eyes were clenched shut. Mel glowered at Del with her eyes narrowed. They all huddled into Persephone, three aspects of Keres holding them against the wall of black rock. Soot streaked her mother's pink robe, and silent tears fell down her face while she shook her head, staring at Del.

Hades alone seemed unsurprised by the betrayal. Mouth set in a firm line, he knelt in front of Nyx with his hands bound at his front. Nothing but resignation pooled in his death-dark eyes. More than anything else, his acquiescence seared Del's heart. Yes, she had always hated him, but after what had happened in the meadow, she had thought things were different. But when she met his eyes through the swirling embers and smoke, she knew he had given up on earning even a sliver of her love long ago. It made her want to scream at him, but if she wanted to save her family, she had to stick to her plan.

Shaking off Than's attempt at a steadying hand, she uncorked the black jar and gripped the tip of the aconite stem. When she pulled out the plant, her mother's eyes widened. Mak elbowed Zag, who blinked through his tears. He fell silent, and Mel leaned against Persephone, relaxing her expression. Only Hades remained impassive while she held the plant toward him. She shook it, and droplets of white water flung from the hood-shaped blooms, sizzling on the rock.

"This aconite," she said, "has been soaked in the river Lethe. If it touches your skin, the water will seep into your soul and suck out every memory you have." She coughed, gesturing the aconite at Nyx. "Whether or not you agree to free Erebos, Nyx will toss you into the pit. The condition in which you arrive, however, is your decision."

Nyx nodded, and Del pointed the aconite at her father again. "If you free Erebos, you will be locked in Tartarus with your soul intact. If you refuse, I will wrap these blooms around you, and your memories will be mine to hold in this flower forever."

She jerked her chin to her mother and the triplets, who avidly watched her movements. "Gone will be your days with the triplets, your courtship with my mother, the moment you realized you were worth something as the underworld's ruler."

She glared down at her father while mortals screamed in the distance. "When Nyx throws you into Tartarus, you will have no memory of who you once were. Even if you eventually find your way to freedom, it won't matter." She smirked at Nyx. "You will never remember your family, even if you see them again. You will be hopeless, alone, and forgotten—the closest a god can come to death."

"So, what will it be?" Nyx grinned at Hades, and Del's heart thundered at the realization of how much power she had. If her father refused to free Erebos, she really would have to take all his memories from him. Nyx would force her hand. This was the most important moment in her plan, and she could not control it. She had to trust her father to make the right decision. Like the rest of her family, she watched him with held breath.

She almost sank to her knees when he lifted his eyes to Nyx. "You don't need to threaten me," he said. "I have regretted what I did to you and Erebos for years. Why do you think I have been so desperate for an alliance? I would have released Erebos long ago, but his bindings were interwoven with your banishment. I hoped we could work together to end it. Thanks to Del"—his eyes flicked to his eldest child—"I can free you both now."

He tipped his head toward his scepter, which Nyx held at her front. She moved it near his mouth, and he murmured to Coronis. The stone raven leaped into the air. He looped once, twice, swirling the embers, then he dove into the pit, straight into the waterfall of fire.

Moments passed. The fire crackled. Than watched Del. Mortal screams echoed off the rock. Keres trained her eyes on Del's family with her arms crossed. Everyone's eyes watered, and they all coughed. Nyx paced back and forth. "What is *taking* so long—"

A wave of darkness exploded out of Tartarus. The triplets screamed, and the darkness crashed onto the alcove. If Del had thought it was difficult to see before, now the shadows were impenetrable. The sudden lack of vision made her stumble, and she fell into Than's arms. "Are you okay?" he asked, but she shoved him away with a growl. The triplets were shouting, crying for Maytare, but the darkness was thinning somewhat.

"My Starlight." Erebos wrapped his arms around Nyx, rocking her gently back and forth. His hair and skin were as dark as the shadows rolling off him, eddying around the intertwined couple. They looked like a silhouette from every angle.

"My Darkness," Nyx murmured against his neck. She held him tighter, and Del felt a twinge of remorse for what she had planned. It was clear how much they loved each other, but Del loved her family too. And to save them, this was what she had to do.

Her thoughts were ripped up by the root when Nyx flicked her wrist, which sent the cords of night that bound Hades dragging him to the edge of Tartarus. Persephone shrieked, and Hades shut his eyes against the angry red light. Letting go of Erebos, Nyx gave him a mocking wave. "Enjoy your stay in Tartar—"

Del spiraled her wrists.

As the soaked stalk of aconite arrowed across the rock and formed a circle around Erebos, she said, "I wouldn't."

Nyx gaped at her, her finger already outstretched to flick Hades into the pit. When she saw everyone staring at Erebos, she turned to him and swallowed. Within the aconite circle, Erebos opened his mouth, but Del sent a vine of bindweed twining around his lips.

Slowly, Nyx lowered her hand. Hades settled back onto the rock, and she looked at Del, whose smile slithered across her face like a snake through a garden.

"Nyx, Nyx," she said, mimicking the singsong tone the goddess had used on her father mere minutes ago, "you did not honestly think I would let you toss my father into the pit of Tartarus, did you, now?" She glided toward Erebos, wagging her finger at the goddess. "You would think, after me kidnapping Than and holding him hostage, you would learn not to underestimate a little flower girl."

"Child." Nyx raised an eyebrow, flicking her finger at Hades in an imitation of her previous bravado, but Del saw her eyes linger on the aconite circle. "You understand that even if you bind Erebos with this plant, I still have the power to dump your father into the pit."

Del cocked her head. "It won't matter, though, will it? You aren't doing this because you hate my father. You're doing it because you love Erebos. What will it matter if you toss my father into the pit, if you can't have him?"

Nyx's eyes darted to Erebos, who stared down at the aconite circle. Shadows rolled off him, but he stood so still that Del wondered if he was holding his breath. "We survived centuries of separation," Nyx said. "We can survive it again."

Del laughed, the sound echoing off the cold, hard stone. "Did you not hear what I just said? If these blooms touch Erebos, it will be worse than before, because he will be right there. You will see him. Touch him. Speak to him."

Her gaze shifted to Than, who stood holding Keres's hand. His wings drooped, and he stared back at Del, his eyes like twin blue lights in the shadows. "He will look and feel and sound the same as he always has, but all the memories that made you mean something to him will be shattered. He will look at you and see just some woman. You will look at him and wonder how he could forget. Forever, you will live like this. Nothing, absolutely nothing, is as torturous as that."

Telling herself the tears dripping down her face were because of the smoke and nothing else, she turned back to Nyx. "Take it from me." She cleared her throat. "I know how it feels. Your son made sure of that." Nyx glanced at Than, and Del hardened her voice. "He made the decision to forget all I meant to him in favor of vengeance. But if you let this aconite touch Erebos, *you* will be making the decision. *You* will doom him. Tell me, can you live for the rest of eternity, knowing you did that?"

"Mother, no," Keres said, but Nyx held up her hand. When she said nothing, only darted her gaze between Erebos, Hades, and her children, Del slowly, daintily spiraled her wrists. The aconite inched toward Erebos. He pressed his feet together, trying to stave off the moment it would touch him. The closer the aconite crept, the more panic twined through Del's limbs. She did not want to hurt him. He had done nothing wrong. But Nyx had hurt her family, and this was the only way to make her stop.

She looked up at Nyx, and her stomach twisted when the goddess parted her lips. She prepared for her answer, but it was Hades who said, "Del, don't do this."

Del stopped growing the aconite. "*What?*" she and Nyx both said.

"Nyx is right." Hades's eyes reflected the flames of the Phlegethon as he beseeched Nyx, lifting his bound wrists. "I deserve this. If you and Erebos want to throw me into Tartarus, do it. For centuries, I have lived every day with the knowledge that I betrayed two of my dearest friends." He addressed the Twins of Death, who still guarded the triplets and Persephone, clutching each other's hands. "I lied to you about what I did. I can apologize again and again, but words scarcely matter." Finally, he turned his attention to his eldest daughter. "What matters is balance. They deserve justice. So, let them have it."

Del stared at her father. This was not part of the plan. Hades was supposed to see the aconite and remember the promise Del had made in Yaya's kitchen. That every time they saw aconite, it meant everyone was going to stay right where they should—

Dread pooled in her stomach at the realization. Her father had not been there when she made that promise. Of course he did not understand she was saving him. All this time, there had been a gaping hole in her plan.

"Free him," Hades said. He closed his eyes when Persephone screamed through the cord of night around her mouth. She tried to get up and run to her husband, but Keres held her against the rock. She sagged against the triplets, who had begun crying again.

"Well, you heard him," Nyx said. "Free Erebos. Your father admits the wrong he did. He knows he deserves Tartarus."

Del swallowed. Her father might be willing to let Nyx destroy their family, but she would not let that happen. "Perhaps he does," she said. "But my mother does not deserve to be parted from him forever. Just as you did not deserve to be parted from Erebos."

"Erebos did nothing wrong!"

"No, but you did. My father hurt you, and in an attempt to remedy that, you locked Eos in the space between realms. Violence begets violence, and I don't want to be responsible for any more of it." She took a deep breath. "I don't want to rob Erebos of his memories. If you vow on the river Styx to free my family and let them live in peace, I will let Erebos go free. If not . . ." The aconite crept closer to the god of darkness.

"Throwing your father in Tartarus will give you everything you want," Nyx said. "Freedom for your mother, for the triplets. Revenge on your father for everything he has done to you over the years."

"I don't want revenge anymore," Del said. "My father is not the only guilty person in my family. We have all hurt each other."

Hades shook his head. "Del, I deserve—"

Del grew a vine around his mouth before turning back to Nyx. "If you want to punish him for what he did to you and Erebos, take his throne from him. I will stay down here and become the queen of the underworld." She gave Persephone a sad smile, who cried silently, holding the triplets close to her heart. "After all this time, I have realized that becoming my mother will not be the worst thing in the world."

Nyx looked at Erebos, who gave a small nod. She closed her eyes and said, "Very well. Than, come here. Help me make this vow."

Than walked toward his mother, and Del resigned herself. She imagined how her life would unfold. She would judge mortal souls alongside him on the throne of bone. She would commune with mortals, telling them the story of how she and Than fell in love. Balance would be restored, and the triplets would continue their magic lessons in the underworld. When it came time for them to reveal themselves to the mortals, she would go with them. She would make sure that day was joyful. It would not all be terrible.

Than stood between Hades and Nyx. "I won't do it."

Del snapped back into the present moment. "What?" She seethed at him. "You are so determined to throw my father into Tartarus that you won't accept this?"

"No." He folded his arms. "I won't accept this because I don't want you to sacrifice yourself. I don't want you to live as a prisoner in the underworld."

Del ran her gaze over him, unsure how to feel. She still didn't trust him, and she lifted her hands in preparation for another betrayal. Than's eyes lingered there before settling on Del's. His lips parted, but when she said nothing to him, he turned back to Nyx.

"Mother," he said, voice softer now, "Hades did awful things to you and Erebos. He lied to Keres and me for years, and I'm angry at him. I'm furious. But we have all hurt people." When his gaze slid back to Del, his voice broke. "Some of us have hurt people in ways that cannot be healed. And I think, if I were to let Del cage herself to save her father from something he already regrets, I would be the worst sort of hypocrite."

"Than." Nyx glanced between him and Del. "If this is about you leaving her Isle this morning, I think you are overestimating—"

She broke off when Keres stepped forward, taking her brother's hand. "I'm with Than."

Nyx stared at her, and Keres said, "I hate Hades, Mother. I hate him for what he did. You know how true that is. But . . ." She met Del's eyes, and her lips trembled. "Today I hurt one of the only people I consider a friend. I can't do that again."

Del swallowed the garden of emotion in her throat while Keres shifted her attention back to Nyx. "I've watched how the banishment has affected you over the years. I don't want to be responsible for putting another woman through that." She gestured at Hades, who still knelt at the edge of the cliff. "Why are we even doing this? You said it yourself." She waved the same hand at the triplets. "One of them might grow up and enact revenge. I don't want to be the reason that happens. The world has enough violence." She turned her trembling smile on Del. "I don't want to harden myself anymore."

A moment of silence, in which the fiery waterfall crackled. "I think," Del said, "when someone has already recognized the wrong they did and now strives to atone for it, they deserve another chance. The world would be a lot lovelier if we all chose to forgive."

Slowly, as though afraid even this small movement would cause the aconite to touch him, Erebos lifted his hand. He pointed at the vine of bindweed around his lips. Del hesitated, but then she disintegrated it. She spiraled her wrists, and the aconite shrank away from him.

"My Starlight," he said to Nyx, "I know you are angry with Hades—as I am. But I don't want to live in the underworld after this. I want us to be free from the memories that will shackle us down here. Let Hades go. Don't punish his daughter for the wrongs he did."

In the wake of his words, Del shrank the aconite back to a single plant. Then she tossed it into Tartarus, watching the sparks flare. Erebos stepped toward Nyx and took her hands. "Forget him," he said. "Let us live for ourselves."

Nyx stared at him. At her children, who used their wings to shield Persephone and the triplets. At Hades, who winced as embers fell on his skin. At Del, who stood between all of them with nothing left to give. Erebos used his thumb to rub circles on the back of her hand. She closed her eyes, and tears cut bright paths through the soot that stained her skin. Without opening them, she dissolved the cords of night that bound Persephone and the triplets.

Before anyone could stop them, the triplets ran to Hades, yanking him back from the edge of the cliff. They hugged him, putting their little bodies between him and Nyx. Del choked back tears. She disintegrated the vine that covered his lips, and Persephone gave him a lingering kiss. Than and Keres flared their wings, forming a barrier between the triplets and Tartarus, and Persephone walked up to Nyx. They mirrored each other, streaked in soot and ash.

"Nothing Hades did to you is okay," she said, her voice strong despite the heat and smoke. This was the voice of the queen of the underworld. "It never will be, and I am sorry for that. But we all contain good and bad. It's like a garden. If we choose to water the bad things that have been done to us, they will grow large enough to choke our goodness."

Slowly, she took Nyx's hand. "But if we make the decision, every day, to turn our anger into love that waters our goodness, it will grow a canopy large enough to overshadow all the bad. The roots of the bad things will still be there. We can never fully eradicate them. But they will never grow beyond that."

Her words hung in the air, and Nyx smiled weakly through her tears.

"I know you have no desire to live here," Persephone said, "but I want you both to know you are welcome in the underworld whenever you wish. If you ever want positions in our palace, they are yours. If you never want to set foot down here again, you need not. Whatever you choose to do, I will support you." She looked to her husband, her eyes rimmed with tears. "And I am sure, given the chance, Hades will too."

Nyx appeared to have a silent conversation with Erebos. Then she turned to where her children shielded Hades and the triplets. She wiped her tears, and in the same motion, she evaporated the cords of night that bound Hades's ankles and wrists. As the curls of night vanished into the smoke, she buried herself in Erebos's shadows. The triplets snuggled in their father's arms, but Persephone turned to her eldest child. Her voice trembled when she held out her arms. "Asphodel."

Del looked down at herself. Through the smoke and embers, she saw red, glowing threads rise from her skin. For a few moments, they encircled her, weaving her into their web. Then they shattered, their glittering pieces tumbling into Tartarus.

Her curse was broken, but she did not run to Than.

Instead, she stepped toward the one person who was more like her than anyone else. Who would fight for what she wanted, no matter the cost. Who understood, more than anyone else, what Del was feeling right now.

With a sob, she collapsed into her mother's arms. "Maytare."

Chapter Forty-Two

No matter how well one tends it, a garden does not grow overnight.

The same was true of Del's healing process. In the days following Tartarus, she helped her family get the underworld back in order. The Furies, who had been trapped in the palace dungeons, went back to guarding the palace. When Cerberus was freed from the gardens, he bounded through the halls, entertaining the triplets.

With the line of mortal souls even longer than usual, Hades was largely kept busy with their trials, but he always made sure to join the family in the grand ballroom for dinner. After the meal, the family played games together, and soon Del discovered she shared a competitive streak with her father. Each night, they led opposing teams, their playful threats wafting up to the tree-root chandelier.

More often than not, Yaya and Cate joined their games. Yaya apologized profusely for not being able to help them during the Tartarus ordeal, swearing that the moment she returned from the mortal temple, she had demanded Cate take them to the underworld. But no matter how many times Cate turned her key in the lock, the spell room refused to travel. Cate said this was because the Fates wanted Del to complete her tasks alone, but Yaya had simply dragged them through the tunnel under the white willow.

As soon as they arrived in the palace, Yaya told Persephone of her desire to bless her marriage. When Zeus stormed into the underworld, half mad and determined to send Mak to the mortals, they had explained their plan to visit the temples together. After a grueling discussion in which nearly everyone lost their temper, Zeus agreed to leave Mak in the underworld, and as the weeks unwound, the mortals rejoiced in the new tale.

No longer trapped in her betrothal, Del strived to think about Than as little as possible. Once, a few weeks after Tartarus, she saw him while she was exiting her new bedroom in the palace. He carried an old hellhound, on his way to help Zag with his magic lesson. They both stopped and stared at each other. He opened his mouth, but Del walked right back into her bedroom and slammed the door. She wondered if he would knock, but he did not. After that, all she knew of him was what the triplets recounted at the dinner table.

In these moments, Del would fall silent. Her smile would dim as her mind filled with images of Than in the bindweed cage, on her sofa, tangled in her bed. She saw his lips part to sing the first notes of his song. Felt his hands pull her close. Heard him vow not to marry her until they fell in love. While her family kept talking over their meals, she would press her hand to her chest and feel the fabric of her robe over smooth skin. It seemed impossible that no one could see her heart beating through the gaping wound in her chest.

Her mother, at least, always noticed her silences. One day while they were tending the palace gardens, she asked if Del would have any interest in improving the Fields of Asphodel. "I don't know," Del said, watching Cerberus roll beneath the lindens. Aconite bloomed beneath his heads. "Than suggested I do that with him."

"Think about it," Persephone said.

It took months of deliberation, but in the end, Del decided she wanted to make death better for the souls who lived in the Fields of

Asphodel. She could see them from her new bedroom window, drifting faceless through the colorless blotch in the underworld. Than might have betrayed her, but they deserved better. He had been right about that.

"I'm named after the Fields," she said to her parents at dinner. "If I ever do decide to reveal myself to the mortals, they will associate me with it. I don't want them to think of it the way they do now. It's dreary. Depressing. I don't want the mortals to mourn being normal."

"What do you think would make the Fields better?" Hades asked. He barked at Mel to stop sneaking filets of whitefish to Cerberus.

Del pressed a bite of barley bread into a tight ball while Cerberus whined beside the table. "I want the mortals to know that being normal does not mean being forgotten." She looked at her mother, who was already beaming. "I know the project will take years to complete, but I want the mortals to know that simply helping each other through their days is enough to deserve eternity in a beautiful place."

Hades nodded and asked the Furies to help him put the triplets to bed. The triplets complained, but he said if they were trying to feed their dinner to Cerberus, they must be finished with it. While the Furies chased them out of the ballroom in a flurry of leathery wings, he told Del and Persephone they should start planning.

The summer after Tartarus, Del and Persephone were in the early stages of the project. Not wanting to disturb the souls who lived in the Fields of Asphodel, they were regrowing it in sections, slowly uprooting the wild asphodel to create artfully placed flower beds. Sometimes they talked, but often they fell silent, losing themselves in the work.

Such was the case one afternoon, when Del sent a cluster of woody stems rising from the base of a hill near the edge of the Fields. She was so focused on making sure the stems grew in the correct formation, their blooms brushing together just so, that her mother had to shout her name a few times before she looked up.

"Keres came to the palace today," Persephone said, her voice carefully casual. "She was looking for you. Have you spoken to her at all?"

Del hesitated before turning back to her handiwork. "Sometimes we talk after she helps Mak with her magic lessons." The first time Del saw Keres after Tartarus, the goddess had apologized for everything that had happened. Ever since, their exchanges had been limited to pleasantries, and stiff ones at that. They were no longer edging toward friendship, but Del was willing to speak with her so long as she did not mention Than.

"But you haven't seen her today," Persephone said.

Del stroked an asphodel bloom to lengthen its petals. "You're being weird."

"Yes, well. She told me Than wants to come visit the Isle this evening."

Del's response was reflexive. "I don't want him there." What she meant was, she wanted him there more than anything, but she didn't want him there like this.

Persephone fell silent for a short while. Del moved up the hill and grew another cluster of asphodel, flinching when one of the faceless souls drifted past her on its way through the Fields. Her father had agreed that all new souls who earned the Fields of Asphodel could drink from the Lake of Mnemosyne, but Del wished she could restore all the souls who had already drunk from the Lethe. After all, it would be no good for the Fields to look beautiful if most of the souls who lived there were miserable.

"Do you want my opinion?" Persephone's voice cut through her thoughts.

"I suppose," Del sighed. She took another step up the hill.

It took Persephone a moment to admit, "I think you should let him visit."

Del whipped her head up to her mother. She had known what Persephone would say, but actually hearing it still filled her with rage. She threw up her hands. "He was going to let his mother throw your husband into Tartarus!"

Persephone waited for another soul to drift down the hill before she stepped toward Del. "Hades banished Nyx for centuries. Think about how you felt your whole life with Yaya telling you Hades had stolen me. That wasn't even true, and you tried to dissolve our marriage vow." She held up a hand when Del opened her mouth. "I understand why you did it, Asphodel. I have forgiven you for it, just as I have forgiven Than for trying to throw Hades into Tartarus. Hades orchestrated his mother's banishment, and what with being locked up on your Isle, Than was already in a vulnerable position—"

"I was going to free him." Del spiraled her wrists so fast they popped, resulting in a cluster of asphodel far too large. "*He* decided to vow not to marry me until we fell in love."

"That doesn't mean it was an easy decision for him." Persephone used her own magic to shrink the cluster of asphodel. "He has loved you for years, but he also loves his work." She took another step toward Del, but Del shook her head and focused on the asphodel, growing clusters faster now.

"If he loved me, he should have told me the truth."

"Yes, he should have."

"He broke my trust."

"You kidnapped him."

Del huffed a laugh, her breath swirling the mists. "I cannot believe you are siding with him, even after everything that has happened."

"Asphodel." Persephone's voice was firm as she took Del's hand in her own. "I am not siding with him. I know you're still angry, and you have every right to be."

Del wanted to yank her hand away from her mother, but she didn't. She was trying to get better about that. "I know I do." She spoke to the row of asphodel she had just grown.

"I'm glad." Persephone squeezed her hand. "And I don't want to make this any harder for you than it has already been . . ."

Del rolled her eyes. "Just say it."

Persephone met Del's gaze with warm brown eyes that mirrored her own. "In his position, I want you to think about what you would have done."

Del wanted to shout at her mother. She wanted to descend into anger. It would be so much easier. But if anyone could be trusted in situations like this, it was her mother, so she thought about it. She watched the souls drift, soft and aimless, scarcely visible in the snow and mist. Black smoke bloomed from Tartarus in the distance. She knew what she would have done in Than's position. She would have done the same thing as him. The same thing as Nyx. It didn't excuse his deception, but despising him made her a hypocrite.

"It would be easier if I didn't love him," she said.

Persephone pulled her into a hug, holding her tightly while stroking her hair. "Why don't you just listen to him," she said in her ear. "You don't have to forgive him. You don't have to say anything back to him." She pulled away, holding Del's hands. "But I think, if nothing else, hearing his reasons will help you understand. Knowing is always better. It will help you heal from what happened."

When they trudged back to the palace, Mak ran up and said that Keres had been trying to find Del, but she had just left for the gardens to head home. Persephone kissed Del's forehead, and Del set off through the halls.

While she walked, she admitted that these past few months had not helped her get over the betrayal. She still dreamed of Than, and she still felt like her chest had been clawed open by a drakone. Maybe it really would be best to talk to him. At some point, they would see each other again, what with him working in the palace. She should get it over with.

Nevertheless, the thicket of panic filled her limbs when she stepped into the gardens. "Keres!" she called as she wove through the flower beds. "Keres, are you still here?"

She strode toward the new elm that rose at the edge of the garden, trying not to think about the last time she had been here with Than. When she passed the lindens, her traitorous eyes dipped to the ground, as though the olive-branch bracelets would still be there. They were not. Tears blurred her vision, and she reached for the knot in the elm.

"I thought you were avoiding me, little flower girl."

Del gasped. She rubbed her eyes and saw Keres leaning against the elm trunk. "I told you not to call me that anymore." She scowled.

"I can't help what you are."

"Do you want to talk to me about Than or not?"

Keres kicked off from the elm. "It sounds like you already know what I came to talk to you about. Are you going to let him come to the Isle?"

"I don't know why he wants to apologize to me in person." Del folded her arms. "It won't change how I feel."

"The truth is a seductive mistress, even when dressed up in teeth and claws."

Del only raised her eyebrows, and Keres sighed, resting her hand on her sword hilt. "Look. I know you hate him, but I promise—he never wanted to lie to you. Please know that. Neither of us thought our mother's plan would come to fruition so fast, and we never wanted to throw your mother and the triplets into Tartarus."

"You would have let it happen." Del tipped up her chin.

Keres's white wings drooped, but she flared them again. "I just don't want him to get hurt more than he already has. Tell him the truth today, no matter how awful it is. I want him to heal, and he can't until he knows you will never forgive him."

"I plan to end it with him."

Keres swallowed. "Yes, well. Whatever happens, don't mention to him that I talked to you about this. He would hate it. He hates himself for what he did to you. He takes full responsibility for it. He reaps his souls, then goes to bed, reaps his souls, then goes to bed. He thinks you deserve an apology, but he doesn't think he deserves your forgiveness."

"And you think he does deserve it."

Keres's red-brown eyes met Del's. "Not so long ago, someone taught me that everyone deserves another chance."

When Del just looked at Keres with her arms folded, the goddess sighed and stepped away from the elm. She flapped her wings and soared into the gloomy sky of the underworld, her words hanging in the air with the snow.

Chapter Forty-Three

Del shook her head and turned the knot in the elm. A few months ago, she had grown this elm with her mother and Yaya, then her father had instructed Coronis to peck a path through the trunk. Wind rushed through it, which made climbing it a surprisingly swift process. Before long, she emerged into the grove of elms on the Isle.

The new tunnel meant the Isle no longer floated freely through the Aegean, and Del was still getting accustomed to seeing the other islands in the archipelago. Their rocky cliffs and flat beaches came into view, golden light bathing the Isle. This far into the summer, the garden was a patchwork of green foliage. Everything was a bit wilder than it had been before, for Del was not here as much anymore. She spent more time living her life than staying in control.

She stepped inside the cottage and took a deep breath. She knew the obol Than had given her was still in here somewhere, but she could not recall where. She stood in the kitchen, facing the wall where the bindweed cage had been. The graphite drawings hung on the wall, rustling in the air. She lifted a hand to her throat and recalled how she had yelled at him. She had yanked the obol off her neck, then his eyes had followed it—

She crouched in front of the oven. It took some time for her to find it, but then she saw the silver glint. It was wedged between the oven and the counter. She pulled it out, and the chain snapped. Her heart pounded, and she looked down at it in the palm of her hand. The pink rose bloom gleamed in the sun.

She drew in a breath and walked out of the cottage. She wanted to be on the beach when Than landed. She wanted this conversation to be as swift as possible, and she didn't want him to come into the cottage. She didn't want to see him there again. It would taint all her memories of them there together, and it would make her feel trapped.

As she sat at the edge of the crocus lawn, she admitted that was how the entire Isle made her feel now. Trapped. Whenever she came here, her memories ate up all the air. She saw Than in the garden, the lotus trees, the elm grove. She saw him on the beach, comforting her while she was overwhelmed. They had sat right here, listening to the waves crash. The wind off the Aegean had kicked up this sand—

A shadow streaked across it. Del squinted up, and there he was, his wings rainbowing like those of a crow as he soared down onto the Isle. His black hair blew wildly as he jogged to a stop. She stood up, and there he was in front of her, looking the same as he always had. His wings twitched when he folded them, shifting his weight from one foot to the other. His lips parted so he could tug a strand of hair from his mouth. The light glanced off his cheekbones, and his eyes were as blue as the waves behind him.

Del's heart pounded, fist clenching the obol in her pocket. She had expected him to launch into some speech as soon as he landed, but he just stood and looked at her. Maybe he was waiting for permission to speak to her. Maybe he was waiting for her to yell that he should leave the Isle and never speak to her again.

She did neither. Instead, she met his eyes and said, "If I didn't love you, I would hate you less."

When he dropped his gaze, she noticed the single pink rose he held. Her heart cracked, but she rolled her hand. "Say what you came to say, then."

It took him a few false starts, opening and closing his mouth, but once the first word dripped from his lips, the rest poured like a waterfall. Just as Keres had said, he made no excuses. He said he had let his anger at Hades grow like a weed, choking all his good feelings. He had felt guilty ever since leaving the cottage with Keres that day. He had panicked the moment he saw they had captured Del's family, knowing he had made the worst possible mistake. He had cried. He had screamed her name. When she had arrived in the throne room, he knew he would never forget the look on her face.

"I say none of this with the intention of inspiring you to forgive me." He met her eyes, twirling the rose by the stem. "I know you cannot. But I want you to know how sorry I am. For the rest of my days, I shall envy the wind that caresses your hair and the ground that kisses your feet, the flowers that shiver under your touch and bloom under your gaze. I am glad, though, that they will never cause you pain."

His words blew away on the wind off the Aegean Sea. Del knew he was waiting for her to say something, but she didn't trust herself to speak. She had planned to give him the obol and be done, but seeing the way his shoulders hunched and wings drooped, she knew he saw the wound in her chest. She knew, because he had one of his own. It shredded the black fabric of his tunic, bright-red blood dripping onto the pink rose he held.

"All right, then," he said with a shaky breath. He glanced down at the rose, then back up at Del. "That—that's all I came to say. I just wanted you to know . . . everything. Thank you for listening. I'll leave—" He held out the rose, its delicate petals fluttering in the wind, then he sank into a crouch. He set the rose on the beach, and sand immediately started to cover it. "I'll leave this here. There." He pointed down at it. "I might . . . I hope to see you again. Someday."

"We will see each other," Del said. "It can't be avoided, now that we both spend so much time in the underworld." The hope on his face was like someone digging their fingers into the wound in her chest, but she said, "If you are ever in trouble, I will be there to help. I do not wish you ill. But I think it would be best to avoid each other as much as possible."

The light in his expression vanished. "Is that really what you want?"

"I think it would be best for both of us."

He scanned her face. "If you're sure."

Del nodded, and after a moment, he turned. He walked along the tide line, leaving deep footprints that filled with water at each lap of the surf. While he moved away from her, Del squeezed the obol so tightly, it hurt. The sun was setting, bright beams of light cutting across the beach as he grew smaller, flapping his wings. She didn't want to see him leave.

She looked down at the rose, which was now almost completely covered with sand. While she watched the grains cover the last of its petals, she imagined how her life would feel when she returned to the underworld.

At first, each time she saw Than, the wound would split open in her chest. Blood would run down her front while her cheeks flooded with tears. But over time, the scab over the wound would thicken. When she saw him, the scar would numb the pain. The skin over her heart would never look the same, but she would heal in a new way. He would become part of her story, and she would have her family. Maybe she would even fall in love again someday. She looked up, hoping he had flown away.

Instead, she saw him striding back up the beach.

"What are you doing?" she yelled over the crashing waves. Without meaning to, she started walking, then she was running until they met in the middle of the beach. "What's going on? I thought you were leaving."

"So did I, but you know what? No." He crossed his arms. "I made a mistake, Del. I admit that with my whole heart. But you don't get to stand here and act like you did nothing wrong."

Del spluttered. "What?"

"You kidnapped me, first of all. And I know. I know I decided to stay with you after making my vow. But that doesn't change how you stole me at the start. You were prepared to destroy the world!"

"When I kidnapped you, I had no idea what would happen to the mortals—"

"And when you learned what would happen, did you let me go? No. I know you were scared. I know you felt like you were losing control. But you still took away my free will. Keres has been trying to explain this to me ever since the day everything broke down. She has tried to show me I am not the only one at fault, but it took me coming here and seeing you to realize . . . she's right, Del. You're not innocent in this. None of us are."

"I know I'm not innocent." Rage-red flowers bloomed up Del's throat. "I made mistakes, and I apologized for them. I made every attempt to right my wrongs. I fell in love. And how do you repay me? By breaking my trust!"

"Fine, then." Than tipped up his chin. They had stepped closer to each other while talking, and less than a handbreadth separated them now. Del watched his chest heave up and down. "Tell me. Look me in the eyes and tell me you never want to see me again. Don't tell me what you think is best. Don't tell me what makes you feel safest. Look me in the eyes and tell me what you *want*, no matter how terrifying it is."

Del opened her mouth and made a small sound, then she closed it. Than watched it close. And she couldn't deny that his small, triumphant smirk went straight to her core.

"I thought so. But *if* we see each other again, we both have things to work on. I have to earn back your trust. And you"—he pressed a finger to her breastbone—"must learn how to cope with not always being in control."

"Does that mean—" Her heart pounded. His face was so close, she could have stood on her tiptoes and closed the gap between their lips. "Are you coming back here? Do you want to see me again?"

His eyes dipped to her mouth, and he scanned her face as though trying to memorize it. Del thought he would kiss her, but then he stepped back, and she blinked in the sudden fiery onslaught of the sunset.

"I don't know," he said. "Keres says I shouldn't. She thinks you are the worst sort of hypocrite—that you claim everyone deserves another chance, but when the person who must give that chance is you, you won't do it." He shook his head, and his voice softened. "Perhaps we have hurt each other too much. I don't know."

With a last look of anguish, he turned and walked up the beach, leaving Del alone.

She watched him fly away, hugging her stomach, which was in knots. He was right about everything. She had taken away his free will. She had been cowardly enough to risk destroying the world. If it wasn't for his help, Zeus would have sent Mak to the mortals. And she was hypocritical. Yes, Than had betrayed her trust, but she had done the same thing to him when she stole him from the underworld. She had done the same thing to her parents when she tried to break their marriage vow. She was no better than any of them.

She was as terrible and as good as everyone else.

She didn't deserve him, she thought while she shook the sand from the pink rose. She ran her fingers over it to perk up its tender petals. Then she took the broken obol out of her pocket and set it on the sand next to the rose. Tears pricked her eyes when she recalled their conversation at the Farewell Festival all those months ago. This flower was a symbol of love. Than had still loved her when he flew here.

She might have ruined that now.

Tears falling silently down her face, she wove her fingers through the air. The stem of the rose lengthened, the new growth twining around the broken chain of the obol. When it had wrapped around the whole necklace, the coin dangled next to the bloom, and she lifted the necklace over her head.

She dried her tears. If she was going to be worthy of this relationship, she had to accept that he was free to do as he wished. She had to learn that he could earn back her trust, and even though she had given him every reason to let go, she had to hope he would choose to hold on.

As she walked through the crocus lawn, she took comfort in the fact that he had always been more optimistic than she was. He had always looked out and seen a softer world, but she worried that the past few months had finally hardened him enough to see its thorns.

The sunlight dimmed when she reached the elm grove. In the shadows, she lifted her hand to her chest, and the rose bloom brushed her palm. She feared, she hoped, she wondered, if he would come back.

Chapter Forty-Four

He did.

Epilogue

It was months of walking along the tide line, of lingering touches on hands and arms, their first kiss as sun-warmed water lapped at their ankles. It was the night summer slipped into fall, their feet crunching on fallen leaves, quickened breaths as her fingers scrambled at the cottage door. It was waking up on a white winter morning to find a kiss pressed to her lips and a cup of tea steaming between her palms. It was making kykeon on a starry night during the spring thaw, three words whispered into each other's smiles for the first time.

It was the summer afterward, when Del wore a white gown in the grand ballroom of her father's palace. She sat perfectly still in one of the chairs at the banquet table, feeling her mother's careful fingers arrange her flower crown. She and the triplets had worked with Del to design the gown. It looked like an asphodel, with its floor-length skirt divided into six panels, each of the pearly-white lengths bearing a light-pink streak down the middle. Her hair had been pinned into an elaborate chignon, which was woven through with the flower crown. The flower crown was composed entirely of asphodel, the star-shaped white flowers holding up the gauzy veil that flowed down her back. The veil was the green of new growth, and her only jewelry was her obol carved with a pink rose.

"Oh, seedling," Yaya said when Persephone gestured for Del to twirl. The pearly skirt caught the faint glow of the tree-root chandelier as it rippled. The panels flung outward, making Del look like a blooming flower. When she came to a stop, the triplets cheered, and Cerberus bounced around the ballroom with thunderous barks.

While Persephone tried to calm them down, Yaya stepped toward Del. Askalabos sat on her shoulder, but the spotted gecko was not the reason she hesitated to pull her granddaughter into her arms. Their relationship was less warm than it had been before, but Del still relished their closeness. Whatever else had happened, Yaya had raised her, and she was grateful to have her here on a day like this.

Careful of the gecko, she pulled her grandmother into her arms. "My heart," Yaya whispered, holding her close, "you are so beautiful."

They were both blinking back tears when Hades swept into the ballroom. He looked uncharacteristically lively in a green cloak that glittered with emeralds. "The boat is all ready to—" he started, but when he saw Del, he broke into a smile. "Asphodel." He strode forward to wrap her in a hug that smelled of balsam and clacked with jewels. "You look . . ."

Del pulled away. "Like an asphodel."

Her father laughed and pointed over his shoulder to the hall. "The boat is all ready for us to head down. Is everyone—" He broke off when Cerberus gave a room-shaking bark. The family turned to the opposite end of the ballroom to find the three-headed dog chasing Gale. The black polecat scrambled across the marble floor. She tried to gain purchase, but she slid in a puddle of Cerberus's drool. Blooms of aconite grew around her paws. The triplets cheered for Cerberus, chanting his name while Gale tried to tug herself free and failed. Cerberus leered over the polecat, opening his jaws.

Askalabos preened on Yaya's shoulder, watching it all.

"All right, that's enough." Del sliced her finger through the air, and the aconite disintegrated around Gale. The polecat dashed to Cate and climbed up her robe. She curled around the goddess's shoulders, face huddled beneath her tail. The triplets whined that they had not played nearly enough with Cerberus, but Hades led them into the hall.

When they reached the palace docks, Del thought maybe she ought to be nervous, but she felt only the giddy excitement of a seed the moment before it bursts through good soil. They all piled into the long black boat, and Cerberus loped along beside them, growing aconite all along the banks of the Lethe.

As they sailed toward the Fields of Asphodel, Yaya leaned toward Del. "Seedling, I am so proud of how you have grown. I suppose all flowers must be buried before they can bloom, and look at you now. I wonder . . ." She waited, and Del raised her eyebrows. "I wonder if you would like to go to the mortals with me this fall. To add your tale to the great story of the world." The boat docked, and she gestured at the Fields of Asphodel. "You deserve to tell them all you have done here in the underworld."

The rest of the family disembarked, but Del stayed in the boat with Yaya. "Let me think about it," she said. "Perhaps I will."

They joined the rest of the family in the Fields, which Del and her mother had completed just over a month ago. Seeing it always made Del smile. What had once been a tangled white sea was now a field of geometric patterns. Del had asked Yaya how she grew her fields on the farm, and Yaya had shown them how to weave the asphodel atop the lush grass that now blanketed the soil. The patterns spiraled toward the center of the Fields, creating pathways where the souls could wander and talk among themselves.

Many of the souls had faces now, their memories restored. While improving the Fields, Del had realized each asphodel flower held the memories of a mortal soul who had drunk from the Lethe. With help from Than and Keres, she had begun to bring the mortals back to themselves. Than sang his song while Del willed their memories forward, and

Keres fed the souls water from the Lake of Mnemosyne. The work was slow, but it was work they loved.

As Del walked to the new pavilion in the center of the Fields, the souls who passed waved hello. Del waved back at them, while Mel tried to convince Cerberus's central head to chase them. Mak and Zag overruled her, urging his two other heads to be patient. Yaya remarked that they were growing into well-mannered youngsters, but when they reached the pavilion, all three triplets leaned forward and chorused for the dog to leap into a gallop.

They dashed into the Fields, but Del was too busy staring at the pavilion to tell them to stop. "I knew you were going to decorate it," she said to her mother and Yaya, "but this is even better than I hoped."

"You see?" Persephone said. "Even in the underworld, flowers grow."

The pavilion, which was composed of wood and ringed like a tree trunk, had been turned into a forest of all the plants Del loved. Olive and laurel trees circled it, their canopies draped with white-flowered bindweed. In the glittering snow, clusters of red and green grapes shone like jewels. Poppies, narcissus, and asphodel covered the ground, and a cloak of pink roses wrapped every tree trunk. Pomegranate trees dotted the shadows, her father's minstrels playing jaunty music while hidden in the branches.

Throughout the pavilion, guests sipped wine and ate from the banquet. When Persephone and Yaya led her through the forest, Del spotted Zeus and his queen, Hera, both of whom chatted with Ares and Athena. Helios and Selene danced around a tree trunk with Eos. They had made amends with Nyx, who now lived with Erebos and Keres in their palace. Along with them, dozens of other nymphs and gods followed Del to the center of the forest, where Than stood on the innermost ring of the pavilion.

He was holding a bouquet, surrounded by his family. Nyx and Erebos looked like twin snakes in their sheaths of green, while Hemera grinned hugely, emeralds glistening in her gold mane. Keres gave Del a wink. In Nyx's arms slept the newest addition to their family, little

Morpheus, the god of dreams. Ever since he was born, Del and Than had been speculating about what sort of mischief would ensue when he grew old enough to meet Mel.

She reached Than now. He wore a white robe rimmed with pink sapphires, along with a cloak that gleamed with emeralds. These were courtesy of Del's father, who stood just behind Than in his matching green clothes. But the bouquet that Than handed Del was a gift from her mother and Yaya. It was composed of poppies, narcissus, and asphodel, all centered around a single pink rose. Del lifted it to her nose, smelling its honey-sweet fragrance as she met the eyes of the man she loved.

She lowered the bouquet to her torso while Hades spoke to the crowd. "This is not a traditional marriage," he said with a gesture to Than and Del, "for one of the parties has already made their vow. It is a marriage of opposites who have discovered they are not opposed at all. After all, it takes darkness to see the light, and warmth to feel the cold." He swept his hand between Nyx and Hemera, then Persephone and Yaya. "It takes the moon to love the sun, and to make a decision means to stand at a crossroads." He gestured to Helios and Selene, then to Cate, who stood next to Yaya.

"Like all these things and more," he said while Than and Del began to smile, "death and life give meaning to one another, because only two equal weights can balance a scale. Than has reached out his hand to Del, and today she has decided to take it—in the grandest show of trust there is for us gods."

In an echo of Hades's words, Than reached out, and Del took his hand. With the other, he held up his clay jar filled with water from the river Styx. She opened her mouth, and he tipped a drop onto her tongue. It tasted of warm ash, and heat spread through her limbs. A hot, dry wind blew through her soul, and she looked into Than's eyes, which began to glow.

"Thanatos," she said, her voice echoing through her bones, "I vow to marry you, joining my soul to yours. Whatever dares hurt one of us will have to face us both. For you and nothing else, I sacrifice my immortal self."

The wind that had blown through her soul encircled them both, whipping their hair and clothes. Shadows engulfed them while their souls rose up their throats and threatened to spill from their mouths. Than leaned forward, cupping the back of her head with his hand, and Del pressed her lips to his.

The kiss was like nothing she had ever experienced. Her entire body was a strummed harp, vibrating across time and beyond. She saw the great orbs of her and Than's souls flatten out, then curl into a pink-and-gray-marbled ball. The colors were so intertwined it was impossible to tell where one ended and the other began. Del seemed to linger there forever, in a place of perfect, harmonious oneness, where nothing could begin or end.

They simply were. Together.

The kiss broke, and their families cheered. Than wrapped his arm around her waist, and she leaned into him. The music swelled loud enough to be heard over the crowd, and she gripped his collar to kiss him again. It was long and luxurious, and the triplets yelled at them to stop being gross, but Del just smiled against his mouth. Cerberus gave a warning bark, and the triplets yanked at Than's cloak and Del's veil, prying them apart. The Furies flapped forward and reprimanded the troublemakers, but Del only laughed and lifted her bouquet over her head. "I'm going to throw it!" she said.

The triplets shrieked in unison. The guests counted down, and Del tossed the bouquet over her head. "I caught it!" Mel yelled. Del turned around to find the little goddess of nightmares waving the bouquet over her head, Mak and Zag trying to nab it.

In the clamor, Keres placed a hand on Del's and Than's shoulders. She jerked her chin for them to follow, and before anyone could see them, she shooed them off the pavilion. "Go on," she said. "Take some time for yourselves."

Del gave her a kiss on the cheek and tugged Than into the Fields. There, with the strains of music and laughter whispering through the air, she took his face in her hands. He plucked her like one of the Fields' flowers, and the panels of her dress split when she wrapped her legs around him. For a very long time, she kissed him with his back pressed against a laurel tree. "Mistress," he said breathlessly, "are you trying to trap me?"

"I don't need to, darling Thanatos," she said as he kissed her forehead, again and again. He smiled down at her while she laughed. "You'll choose to stay."

And he did, walking with her through one of the pathways long after they should have returned to the pavilion. At one point, he plucked some of the grass and made her a bracelet. She kissed him while he slipped it onto her wrist. When that earned some hoots from the souls drifting around them, they laughed. As they wandered aimlessly, holding hands, she said, "Yaya asked if I would like to share my story with the mortals this fall."

Than swung their hands between them. "What did you tell her?"

"I told her I would think about it, but I think I will." She gestured at the Fields. "I can tell them about all this now. And I can tell them about you." She kissed his flushed face and giddy smile. "Someday soon, we will have a story all our own. But for now . . ."

She rubbed the space between his forefinger and thumb. "I have had enough conflict. Enough vows and quests and spells. I think other gods have given enough story to the world. For a while longer, I would like to be normal. If it's all right with you, I would like to live our life and not care who knows."

She looked up at the man she loved, and he smiled. He cupped her face in his hands and brought it to his own. "With you," he said between kisses, "I would love to be normal. Let the other gods seek mortal favor and revel in their tales. You and I, we will linger in the peacefulness that follows a good story's close." He pressed his forehead to hers, his voice sonorous and low. "In life's never-ending chaos, let us be still."

Del kissed him sweet and soft, and he ran his hands down her waist before picking her up. She shrieked a laugh as he gave her a twirl. Her laughter swirled through the mists and snow, her gown blooming around her when he set her back down. Around her, new stalks of asphodel split the ground. She let them grow.

Acknowledgments

Of all the characters I have written, Del is the most like me.

Throughout the story, she resorts to anger rather than admit she feels less than. She makes an island of herself, cutting off others in an attempt to maintain control. Only after Than helps her realize her worth can she become who she was meant to be.

This book would not exist without all the people who believed in me.

First comes my family. Thank you to my dad, who made up a new bedtime story each night before I went to sleep. My mom, who took me to the library every week. My sisters, Katie and Janie, who wrote stories on stapled notebook paper with me.

My grandparents have always been the greatest champions of my writing, and if you look closely, in these pages you will find my grandfather's description of a stately oak tree. He gave me that description for a short story I wrote in high school, and although he has since passed away, I swore I would include it in my first published book.

I wanted to write my first book in college, and a handful of professors made that possible. Charles, Laura, and Darby—your feedback will encourage me for the rest of my life. I will never forget the day I received my first offer of representation from a literary agent while in the school library, and all three of you helped me reply to the email.

Thank you to my literary agent, Jenissa Graham, who took a chance on my first book and stuck with me for *Fields of Asphodel.* I am forever grateful that when I had the idea for a Hades-and-Persephone role reversal, you suggested I write about their children instead. Without you, Del and Than would not exist.

Writing a book often feels like a solitary endeavor, but throughout the process, my friends have been indispensable.

Thank you to Tallie, who read chapter by chapter while I wrote the first draft. Your Wattpad-level comments still make me laugh.

To Clara and Chandler, who provided the comfort of childhood friends. If someone asked me if I loved you like family, I would say, "Yes, quite." You understand.

To Megan Murphy and Noelle Monét, who believed this book would be published even when it was littered with my most unusual crutch word: *tents*.

To Bella Galbraith and Morgan Forté, who understand the grueling wait times of the publishing industry all too well. Our rise might be slow, but it is inevitable.

To Saint Gibson, for giving me a sensitivity read in record time. I can't wait to return the favor for your next book, and the one after that, and so on.

Most of all, thank you to my critique partner, Sydney J. Shields, who has made me a better writer and person every day since we became friends. I cannot believe I get to write books with you, and I cannot imagine writing them without you.

Sydney was who I called when, halfway through a workday at my day job, I received an email saying that Elizabeth Agyemang, an acquisitions editor at 47North, wanted to publish *Fields of Asphodel*. Thank you, Elizabeth, for seeing the beauty in this book when it was still in the bud; thank you to my developmental editor, Wendy Muruli, for helping it grow; and thank you to my copyeditor, Davy, and proofreader, Jill, for pruning it into the bloom it is now.

Thank you to my cover artist, Edward Bettison, for creating a piece of art so stunning that the first time I saw it, I nearly dropped my laptop. It is better than anything I could have hoped for, and my coworkers at my day job were kind enough to print a poster-size version for me to hang on my wall. Special thanks to my Cavity Corner desk mates, Mikey and Lydia, who supplied me with endless lattes and sweets, and to my boss, Jason, who always let me gush (or rant) about writing in our one-on-one meetings.

And to Tate—every day, you help me understand the sort of love this book is about. With you, I would love to live in the stillness and in the chaos both . . . and if it wasn't anachronistic, I would have given Del's cottage a Dutch door.

Publishing my own book has been my biggest dream since I was stapling stories on notebook paper as a little girl, but I never would have achieved it without the authors I read between then and now. To name only a few:

Rick Riordan, my passion for Greek mythology is because of you.

Rainbow Rowell, my dialogue pales in comparison to yours.

Robin Hobb, I hope my characters feel half as real as your own.

Thank you to my cat, Lewis, for all the snuggles . . . and for all the ankle bites when I needed to take a break from writing so I could chase you around the house. Publishing deadlines are not for the faint of heart, and I never would have made it through mine without the baristas at Sunergos Coffee, who make the best iced mochas in the world. (I also watched a lot of BBC *Sherlock* and Dan and Phil. Yes, I am a fangirl at my core.)

I could fill an entire book with names, but suffice to say, if I have known you, you are somewhere in these pages. Everyone I have ever met has made me who I am now, and *thank you* is not large enough a phrase to express what I feel.

Lastly, thank you to every reader who has made room for *Fields of Asphodel* in their heart, home, or Kindle shelf. You are the people I thought of while typing the first words of this book nearly two years ago, and you are the ones I'm thinking of as I type these last words now. I hope you saw part of yourself in this story, and I hope that part of you healed.

For me, writing this book felt like coming home.

About the Author

Photo © 2025 Katie Rowland

Callie Rowland lives in Louisville, Kentucky, where she spends most of her time reading and writing. When she's feeling brave, she even hangs out with other people. She is the proud mother of a spider plant named Lucifer, a pothos named Lilith, and a cat named Lewis (who she is convinced is the guardian of realms). You can find her across social media @calliemrowland or on her website, www.callierowland.com.

PRAISE FOR *FIELDS OF ASPHODEL*

"This lyrical debut is blooming with unique floral magic, intricate world-building, and pitch-perfect forbidden love. Fans of spicy fantasy romance and Greek mythology will be completely obsessed. *Fields of Asphodel* is a romance with Death like you've never read before, and you will not be able to put it down."
—Sydney J. Shields, *USA Today* bestselling author of *The Honey Witch*

"An epic and grand love story, worthy of the myths that inspired it! *Fields of Asphodel* weaves beloved Greek myths with coming-of-age and family drama to create a story that feels both fresh and classic."
—Sarah Beth Durst, *New York Times* bestselling author of *The Spellshop*

"A sultry, sweet inversion of the Hades and Persephone myth, wreathed with flowers and rooted in the belief that generational cycles can be broken."
—S. T. Gibson, international bestselling author of *A Dowry of Blood*

"By turns sweet and steamy, *Fields of Asphodel* is a refreshing take on the Hades and Persephone myth, where their children reverse their parents' dynamic (with healthier results)."
—Caitlin Rozakis, *New York Times* bestselling author of *Startup Hell*

"A captivating, tender, and romantic tale, *Fields of Asphodel* spins a lyrical world that explores the strength of being soft and the dangers of love. When the fierce goddess of flowers and the alluringly gentle god of death must fix the chaos they've caused, flowers will not be the only thing blooming between them. Whimsical. Warmhearted. And a stunning debut."

—Taylor Epperson, author of *Second Time's a Charm*

"With a lush story that twists and ensnares like a vine, readers will be captivated by *Fields of Asphodel*."

—Mai Corland, *New York Times* and *Sunday Times* bestselling author of the *Five Broken Blades* trilogy